DEMON CARD ENFORCER

JOHN STOVALL

Published by
CS BOOKS, LLC

This is a work of fiction. Names, characters, places, and incidents either are the product of author imagination or are used fictitiously, and any resemblance to actual persons, living or dead, business establishments, events, or locales, is entirely fictional.

Demon Card Enforcer
Copyright © 2024 Capital Station Books
All rights reserved.

Cover Design: Michael Gladigau

Editors: Amy McNulty, Nia Quinn, Celestian Rince

IF YOU WANT TO BE NOTIFIED WHEN JOHN STOVALL'S NEXT BOOK RELEASES, PLEASE VISIT HIS WEBSITE OR CONTACT HIM DIRECTLY AT

John.W.Stovall@gmail.com

Dedications

*First, as always, to my wife, **Shami Stovall**, who has made this career, and many other things besides, possible. You are the most amazing person I know. With, and because, of you my life has elevated multiple times.*

*Secondly, to the other members of my writers' group. To **Dana, Ryan, Mary, Emily, James, and Scott**, thank you for the efforts you put into this as well. Especially Ryan, whose own card game efforts led to this book directly.*

*Third, to my parents, **John and Gail Stovall**. Your support throughout my life has been over the top, and you are the perfect parents everyone else wished they had. And, in my "Master's degree in English" mother's case, one of my editors as well. This dedication, unfortunately, comes too late to reach my father, who passed away. I hope you were isekai'd to some place with a really awesome map, perhaps an alternate magical earth, to fight for the good one more time.*

*Fourth, to my editors **Celestine Rince** and **Amy Mcnulty**.
Thanks for doing this, I know I don't make it easy.*

*Fifth, I'd like to thank **Chris Zinn,** who supported me on patreon
for multiple years as my single, sole patron, and provided bonus
editing, before all this took off.*

*Sixth, I'd like to thank the giants that came before me. When
Shami picked up authoring, I picked up Kindle, just to see how her
books were doing, and I became addicted to a whole new
generation of amazing authors through Kindle Unlimited. A
friend recommended the Cradle series, by **Will Wight.** I loved it,
and the Also Boughts led to the Chaos Seeds series, by **Aleron
Kong,** and I discovered Litrpg. Also Boughts of that led to Divine
Dungeon, by **Dakota Krout**, what I still consider the premiere
example of Dungeon Core in this genre I came to love so much,
which I discovered from him. Every few months I read that series
again. And the Also Boughts of Divine Dungeon led me finally to
the Hapless Dungeon Fairy series, by **Jonathan Brooks**, which
had many of the ideas in it that led me to dream about cool things
enough to finally write my first novel, Corrupted Core.*

*So, again, I'd like to thank the giants that came before me, for
giving me the books I loved that made me dream. I raise a glass to
you. **Will Wight, Aleron Kong, Dakota Krout, and
Jonathan Brooks**—thank you. Truly and deeply. Also, p.s....
when are your next books coming out?* 😊

CONTENTS

CHAPTER 1

BEELZEBUB'S PARTY

"**The Great Game Rule #1**: Every ten years, the gods will grant one in five hundred people over the age of thirteen a deck of ten cards, and that person shall become a deckbearer."

Drop Night—when the new card set was released by the gods—was the single biggest holiday for everyone around the world. The one night every decade when they might receive a deck of cards, and become a deckbearer.

Everyone desperately hoped that they would be chosen, and every single person did something to prepare for or celebrate the night. Perhaps sit in the dark, hands clasped, hoping fate would change their lives. Perhaps performing last-minute deeds that they thought would convince one faction of the gods to reward them with a deck.

But most people threw a party. Alcohol and drugs worked equally well for celebrating good luck and drowning sorrows, after all.

Wolfe strode through the massive rave he was required to

attend. He shoved his way across a fog-filled dance floor shining with red strobe lights that flashed between statues of demons and giant flies, his bones reverberating from the loud club music. Wolfe did his best to weave his way among the partiers as he made his way to the VIP section, but that was difficult, given the number of drunken, half-dressed dancers.

He couldn't help but think that while the gods had never talked to anyone, it was still painfully obvious they had favorites. This whole party was a celebration for one man, Wolfe's employer, Big Man Grimm, who ran the Grimm crime family.

Big Man Grimm was clearly favored of Beelzebub, a dark god of the Infernal faction and Master of Gluttony. That was why fly statues and décor covered every inch of the nightclub.

Wolfe's thoughts were interrupted as a petite girl bumped into him. She wore a black miniskirt and bra, and had her blonde hair shaved on one side. She craned her neck in order to stare up to Wolfe's six-foot-two height.

Her drink had spilled onto Wolfe's gray Armani suit—a gift from Big Man Grimm himself.

"Why'd you shill—spill—my drink?" the girl slurred, slapping his arm, practically hurting herself in the process. Wolfe was two hundred and thirty pounds of rock-solid muscle. "I'm gonna ge' a deck tonight!"

Wolfe stared at her for a moment, then glanced up at the man who was dancing with her: Richard 'Rich' Cordova, one of the many other enforcers who worked for Big Man Grimm. Wolfe met the other man's brown eyes with his own hazel gaze, and Rich shuddered.

He grabbed the girl, pulling her away. "I'm so sorry, Wolfe. Um, Tiffany is just havin' fun. I'll pay for the—"

"Don't bother," Wolfe growled. "Just get her out of here."

Tiffany pouted. "But I still want to—"

Rich put his hand over her mouth, hissed, "Shut up!" Then glanced at Wolfe. "We were just heading out."

Wolfe turned away, irritated at himself for being irritable. But he was—and he knew why. The gods didn't care about people like Wolfe. He had been to these parties twice, once when he'd been eighteen and newly in the family, and once when he'd been twenty-eight and still full of adrenaline. He had never received a deck on Drop Night.

Truth was, Wolfe wanted to be at home tonight, even though it was empty. Pierce, his dog, had recently died, and Wolfe only had his shadow for company now. He still preferred that over the blaring music and drunken nincompoops.

But Big Man Grimm wanted all the important members of the family's business here at the Ekron Eternal. The club was the heart of the Grimm family business.

Unfortunately, 'all the important members' included his head enforcer, Wolfe.

Wolfe sighed and went back to making his way past other drunk-ass girls and men who thought they were dangerous to reach the club's most important table, the one with the people who mattered: Big Man Grimm, his inner circle, and his family.

Two large, rough-looking thugs who could have been brothers—Harry and Dan—were guarding the table.

Neither batted an eye as Wolfe slid into the last place on the outside edge of the VIP table. They knew Wolfe belonged there. He did get the stink eye from the other members of the table— the Big Man's children and a couple of his remaining lieutenants.

"Sorry I'm late, boss."

Big Man Grimm—Thaddeus Grimm, Senior—looked and sounded like his name. He was big... and grim. He was sixty years old and two inches taller even than Wolfe, but he had stayed healthy in an old-man way. He had a lean body and large muscles that still couldn't hide his nearly white hair and wrinkled skin. Big Man Grimm almost never smiled, and when he did, it wasn't a good thing.

But the scariest thing about him was his voice.

"We were just talking about my children," Big Man Grimm said in a tone that was heavy, deep, and the stuff of horror movies. "Do you think they'll get a god-gifted deck?"

The boss swept his arm to take in his three children.

The Big Man's oldest son, Thaddeus Jr., who was thirty, had been watching the girls dance. At his dad's voice, he turned back to the table. "What?"

Thad Jr. was extremely handsome in a lean way, and once he had been the apple of his father's eye. But his own eyes were blank and he seemed perpetually surprised.

And he's wearing a football tie with the Armani suit. Even I know that's tacky.

Damian Grimm, the middle child, was younger at twenty-six. He resembled a demented hobbit—four and a half feet tall with fat rolls under his chin he tried to hide with a black goatee. He wore a burgundy suit, near blood-colored, and he fingered his 'demon-fly' cufflinks.

Damian smiled at Wolfe as Wolfe. Grimm's middle child loved stories of Wolfe's exploits, especially the times Wolfe had taken down deckbearers without a deck of his own.

"Maybe our own Wolfe-y will finally get a deck." Damian smiled at Wolfe with perfect white teeth, the only thing about him that didn't scream 'beaten near to death with the ugly stick.'

Miriam was Big Man Grimm's youngest child. She was tall and slender, and her naturally black hair was complemented by black eye makeup and an equally black mortuary dress. If there was a "goth pride flag" she would be waving it.

Or perhaps she's hoping the gods of undeath will give her a deck tonight.

Miriam stared at everyone around the table with an expression of amused condescension, but when her gaze reached Wolfe it lingered, her stare intense. "Yes, Wolfe, do tell me whether you think I'll deserve a deck this year. Have I been a bad girl? At least bad enough these last ten years to curry the favor of the dark?"

She smiled and pulled up a necklace with a dagger pendant from the depths of her black dress. Her tongue flicked out to briefly lick it, her eyes boring into Wolfe.

Wolfe ignored her antics—Miriam was twenty and head of her class at law school, with all the intelligence and verbal skills that implied—she just had a nasty habit of dragging people into conversations that could get them in trouble.

Why? Because it amused her, for all Wolfe could tell.

Miriam leaned back, narrowing her eyes when Wolfe didn't answer, but she raised her wine glass to him as if acknowledging his victory for not getting roped into her game.

"Might be someone's lucky night," Wolfe said as he glanced over to Big Man Grimm. "Even your children, whom you've already bought decks for, could get a god-gifted one. On the other hand..."

Wolfe paused before he finished his thought. "It's not the best odds, though. 'The Great Game Rule One: Every ten years, the gods will grant one in five hundred people over the age of thirteen a deck of ten cards, and that person shall become a deckbearer.'"

A weaselly man made his way to the table, passing the guards with a huff and roll of his eyes. He wore a suit that said, "*Yeah, you can beat me up, but my daddy will sue,*" and walked with the same haughty confidence.

Heinrich Grimm. The family accountant.

"I'm here, I'm here," Heinrich said, his voice nasally.

Big Man Grimm nodded.

"Ah, cousin," Heinrich said with a smile. "It's almost time. You've given much to advance the causes of Beelzebub. I'm sure he'll continue to favor our family greatly. Do you want to make a speech? You're so good at speeches."

Wolfe scowled at Heinrich. *What an ass-kisser.*

"I'm here to enjoy my family," Big Man Grimm stated, then nodded to Wolfe. "And my friends."

No one else said anything after that, the conversation stalling.

Then Thad Junior piped in. "Hey, has anyone seen Johnny? I thought he'd be here tonight."

Wolfe pinched the bridge of his nose and shook his head.

Big Man Grimm didn't answer his son, just frowning at him with a brow so furrowed, it threatened to split his face in two. Miriam laughed loudly into her wineglass, and Damian shook his head in theatrical disgust at his older brother and fiddled with one of his fly cufflinks. A few of the other, lower-ranking lieutenants around the table looked away, unwilling to get into the conflict.

Johnny, a long-time supporter of Big Man Grimm and his best drug courier, had been killed in an ambush last week, along with his entire team. The drugs he had been moving for the Grimm family had all been stolen. The Cobras, a stupid jumped-up street gang that had been making waves, had brazenly left their calling card at the scene. No one knew how the Cobras had found out what Johnny was doing, or where he would be. Millions of dollars in product had gone missing.

To judge by the claw marks and the couple withered, horror-faced corpses they had found, it had been a deckbearer who did the killing, most likely the Cobras' head enforcer, Nico. Somehow, the Cobras street gang had *six* deckbearers, the real reason they'd been able to move into Grimm family turf.

Wolfe sighed. Thaddeus Jr. was a decently likeable guy, and he had always admired Wolfe. But the man's I.Q. sat squarely at room temperature. How did he not know about Johnny's death?

Big Man Grimm turned to Wolfe. "I didn't want to spoil Drop Night, but I'm going to need you to do what you do best.

The Cobras have been cutting us to pieces. It's time for you to hit back."

Wolfe's scowl deepened. He had managed to kill two deckbearers in the past, but he had almost gotten nixed in the process. Now Big Man Grimm wanted him to do it again?

Big Man Grimm had taken the cards from the dead deckbearers to make his own deck, and his children's, stronger. Without a deck of his own, Wolfe would be at a disadvantage...

Wolfe's eyes flicked to Big Man Grimm. He owed the man everything. But Wolfe still wished Big Man Grimm had allowed Wolfe to keep the cards he had killed, so to speak.

Wolfe's boss must have sensed his mood, because he took a package from the seat next to him and passed it across the table to Wolfe. "Here. I was gonna give this to you after midnight, when the new deckbearers had been picked, but have it now. We don't need both of us scowling and ready to kill everyone."

"What is it?" Wolfe asked, picking the package up. It was the size of a shoebox, and it weighed quite a bit. But when Wolfe surreptitiously shook it, nothing moved inside.

Big Man Grimm shifted in his seat, glowering out at the floor, where the bodies of the dancers were visible as silhouettes through the smoke and lights. "Bonus and a promise, for my best and most loyal packmate."

Heinrich huffed at that statement.

Big Man Grimm ignored his cousin. "Take it and open it alone. In fact, use Suite Two on the upper floor. Also, I give you my word: You can have the cards of the next deckbearer you end. I know you've balanced the sheets between us, and you've been with me for twenty years. I'll have your back."

It was Damian's turn to huff. He picked up a shot glass and threw it back. "I need to be able to look at any cards he gets first, especially if they're Infernal. I *need* the best cards possible."

"You can take the cards when you've done as much as Wolfe,

and not before. You don't lead yet, son," Big Man Grimm said in his most menacing tone.

Damian glowered to the point his eyebrows appeared to be trying to forge a dynastic union with his nose. But he didn't speak any further.

Wolfe's heart warmed. He appreciated that Big Man Grimm was siding with him over his spoiled son.

Wolfe picked up the package from the table and stood. "I'll be back."

He got a respectful nod from Big Man Grimm and Damian, a corny salute from Thaddeus Jr., and a glare from Heinrich. The other, lower-ranked lieutenants at the table didn't acknowledge him.

Wolfe walked around the outside of the dance floor—hoping to avoid any more 'Tiffanys'—and reached the elevator. He rode it to the second floor and exited. It was the big man's private set of suites. Suite Two was his best guest suite in the entire Ekron Eternal.

Wolfe entered the spacious room and shut the door. There was a bar, circular couches around a central table with a statuette in the middle, even a goddamn indoor jacuzzi.

That was just the front room—it also had a bedroom and bathroom. Most of the suite was done in garish red and black, thick curtains and velvet, with art—a sort of baroque-style depiction of the Infernal in both painting and statuary—liberally spread around. An iron clock with its gears showing hung on one wall, its style out of place.

Wolfe imagined he could almost smell blood and incense from the overly themed room. There wasn't any, of course. But the décor tickled his brain and summoned his memories of the smell.

The sounds of Drop Night celebrations and a few early fireworks outside the window really mute the evil vibe, though, Wolfe thought with a sardonic grin.

Wolfe put his package down on the marble bar top and then sat on one of the barstools. He grabbed an ashtray, pulled a half-full cigarette pack from his pocket, removed a cigarette, tapped it, then pulled his lighter and lit it up.

Once he had smoked for a few seconds, he glanced at the clock on the wall.

11:58 P.M.

He was tempted to wait for the very moment of Drop Night but then cursed himself for a fool. He tore open the package and stared at it.

The majority was a thick stack of *thousand-dollar* bills... and the top was a stylized card that appeared to be a blank creature card.

Wolfe was pretty sure it was a promissory note—promising him that he would receive at least some kind of deck and become a deckbearer. Big Man Grimm could do it if he wanted—and he'd been there for Wolfe when—

A fiery pain in his chest caused him to yank his shirt open, a button shooting off to disappear in the plush red carpet. Wolfe stared at the huge, raised-off-the-skin scar that marked his chest. There was a brief flash of flame, then chains and a pentagram appeared above his chest. After a second, they sank into his scarred flesh and disappeared.

His own eyes wide in shock, Wolfe slowly touched his chest with a trembling hand splayed open in the gesture everyone knew from watching hundreds of TV shows about deckbearers. A sense of fire and eternal hunger, as well as a controlled rage and purpose, filled Wolfe, all of it tempered by a feeling of limitless possibility.

His heart beat so fast he thought it might burst. Wolfe held his hand out, still splayed open.

A red, fiery light pushed out from his hands and manifested as three cards, each the size of a normal playing card, hovering in front of Wolfe, just like it would have for every newbie deckbearer ever. A fourth card also manifested, hovering in the air off to the side—which wasn't normal.

He mentally called up a list of his cards. He had:

Two Escaped Damned, creatures.

Two Tormentor Imp, also creatures.

One Loyal Guard Dog, and One Rescue Pup, both creatures.

Two Return to the Pit, which was an immediate spell.

One Soul Hunter, his mantle card—something that empowered *him* whenever he played it.

And finally... A named card. Cereboo.

A piece of him was concerned he had received an Infernal god-gifted deck, which probably said some pretty bad things about him. But in that moment, he was just overjoyed to have received a deck at all.

Wolfe's eyes strayed to the last card, the fourth one hanging by itself in the air even through his swipes. He knew instantly it was different... It had no power cost, it was labeled as a companion card, and it was unique. Cards had both rarity and tier. Rarity tended to reflect starting strength compared to its power cost, and each tier was just a slightly stronger version of the same card—and cards could normally be combined to form higher-tier cards.

Unique cards could be nearly any effective rarity in quality, and since they couldn't be raised in tier, were assigned an 'effective tier' to explain their total strength. Tier-seven was... ridiculously high.

Wolfe stared at his card, Cereboo.

Cereboo
Unique Beast/Infernal[Canine] Companion Effective Tier-7
0 Power
Health: 12
Attack: 5 x3

Magical Attack: 7
Defense: 7
Magical Defense: 4

Special: While in play, Beast and Infernal power may be spent as if they were the other.
Special: Guardian of the Gate: +100% attack and magic attack against other Infernal cards.
Special: Preferred Typing: Gains all the better type matchups of both Infernal and Beast.
Special: One of the 'Gate to the Underworld' cards. If all 6 are possessed in the same deck, the bearer will gain 7 Legendary Infernal or Beast card pulls. Additionally, the deckbearer may either gain the Mythic 'Gate to the Underworld' Building Card or evolve Cereboo. Each card was given to a member of the Noimoire underworld.

"A pup of Cerberus, who was born into a particularly frisky litter. Cereboo was the runt—not quite as strong, nor as tough, as his litter mates. But his heart was the heart of a huntsman, and the blood of Cerberus runs in his veins. He hunted across the fiery plains of the first infernal realm, chasing the damned that tried to escape their fates. Now, he chases many things, but his soul is still called to chase those that belong in the Infernal Realms."

Wolfe was intrigued by the part where it claimed it belonged to a set that would unlock other, even more powerful cards... If Wolfe could acquire the other five. Cards came in five rarities—common, uncommon, rare, legendary, and mythic. Legendary cards were so rare that only the most famous card users had more than one or two, and Mythics were almost always out of reach of all but the insanely powerful deckbearers or the leaders of nations and the ultra-rich. *The gods might have power crept this season*. Wolfe's mind raced with the possibilities.

Before he could do anything, however, his spine crawled with danger. Hot, fetid breath, smelling faintly of decay and incense, washed across him. Wolfe dropped his hand to his pistol and turned, but nothing was there in the empty hotel room.

Despite seeming to be alone, Wolfe's skin still prickled. A sudden premonition filled him. He saw, in his mind's eye, the indistinct outline of the five other people that had all gotten the cards that was part of Cereboo's card set. They fought one another, until only one was left, and from that person a miasma of darkness, evil, and pain spread.

"This is the fate if you do not hunt them down, and claim the cards for yourself. It will be as your failure from before, but far, far worse."

Wolfe could not have put a name to the voice that entered his mind, but it was hungry and vengeful... but somehow not evil. Or not entirely.

Wolfe shuddered as the room returned to normal.

He stared at the Cerberus puppy card for a moment, gathering himself. The picture of the pup reminded Wolfe of his late dog, Pierce, but with three heads, and it calmed him. He had been in numerous life-death-situations, but it took him a moment to gather his normal sardonic wit after that voice.

"Pierce better not be in some hell," Wolfe quipped. Then he gave a dark chuckle—he knew damn well his dog hadn't gone to any bad place in the cosmos. He was the only purely good being Wolfe had ever known, even if he had been a bit of a doofus.

Wolfe reached out a hand and touched the Cereboo card. Immediately, the card turned into red light and rushed to the carpet. In less than a second it spread out, intensified, and then disappeared, leaving a massive three-headed, black-skinned boxer puppy that appeared to weigh around two-hundred pounds in its place.

Wolfe was stunned. *I just summoned a card, like a real deckbearer!*

The puppy woofed from its right head.

Pierce reached out and pet that head, and the left head pushed at his right hand. Wolfe reached out and scratched that head behind the ear. Both the left and right heads were now panting happily, and the dogs tail was wagging.

In that moment, when Wolfe was fully occupied, the middle head licked his face.

"Blargh," Wolfe said, grabbing the bed cover and wiping his face. "Infernal you might be, but a dog you remain."

Cereboo woofed happily and bounded around Wolfe in a circle.

Well, I've been ordered after the Cobras, so maybe I'll find one or more of the people I need to kill with them.

How the hell am I supposed to find out who has these cards?

Wolfe put it from his mind for the moment, and was about to pull up his status sheet when his phone went off. *What the fuck? It's been like four minutes since the drop! How the hells can someone already need me?*

He pulled it out to see who was calling, then answered immediately.

"What's up, boss?"

Big Man Grimm's voice came through the phone. "Get down here. You need to deal with this."

Chapter 2

Aeshma's Bid

"**The Great Game Rule #2**: When a deckbearer is defeated, anyone may take their cards."

A few minutes later, and after sending Cereboo back to the deck, Wolfe slipped back into his seat at the table with a nod to Harry and Dan. Heinrich was missing, but the rest of the inner circle was still at the table.

"What's going on?" he asked.

Damian had four cards out, each floating in front of him. Most of his cards glowed a fiery red, and every minute, he swiped them to the side, switching them for others and staring at them. Four cards at a time was impressive—that was one more card out than a Level One deckbearer would normally possess.

Wolfe wondered when the fuck the miserable little man had been able to level up and improve his hand size. Damian was sifting through cards laid out on the table, and even as Wolfe watched, he removed one from the cards floating in front of him and replaced it in a single swap.

"He got new cards?" Wolfe asked over the music that still thumped through the club.

Big Man Grimm nodded, a tight smile on his face. "Yes. My son was gifted a deck with some Beelzebub cards in it. Just like his old man before him."

Wolfe glanced over at Damian's robust frame and chuckled. *And at least one of you favors gluttony in turn.*

Damian glanced up, his face flushed. "Wolfe, I got a companion card. They're new to this drop. They cost no power to use, so they make any deckbearer that has them, like me"— Damian tapped his own chest with a ring-encrusted, pudgy hand, smiling broadly—"*very* powerful."

I bet you love the idea of finally being powerful, Wolfe thought, keeping his sneer from reaching his face. It wasn't fair to Damian to judge him for wanting the cards so desperately, Wolfe knew. What the gods had taken from Thad in the brains department, they had taken from Damian in the brawn department. *Of course* the big man's son wanted to be powerful, and if his lust for cards was a little unseemly, well, at least it made sense.

Wolfe raised an empty glass at Damian. "Congratulations."

Big Man Grimm turned to Wolfe, his question on his face.

Wolfe hesitated but then said, "I got a deck as well."

A couple of the other gang members around the table clapped, but Thaddeus Junior exploded and swiped a half-empty brandy glass from the table. "What? How is that possible? I'm the oldest son! Damian got a deck, Heinrich got a deck, and our *dog* got a deck?. How come I didn't, Dad? What a crock of shit."

Wolfe gave Thad Junior the eye as a nearby waitress came over and started to clean it up. *Daddy already bought you one, you spoiled little shit.* Wolfe had known Thad Jr. since Wolfe was eighteen and Thad Jr. had been ten. He had been spoiled then too.

Damian stared at Wolfe with curiosity.

Miriam had her arms crossed over her chest. She reached one

slender arm out and languidly took a wineglass, raising it and a black-dyed eyebrow at Wolfe. "Congratulations. Welcome to the true aristocracy, the only one that really matters."

Big Man Grimm raised his own eyebrow in a near mimicry of his daughter.

They went way back, Wolfe and his boss. Just over twenty years.

Big Man Grimm had saved Wolfe, and they had fought on the streets together in the early years, where Wolfe had saved Big Man Grimm's life in turn, and the Big Man had been mentor to Wolfe, showing him what he needed to know about the new world Wolfe had found himself in.

It had been many years since they had fought side-by-side, and their relationship was mostly boss and his right-hand man these days, but both trusted the other implicitly.

"What did Heinrich get?" Wolfe asked, thinking about what Thad Jr. had said.

"He claimed he only got generic Infernal and Psychic cards," Damian said, running a finger across the table. "Then he ran off with some whore, like he always does to celebrate. What cards did you get? I can't wait to tell you what I got."

Big Man Grimm chopped his hand through the air. "Enough of this. I'm glad so many of us got decks, but we can compare cards later. Wolfe, I'm sorry, but I called you down here because I'm having a feeling... I want you to go and provide back-up at the docks."

Wolfe sighed.

Big Man Grimm frowned. "I know, my friend, and I'm sorry. We can't afford to lose this shipment. If it goes away, we're fucked. A few years ago, we were the strongest family in Noimoire, but we're losing it. It stops tonight—this new year, with our new deckbearers, we will remake ourselves."

Wolfe sighed again, but stood from the table. He really wanted to figure out what being a deckbearer *meant*. To sit at some computer and learn about the new companion system and what cool cards had been released with this current set. Check out card combos that might work with his deck. Wolfe had already had a ton of money squirreled away, from his time as Big Man Grimm's top enforcer. He'd just gotten even more. Before now, he hadn't had a reason to spend the money. Cards that helped him in his job, though...

But Wolfe wouldn't say no to Big Man Grimm. He owed the man too much.

"I'll be at the docks in fifteen," Wolfe said, stepping away from the table and heading for the elevator to the garage.

On his way, he avoided the couple people that were sobbing over *not* having gotten decks and *not* becoming special in a single moment.

Wolfe had problems of his own.

Three minutes later, Wolfe stepped into his beat-up black Chrysler 300 SRT. Wolfe liked his car—it appeared to be a boring sedan, but it had a ton of power under the hood. He even left a few dents and scratches in it to encourage the view he was poor and harmless. Even if most of the players in the Noimoire underworld—and even a few in the larger circles within the greater rust belt—knew him, the street-rank thugs didn't know him on sight, so it was still possible for Wolfe to appear unimportant occasionally, and take people unawares.

Plus, an expensive car in the bad parts of Noimoire got the cops on you faster than shit got flies.

Wolfe had also paid good money on some modifications— armor plating in the door, bulletproof windows, and a couple of small, hidden compartments in case he ever needed to smuggle something.

Wolfe reached back and put his gift from Big Man Grimm in one of the smuggling compartments. Then he drove out of the underground parking garage and onto the usually dark and rain-filled streets of Noimoire. It *was* raining, a cold drizzle, but it wasn't that dark in this part of the city—the part where the city spiked vertical. The glittering lights of the club district plus the flashes of fireworks lit the place up decently.

Even if they hadn't, all the billboards had their own floodlights, which would have kept the streets lit. Wolfe could practically drive the city by the insane billboards.

He glanced up at the floodlit signs through his rain-slicked windshield. To get home, take a right at the giant 'soap' card billboard, with 'germ attack' listed where the magic attack stat would normally go. So clever, no one has ever done that before. Then take a left at the advertisement for Gavin's, the online card buying site. It actually makes sense to advertise here, I suppose. Noimoire, and similar cities, are the only places with enough money to justify blanket advertising a site for buying cards when the minimum price of a card is fifty K, and the cards get more expensive rapidly from there. Wolfe has nearly half a million saved up from his life as an enforcer, and briefly wondered about whether he could buy the other five cards he needed.

Wolfe laughed and met his own eyes in the rear-view mirror. "Sure, buddy, you can just buy these five ultra cards when some legendary and mythic cards have gone for hundreds of millions of dollars or even caused wars. Sure. It'll be that easy. Face it, this is gonna be a whole *thing*."

The lights faded as Wolfe left the glitzy nightlife district and headed to the docks, and the billboards began to advertise alcohol. There were a lot of docks in Noimoire's crescent-shaped harbor, but the ones Wolfe was headed to were in the poor part of town. Far fewer cars and people were out at night here, and the ones who were mostly wanted—or purveyed—illicit drugs or sex.

Wolfe chuckled quietly to himself, noting that they were doing it from under awnings at the moment, trying to stay dry in the rain.

He reached into his pocket and pulled out another cigarette, lighting it from his car lighter and then puffing. He didn't expect trouble on Drop Night, not till he got to the destination, at least, but his eyes scanned for danger through the rain and his wiper blades all the same.

He noted the car idling down a side street with its headlights on as he turned onto Main Street, but his danger sense didn't flare until it sped toward him. *What the hell?*

Wolfe yanked his steering wheel to the left. The oncoming car sideswiped him, and they both spun out, the sounds of metal crunching filling the night air. Even before the collision, and despite having never been a deckbearer before, Wolfe had already placed his hand on his chest, and before his car had fully come to a stop, he had his cards up.

Wolfe had always been an intuitive killer with whatever tool came to hand.

He saw two Escaped Damned cards and a Loyal Guard Dog card floating in front of him—as well as his ever-present companion card. *Fuck. Of course I didn't get my mantle card. Well, we're doing this without the added personal protection, I guess. Never stopped me before.*

A notification popped into his vision, claiming that a deckbearer had drawn their deck. A fierce predatory glee filled Wolfe. *Another deckbearer. Which might mean more cards, even if it means more danger. And I haven't even seen all my own cards yet.*

He grabbed his companion card, Cereboo, and willed it into existence just outside the car door even as gunfire erupted from the opposite vehicle and a series of spiderwebs formed in his windows where the bullets had been caught by the bulletproof glass.

Wolfe ducked below the window level and released his seatbelt. Then he opened the passenger-side door and slapped his glove box open. He grabbed his firearm—and STI international Edge 40 caliber with a 14-round magazine—from the glovebox and rolled out of his car, onto the rain-slick cement of the sidewalk. Less than five seconds after the collision, Wolfe came to his feet in a crouch, his pistol pointed at his opponents' car, watching through the rain-splatters on his hood for a target.

His companion card, Cereboo—now a two-hundred-pound, black-skinned boxer puppy with three heads—woofed excitedly and leapt onto the first thug out of the car, grabbing both arms in his left and right mouths and chewing on the guy's shoulder with his center head.

Wolfe wasted the second thug that came from the car—the back passenger side, facing him—with three shots to the chest from his slightly-more-powerful than cop guns pistol. He noted the snake tattoo on the thug's exposed shoulder. *The Cobras. Of course.*

He also received a hundred experience and a level notification overlaid across his vision, but he dismissed those.

But both of the ones to come out of the car side facing Wolfe were now out of the fight—one being chewed on by Cereboo, the other dead.

I've still got it! These fuckers ambushed me and I'm the one that got first blood!

Someone still inside the car shot Cereboo in his left head, screaming "Kill the fucking card!" and blood splashed from the dog's head, but Wolfe's new mutt didn't go down. A guy came out of the back driver's side and shot over the hood of the car, screaming "I'm taking out their deckbearer!" Wolfe cussed as the shot grazed his arm.

Four total mooks, three I still need to kill, Wolfe catalogued automatically.

Wolfe's first-ever combat log appeared in his vision, but he mentally pushed it aside—it wasn't helpful in the middle of combat.

As he ducked back behind the car, he grabbed his next card: the Loyal Guard Dog. He was tempted to pull the Escaped Damned, as it had immense physical defense, but it had almost nothing else, and Wolfe needed damage output to finish the fight since the momentum had shifted in his favor. *Never give your enemies a chance to recover.*

Magic flowed from him as he brought forth his card, a tickling sensation running from his chest along his arm and out through his hand.

Loyal Guard Dog
Common Beast[Canine] Creature Tier-1
1 Beast Power
Health: 10
Attack: 5
Magical Attack: N/A
Defense: 5
Magical Defense: 2

Special: May remain on the battlefield for twice as long as the caster's 'base length of play' stat.

"A Powerful mastiff guard dog. A basic low-level Beast creature, common throughout the world in junkyards and the homes of people that want to look dangerous."

The dog manifested. It hit the ground and ran around Wolfe's car. Another creature also manifested—an enemy spirit obviously summoned by one of the thugs. It was a yellow-red spirit that appeared to be on fire. It floated around the thug's car, its arms outstretched. Wolfe cussed. *He brought his own Escaped Damned to the fight.*

Both his dogs attacked the Escaped Damned.

Wolfe grimaced and muttered to himself, "The Great Game Rule Fourteen: Summoned creatures *must* attack opposing summoned creatures *first*, before they can target enemy deckbearers or mortals."

Fortunately, deckbearers could attack whomever they wanted.

Wolfe popped back up and finished off the wounded thug that Cereboo hadn't quite put away, noting that the experience was reduced to fifty this time. He dove back behind the car as a fusillade of bullets whistled through the air where he had been. His driver-side window finally broke.

Wolfe also got a notification that his Cereboo had finished the Escaped Damned off, briefly surprising him. Then he remembered the card. *Right, Cereboo gets a huge bonus to his attack against other Infernal cards. Convenient.*

Wolfe ejected the magazine from his pistol, pushed a new one in, and then swiped his cards away, bringing the next three up for use. He got a Tormentor Imp that cost one Infernal power, a Rescue Dog that cost one Beast power, and a card called Return to the Pit that only required one available Infernal power to use. The last was a persistent activated card.

Wolfe was pretty sure he had the advantage at the moment— but he needed to hold it for a few more seconds. He couldn't give the enemy deckbearer a chance to change the flow of combat with his deck.

Hoping the Cobra gang enforcer would pull a second Infernal creature, Wolfe played the Return to the Pit card, spending his last power. And then he fired over the hood of the car to distract his enemy.

For a fraction of a second, as he huddled behind his shot-up and dented car, Wolfe's mind wandered away from the combat, something that almost never happened to him. *I'm a real deckbearer! I just ran a tribe-specific shutdown strategy, something my deck seems built for! It's like the* king-of-cards *comic!*

A brief yellow and red flash of flame appeared—another Escaped Damned; the guy wasn't that creative—and then the Return to the Pit card activated, wiping the creature card out and trapping the one Infernal power his opponent had used for five minutes. The card briefly manifested as a pentagram, then dissipated, the energy flying back into Wolfe's chest and disappearing. *Returning to my deck.*

It's just you, me, and my doggo, assholes! I'm betting you're fucked.

The third thug was covered in bites but tried a wild kick to fend off Cereboo. His planted foot flew out from under him and he slammed down back first onto the rain-slick pavement. The Loyal Guard Dog and Cereboo both leapt forward and ended the last thug with four bites, one to the thug's neck. Wolfe got another fifty experience and went to level three.

Wolfe lurched to his feet, throwing his Rescue Pup card out as well.

A decently sized dog, maybe forty pounds, emaciated but with huge cute eyes, appeared. Wolfe fired rapidly at the enemy deckbearer, who ducked and brought forth a Tormentor Imp.

Those have got to be the Infernal common baby drops for this drop season, Wolfe thought to himself as he raced around his own car. He swiped his cards again, and his mantle—Soul Hunter—another Rescue Pup, and a second Return to the Pit appeared.

His Loyal Guard Dog and Rescue Pup was still in play, as was Cereboo. Wolfe had the upper hand and meant to keep it, which in this case meant doubling down on his shut-down strategy. He pulled the Return to the Pit to prevent an enemy creature from appearing. If his creatures could attack the enemy deckbearer, he would win, and he was pretty sure they'd finish the enemy imp off quickly.

As he came around the enemy car, however, his preparation proved unnecessary. The deckbearer was firing at Cereboo while trying to dodge the three dogs. What he wasn't doing was keeping his eye on the guy with the gun.

"Good-bye, fucker," Wolfe said, satisfaction in his voice as he held his pistol out. The man turned, his expression a focused snarl. Wolfe hit him with a couple of shots to the chest. The enemy deckbearer went down, a red mist briefly marking the space the bullets had hit him. The Tormentor Imp disappeared in a puff of red smoke.

Wolfe ejected the clip and reloaded his pistol a second time, storing his empty while standing over his dead assailants. "Fuck around and find out," he muttered to their uncaring corpses.

Wolfe had gotten sixty-seven experience for his last kill—he was pretty sure it had been sixty-six point six, which felt appropriate and caused him a brief, black chuckle. The deckbearer's cards appeared on the ground next to the corpse. Wolfe scooped them up before the seeping blood got on them. Wolfe didn't know if they could be stained or not, but he didn't want fucked-up cards in his deck.

As he picked the cards up, the rain beaded on them but never soaked in. *Probably can't be affected by normal things, then.*

Wolfe scanned the scene—four corpses with snake tattoos on their arms, pools of blood everywhere slowly diluting in the rain, guns, and a car with a dented front. Plus, his own busted vehicle. He sighed. *All right, more like twenty minutes till I reach the docks.*

Also, how the fuck do the Cobras keep getting the drop on us?

He frowned at his expensive suit, torn and stained and now getting wet.

The Loyal Guard Dog and Rescue Pup waited, doing nothing, but Cereboo ran up to Wolfe and planted his feet on his chest, all three heads licking him. Each had the oversized idiot grin of the boxer, as well as the enlarged jowls even the puppies got. Wolfe was again powerfully reminded of his old dog, Pierce. Despite the setting, he was warmed by his new companion's presence. "Who's a good boy, helping me put down the Cobras? Is it you?"

Cereboo woofed with all three mouths.

I wonder if Cereboo playing with me, rather than waiting like my other summons, is a sign of his personality?

Wolfe put the question from his mind as he laughed at his enthusiastic new demon-puppy. He had work to do, so he wrestled Cereboo aside, then pointed to the ground next to him. "Sit."

Cereboo sat, all three heads panting happily.

Wolfe pulled his phone out and called Rich while he rooted for and found his own ejected empty clip.

"Wolfe?" the voice answered.

"We have a situation, and I'm needed elsewhere. Get a cleaner crew to Main and Thirty-First, near the local Cardless Café. Four bodies, all Cobras, and a dented car. Disappear the bodies and repurpose the car and guns."

"I'm, um, about to... you know. With Tiffany."

"Take her or leave her—get road head, for all I care—but get out here and get it done."

There was a brief pause, then Rich's annoyed voice came through the phone. "All right, I'll be there."

Wolfe ended the call, and mentally dismissed his two other summoned cards. Both dissipated into a brownish light and flowed back into Wolfe. Then he looked at Cereboo. "I'm sorry, buddy, but I need to put you back in the deck, okay?"

Cereboo whined.

Wolfe grimaced. "If any deckbearer sees you, they'll be able to read your card. Then they'll try to take you from me, boy, because you're part of some super rare card set. I'd rather not deal with that shit, okay? I already lost one dog this month."

Cereboo flopped to the ground but quit whining, and Wolfe took the action as acceptance. He unsummoned Cereboo, who became red energy and rushed back into Wolfe's chest.

He went to his car, swept the glass from the driver's seat, and continued to the docks, eighty percent of his brain thinking about the strategy he had almost instinctively employed against the enemy deckbearer, and other things he might be able to do with his deck.

But the last twenty percent was occupied with a fierce joy at his victory. Wolfe still had it. And he wasn't about to lose his cards *or* fail Big Man Grimm.

CHAPTER 3

WRATH OF THE PIT

"**The Great Game Rule #3**: Anyone who acquires ten cards
outside of Drop Night becomes a deckbearer and is bound by
the rules of the Great Game."

Wolfe pulled into the parking lot at Dock Eighty-Seven with his dented but still functional car and turned his engine off. He waited for a moment in his car, remembering what it was like to be young and on a product run. It was nerve-wracking. He could see a couple guys out near some shipping containers, and he didn't want to spook them into using their guns.

Besides, Wolfe was still quite excited that he was a deckbearer, and, thanks to the few Cobra jerks he'd just made the acquaintance of, already level three. Excitement outside of a fight was an unusual sentiment for Wolfe, and he treasured it, trying to hold on.

Although said excitement was muted a bit since the rain had been soaking Wolfe through his shot-out window the whole time he had been driving, and his car had a few too many bullet holes for his taste now.

It's gangland chic, Wolfe thought to himself with a snort, surprised by his own whimsy.

He glanced around. Dock Eighty-Seven was one of the many, many docks of Noimoire, which had both lake- and river-side docks. This one was lakeside, and had a medium-large ship at port—a smaller container carrier, with a pile of unloaded shipping crates on top, and a few large cranes near the ship.

A couple of the containers had been unloaded onto the dock and left there, and a couple cars were parked around the metal shipping crates. Wolfe was only about two hundred feet from the set up, and finally, a few men left the five Wolfe could see and approached.

He grabbed his pistol, stuck it in his belt, and got out of his own busted car just as the Grimm family men arrived at the vehicle, keeping his own empty hands visible. Wolfe didn't recognize the first guy coming up, a tall, wiry man with coffee-colored skin and hazel eyes to match Wolfe's own. Guy moved like he could fight, however, and had his hand on his pistol at his belt, which Wolfe approved of.

The second guy, however, Wolfe knew. "Hey, George, everything going alright? The boss sent me to oversee everything."

George was a long-time member of their organization, and his loyalty to the boss was unquestioned. But over the years he had gone from a tan, hulking bruiser to a grossly overweight pasty dude. He was out in the rain sporting sweatpants and a wife beater, despite the drizzle still going on.

Wolfe frowned—guys with moobs shouldn't wear wife beaters. Or lead runs for the family, no matter how loyal they were.

Although he was legitimately impressed by George's ability to ignore the wet, cold weather.

I wonder if his fat insulates him? Wolfe thought with genuine curiosity. He was uncomfortably cold, himself, but didn't allow himself to shiver or otherwise acknowledge his cold in front of his compatriots. His reputation for ignoring pain and discomfort kept him from a lot of actual fights.

The flash of headlights cut off any answer. A car turned onto the pier-side road, weaving drunkenly. *Probably sad they didn't get cards,* Wolfe thought with a glance over his shoulder to make sure it wasn't a threat. It passed the dock without slowing down.

Once the car was gone, George responded. "It's good you're here, Wolfe, but there's no need. Everything's quiet."

"Hmm," Wolfe responded, his eyes scanning the night despite the reassuring words. There was little light, only that provided by the streetlamps on the side of the road, plus a tiny bit through the drizzle from the city itself, which he could see along the shore.

George hooked his thumb back at some men working on the shipping containers. "Our boys are over there right now, getting the product. We're mantled."

Wolfe chuckled at the common expression, which referenced a deckbearer that was wearing a mantle—they were almost always far stronger than one that hadn't gotten a mantle on yet.

George cocked an eyebrow and scratched at his gross chest, but didn't pursue when Wolfe declined to comment.

"Who's the new guy?" Wolfe asked with a jut of his chin at the man next to them.

"I'm Derek." The man held his hand out. "Derek Washington. I carry a gun for the family. Really glad to meet you, Wolfe. Everyone around here really talks you up."

Wolfe just glanced at the offered hand, then raised his own eyebrow.

"He's new," George explained. "Hired to replace some of the men we lost with Johnny."

Wolfe nodded and started to hold his hand out in turn, but a flash of headlights pulled his attention away.

Another car turned onto the pier road, driving slowly. Then another. And another.

Wolfe's hand dropped to his Edge pistol almost automatically. He turned to get a better view of the cars.

In the dim light of the street lamps, through the misty air and drizzle, he couldn't make out much, not even the exact color of the cars, although they were all darker. But a metallic glint of light where there shouldn't be any metal, in a back driver-side window, warned him.

"Down!" Wolfe screamed, throwing himself to the rain-slicked concrete of the parking lot, grunting as he jostled his already-bruised-and-shot shoulder.

Derek followed him half-a-second later, leaving George standing.

From the back window a series of lights flashed, and loud bangs rang out across the docks—the sound of an automatic rifle. Wolfe stared in shock. *Where the fuck are people getting military rifles?*

Two large red holes appeared on George's chest, and his back exploded in a shower of gore. He slammed into the ground with finality, almost certainly dead from hydrostatic shock before he hit—and if not, he would be in seconds as blood *poured* from the massive wounds in his back.

Hollow-point rounds? This gets better and better.

Even through the rain, the coppery smell of blood was over-powering, and a shit-stink of death joined it.

Wolfe rolled to his back across the wet asphalt and put his hand on his chest as the three cars turned into the parking lot. He had three cards—a Return to the Pit, an Escaped Damned, and a Tormentor Imp. And he always had Cereboo available.

No mantle in my first pull again. Of course.

Wolfe was very briefly tempted to put the Escaped Damned

into play, as it had powerful defense and health stats for a tier-one card.

Escaped Damned

Common Infernal/Undead Creature Tier-1
1 Infernal Power
Health: 10
Attack: 0
Magical Attack: 3
Defense: 8
Magical Defense: 1

"A soul that somehow escaped the Infernal realm and wants to remain free"

Cereboo was treated as Infernal for purposes of resistances, which meant he was fifty-percent stronger against Mortal... including *actual* mortals and their guns. So Wolfe ignored his weaker cards and tossed Cereboo into the fray once again. The red light left his card and formed into his dog, who ran toward the Cobras gleefully.

As soon as Cereboo was in play, Wolfe sprang to his feet. "Get to the crates!" he screamed at Derek, who followed him almost step-for-step. Wolfe kept his own car between himself and his enemies as he moved, making sure he had cover.

More gunfire, and the sound of exploding glass, caused him to grit his teeth. He was pretty sure his car's repair bill was gonna rival the national debt.

He reached the containers and slid to a halt half-behind one. He saw three more of the Grimm family men and another corpse—the head was blown through.

Two guys killed in a spray-and-pray, in the darkness, in the rain? And I didn't get my mantle? The gods must really hate me.

Derek slid in next to Wolfe and then scrambled around to the other side of the container, his gun out.

Wolfe fired blindly in the direction of the enemy cars, just to keep their heads down, but a round of cussing told him that not all his luck was bad. It was followed by a combat log showing four damage against an 'unknown enemy thug.'

Derek fired from his side of the big shipping crate, but the other three were just hiding.

Wolfe glanced over at them. "Fight back, you dumb fucks!"

"They have a gun!" one called back.

Wolfe pointed his pistol around the corner again and fired another couple rounds off. "You idiots, we *all* have guns!"

Three howls, that sounded suspiciously of glee to Wolfe, rang out from the darkness, and someone yelled, "Dogs!"

A series of screams sounded, and Wolfe got another combat notification that he summarized as Cereboo turning someone into an involuntary chew toy. *These notifications are really helping out, since I can't see a gods' damned thing out there in the dark and rain.*

His remaining cards became available again, and he threw an Escaped Damned out. A screaming soul, yellow, with red fire around it, appeared a few feet from him.

The Escaped Damned cards were extremely strong on the defense, but weak on the attack.

And I didn't bring a spare magazine, Wolfe thought to himself, desperately wishing he had access to his car glove box and trying to remember how many rounds he had fired. He couldn't, although he usually fired three-round bursts to keep people's heads down... so probably eight shots left. Probably.

He turned around the corner of the metal shipping crate he was still crouched behind.

Three men ran up fast, one carrying the automatic rifle. They were close enough that Wolfe could easily make them out in the dark. He casually pointed his pistol and shot the guy with the big gun in the head. He got a notification of another thirty-three experience and level four.

I really should level. I could have used being stronger right about now. Although, I hate the idea of not sitting down and carefully planning my growth as a deckbearer.

The other two men leapt to the sides, and one pulled a grenade from his jacket and tossed it toward Wolfe, rolling it behind the protection of the crates. "Die, fucker!"

Wolfe's eyes involuntarily widened. *A grenade? In a gang war?*

Wolfe was so shocked by the incongruity of the weapons in this fight that he almost didn't act, but his instincts carried him through. He leapt behind his Escaped Damned just as the grenade went off, praying his summoned creature would be enough.

CHAPTER 4

AN EYE FOR AN EYE

"**The Great Game Rule #4**: Cards cannot be destroyed."

The explosion ripped through the box, sending shrapnel everywhere. All three of the Grimm family enforcers collapsed to the ground, two screaming, one unmoving. Derek grunted and dropped his gun. He grabbed his thigh as blood gushed between his fingers.

But Wolfe was fine—utterly untouched. The high defense of the Escaped Damned provided a strong enough barrier to stop the shrapnel, although it was chewed to pieces itself.

The two Cobra thugs had kept moving forward, and Wolfe was *really* close to his two assailants, less than thirty feet from each man. He shot both, a cluster of three bullets to each, although he clicked on empty on the very last shot. A double notification of twenty-five experience each told him that the men were down.

At the same time, his notification chart included Cereboo finishing off a thug, giving another twenty-five experience as well. But the gunfire was starting to add up on Wolfe's mystical new pooch, who was almost dead.

Wolfe's eyes fell to the rifle at the feet of the first Cobra thug he had shot.

"I'll be back for you!" Wolfe called to Derek, the only jackass on his team that had been doing what they were supposed to be doing—fighting the Cobras.

"I'm fine!" the man called out. "Just take those fuckers out!"

"I intend to," Wolfe muttered under his breath.

He ran and grabbed the assault rifle, which felt uncomfortable in his hands—he'd fired one at a local gun range years ago, but that was his only experience using the heavier weapons. He didn't even know the make or model, and he considered himself something of a handgun expert.

As an afterthought, he also grabbed a second pistol from one of the dead Cobra thugs. "I'd say sorry for taking your shit, but I figure you don't give a fuck anymore," Wolfe quipped to the corpse.

He stuck the weapon in the back of his pants, violating nearly every gun safety rule, and rushed toward the sounds of snarling, barking, screams, and gunfire.

Cereboo is being a very *good boy.*

Right as he thought that, the growls ceased, and red light poured back into his chest. Cereboo had been defeated.

Cereboo wasn't in his 'hand' of cards, and Wolfe no longer had the option to summon Cereboo as a companion. He wondered how he got back into circulation in his hand— perhaps Cereboo was a random pull now that he had been 'killed' once?

Someone ahead of him called, "The gods' damned dog is finally down."

Wolfe vaguely saw four people standing together in the rain under one light, near all the cars. He stopped running near a car that he could use for cover if things went south.

Then he swiped his cards. He passed on the Escaped Damned that came up, as it would light everything up and reveal his position. Instead, he grabbed a Tormentor Imp and threw it down. A small red humanoid, about three feet tall, appeared. It had oversized hands that ended in sharp claws, and it rushed into the darkness, toward Wolfe's enemies.

One of the thugs, taller than the rest but otherwise indistinguishable in the darkness and rain, started yammering at his associates. "There's a deckbearer around, let's go kill him so I can get a new deck and join the rest of our—"

Wolfe opened fire at the clumped targets with his rifle. Two of them went down fast but two more managed to hit the ground and start scrabbling across the pavement toward nearby parked cars. Wolfe released the trigger.

Two can play the unfair weapons game, assholes.

Both the thugs brought pistols out as they scooted for safety, but obviously hadn't gotten their bearings yet, staring out into the darkness with light-blinded eyes. Wolfe took careful aim, squeezed the trigger, and ended a third.

Level Five. He dismissed the notification.

From where he lay on the ground, the last man pointed his pistol in Wolfe's direction. Wolfe ducked behind the car he was using as cover with a curse as the man fired at him, and the bullet whizzed through the space he had just occupied.

Wolfe mentally directed his Tormentor Imp to attack, and a few seconds later the man started yelling.

"I need one to question," Wolfe muttered to himself. He rushed around the car, low, hoping the yells meant the Cobra thug was distracted.

A notification of damage to his enemy told Wolfe that he was, in fact, distracted—not that Wolfe needed it now that he could see the Cobra gun carrier. The imp was on Wolfe's target, biting and scratching, and the man was on his back, punching and kicking, his handgun on the ground next to him.

Wolfe dropped the assault rifle and pulled his new pistol. Then he ran across the wet asphalt of the parking lot to the thug.

He kicked the guy's weapon away and stuck his borrowed weapon in the man's temple.

The thug dropped his hands but kept trying to weave his head as he yelled, "Alright, you got me, Wolfe! For all the gods' sake, call your imp off, and please don't shoot me!"

Not sure if I'm proud or concerned that this fucking dipshit knows me on sight—the other families' mooks don't usually. Little of column A, little of column B, I suppose.

With a mental command, Wolfe urged his Tormentor Imp to back away. The red imp leapt from the Cobra thug's chest to the ground.

Wolfe winced as he glanced at his imp—one wrist was clearly broken, and a huge purple bruise was already forming on its side. The thug was better, but still had multiple scratches on his balding, broken-toothed mug, and the Noimoire Jackals windbreaker over his chest was ripped up.

"How did you know we'd be here?" Wolfe pressed his pistol hard into the thug's temple.

The man's eyes were wide as rain splattered across him, and even through the downpour Wolfe got a taste of near-deadly halitosis as the thug spoke. "I got no clue, man! Nico just told everyone to be ready—he said that Drop Night would be a good day to catch all you stuck-up Grimm boys with your pants down!"

A chill ran through Wolfe. *Nico. The head enforcer for the Cobras, a deckbearer that has had ten years to build his deck and levels.* Wolfe scratched at the scar on his chest. *The man who gave me this.*

Although, Wolfe had his own deck now—a rematch might be a bit more interesting. Wolfe was pretty sure he could take Nico alone, but he had never been able to take Nico plus Nico's deck.

The sound of sirens infiltrated Wolfe's thoughts. *I've got a few seconds here at best.*

"Where else is everyone hitting?" Wolfe asked.

The guy reached up, probably to wipe rain from his face, but Wolfe shook his head *no*. He might have been reaching for Wolfe's gun.

The guy grimaced. "C'mon, man, I'm just a carrier. I don't know the plan! We were all just told to gather at the Snakebite Club, and we did, and then Nico sent us all away on missions! We're supposed to gather there when we're done."

"Anyone there now?"

"I..."

Derek came limp-jumping from the darkness on one leg, using the assault rifle as a crutch.

Wolfe raised an eyebrow at him, and Derek frowned. "Other guys didn't make it."

The thug's eyes flickered to Wolfe's fellow Grimm employee, but Wolfe poked the thug in the side of the head with his pistol again. "Focus. The club? Who's guarding it?"

The man gave the slightest nod of his head "Well, Frankie's there, and maybe one or two of his guys."

Wolfe felt a jolt of excitement go through him. Frankie 'the Frog' Fodorvich was a Cobra lieutenant, one of their original members—he'd been head of one of the gangs that had merged to form the Cobras, back when they had all been little upstarts unhappy with how Big Man Grimm was running things. In fact, he'd been the one to call for everyone to make one big gang under Jason Klaus, the head of the Cobras.

And he was a deckbearer. With more cards.

If he was nearly alone, in the Cobras' old club... Wolfe could perhaps take him out, get even for Johnny. And whomever else the Cobras had managed to kill tonight, since apparently the Grimm family was under attack.

Speaking of...

"Derek, call the Big Man, tell him that the Cobras are making a move across the whole city. Tell him to get everyone he can off their drunk asses and somewhere safe, and then then tell him that the product is about to go into police custody."

"Right. Will do."

Wolfe shook his head and frowned. "You know what? Just explain the whole fucking situation, you seem like you've got a few brain cells to rub together and can handle that much."

"Thanks for the vote of confidence," Derek said sardonically, despite the situation and his own wounds, raising Wolfe's estimation of the man again. Derek pulled his phone out, then motioned to the thug lying on the ground. "What about him?"

I don't have time to deal with him properly. "Four of our men won't go home to their families tonight. This thug made his choice, and it was to orphan our people's children. The sentence is death."

"No—" the man started, but Wolfe pulled the trigger, and blew the thug's brains out sideways across the pavement. The body jerked once and then went still.

"Damn, man..." Derek said, trailing off. The sirens were loud in the new silence.

Wolfe motioned to the phone held in Derek's hand. "Do your job. While you're at it, limp your bullet-ridden ass to my car —I'm going to take you to the family doctor, and we need to go fast."

Derek glanced at his leg as he dialed. "This hurts like a sonofabitch, but I don't think I'm gonna *die* from it."

"Yeah, but I have business to take care of. I can't leave you here for the police to interrogate, so I've got to take you somewhere soon where I know you'll get your butt fixed all shiny and new... without a police interrogation."

"Cute." Derek frowned, but then slumped slightly. "And thanks."

Wolfe nodded, and pointed to his car, which was now missing its rear window as well. "Try to get as little blood on the seat as you can. Poor girl has already had far too much damage done to her."

A bit less than ten minutes later, with all the shit that would have gotten Derek immediately arrested at the hospital lying in the back of Wolfe's car, Wolfe stared at the Snakebite Club through the hole where his driver's side window had been.

It was in the *worst* part of town, and a couple homeless people were huddled in the overhang of a chop shop, around an oil drum with a fire in it to keep warm.

Those guys are living like it was still the eighties. There's a 'no-questions-asked' homeless shelter a few blocks down, for fucks' sakes.

Although one guy appeared to be actively doing something with his inner elbow so maybe he wasn't ready to go there just yet.

The Snakebite Club itself had a corrugated-metal roof with an overhang, and a few dirty windows—and one broken and boarded-up window—fronted the place, filled with flickering display signs for booze and cigarettes, and one trashy neon outline of a girl. A few motorcycles were out front, as well as a beat-up car that was held together by its rust, from the looks of it. A pile of broken bottles and cigarettes was near the door, and a rat was digging in it—for what, Wolfe couldn't fathom.

Maybe even the rats are alcoholics in this part of town.

No one was guarding the place on the outside, and Wolfe didn't see anyone in the windows either. *Maybe it really is as abandoned as hole-in-head said it was. I hope I get to put the frog away for good.*

The Cobras had six deckbearers that worked for them, each with a deck built around some dark collection of gods—

43

Infernal, Undead, Elder, and Corrupted. The dark powers, the ones associated with evil.

Wolfe frowned to himself. *Like my own deck.*

He shook the thought away, refocusing on what he needed to do. Frankie 'the Frog' had built his deck around corruption—cards that caused wounds that lingered and festered. He was called 'the Frog' because he had four tier-2 common Caustic Frog Demon cards that were mixed Infernal and Corrupted, and because of his mantle. Which turned him into a bipedal frog.

Wolfe paused. The rest of Frankie's cards were known to be Corrupted, not Infernal... Cereboo would do okay, but his 'Return to the Pit' cards probably weren't the best, even if they'd keep the Frog Demons out of play for a moment.

A stench of sour wine and enough body odor to shame a teenage football team wafted in through the broken window. A man that looked like he had used *all* the drugs and was now held together by pickling and prayer was staring at Wolfe. The gross apparition smiled, showing off about half a mouth worth of teeth, all black nubs.

"Spare sum change? You look healthy an' tough an' shit, you can spare sumthin', right?"

Wolfe sneered. He didn't like panhandlers, and his demeanor usually kept them away. On the other hand, at this moment, he had very little time and a lot to do, and didn't want to call attention to himself by getting in a shouting match with a bum.

He passed a twenty out the window. "Here."

"Thank 'e." The man smiled near toothlessly, took the twenty, and ambled away back toward the oilcan fire the hobos had going.

Wolfe quickly flipped through the deck he had captured from the jackasses that had ambushed him on the way to the docks. A pair of Escaped Damned cards, *four* Tormentor Imp cards, an Imp Master mantle card that empowered imps, a Tiny

Pitchfork equipment card, and two cards called Punish the Sinner that allowed an Infernal creature card to attack a deckbearer directly, regardless of creature cards on the field.

Wolfe looked at the Tormentor Imps side by side with the Punish the Sinner cards.

Tormentor Imp
Common Tier-1 Infernal Creature
1 Infernal Power
Health: 7
Attack: 4
Magical Attack: 4
Defense: 3
Magical Defense: 3

Special: If any enemy deckbearer with *any* Infernal, Undead, Elder, or Corrupted cards in the deck is damaged by this creature, they cannot use any of those card types for 2 phases.

"A lower tier of imp, innumerable within the infernal realms, used to punish sinning souls with the burning fires of the hells."

Punish the Sinner
Uncommon Tier-1 Persistent Enhancement
1 Infernal Power

Special: This card allows any one creature to attack a deckbearer directly, regardless of the cards on the field. Once the enhanced creature inflicts at least one actual damage, this card returns to the deckbearer's deck.

"It has long been speculated that the Infernal realms have a purpose, and that purpose is deterrence. Regardless of the truth of that matter, this card can bring the power of the Infernal to bear on those that have displeased the pit."

A plan began to take form in Wolfe's mind. He quickly pulled his deck out, and switched it almost wholesale. He kept Cereboo, as his pup would be critical to the build. The remaining nine cards were *six* Tormentor Imp cards—his two original and the new four—two Punish the Sinner cards, and the Imp Master mantle card. He was tempted to keep his original Soul Hunter mantle, as it made him stronger... but he wanted to optimize the deck for the fight.

I can't believe I'm running an Imp Tribal deck. Weakest basic creature in all of the Infernal builds... Still, this is just for this fight, then I'll switch to something else, especially if I get better cards from murdering my way through the Cobras.

Wolfe paused.

He had four leveling pips available to him. He *really* wanted to look at all his cards and think about his leveling choices in detail, but a bit of extra power right now could really go a long way. He compromised by spending a single leveling pip to raise his Infernal power from one to two, giving him four total power. *If I live through this, I'll probably make some levels anyway.*

His choices made, Wolfe put his hand on the door handle and prepared to exit the vehicle.

He stared, feeling his eyes widen, as a girl walked across the trash-filled streets.

She was five feet and a couple inches, with red hair and fair skin. It was too dark to see more than that, and she wore a huge wind-breaker and jeans as she walked through the drizzle.

The girl reached the door to the Snakebite Club, took an obvious deep breath, the touched her hand to her chest. She pushed her hand out and four cards manifested in front of her, each suffused with a soft golden light.

A notification appeared in Wolfe's sight.

A deckbearer has drawn their deck near you.

The girl yanked the door open and strode into the club, her hands touching one of her cards.

CHAPTER 5

THE BAR ON THE ROAD TO HELL

"**The Great Game Rule #5**: Cards will vanish from the world
ONLY if the deckbearer is killed by a (1) a free-roaming
monster, (2) a dungeon, or (3) their own hand."

Wolfe pushed his car door open and rushed across
the cracked asphalt of the street, wove past some
motorcycles, and hustled up to the dingy door of the
club. Even as he rushed toward the front, he got a second,
"A deckbearer has pulled their deck," notification.

Wolfe peered into the window, but a flash of light caused
him to hit the filthy pavement outside, barely missing the
broken-glass-and-cigarette pile.

What the fuck?

A croaking roar, one of the oddest noises Wolfe had ever
heard, echoed from the club, followed by a feminine scream.
Something exploded through the club's front window in a
shower of glass, hitting the ground with a thump and high-
pitched grunt.

The figure rose—a beautiful woman with giant dove wings

flaring behind her. She had a halo over her head and an old-fashioned lantern held in one hand, chained to her wrist, but she had rents across her face and through the sleek black dress she was wearing—rents that leaked blood. Even as Wolfe glanced at her, a card appeared to hover over the woman.

Sorenia

Unique, effective Tier-7 Divine/Light companion
0 Power
Health: 10 (3 remaining)
Attack: 0
Magical Attack: 9
Defense: 8
Magical Defense:

Special: While in play, all Mortal creature cards gain divine typing and +25% (minimum 1) to all stats.
Special: The benefits to Mortal cards stack with the other three named companion lantern angels. If all 4 are possessed the card, Zarachiel, Commander of the Lanterns, a 4-power mythic tier-8 equivalent divine companion card will be gained as well as a free companion card slot.

"A particularly zealous and dedicated member of the hundred thousand lantern angels, she tries to guide mortals to right behavior—and victory over the Infernal, Undead, and Elder gods. Through her zealous efforts to make the Mortal world better she once earned a lesson at Archangel Raphael's knee, her proudest memory."

The angel card—Sorenia—glanced back at him. She started to raise her lantern at Wolfe.

"I'm on your side—and even if I wasn't, I wouldn't beat up a woman," Wolfe said.

He rushed past her, placing his hand on his chest and bringing forth his deck. He leapt through the now-broken window, throwing Cereboo's card out to the floor of the club and pulling his pistol even as he did.

"Club" wasn't the best descriptor for the place—"Dingy Bar" was closer to the truth. Most of the tiny bar tables and flimsy chairs had been knocked down, and many smashed, and the floor was covered in the wreckage of the furniture. The couple overhead lights swung wildly.

Two thugs flanked what could only be Frankie 'The Frog' Fodorvich, an eight-foot-tall, grossly fat bipedal frog that dripped black liquid. When a mantle was active on a deckbearer, the magic soaked their body completely, changing them physically.

Frankie's mantle had obviously transformed him into some sort of freakish frog creature. Nothing could've been more appropriate.

With his new mantle-increased strength, Frankie whaled on a girl held in one of his gross hands.

The girl had three eyes—one of which was glowing. She, too, must've activated her mantle. Her divine magic had changed her appearance and given her increased defense, but it clearly wasn't enough. Frankie slammed her against the bar, and she screamed.

The girl's arm was lacerated and bruised, but far less than it ought to be—the third eye and a soft, golden glow seemed to be providing healing.

She wasn't with the Cobras, that was for sure.

The smart move was probably to take out the thugs first, but visions from Wolfe's own past, a girl with brown hair and hazel eyes cowering beneath a man that looked like Wolfe in a power suit, flashed behind his eyes. His sister, gone now.

Wolfe aimed his Edge at Frankie and then pulled the trigger rapidly. The first bullet hit Frankie's spine, but despite the decent stopping power, did almost nothing. The Cobra lieutenant grunted but still managed to punch the girl again.

The girl collapsed to the floor, completely still. But her companion card didn't disappear, so Wolfe knew she was still alive. For the moment.

The next shot struck Frankie's head, and even though the man wore a powerful mantle, the shot did some significant damage. The bullet left a divot in the man's cranium.

Frankie turned away from the girl, and locked eyes with Wolfe. "Fuck, that hurt!" His eyes focused. "Wolfe, is that you? Wha the fuck're you doing here, old timer?"

"You're hilarious, you fat sack of sad, but I'm *at least* twenty years younger than you."

The two Cobra thugs pointed their handguns at Wolfe.

A beam of light hit one in the neck, slicing through the side of it. That thug grabbed his neck and dropped his pistol before falling to the floor.

The angel card outside had released some sort of Light energy-based attack. Cards would still fight until their deckbearer died.

The second thug ignored the girl and shot at Wolfe, grazing his already-bruised shoulder. Wolfe cussed and dived behind the tiny bar tables, getting shot in the side for his troubles. He took two and eight damage respectively, dropping his health from his boosted thirty to twenty.

Cereboo gave an antiphonal chorus of snarls and launched himself at Frankie. He bit him twice before Frankie grabbed Cereboo with his claws—*why claws on a frog?*—and hurled him over the bar into the wall of liquor there. Everything shattered and Cereboo fell to the ground amid a waterfall of booze, letting out an awkward woof when he hit.

Wolfe winced, wondering if his companion could really feel pain.

Frankie stalked toward Wolfe through the wreckage on the

floor. "Ah, and you brought me a new pooch, Wolfe! A companion card that'll let me include Beast cards in my deck and maybe even get some uber cards. I really should remember to get you a gift this next Arbor Day!"

Arbor Day?

Wolfe pushed his injuries to the back of his mind. He fired over his shoulder, causing Frankie and his thug to take cover. Wolfe stared at his own cards as they hovered in front of him, their ethereal form glittering. But none of them were useful. None. Wolfe needed some luck. He needed it yesterday.

"Ooh, you're a terrible shot," Frankie called.

The Great Game Rule #10: The deckbearer can only summon a new hand of cards every sixty seconds. The instant Wolfe had waited sixty seconds, he swiped away the three useless cards and gained access to three more from his deck.

His Imp Master Mantle was now in his hands! That would give him two additional defense and empower any imps Wolfe summoned. He also had two Tormentor Imp cards. He would only get one pull from the deck before it switched since his first pull had been Cereboo. He needed a Tormentor Imp and a Punish the Sinner in the next set of cards if he didn't use an imp now, but given what he had left in the deck, that was considerably more likely than not.

And he needed to *survive* the next minute most of all.

He touched the Imp Master Mantle card. Instantly, the red energy flowed across him. Patchy red scales sprouted across his skin, and his back twitched as small wings sprouted and ripped through his jacket. Thankfully, they were wings he somehow knew how to use.

The mantle gave him two to his physical defense, and raised the power of his imps by one in every category.

Wolfe rolled again, taking another grazing hit, again to his side, but his toughened skin reduced the damage to almost nothing. Almost involuntarily, he rose into the air on his tiny wings.

Frankie tossed a Caustic Frog Demon onto the field—a strong four-power card with tens in most of its stats and a damage-over-time acid effect. The card Frankie was famous for.

"Wolfe!" Frankie shouted, spreading his arms and smiling wide with his frog face. "I'm Level Eleven! I've got *seven* total power—one of my personal merits gave me an extra power and I've spent ten of my leveling pips in the category. You've been a baby deckbearer for like ninety minutes—you can't hope to face me! Give me your cards and swear to serve the Cobras, and I'll let you live."

Wolfe ignored the old man, and similarly ignored the Caustic Frog Demon as it charged out the window to fight Sorenia, the girl's Divine companion card. He focused on evening the odds, and shot the second thug repeatedly in the chest.

As the thug dropped in spray of his own blood, Frankie's false cheer dissolved into a snarl. He grabbed a pool stick from the floor and charged Wolfe, swinging the stick wildly. "He was my friend, asshole!"

"Then he shouldn't support people who beat the shit out of girls," Wolfe said as he ducked under the pool stick and uppercut Frankie, whose head barely moved. "Or kill our men," Wolfe continued as he shot Frankie in the stomach at point-blank range.

Blood welled around the hole, and Frankie half-bent. Before Wolfe could fire again, the deckbearer backhanded him hard, sending him back to the floor, his Edge skidding from his hand. Even as Wolfe's head reeled from the powerful, magic-backed blow, he switched his cards and threw a Tormentor Imp out.

He grunted as his cheek sizzled, acid eating at it, courtesy of Frankie's mantle's magic. But he still had the presence of mind to barely roll to the side as Frankie fell from the sky feet first, obviously trying to crush Wolfe.

He grabbed the deckbearer's leg and yanked, using the leverage to spin himself on the floor. While still holding the leg, Wolfe kicked up into Frankie's balls. Frankie yelled and crashed back onto the floor.

Wolfe scrambled across the floor and grabbed his Edge pistol. He saw golden light filter back to the girl on the ground. *Her angel, Sorenia, must have been defeated.*

Cereboo had recovered and was already fighting the Caustic Frog Demon alongside the Tormentor Imp.

But Frankie's card was too powerful for Cereboo and the imp to handle, he knew—and once it died, Frankie would just summon another, since he had three more in the deck. Wolfe assumed Frankie's lack of power with which to summon was the only reason Wolfe wasn't already facing more of them. The bastard did have a powerful mantle and creature card both on the field already.

Great Game Rule #12: Deckbearers use power to activate their cards. Once a card is brought forth, the power used to bring it forth remains used up as long as the card is in play. Once the card returns to the deck, the power is restored.

If Frankie had summoned seven 1-power monsters, the whole club would've been filled with claws and fangs, but Frankie obviously preferred size over quantity. The Caustic Frog required 4 power, more than half of Frankie's total, to maintain.

Frankie touched his cards and threw a bubbling cauldron onto the battlefield—it settled into some wreckage of tables and chairs. A thick miasma filled the air, weakening anything not from the Corrupted faction. Wolfe was affected by the terrible magic and started coughing.

But Wolfe's deck wasn't affected, nor was his trusty gun. Wolfe played his Punish the Sinner card, using his one Beast power as if it were Infernal thanks to Cereboo's special ability—

his mystical pooch allowed Infernal and Beast power to be used interchangeably. Wolfe raised his gun and fired on the frog demon at the same time as he ordered his Imp to attack Frankie.

Thanks to Punish the Sinner, the imp got one hit in on the bastard, not having to fight the Caustic Frog Demon first.

"What?" Frankie roared as he stood, staring down at the imp. He touched the cards in front of him, but nothing happened. "What did you do, Wolfe? What did you do?"

Wolfe smiled. "Win."

The one hit from the Tormentor Imp had removed Frankie's ability to play both Infernal and Corrupted cards for the next sixty seconds—and the inability to play a card for a full minute was forever in a deckbearer battle.

Surrounded by the faint red haze of his mantle, Wolfe shot the Caustic Frog Demon with a hail of bullets. Wolfe's mantle made his attacks considered Infernal, and not the Mortal attack the demon would resist. Between the earlier light beams of the now 'dead' Sorenia, the empowered bites of Cereboo that did double damage against Infernal, and Wolfe's gun, the demon finally expired, the power rushing back to Frankie's chest.

And now, the old bastard had no creatures. Wolfe, on the other hand, had his companion, an imp, and himself.

Wolfe turned to the giant, fat frog man. The Tormentor Imp was already clawing, nearly ineffectually, at the frog. Cereboo was at Wolfe's own side.

Frankie ignored the imp. He snarled wordlessly and charged.

Wolfe was surprised that Frankie didn't quip, plead, beg, or try and negotiate, given how wordy he had been earlier. But it made Wolfe's job a touch easier.

Wolfe fired the last of his bullets into Frankie's chest and then leapt to the side, barely dodging the Cobra founder's clawed swing. They did quite a bit more damage now that Wolfe was considered Infernal, but they still didn't drop the Cobra lieutenant.

Cereboo leapt at Frankie, grabbing him with three heads and ripping at him—with the plus one-hundred-percent damage bonus against other Infernal cards. Frankie began screaming even as he fought, and Wolfe rapidly put another clip into his Edge and then emptied that into Frankie from behind—a mercy at this point. The deckbearer fell forward, landing face-first amidst the ruin of the bar.

"I guess it's frog legs for dinner," Wolfe quipped, then cringed. *That was bad. I'm glad everyone else was knocked out or sent back to their deck that could hear that.*

He glanced over at Cereboo, who stared at him with three pairs of eyes, not panting happily like usual.

Okay, not everyone. "Don't judge me," Wolfe growled, his cheeks heating.

He was saved from any other embarrassment by a notification that he had killed a Level Eleven deckbearer and gained three-hundred-and-thirty-two experience, evenly split with the other deckbearer.

Wolfe whistled, and Cereboo gave a happy bark. *Level Eight. Fuck. I only got my cards about an hour and a half ago.*

Wolfe did a double take. *Can Cereboo see my notifications?*

Frankie's deck manifested on his back, some of the cards briefly glowing with red light, others with a sickly green light. There were ten, which didn't surprise Wolfe, since Frankie had admitted spending every single leveling pip he had gotten on his power stat to play powerful cards.

Wolfe put all his unimportant questions from his mind, picked up the cards and then went over and checked on the girl. Cereboo sniffed at her and whined, then licked her with two heads.

"It's okay, boy, she'll be fine—I think."

The girl was clearly banged up.

Wolfe picked her up in his arms and carried her out through the rain to his car, Cereboo following behind him, two heads hanging, and one making odd half-woofing noises in the direction of the hobos. Wolfe gently put the girl in the back seat after awkwardly brushing some of the shattered glass from it. He wasn't in the best of conditions himself, with over half his health gone—wounds to his side, his shoulder, and his cheek—but he really didn't want to risk injuring her further. He would heal.

And chicks dig scars.

Cereboo jumped into the car through the busted driver's side window, squirming and barely making it, and then crossed over and sat in the passenger seat, dominating it with his bulk and panting happily with one head, watching the hobos with a second, and watching the girl with the last one.

Wolfe had one more matter to handle. He went back inside the Snakebite Club, then went back behind the bar and glanced at the booze that was everywhere from when Cereboo had been thrown into the bottle display. Wolfe took his lighter, and set the alcohol on fire. Alcohol fires weren't the hottest, and it was raining, so Wolfe doubted much would come of it—but Frankie and his two aides dead and the Cobras' club gutted would at least do something to let them know this wasn't going to be a completely one-sided war.

Not if I have anything to say about it.

A minute later, Wolfe drove from the Cobras' territory, the flickering fires of the Snakebite Club behind him, the homeless man staring at him with wide eyes as Wolfe disappeared into the rain and darkness.

CHAPTER 6

THE FALLEN ANGEL

"The Great Game Rule #6: On each Drop Night, the gods shall create a number of reward cards based on the number of deckbearers. These reward cards will be (1) held by free-roaming monsters, (2) present within dungeons, and (3) contained inside puzzle boxes."

"Uh...wha? Where?" came from the back seat a few moments later.

Wolfe glanced in his miraculously still intact rearview mirror to see the girl sitting up in the car.

He cast a critical eye at the image the girl presented.

She would have been gorgeous if she wasn't so beat up. She had fiery red hair, now matted to the side of her head with blood. Her face was pale but for a smattering of freckles—and a large bruise. She also had a cute snub nose that appeared like it might be broken. Her brilliant green eyes that were fuzzy, and one might have been a touch larger than the other.

Shit, I'm gonna have to take her to the hospital after all. Wolfe put his blinker on and turned off Main, avoiding the drunk man stumbling through the intersection. He turned into a small alley. He needed to head in the other direction.

Wolfe held one hand out and up, open and fingers splayed, where the girl could see. "Don't freak out, girl. You're alive and Frankie's dead. I didn't want to leave you in the club when I left —it was on fire."

She blinked at him. "Why... I feel slow, like I can't think. Does... does your dog have three heads?"

Wolfe chuckled. "That's Cereboo, girl. He's my companion card, like your Sorenia. As to why you feel odd, well... You were beat within an inch of passing to the next realm, or whatever poetic bullshit you want to use. I'm almost positive you have a concussion. Don't get your panties in a bunch though, you'll be fine. I'm gonna drop you off at a hospital."

She reached forward, slowly, and gently touched Wolfe's shoulder where he had been shot. "Wha... about you? You... okay?"

No wonder she has a Divine deck. Beat half to death, with a concussion, and next to a three-headed demon dog—but her first thought is to worry about me. She has 'martyr' written all over her.

"Never mind me," Wolfe said. "I'm tougher than I look, and I *look* plenty tough. *You're* the one that just knocked at the pearly gates. On a scale of one to dead, you got more beat than a rap battle."

"It's... okay," she slurred, and pulled her deck.

Wolfe's hand fell to his pistol, but her closed eyes and the hand she put to her face convinced him she wasn't about to attack—and Cereboo was still in play.

She touched a card, and a golden light covered her. The skin on her forehead parted, revealing an open third eye—which promptly began to weep crimson. But her head stopped leaking blood, and her nose straightened—her wounds were slowly healed.

That's not a great in-combat mantle, but damn is it useful after the fact.

Cereboo gave a quiet woof and leaned one head back, licking the girl, then nudging her gently. Wolfe wasn't sure if it was a good or bad thing that his demonic puppy seemed to like the waif.

The girl completely healed over about three minutes as Wolfe drove, except for a patch of burns on her shoulder and face, where Frankie had hit her. The whole time she was quiet, but when it was done, she stared up.

Her eyes were now normal sized, and flickered around the car rapidly, taking in details. She also shivered in the cold.

"The burns on my shoulder and face can only heal a point a day... but we don't need to go to the hospital."

Wolfe nodded. He had already turned back once she started healing, and was most of the way to his house.

"What happened?" the girl asked as Wolfe left Main for Poplar, the second-to-last turn before they reached his house.

"What's your name, girl? I'm Wolfe."

"I'm Shel... well, Rachel Lyons, but I just go by Shel."

Wolfe sighed. "As to what happened, you walked into one of the Cobra gang territories and attacked a Level Eleven deckbearer that actually knows something about fighting and had back-up thugs. You, rather predictably I might add, promptly got the shit kicked out of you. What the fuck did you think would happen?"

"I had a deck..." she mumbled, her cheeks crimson in the rearview mirror.

"How'd that work out for you?" Wolfe quipped.

"I can't remember any of it..."

"Well, can you remember *why* you decided to attack Frankie? Not that I don't admire your spunk, but what the hell were you thinking?"

"Spunk?" she asked, a hint of mirth in her voice.

Wolfe frowned, mildly annoyed at being reminded of his age. "You get my point, girl. Now answer the damn question."

"They—the Cobras, I mean—killed my brother. I don't know who, exactly, but one of them did it."

Wolfe's hands tightened on the steering wheel. "Why'd they kill him? Was he some police officer that was trying to put them all behind bars? Or maybe a D.A. willing to prosecute?"

Shel shook her head, and another tear slid down her face. "No. He was just my brother, and he was a colossal fuck-up."

"Still not getting it."

"Against my advice, he actually joined the Cobras."

"And they... killed him?" Wolfe asked, confused.

Shel nodded. "Yeah. No one I can find knows why, or who did it. I talked to a few of their drug dealers... and to the police. The dealers thought maybe he was a snitch, but the police say he wasn't working with them. The detective I talked to about his death—Detective Amber Young—thinks that he might have fucked up so bad that the Cobras killed him as an example. But the dealers never heard of anyone making an example of him."

Wolfe nodded. *They'll kill for snitching, or stealing from the gang, but most thugs start damn low on the 'not fucking up' scale and never climb higher. You have to screw the pooch truly badly to be killed for not being talented enough. Seems unlikely.*

Shel was still talking, and a few more tears slid down her face. "I don't actually know what the reason was. But he was found behind the Venom Arena, his throat slit, almost entirely exsanguinated."

The whole thing stank to Wolfe. *The Venom Arena was Jason Klaus' personal business, like Big Man Grimm had the Ekron Eternal club. Why would they leave the body near their main hideout?*

Wolfe stared in the rearview mirror, meeting Shel's eyes. "So the gods gave you a deck and you decided that you were now an avenging angel or something, and that you'd just go kick ass and take names? Against people that have had their cards for ten to twenty years, and also, by the way, have guns?"

"Well, I mean..."

"Whatever, it's a moot point now. I flambé'd Frankie for you. You can spend the night at my house—"

Shel flinched.

"Not like that, girl. I've got a code, and high on the list is 'don't hurt women.' Got it?"

Shel blushed again and nodded. "I got it. Sorry." Then she stared at him quizzically. "So, your dog, Cereboo—he's an Infernal companion, right?"

Wolfe's tensed—he was pretty sure he knew where her line of questioning was going. "Yeah."

Shel fidgeted with her hair. "How did a guy like you—that seems nice and... well, nice... get an Infernal deck?"

"I'm not *nice*. I've killed more people than cancer."

Shel half laughed, half snorted.

Wolfe sighed. *Alright, that was terminally cringy. I need to work on my one-liners. Although in all fairness, I've been up way too fucking long.* "Fine, it wasn't my best quip. The point is that I've caused a lot of mothers to bury their sons. I've legit killed more than thirty people now—eleven of them in the last couple hours. It makes sense why the Infernal would give me a deck, even if I have a code."

"What's your code?" Shel asked.

"All that matters to you is that I don't hurt women."

"Why?"

"I just don't. Leave it."

Shel went silent, and Wolfe focused on his driving.

Wolfe stared out the window. Trash littered the wet roads between the large warehouses and multi-story apartment buildings as Wolfe drove through the rain, detritus from general neglect and the more recent Drop Night celebrations both. It had been an odd little zoning thing that ran all the poor people's residences up against the working area with the big trucks roughly twenty years ago, and it had never been fixed.

Loud vehicles were the least of the residents' concern, of course. Number one was all the crime. The criminals were still out and about, even two hours after the drop. He saw obvious streetwalkers, as well as dealers he personally knew, almost all of whom worked for the Grimm family. Either directly or, more often, indirectly—thinking they were a gang owning turf, rather than just the hired distributors of Big Man Grimm, whom he could wipe out merely by not providing product.

And if they ever got really uppity... *Well, that's what I'm for*, Wolfe thought with a grimace.

He turned past the small Sanctuary Hospice, the slightest smile tugging at his lips as he gazed at its rundown wooden façade.

The hospice was run by David Torres, a rat tribal deckbearer who had Beast and Life power.

David Torres had gotten the sanctum as a building-type card in his deck. Building-type cards had been introduced almost fourteen hundred years ago in a set release but still showed up in new sets as well. They were quite powerful, reducing your available power or occupying card slots but adding permanent bonuses if you were inside the building—and usually benefits everyone could use.

The hospice was a haven for the poor and sick in Noimoire, a tiny light shining in the darkness that provided healing, a place to stay, and some food from whatever magical energies sustained the cards.

It was also fairly close to Wolfe's own house, and a second later, Wolfe turned into his driveway.

CHAPTER 7

DEAL WITH THE DEVIL

"The Great Game Rule #7: New card types and subtypes may be created each Cycle, each with their own new rules and advantages."

Wolfe's home was a small rental composed of two bedrooms, one bath, a half-kitchen, and a living room. Wolfe parked his busted car next to the low chain-link fence around the yard. That was where he had used to let his dog, Pierce, have the run of the place before the mutt had died of old age a couple of weeks ago.

Pierce's food bowl was still in the yard, just outside his doghouse and next to his favorite blanket and a few half-eaten bones. Wolfe hadn't gotten around to removing them yet. He put his old friend from his mind and turned to the car's occupant.

"Let's go, girl." Wolfe reached in front of Cereboo, opened his glovebox, took the package, and stepped from his car. Cereboo followed him out the driver side, squirming over the console to get out.

Shel exited after only a cursory glance at the package Wolfe had grabbed, and Wolfe clicked his car locked on his keychain fob, shaking his head as he thought about how useless that autonomous response was now. After all, his car was 'naturally airconditioned' through two windows.

Wolfe lifted the latch to let Shel and Cereboo into the yard. Even in the rain and two weeks after the fact, Wolfe could still pick up the slightest smell of dog. It reminded him further of his old friend.

"You have dogs?" Shel asked, then glanced at Cereboo. "I mean... normal dogs?"

Cereboo woofed once, a short one that Wolfe swore sounded offended. Shel reached out and scratched the mutt behind his left-head ear. Cereboo licked her with his central head—acceptance of her peace offering, Wolfe guessed.

"Used to. One. He died."

She nodded and didn't say more until Wolfe had unlocked his front door and entered the house.

Wolfe grabbed a hand towel off a hook near the intersection of the front door and the living room and tossed it to her. "Bathroom's down the hall. Go clean up and dry yourself off. You may be mostly healed, but you still look like shit."

She glanced at him, opened her mouth, then shut it. She nodded and headed to the back.

When she had gone, Wolfe went to his room. It was fairly plain—one queen-sized bed, a small desk and computer, and a single piece of art—a giant, framed poster of a grim reaper, stats and all, signed by one of his favorite bands. A reminder of the part of his youth less misspent than the rest, he thought to himself with a sardonic grin.

Cereboo leapt onto the bed and lay down, watching Wolfe from three pairs of half-lidded eyes.

As he heard the water splashing in the bathroom, he pulled the picture away from the wall and revealed the safe behind it.

He turned the dials to Big Man Grimm's birthdate, then opened it. Inside, he had almost three hundred thousand dollars—the benefits of being the head enforcer for a major gang.

He took the package out, opened it, and counted the money into the safe. *A hundred thousand bonus. Big Man Grimm really does take care of me.*

Most of his pay came in 'benefits'—examples included doctors on staff, free food on missions and at Big Man Grimm's mansion, and the ridiculously low-rent house he was currently staying in. But the bonuses... he had thought that someday he might retire, and he needed a lot of dough for that.

Lately, his life had been feeling... pointless. Back in the day, when he and Thaddeus senior had been building the empire, it had all felt more worthwhile.

Although the new deck, and the attack on the Grimm family, were both thrilling in their different ways. As was the command of the voice Wolfe had heard when he first got a deck.

Wolfe thought about the deck he had been given, specifically. *The Infernal clearly decided that I was evil, and gifted me a deck. I mean, I'm excited I have cards, but I guess I foolishly thought my code, and the fact that Big Man Grimm kept our business away from the normies, meant I wasn't on the side of darkness. Although my patron seems to want me to slaughter other evil people, so there's that at least.*

Wolfe stared into his safe at the pile of cash, now nearly half a million dollars made in service of that business. A business that made one of the evil card factions, probably the *evilest* faction, give him a deck.

Wolfe continued to stare at the huge pile of cash in the safe, but he wasn't seeing it. His mind was elsewhere, arguing with itself.

I may not be on the side of good, but I can do the angels a solid.

Wolfe's hand involuntarily tightened on the safe handle. *You're a fucking idiot, Wolfe—trying to play the hero is what fucked you the first time. Everyone would have been happier if you'd just been selfish and minded your own damn business.*

Wolfe's mind saw the terror-filled eyes again, and he cursed himself for a fool. But he wanted, *needed* to save one. *Just one*, he promised himself. If only to banish his own demons.

I'll just help a little. Wolfe counted half the cash back into the box and put it on the small computer desk, then sat in his office chair, feeling almost as drained from his memories and thoughts as he had from being shot.

Wolfe pulled his phone out and pulled up the internet. A news alert told him that a monster had attacked the shopping mall—a very large dragon that a couple of the elite Card Police had been required to take out. Like most of the free-roaming monsters that appeared on Drop Night, it had dropped a card when slain, which the elite Card Police hadn't revealed to the public yet.

Wolfe wasn't looking for the news at the moment, but it reminded him to try and find any monsters, or even better, dungeons. He could use them to try and get experience and cards. He'd call some of his contacts tomorrow—maybe Victor.

That guy owed Wolfe big.

But Wolfe put that aside and looked up decks, combining cards, and leveling as a deckbearer. He needed as much information as possible since he was sitting on six levels and twenty cards he would need to do something with.

The water shut off, and Wolfe, still sitting, closed his phone and turned to face the door.

Shel walked in.

She had scrubbed her face and tried to wash her shirt but had only succeeded in smearing the blood and turning the front of the shirt slightly transparent—and acid had eaten part of the sleeve. It was nearly as dead as the guy that had damaged it in the first place.

Even as beaten up as Shel still was, she was gorgeous. She had fiery red hair hanging almost to her waist, emerald-green eyes, and a light dusting of freckles... all on a frame thin almost to the point of boyishness but still clearly on the side of feminine. As well as nearly perfectly symmetrical features.

"Do you have a shirt I can borrow?" she asked. "I can't fix this one."

He pointed to his closet. "Anything I have will sit on you like a poorly made dress, but you're welcome to it. They're mostly blood-stain free, so that's a plus."

Shel nodded, then went to the closet. He barely paid attention, simply fidgeting with the shoebox—until she stripped the shirt over her head. She was faced away from him, so he didn't see much, but even her back was feminine and beautiful.

Shel took one of his black T-shirts down and put it on, then turned back to face him. It was ridiculous how much of a tent the shirt was, but it did its job. She didn't have any visible blood on her, despite the large facial burn, and the shirt was so large it even covered the spots on her jeans.

She stared at him, and it seemed neither had any idea what to say.

Wolfe grabbed the shoebox and held it out brusquely. "Here."

Shel didn't move to take it, her eyes flicking to his face, then his poster, and then back to the box. "What is it?"

"It's fifty thousand cash."

Shel held the box, her eyebrows knitting. "Why?"

"Take it and get the fuck out of town. I'm sorry about your brother but the issue is moot. He's dead. You're not. Let's keep the second part that way. Because you're not gonna pull revenge off with your skillset. Especially since you don't even know who killed him, or why."

"Moot?" Shel tilted her head. "You've said that twice. That's an odd word for a thug, even a... high-ranked one."

Wolfe frowned at the utter non-sequitur. "My dad was an

attorney, a senior partner at a very large firm. Plus, I was in all the most expensive prep schools, before."

"Before what?" Shel asked.

Wolfe tensed, anger rising up that he had to throttle down. "Girl, I just saved your life. If your thanks is just gonna be twenty questions about my life, then get the fuck outta my house. I don't want to deal with this shit."

Shel nodded, her cheeks pink. But then she hardened her expression, and gripped the box tightly. "Well, I can't leave town. Not yet."

He sighed. The longer she stayed, the more likely she was going to get herself into trouble. "You don't need to go back to your place to grab things. Just go. As fast as you can."

"*No*," Shel snapped, much to Wolfe's surprise. Then she rubbed her hand over the box of money, her gaze falling to the floor. "I need to get revenge. For my brother. And I need to make sure those... bastards... don't do anything like this ever again."

She said the word *bastards* like it was spicey and she didn't like the taste.

Wolfe rolled his eyes. "What's your plan, huh?"

"Fight them." Shel had spoken with an icy conviction.

"No offense, but you were worse than useless at the Snakebite Club. I'd have done better just ambushing Frankie before he'd gone full frog. Saving your ass nearly got me killed."

Shel shook her head. It clearly took her a few moments to form the words she needed to explain herself. "If I don't avenge my brother, no one will. I have to do it. I have to find a way. I think that's why I got a deck on Drop Night..." She touched her chest. "I... I have power now."

"Your power didn't help you fight the Cobras," Wolfe stated.

Shel stepped away, her expression shifting to anger. "Well, you gave me fifty thousand dollars, right? I'll use this to help me! I'll do whatever I need to do. My brother..." Sadness replaced all her emotions once again. "He meant a lot to me. I can't believe people like the Cobras just get away with... all their evil."

A lot of evil was never dealt with in the world. Wolfe was surprised to find someone who actually cared about correcting it. It genuinely made him wonder why she was in the same room as he was—it wasn't like he was a nice guy.

"Fifty thousand isn't going to get you much in the way of weapons or cards," he muttered as he half turned in his office chair. "Just get a car and go."

With water glazing her eyes, Shel held the box out and then thrust it toward him. "How about... I hire you? *Help me.*"

He pushed the box away. "I can't help you."

"You beat that Cobra frog guy! You just... jumped into the fray... and fought him off. You're clearly strong! And you know the rules of the Great Game already. *Please.*" She shoved the box back into his chest. "Fifty thousand to fight them—to help me avenge my brother. You're opposed to them already, right?"

Wolfe sighed as he took the box. He fiddled with the outside, drumming his fingers on the wood. "This is like paying one crook to off another crook. You don't want my help."

Cereboo jumped down from the bed and licked Wolfe with all three heads, then the giant pup whined.

"I'm fine," Wolfe growled to his new pooch.

His companion leapt back onto the bed, the dog's ears drooped.

"I'm not trying to fight all the crooks of the world," Shel whispered. "I'm trying to fight the ones who hurt me. Who killed my brother. Please. This is personal."

"Fifty thousand isn't enough," Wolfe stated.

Fighting an entire gang so they could track down one killer? Fifty grand was way too little for that type of assignment, especially when Wolfe thought about all the deckbearers the Cobras had.

Hopefully, the girl would take the hint and just leave.

But she didn't. Instead, Shel took a hesitant step closer. She knelt between Wolfe's legs and then stared up at him through her eyelashes.

Tense, and a little caught off guard, Wolfe held his breath. What was she doing?

"If fifty thousand isn't enough, I can pay you in other ways," she said, her voice just below a whisper.

She placed an unsteady hand on Wolfe's knee. He felt the trembling of her fingers through the fabric of his pants.

Wolfe hadn't been with anyone in a while. He had been busy with street gangs, and prepping for Drop Night. Shel's sudden offer caused his blood to race.

She scooted closer and reached for his zipper, but that was when the shock wore off for Wolfe. He grabbed her wrist and lifted her hand away.

"*Don't*," he growled.

"W-Why not?" Shel asked. She stared up at him, her brow furrowed. "Am I not... pretty enough?"

Wolfe stood from his chair, his heart hammering. He needed to distance himself from her. He really didn't like being caught off guard. After running a shaky hand through his hair, and turning his back to her, he said, "You're plenty beautiful. That's not the point. Get off the floor."

He heard her stand, but she didn't say anything after that.

"I'll help you," Wolfe finally said, almost hating himself for doing so. "But for fifty grand, you have to fight with me. You *are* a deckbearer. Maybe—if you weren't such a chump at fighting—taking down the Cobras would be easier."

"Really?" Shel asked, breathless.

Wolfe whirled on his heel, glaring. "You heard me, didn't you? You have to help me fight. That's part of the deal. You were right—I need to fight the Cobras regardless, so I might as well have some backup. I suppose an angel deck might be just what I need."

Shel nodded along with his words. "I'll help. I swear." She pulled out her deck, and swiped through it. Wolfe ignored the notification, curious as to what in the various realms she was doing, but trusting that she wasn't about to attack him.

After a moment, a card appeared—one that was both gold and red.

Shel fiddled with it, casting it to the ground. As she did, she gasped. Wounds opened across her body.

A woman appeared, different than Sorenia. She was tall and almost perfectly made, with wings coming from her back. But her wings were black, and feathers were dropping from them—and she sported a pair of red horns poking out from her golden hair. Tracks of crimson ran down her face, like she had wept blood.

"Are you okay?" Wolfe asked, his attention on Shel's injuries.

Cereboo leapt off the bed and growled, but the new angel didn't attack.

Shel took Wolfe's hand and nodded. "Yeah... look at the card, it'll make sense. And as soon as I find my mantle, I'll be fine again."

Wolfe stared at the card.

Fallen Angel
Rare Tier-1 Infernal/Divine creature
2 Infernal or 2 Divine Power and 5 Health
Health: 20
Attack: 9
Magical Attack: 9
Defense: 6
Magical Defense: 6

Special: Gains the best type match-ups of being Infernal or Divine, and additionally gains all positive modifiers that any Infernal or Divine being in the deck would gain.

"Occasionally, even the Divine may fall, twisted from the path of righteousness by a need—perhaps even a noble one, such as love for another, or the need to protect them."

A golden glow distracted Wolfe, who looked over to see Shel with her mantle on—healing. She smiled at him. "Look, I wanted to thank you, for saving my life. I know you didn't have to do that, and it would have been easy to leave me. Most people would have."

Wolfe nodded along to her statement, thinking about how most people had treated him in his life.

Shel continued. "Also, now, you can think of this card partially as payment for helping me. It's an extremely valuable card... but you'll need to give me a cheap card so I can shift it out of my deck, since I need ten minimum."

Wolfe smiled. He appreciated people that tried to honor a debt.

But...

"Look," he muttered, "keep the card for now. I'll grab it from you later, when, and if, we get a card that fits your deck. I saw your companion—you need Mortal and Divine cards, not my weak Infernal card cast-offs."

Shel nodded along with his words. The Fallen Angel card flowed back into her chest. "I can help with something else as well."

Wolfe nodded at her to go on.

Shel raised a hand and swiped it through the air sideways. Three of the cards disappeared to the side, fading into nothing, and three more came from the nothing on the other side. She still hadn't stood up for some reason.

She touched one of the new cards, and a nervous-looking woman in a blue jumpsuit with a white plus symbol on it appeared. She raced over and touched Wolfe. Wolfe felt a surge of health and wellness pass through him, and the strange sensation of his flesh crawling around his wounds filled him. He stared at the woman in front of him, and the card appeared.

Rookie EMT
Common Tier-1 Mortal creature
1 Mortal Power
Health: 8
Attack: 1
Magical Attack: 0
Defense: 5
Magical Defense: 5

Special: When the Rookie EMT enters play it may fully restore one creature card or restore 3 Health to any deckbearer. Deckbearers may not benefit more than once every 24 hours from any singular copy of this card.
Special: If on the field with any 'Veteran' card, this card heals twice as much to Deckbearers and may heal a creature card every 30 seconds.

"This trainee just got her certificate and really wants to save lives. Just as soon as her hands stop shaking."

Wolfe still felt the burn on his face, and his side still hurt a bit—but less. His shoulder felt fine.

"Thanks, that really hit the spot," Wolfe said and reached down to grab Shel's arm. "Okay, if we're doing this, you—"

Shel grunted and half-screamed as he grabbed her left shoulder.

"Sorry," he muttered, transferring his grip to her unburned right shoulder and pulling her to her feet. "As you said, if we're going to do this, if you're going to help me, I need you to be in fighting shape."

She glanced down at her hundred-pounds-soaking-wet

frame, then stared at him with determination in her eyes. "How are we going to do that?"

"Your deck, girl. We need to train you to use your deck. Magic is as great an equalizer as a gun. Better once you get high enough level. I'll need you to learn both."

CHAPTER 8

THE ABOVE AND THE BELOW

"**Great Game Rule #8**: Deckbearers can never have less than ten cards."

Wolfe pointed around his barren living room. He had moved the electronics to the kitchen, pushed the couch against the wall, and piled his weight set in one corner on top of the duffel bag that had come with it. That was all that had been in his living room—he didn't really live to keep up with the fucking Joneses.

Cereboo watched from his perch on the couch.

"We need to train," he said. "How much do you know about using a deck?"

Shel frowned. "I didn't really have a chance to learn anything, before I..."

Foolishly attacked an experienced deakbearer ninety minutes after you got your deck, Wolfe finished in his mind. *So nothing, which is barely less than I do. Still, I researched how to take out deckbearers once upon a time. And I just spent ten minutes on the internet... so, a touch more than nothing, at least.*

"Alright, well, the most important thing to understand is your mantle. Remember what happened in the fight with Frankie?"

Shel shook her head. "I still can't remember any of it."

"Fuck..." Wolfe muttered. Apparently, her healing didn't restore memories that hadn't implanted due to physical trauma.

After a moment, he shrugged. "All right then, not gonna lie, this first lesson's gonna hurt. But it's the only way to truly, in your gut, understand what a mantle does for you. Come stand here," Wolfe said, motioning to the center of the room.

She approached cautiously, and when she got close, Wolfe abruptly kicked out with a simple push kick to her stomach. It wasn't even full power—he knew that against this waif of a chick, he would do damage if he used his full strength. But he needed her to lose her fear, and fast, and this was the simplest way.

Shel went stumbling back and then fell against the couch, half on the floor. She yelled as she hit—without training, Shel fell hard. Something else he would need to fix, but not yet. First things first.

Cereboo woofed and stood back—she had almost crashed into him.

Despite her ignominious drop, the girl leapt to her feet, her eyes watery, her lip trembling. But Shel stood firm in front of him, not letting a single tear fall.

"Why?" she asked.

"I just told you—training. You need to understand your new capabilities. This is the easiest way to train people how to fight. First, show them without training or gear, then show them with. It's nothing personal, girl."

Shel nodded at his explanation, her face firming further.

Shel's weaker than a geriatric purse puppy. Still, girl's got spunk and a deck. She can be made dangerous with that much.

Maybe she was right about being able to help me... guess I'll see soon enough.

"Summon your deck now," Wolfe said.

Shel summoned her deck with the ubiquitous pattern almost every deckbearer used. She touched her hand to her heart for two seconds and then held her hand out palm forward.

Three cards manifested in front of her, glowing with a soft, golden light and floating in the air. They were the size of standard playing cards. Off to the side, a fourth card also manifested, but Wolfe ignored that. It was her special-to-the-season companion card, like Cereboo—he would talk about Sorenia later.

Wolfe received a notification: *Deckbearer Rachel Lyons has pulled a deck near you.* He then addressed Shel. "All right, play a mantle card. Don't play any other types."

"Persistent card, mantle sub-type?" she asked.

"There isn't any other type of card with 'mantle' in the type."

"I... don't have one," she muttered.

Wolfe held up a finger. "*The Great Game Rule #18: Every new deck shall contain a persistent mantle card.*"

"You know all the rules to the Great Game?" Shel asked in awe.

Wolfe narrowed his eyes. "Of course. I've had to fight deckbearers in the past. Even if I didn't have any cards, I needed to know what I was up against. And knowing a deckbearer's limitations is key to defeating them."

Shel ran a hand through hair. "So... Everyone has a mantle in their deck?"

"There's been no known exception in all of fucking recorded history. Besides, I *watched* you use one three times now. Don't lie to me."

"I had just meant in my hand," she said, frowning at Wolfe with a cute scrunch of her freckled nose.

"Oh. Sorry. That makes more sense. It's super late and I'm tired." Wolfe yawned and motioned to the windows, where the almost three a.m. sky was still nearly black.

Shel nodded.

Wolfe continued. "Just wait a minute. You'll get the option to swipe and draw the next three cards. That's how it works. *Great Game Rule #9: Deckbearers may play a card every thirty seconds from their hand,* and... *Great Game Rule #10: A new hand of cards may be drawn every sixty seconds.*"

They both sat there for a bit longer, then Shel swiped the air near the cards sideways, and three cards rolled from nothing into view and pushed the other three back into nothing.

She reached out and touched one, and it flared to life. Blood began to bead around the corner of her eyes, and a third eye appeared on her forehead, but all of her other wounds healed. Most importantly to Wolfe's demonstration, a faint, golden haze appeared around her.

He focused on Shel's aura, and the card for the mantle she was using appeared, semi-translucent and overlaid around her.

Resilient Martyr
Common Tier-1 Divine Mantle
1 Divine Power

Special: This mantle grants +5 Defense, a pool of 5 Health, and restores 1 health per minute active. All Mortal cards played, and all Mortal cards allies have played, heal 1 life every minute as well while this mantle is active.

"The gifted of the archangel Raphael exist to ease the suffering of others, even if that means taking the suffering for themselves. His grace helps them to endure what they must..."

Wolfe glanced at it. Strong for a one-power card, although it didn't grant any attack power.

He walked up and pulled his foot back again. Shel flinched, but Wolfe kicked out with about the same force as before. It hit, and she stepped back once, but nothing else happened. Wolfe dismissed the combat log—he would discuss it with her in a moment.

Shel's eyes were fuzzed out, staring at nothing. "It says—"

"We'll get to the log in a moment," Wolfe said. "Don't get distracted trying to read log information in battle. It's a good way to get killed."

Shel nodded.

Wolfe continued. "The important thing to know is that you have a mantle now. Without it, you're a tiny waif of a girl, less dangerous than a ham sandwich."

"Why a ham sandwich?" Shel asked with a laugh.

"Ham sandwiches have killed a few people, which is more than you, girl. Also, don't interrupt. As I was saying—without a mantle you're vulnerable. With it you can fight. Survive, really. Almost every single deckbearer uses a mantle in their deck. Or even multiple ones."

"Can you wear multiple mantles?"

Wolfe shook his head. "No. *The Great Game Rule #20: No Deckbearer may be equipped with more than one mantle*."

"Then why have multiple mantles in a deck?" Shel asked.

"To be able to pull one faster, or have different ones for different situations. Mantles are *important,* girl. It all comes down to the Great Game, Rule #6: Summoned creatures *must* attack opposing summoned creatures *first*, before they can target enemy deckbearers or mortals. But what's important is what it doesn't say—that an enemy deckbearer, or just some random schmoe with a nine-mil, can. So, if there's any fighting, get your mantle on as fast as possible. It'll help make sure you survive in a way that just stacking up creatures won't guarantee."

Shel focused on him, her lips silently repeating parts of what he was saying.

"I know you can't remember, but the fight at the Snakebite Club was all about how good mantles are. The average schmoe human has five defense—I'll talk about all that in a minute—and your defense was raised to ten. That means that every attack against you did half the damage, essentially. Which is why when Frankie was beating you, the bar gave out and died before you. Barely before you, but still."

Shel twirled her finger in the long red hair she allowed to fall across her face. "I'll, um, I'll keep that in mind. New subject... Can you please talk to me about the combat log?"

He rooted around his kitchen until he found a rolling pin and tossed it to her. She fumbled and dropped it, blushed even darker, and then picked it back up.

Wolfe put his hands on his hips. "Okay, try to beat me to death."

"What?" she said, her expression horrified.

Wolfe laughed at the shock on her face. But the idea of her taking a skilled brawler like him out with a rolling pin was just too much. He had just finished a fight outnumbered four to one after being ambushed, survived an ambush with military weapons shortly thereafter, and then taken out a deckbearer and his mooks—a deckbearer that was far more experienced and had a higher level than Wolfe did. He was fine—well, basically fine—and no one else had walked away.

"Trust me, you won't succeed in hurting me. But try. It'll be a good lead-in for the discussion."

She attacked with a haymaker pin swing, the golden haze still around her. Wolfe swept the pin to the side with an open palm strike, then swept her leg in turn. She went crashing to the ground but leapt up, no worse for the wear thanks to her mantle.

Shel came at him again with a wildly telegraphed overhand strike and he caught the pin arm above his head with a crossed-arm block. She kneed at Wolfe—surprisingly creative—and he twisted and caught it on his inner thigh, then swayed back from the punch she threw with her unblocked left hand.

The pin hitting him in the head hard enough to sting was a surprise—she had dropped it from her trapped right hand. Hardly a debilitating blow, but Wolfe was impressed she had gotten even that much.

The combat notification appeared. "Back and hold," he said.

She dropped back, already breathing hard, but her eyes were crossed—likely looking at her notification again.

Wolfe stared at his own in turn.

Deckbearer Ethan Wolfe and Deckbearer Rachel Lyons engage in physical combat.

Ethan fights derisively—takes a negative maximum (10) to his attack. Makes a Physical Attack at 0 against Deckbearer Lyons' Physical Defense of 8. Damage dealt is 0 (0 * (0/8)).

Deckbearer Rachel Lyons makes a physical attack at 3 against Deckbearer's Physical Defense of 10. 0 damage taken to Deckbearer Wolfe's 30 Health. (3 * (3/10), rounded down)

Hmm, I did underestimate her a bit. I shouldn't do that. She could have gotten a higher random add score.

Shel, still fuzzy eyed, asked, "What does this all mean?"

Wolfe pulled a cigarette from his pants and lit it up. "When you're attacked, by either a summoned creature, a deckbearer, or some random thug, they make an attack against your defense. Creature cards always get whatever their base attack score is. But the jackasses who can think can also get lucky—or unlucky. They get a random chance to go up or down. Then that score is compared to your defense, and the result is basically your enemies' attack squared divided by your defense—that's how much damage you take."

Shel coughed and waved the plume of smoke away. "The square of the attack?"

"Yeah. Which means that increases to attack are more dangerous than you might think. A five attack against a five defense does five damage—five times five, divided by five. But a seven will do nearly double that. Because seven times seven divided by five is just shy of ten. A small difference in attack can be huge."

Wolfe had gotten through algebra two, but he hadn't used math in ages. His pithy answers came from the internet research he had done the few minutes he was waiting for Shel to get out of the shower, as well as his analysis of his own combat log.

Shel stared at him intently. "Does defense go up and down like attack does?"

"Attack gains a random modifier from negative one hundred percent to positive one hundred percent," Wolfe said, confidently spouting more information gained less than an hour ago.

"So complete whiff to double?"

"Brilliant restate." Wolfe raised an eyebrow while taking a deep drag on his cigarette.

Shel blushed but said nothing else.

Wolfe walked into the half-kitchen as he talked, fishing an ashtray from his cupboard. "Defense goes from negative fifty percent, rounded up, to positive a hundred percent. So half defense to double defense, to use your restate terms. Got it?"

"I got straight As in school and graduated valedictorian. Well, one of four valedictorians," Shel said.

Wolfe was tempted to make another sarcastic comment but held back, just taking his ashtray back to the living room and continuing his explanation instead. "A basic human, no skills, has a five in both attack and defense. Training can modify it quite a bit higher, and weapons can as well. Like a gun."

"A gun?" Shel asked.

"Yeah, a gun, like my trusty Edge. Don't think that just because you have your martyr ability, you can stand in front of a gun. You'll end up deader than a doornail. People make a big deal about the fact that I've killed deckbearers. But both times I did it, the idiots had gotten cocky, thinking that their status made them invincible. But unloading my Edge into the chest of a monologuing asshat isn't that hard, and they go down almost as fast as a normal schmoe who's been shot repetitively in the chest—which is to say, faster than a pre-paid whore."

"Such colorful colloquialisms," Shel muttered.

Wolfe took another drag on his cigarette. "Cute. But enough of your supposed witticisms. Bring up your status chart."

"How?"

"Seriously? Just think 'Status Chart' really hard. That's it."

Wolfe followed his own advice and stared at his chart for the first time.

CHAPTER 9

THE MARKS OF THE FALLEN

"**Great Game Rule #9**: Deckbearers may play a card every thirty seconds from their hand."

W olfe's status chart was a bit more complicated than the cards were, and he was fairly excited with the information presented. *A lot here I can work with. Some great personal overlaps to my deck.*

Ethan Madison Wolfe Status:
Level 2 Deckbearer (6 Levels pending)

Deckbearer Perks:
Deckbearer Perk 1: In the Thick of it: +50% to all numerical benefits gained from mantles
Deckbearer Perk 2: Man's Best Friend's Best Friend: Gain 1 Beast Power. May have one extra card in play so long as it's a Beast(Canine or Hybrid Canine).
Deckbearer Flaw: Fallen: May not gain Divine Power, nor use Divine cards unless they are also Infernal or Corrupted.

Deckbearer Stats:
Cards in Deck: 10
Cards in Hand: 3
Cards in Play: 2
Length of Play: 5 minutes
Specialty Cards: Companion: 1
Type 1 and Power: 2 Infernal (1 pip)
Type 2 and Power: 1 Beast
Energy 1 and Power: 1 Fire

Personal Perks:
Inborn Perk 1: Vicious Predator: +25% to all Attack and
Defense, check twice for Attack modifier and take the best
Inborn Perk 2: Tough as Nails: +10 Health
Acquired Perk 1: Crafty Street Fighter: +3 Attack and Defense

Personal Stats:
Health: 30
Attack: 10
Magical Attack [None]: 0
Defense: 10
Magical Defense [None]: 5

Wolfe had Infernal power, and Divine was forbidden to him. He had already known it, but seeing it displayed so blatantly reminded him of his status. The gods tended to pick people who aligned with their values, and he had been picked by some being in the Infernal faction. Although his patron seemed to want him to kill other Infernal deckbearers, at least. Wolfe sighed and put the thought aside to focus on what was important.

"What does this all mean?" Shel asked, her eyes fuzzed out as she likely stared at her own chart.

"You didn't just Google it? I mean, this is known stuff—a lot of famous people make their living selling guides to it. Hell, you play a deckbearer in a ton of popular games... ever played *Deckbearer Car*? *Beast Summoner*? The Thirteen Series? *Deckbearer Car 2*? Or *3*?"

Shel shook her head. "I focused on my studies a lot, and my family really needed money, so I got a part-time job as a shelver at the local grocery store... and I studied to take the SAT, and learned about creating a college application..."

No one gives a shit about the child labor laws in these parts. Or tax laws. They probably paid Ms. Goody-Two Shoes under the table as well.

Wolfe took another drag on his cigarette, then put it into the tray gently, tapping the ash off the end once. *Damn shame her brother dragged her into this world, and damn shame she was stupid enough to try and seek revenge. Sounds like she coulda made something of herself in the corporate world. Or with those looks and that kindness, grabbed some soft but smart dude pulling six figures and had a great life raising a bunch of overachieving rugrats. Not my fucking problem, though—I'll do my last good deed, just to flip the Infernal the finger. Get her the vengeance, then send her off with a second chance. Then it's in the gods' hands.*

"So...?" Shel asked.

"Right. Quick course. At the moment, you've got ten cards in your deck. You also have a maximum of ten cards. You can increase the maximum by five when you level—I'll get into that in a moment. With me so far?"

"Yeah, but, I mean, if you had a great set of cards, why wouldn't you want to just keep it to ten?" Shel asked.

Wolfe shrugged. "Some people do. But a lot of cool shit is gained from having more cards. Enhancer specialty cards add to your personal stats, but are null cards for the Great Game. They can even add years of life per card in your deck, so gathering levels and cards could theoretically make you immortal. Some fucked-up people go around trying to murder deckbearers to gain experience to keep buying more cards and gain that next five years of life."

"I've heard about the Thousand Card Killer," Shel said.

Wolfe gave a second shrug, then picked up his cigarette. "Yeah. But other people too I'd bet. More commonly people want a lot of cards because they can affect the outside world, like getting a cool mansion with magical flowers or a waitress card so you just have a magical worker in a restaurant that you can pay even less than minimum wage. Shit like that. If you want a lot of those types of cards so you don't have to work and stuff, but you still want to kick ass, you need to have a lot of cards in deck. The gods set the system up to encourage large deck sizes, I'd bet. Also, to encourage deckbearers to kill each other. At this point, I think the gods might all be sadists."

Shel shuddered at Wolfe's musings but nodded.

"Next item is cards in hand. Every minute, you can switch to another draw of cards, equal to your cards in hand score, drawn randomly from your deck. You can play a card every thirty seconds. So, the more cards in your hand, the more options each switch phase, since you can still only play two cards a minute. But having more options each pull is better, right? Especially if you have some devastating combo that requires very specific cards."

Shel nodded.

Wolfe continued. "You can increase the total hand size by spending level points as well, one extra card for each time you increase it. One of the better choices, in my opinion."

Shel waited.

"Cards in play is just total cards you can have in play at one time. More monsters. More mantles. Things like that. The more you have in play, the better, obviously. For most people, their total power is the bigger restrictor, but some need a lot of cards in play specifically. Like goblin tribal deckbearers."

Shel nodded again and Wolfe continued. "Length of play is

how long a normal card can remain in play. A powerful creature staying on field is great, obviously. A mantle lasting longer is also great. Five minutes is forever in a close-in fight, but it's nothing in a chase or gang war. It can help a lot. You can raise time in play when you level up as well, at a minute per pick."

Shel nodded a third time. She was starting to look like a bobblehead, but Wolfe ignored it. At least Shel wasn't making more wisecracks, and he could almost see the wheels going behind her eyes. *She'll probably be a great deckbearer someday. If the frail girl makes it to 'someday.'*

"Power types are the types of magic you can use to cast your cards. There are technically two subsets: type power and energy power. I have Beast and Infernal for types. I also have a Fire energy type, so three types. I already raised my Infernal power a point, so I actually have four power. But I couldn't play a card with a two Beast power cost, for example, because I only have one Beast power. But I could play one with one Beast power and three any-power cost."

Wolfe took another drag of his cigarette, the smoke now a slight haze around his living room. He leaned forward a bit. "Now, the most important thing is this: Most cards have *drawdown*. That means that when you play them, you don't get the power back until the card is killed or the time is up. Also, lost cards don't return their power until the next card switch, when you draw a new hand. Managing the timing is extremely important if you don't want to die."

"Why?"

"Because creatures fight in thirty-second units of time. So, if you lose your creature in the first thirty seconds of a card switch, you won't get another creature out to defend you, and their creatures can just whale on you. But if you lose your creature in the last half, you can play another creature card... assuming you have one to play. Make sense?"

Shel ran a hand through her hair.

"All right... the last thing. This season apparently opened up a new specialty card, the *companion* card. You've seen mine, Cereboo. You may not remember it, but I've seen yours as well—Sorenia. I assume you got a companion card slot as well?" Wolfe grimaced at his words. *Of course* she got a companion card slot, or she wouldn't have been able to use Sorenia.

Shel didn't notice his slipup, answering normally. "Yes. My chart has a starting companion card slot."

"Perfect. I checked online, and there's already a small guide written by some nerd deckbearer. Apparently, companion cards are solid increases for most deckbearers who got one. They're creature cards that have no time limit. Just summon the thing and it can hang out like the world's most demented purse puppy. Also, they can remember shit, like a real person, from summon to summon. So, Sorenia might be a bit miffed about being murdered by a Caustic Frog Demon in your last fight."

Shel's cheeks grew redder and her voice softer. "Oh."

"Companion cards also don't have drawdown, and everyone says they're about as strong as a tier five to seven, two-power card, which is *huge* for a zero-cost creature. So the gifted deckbearers for this season are a lot stronger at the start. Still nothing compared to the insane high-level champions and other asshole bigwigs, but stronger than most starting deckbearers. I'm going to summon mine. You do the same."

"How do card tiers work?" Shel asked.

Wolfe took one last puff and ground his cigarette out. "I'll talk it over with you in a minute, since I have some cards I want to screw with. If we start deep-sixing a bunch of deckbearers, or if we get rich and can buy cards, or if we get lucky and find one of the new dungeons that came with the season, you can do the same. Now summon your companion card. It's supposedly your best."

Wolfe stood and placed his hand over his heart. He felt his deck, and his power. Dark, angry, and hungry. He pushed his hand forward and brought forth his deck, willing it into existence. He had ten cards in it, and three came up—a Tormentor Imp, an Escaped Damned, and Imp Master, his persistent mantle card.

Wolfe glared at the mantle card. *Now you show up on first pull*.

He was curious about his other mantle, the Soul Hunter, for a long-term build—it could make *him* extremely dangerous, especially with the mantle-increasing perk he had. But he ignored it for the moment, focusing on what he was talking about right now—his companion card, Cereboo. Which hadn't come with his pull.

Feeling silly, Wolfe glanced over at the couch, where Cereboo was just sitting quietly. *Right, he's already out. What with all the training, I'd forgotten.*

Wolfe smiled as he stared at his new doggo. Cereboo was special, and had already proven his worth multiple times over in three fights. Although he had been defeated in one of them—it wasn't just Sorenia that had paid to keep her deckbearer alive.

"Hey, um, you okay, Cereboo? I didn't mean to let them... kinda kill you in the ambush. The second one, I mean. We did great in the first one."

Shel glanced over at him, but Cereboo stood up on the couch, all three mouths open in the 'happy dog' expression, his tail wagging furiously.

"I think he likes fighting, the same way most dogs like chasing a ball," Shel said dryly.

Cereboo woofed happily but shook his heads.

"You like fighting bad guys?" Wolfe asked, his intuition kicking in.

Cereboo woofed happily again.

Wolfe checked the stats on Cereboo again, noting the attack, defense, and magical version scores... but he remembered that its real value had been its resistances and strengths. It reduced damage from Mortal sources, including actual mortals, thanks to its Infernal typing. But the card's special powers gave it a bonus against its *own* card type of Infernal.

In short, it was an absolute perfect card for someone who spent most of his time punking or fighting thugs and other Infernal deckbearers.

Cereboo

Unique Beast/Infernal[Canine] Companion Effective Tier-7
0 Power
Health: 12
Attack: 5x3
Magical Attack: 7
Defense: 7
Magical Defense: 4

Special: While in play, Beast and Infernal power may be spent as if they were the other.
Special: Guardian of the Gate: +100% attack and magic attack against other Infernal cards.
Special: Preferred Typing: Gains all the better type matchups of both Infernal and Beast.
Special: One of the 'Gate to the Underworld' cards. If all 6 are possessed in the same deck, the bearer will gain 7 Legendary Infernal or Beast card pulls. Additionally, the deckbearer may either gain the Mythic 'Gate to the Underworld' Building Card or evolve Cereboo. One card is held by each of the crime families of Noimoire, and the sixth is held within the city by another.

"A pup of Cerberus, who was born into a particularly frisky litter. Cereboo was the runt—not quite as strong, nor as tough, as his litter mates. But his heart was the heart of a huntsman, and the blood of Cerberus runs in his veins. He hunted across the fiery plains of the first infernal realm, chasing the damned that tried to escape their fates. Now, he chases many things, but his soul is still called to chase those that belong in the Infernal Realms."

"Hey, what's your magical attack?" Wolfe asked Cereboo.

The two outside heads woofed, and the middle head faced downward and breathed a gout of flame across the floor.

"No, bad dog!" Wolfe exclaimed. He rushed over and grabbed a couch cushion. Then he smothered the tiny fire that had started.

Shel was wide-eyed, but after a second, she started laughing.

Wolfe pressed the cushion down on the burned spot, making sure everything was properly snuffed. With a frown, he shot her a sardonic glare.

She flushed red and glanced away, twirling her finger in her hair.

"You've been a bad boy," Wolfe said again as he stood. He shook his finger in Cereboo's unrepentant face, adrenaline racing through his body for the 'one too many-eth' time.

Then Wolfe started to laugh himself. Wolfe wished he could have named Cereboo 'Pierce' instead, after his old dog. They both had the 'mostly good doggo but—' vibe. His new companion was already named, however.

A pure white light with gold at the edges shone, and a woman appeared next to Shel. She was six feet tall, with blue eyes, and she carried an old-style ironmongery lantern in one hand, chained to her wrist with no obvious way to take it off. But her most notable features were the white wings that spread back from her body and the oversized purple halo above and behind her head. She faced Wolfe and bowed, deeply.

"We meet again, Infernal Deckbearer. Thank you, from the bottom of my heart, for going against your nature and saving my own Deckbearer."

Cereboo ignored the Divine card, something that surprised Wolfe.

"I'm happy Shel's okay," Wolfe said, staring at her until her card appeared.

Sorenia
Unique, effective Tier-7 Divine/Light companion
0 Power
Health: 10 (3 remaining)
Attack: 0
Magical Attack: 9
Defense: 8
Magical Defense:

Special: While in play, all Mortal creature cards gain divine typing and +25% (minimum 1) to all stats.
Special: The benefits to Mortal cards stack with the other three named companion lantern angels. If all 4 are possessed the card, Zarachiel, Commander of the Lanterns, a 4 power mythic tier-8 equivalent divine companion card will be gained as well as a free companion card slot.

"A particularly zealous and dedicated member of the hundred thousand lantern angels, she tries to guide mortals to right behavior—and victory over the Infernal, Undead, and Elder gods. Through her zealous efforts to make the Mortal world better she once earned a lesson at Archangel Raphael's knee, her proudest memory."

Wolfe whistled. *Okay, that's strong as heck—she could make an absolutely badass Divine Mortal combination deck, but how much would three additional companion card slots cost? A ridiculous amount of leveling points, I'm guessing.*

Although the gods made decks a lot more specialized this

season. It feels like she almost has *to go into the Divine and Mortal split... Plus, to really become powerful, she probably has to whack other Divine deckbearers.*

Wolfe frowned. *The gods really are dicks.*

"Nice companion, girl. I think I see where your deck is going."

The angel frowned. "I am Sorenia, dark deckbearer. A guiding light to mortals from the realm of the Divine. I do appreciate your aid, truly, but I would still appreciate it if you not act as if I weren't here."

"Sure, whatever," Wolfe said.

Cereboo gave a half-woof, more playful than anything, and went up and licked at the angel. She tried to fend him off and look regal but couldn't seem to put down the lantern. The 'one hand to three tongues' matchup resulted in Cereboo transferring quite a bit of slobber.

Wolfe laughed and turned his attention back to Shel.

Shel stared at her angel for a bit longer but then faced back at Wolfe. "How do I get more companion card slots?"

"Level a whole bunch and save your leveling. Each time you add a specialist card slot, it costs five leveling per slot, except for minion and enhancer cards, which are one each... and then it goes up by an equal amount each time you level."

"And you level by defeating other deckbearers in the arenas?"

Wolfe yawned. "Girl... there are a lot of ways to level. I got two levels by killing some thugs who tried to off me on the way to the docks. Then I got another two from thugs that tried to off me when I arrived at the docks. And Frankie and his thugs gave me three more after that. You only get three challenge options at the special arenas each season. It's very limited. But there are other ways—like killing people."

Wolfe remembered the fight, and its ending. "Speaking of killing, you technically helped me take down Frankie the Frog. You should have a couple levels—probably about four, since I got three and was higher level to start. You can already improve yourself with leveling pips."

Wolfe yawned a second time. "But I'm tired. It's three in the morning and I'm still awake, something that is at least half your fault. How about, we instead go to sleep, and we can talk about card combinations and leveling tomorrow, okay?"

"Right," Shel muttered.

"You can use the bed." Wolfe gestured back to his room. "I'll take the couch."

"I-It's your home. You should have your own bed. I'll just take the couch." Shel hurried over to it, her face red.

Wolfe wasn't about to argue with her. He liked his bed. But the way she avoided his gaze and fumbled with the cushions made him curious as to her thoughts.

Wolfe glanced over and saw that Shel's angel was now just petting Cereboo, who was panting happily.

Wolfe turned back and shook his head. "Listen, I have a guest room in the back with a futon. It's not the most comfortable, but it is at least private. And if you change your mind, because it's so lumpy, you can always come back to the couch."

"Really?" she asked.

Wolfe growled an affirmative.

"Th-Thank you. So much." Shel wrung her hands. "But... You're just going to leave me alone in your house? While you sleep? You're not going to chain me up to something?"

"Do you *want* me to chain you up to something?" Wolfe asked, borderline baffled.

"*No*. O-Obviously not." Shel turned away from him as she fidgeted with the ends of her hair. "That's not what I meant. I mean—I just figured—you wouldn't trust me. And you would demand to keep me locked up. Or something. Isn't that what... what gangsters do?"

Wolfe wanted to point out that, if she was being held

captive, he wouldn't have taken her to his personal home, but he kept all that sarcastic commentary to himself. Shel clearly didn't understand how organized crime operated.

"Listen," Wolfe said with a sigh. "You're smart, right?"

"I mean... yes?" Shel said, her voice rising on the last part as if it were a question.

"Well, I'm sure a super smart girl like you can figure out what'll happen if you steal my shit or fuck with me while I sleep. Now quit bothering me. I'm going to bed."

CHAPTER 10

DARKNESS SEEPS ACROSS
THE LAND

"**Great Game Rule #10**: A new hand of cards may be drawn every sixty seconds."

It was barely light outside when Wolfe's phone went off. He reached over from his bed to the computer desk, three-fourths asleep, and knocked the phone onto the floor—as well as jiggling the mouse, turning his computer on.

6:33 in the morning. No sane person should be up at this gods' forsaken hour.

He leaned off the bed and grabbed the phone. *Big Man Grimm again? What the hell is going on? We don't operate in the morning!*

Wolfe hit *accept* after the brief half-second of disbelief and answered as non-groggily as he could while scratching the massive scar on his chest. "What's up, Thad?"

Big Man Grimm's heavy voice came through, and Wolfe could hear the throttled rage. "Get up, Wolfe. We have another situation. Melissa says Heinrich's been murdered."

"Shot during the fighting last night?"

"No, Derek's warning—really from you, I know—helped a

lot. We got most of our guys to safety. Most. But Heinrich was murdered in a motel bed. I'm sorry, but I need you to deal with that."

Wolfe stared at his phone. "Fuck."

"We're gonna need to get you some new clothes soon. You look ridiculous in yesterday's sweat-and-whatever stained jeans and my giant T-shirt. Perhaps we should stop by your place."

"That won't work," Shel said, rubbing her eyes, which were red and puffy, and then leaning against the car window. "Can we just talk about how we level and combine cards?"

Someone else has some skeletons in their closet. "No."

"You said we'd talk about it today," Shel said.

"Girl, I said we'd talk about it tomorrow at three A.M. today. Now, I'm not trying to play here—I admit I *meant* when we woke up. But I also thought that would be after more than three hours of sleep. So I'm gonna fall back on the real definition of 'tomorrow.' 'Cuz I'm too tired to talk about this shit."

"Can we get something to eat?"

"You got money?"

Shel shook her head.

Of course. "Yeah, sure, one sec."

Wolfe pulled the car into the first fast food place he saw, a Deckburger, and pulled up to order. He lowered the window, receiving an odd stench of rain and garbage. The Deckburger menu was... questionable, however.

Deckbugers!! Where Every Bite is a Winning
Hand!!
Try our new special!
The Creature C-C-C-Combo:

2 Deckburgers, "2 Pair" Tacos, and 2 Grape
Graveyard Milkshakes

Wolfe inwardly groaned. The rest of the menu was filled with an equal number of cards puns, including the Cesear-Mantle Salad, and the 6-Draw Sliders.

No plain black coffee, though.

Pretty sure everywhere has plain black coffee, Wolfe thought.

"Good morning, can I spice up your day with a c-c-combo?" the speaker asked, obviously hating every second of her rehearsed script. She spoke each word like it were slowly killing her.

Wolfe turned to Shel. "Whaddya want?"

"Um... a vegan Winning Hand Wrap and an orange juice."

"The fuck? A vegan breakfast?"

Shel just half shrugged and remained quiet. Wolfe was glad she had decided to put Sorenia back in the deck at some point. Wolfe had also reluctantly put Cereboo back in his deck, since he didn't want people finding out about his special status.

Whatever. Wolfe turned back to the speaker. "One Sausage Creature Roll, one... Winning Hand Wrap, an orange juice, and a black coffee."

"Um... you mean the *Infernal Juice*?"

Wolfe scratched the scar on his chest. "I don't have time for your pun nonsense. Just give me a damned black coffee, strong as you can make it."

"Ugh... Look, you have to say you want the Infernal Juice if you want the blackest coffee we have. Otherwise, I have to give you the coffee with cream. Company policy."

Wolfe throttled his anger. "Fine. Infernal Juice. *Strong*. Your largest size." Something about calling coffee *juice* made him disgusted. Bean juice? What kind of pun was this? A lazy one.

Shel giggled from the seat next to Wolfe, but when he looked over at her, she stared ahead and tried to assume a straight face, twirling her finger in her red hair.

"That'll be thirteen dollars and nine cents."

Wolfe pulled up and they got their food. The Infernal Juice was actually good, although it didn't taste exactly like black coffee. Stronger, somehow. Wolfe didn't want to know why. Ever.

"I'm surprised," Shel said as she nibbled her wrap.

"About what?"

"They made you say Infernal Juice. I thought, well, you'd get angry and flash your gun or something. Maybe threaten them."

Wolfe sighed. "This isn't the movies. Contrary to popular belief, you don't want to go around announcing your criminal status. It's a fast food joint, not a back alley transaction."

Shel hemmed and hawed for a moment before muttering, "I don't know. You were just nicer than I thought a gangster would be, that's all."

Wolfe didn't know what to say to that. Noimoire had hit a new low if keeping his pistol in its holster was considered *nice*.

After that, Shel was too busy eating to ask any more questions, which Wolfe was also fine with. She finished whatever nasty vegetable roll she had ordered by the time they'd arrived at their destination: The Morning After Inn. It was three stories of sleazy rooms packed into a long, thin building. Wolfe had been there a couple of times, for one reason or another.

He wished he had stopped for a cigarette before getting here, or smoked in the car. He was feeling jittery.

Wolfe got out of the car, stomped his legs, and entered the front of the building. The paint was off-white, old and cracked and covered in dirt. A beat-up sign hanging in the front window declared, "Rooms rented by the hour, available now!"

There were very few reasons to rent a room by the hour, and most involved getting your rocks off.

Wolfe walked into the front room, swinging the door open wide as he pushed in, and Shel followed in his wake.

The woman at the front desk smiled widely upon seeing

him. "Wolfe! I knew they'd send you, hon. What took you so long?"

"Melissa, how's it going?"

Melissa was a kinda used-up-looking woman of forty with brown hair and blue eyes. She had enough makeup to look bangable without looking *good*. She was in a loose, white chemise with food stains on the front and pink bra straps showing.

Her eyes immediately went to Shel. "Bringing in some local competition? Or did you want an expert to help you both?"

Wolfe grit his teeth. "Melissa, *please*. *You* called *us*. This is very serious."

Shel glanced around, taking in more of the décor that Wolfe's eyes had just passed over. Pictures of half-naked women on the walls. The rooms, listed by bed type—including water and vibrating. Melissa herself. "What kind of place is this?"

Melissa lifted an eyebrow. "Wow, she's green. Who *is* this kid?"

Shel furrowed her brow and scrunched her nose. "I'm not a kid." Then she held her hand out to Melissa. "I'm Shel. Pleased to meet you."

Melissa was a bit nonplussed but took the hand. "Wow. So, now I *know* you aren't local competition. What're you here for? You can't possibly be Wolfe's replacement, slip of a girl like you. Even if he is getting old."

Wolfe ground out, "Melissa..."

"How old is he?" Shel asked.

"Old enough. He's been around forever, solving—and sometimes making—problems. *Way* longer than most people make it in this life, longer than the twenty years I've been doing this. Getting old. We both know that Big Man Grimm is gonna need a new enforcer soon."

Normally, that would have pissed Wolfe off—because it

would have been true, he admitted to himself. But now... now he had a deck. He gave Melissa a smug smile. "We'll see."

Then he leaned forward on the counter, tapping his fingers on it rapidly. "Now, please, just tell me where I need to go."

She sighed. "You used to be more fun, hon. What happened?"

"You got a bit long in the tooth to be plying with lies." Wolfe's weirdly building anxiety and irritability was getting the better of him, and he had no idea why. "*For fuck's sake*, Melissa, just tell me where the problem is. I have a lot on my plate and almost no sleep at all."

She sighed again. "You seem wired, hon, but sure. D3. I've closed the whole floor till you can handle it."

Wolfe gave her a single upward jut of his chin. "Thank you. I'll deal with it."

He stepped to the elevator and hit the *up* button, tapping his foot as he did. A moment later, it chimed and the brass doors opened. Wolfe, followed by Shel, stepped inside. The place smelled like ass for some reason. Wolfe hit the '3' on the panel, trying to breathe through his mouth.

"How old are you?" Shel asked.

Wolfe sighed. *Why, by the gods, did they need to talk about this?* "Thirty-eight."

"That's not that old," Shel said. "I mean, you look a lot younger than she did. Really good for your age."

Wolfe grunted but didn't say anything. Thirty-eight was damned old to be a street enforcer. He absently touched his chest, a comforting sense of flame and hunger rising. *Not that old now, though.*

His scar still itched, however.

"Who was she?" Shel asked.

Wolfe shrugged. "Melissa was just some working girl once. I have no idea of her fucking backstory prior to that. But she was an unusually pretty and sociable whore. She made some decent money and then cut a deal with the Singh family, who run most of the prostitutes and not totally legal brothels. She somehow fucking *financed* this place—like with a damned bank—which she now owns outright. That was about sixteen years ago. She gives money to the Grimm family for protection and still works with the Singhs, keeping this as a place they can send their whores and johns. Knows to tell the cops they aren't welcome and has a deal to call the Singhs when someone asks about prostitutes. She knows half the players in the city, even if she isn't much of one herself."

The elevator dinged and Wolfe got out.

He walked over to room D3 and opened the door. Immediately, the rank, copper-and-shit smell of death hit his nostrils.

Wolfe grimaced. *Just as Big Man Grimm said. Don't know why I keep hoping people will be wrong about this shit.*

Shel gagged, like she was trying to keep from throwing up.

"You going to be able to handle this?" Wolfe asked.

She nodded, keeping one hand over her face. With her other hand, she offered him a shaky thumbs-up.

Wolfe walked in. After half a second, Shel followed.

Wolfe glanced around the room, a frown on his face. It was like every fleabag motel room he had ever seen, only with a palette swap and a bucket of red paint. Cheap carpet, check. Old-ass bed whose mattress looked like it was begging for death, check. World's most boring round table and flimsy-ass chair by the window? Another check. Nightstand with a built-in ashtray, the height of class? Also check.

The dead guy and girl, however, were unusual. Not exactly mythic, but still uncommon.

Dead guy was lying faceup, completely naked, half-off the bed. Without even the slightest hint of a forensic degree—or finishing fucking high school—Wolfe could tell he had been shot right after 'dismounting' the girl. His head was perforated, but it wasn't a clean shot. It was slightly off-center. A pro would have aimed for the torso, which was a bigger target, or gotten the perfect headshot at five feet if they were odd enough to go for it. This was mostly likely a gang hit, but why?

Wolfe sighed as he stared at the still-present perfect teeth and salt-and-cinnamon hair. Heinrich Grimm, all right, even with the hole in his face. Big Man Grimm's cousin and accountant, and a new deckbearer a mere eight or so hours ago. *There's gonna be hell to pay for this.*

He didn't know the girl, but as he looked at her, he clenched his teeth. She had been shot three times in the chest, at close range. There were smears where she had flailed in Heinrich's blood before dying. The sick fuck who had done this had reveled in killing her, and more. He had reveled in her terror before she'd died.

Her hair matched his nightmares, and Wolfe silently promised himself that whomever had done this would die.

"Why does her death bother you, but the guy's doesn't?" Shel asked. "Is it because she's a woman?"

Girl's too fucking perceptive for her own good. "Shut up. We have work to do."

He moved closer to the bed, careful not to step in the spreading blood, and glanced about. On the sheets was a card with the stylized snake symbol on it.

The Cobras. Of course. They were everywhere the Grimm family was having problems, somehow.

Why announce this? That makes zero sense, unless they want a war... but between this, our dead drug mover, Johnny, the attack on me, and last night's kill fest, I can't come up with any other conclusion than they do, in fact, want one... but still, why claim this kill?

Wolfe put that aside and kept looking. Knowing which gang didn't tell him a lot.

There were odd smears on the floor, faint, as if something

had gotten blood on it, dropped on the floor, and then been picked up. Including some partial prints with blood. *Sucks we can't go to the cops for this.*

"Hey, Wolfe?" Shel asked again.

"Yeah?"

"Shouldn't I understand more if I'm going to help? You're not..." Shel waved her hand in front of herself as she obviously searched for the right words. "You're not helping me to help you. This whole thing was for me to help you take the Cobras out, and I *am* a deckbearer."

Wolfe started to grit his teeth but then relaxed. *Can't hurt, might help.* "Yeah, you're right. I should teach you so we can make sure your cute ass stays alive till we can finish the Cobras off. Sorry. To answer your first why—of this room—it bothers me because she isn't running with the gangs, not because of her gender—although her being a girl makes it worse for me."

"Oh."

Wolfe exhaled noisily. "I mean, the families and gangs fight over turf, sure, and I'll waste any idiot punk who tries to take Grimm family territory. Heinrich knew what he was getting into. But killing the working girl is just... classless and... wrong. She wasn't involved."

"Big Man Grimm's rule?" Shel asked.

Wolfe shook his head, then frowned. "Well, yeah, it's his rule. I just mean I feel the same way, regardless of his rule. I'd be pissed with or without Big Man Grimm weighing in. It's not right."

Shel nodded.

Wolfe pointed to Heinrich. "This dumb fuck, who never could stop screwing prostitutes—he lost two wives over it—is Big Man Grimm's cousin. Also, the big man's accountant. There's gonna be hell to pay over this killing, although I guess we're already in a war with the Cobras. Which I'm *really* not looking forward to, like I would have in my younger, dumber days."

Even as Wolfe said it, he felt a slight stirring at his words. Two days ago he wouldn't have been looking forward to it, but now... *levels, cards, and a chance to take out the trash that thinks they can replace us with their thug tactics.*

Maybe I am looking forward to it, somewhat.

Shel quirked an eyebrow at him as he paused.

Wolfe shook his head and continued. "As I was saying, at least Heinrich here was in the game, so to speak. He knew the risks and made a lot of money—and slept with a lot of working girls—for taking part. With the rewards goes the risk. But the girl didn't deserve it."

Wolfe blew out through his nose. "Anyway, we have to clean this up so that Melissa can get the girls back into the third floor. We still have business."

Shel glanced around again. "What if we pinned this more directly on the Cobras?"

"What do you mean?" Wolfe asked.

"Well... you could move the bodies. I see there's a partial fingerprint on the sheet"—she pointed to one Wolfe had missed —"and if we move the sheet and the bodies to some part of the Cobras' territory, I can call the cops on them. I mean, I've already been working with Detective Young."

That... isn't the worst idea ever. "All right, that's not a bad plan. But just the girl."

"Why?"

"Because if a known Grimm family member is murdered and ends up at the police station, it gives them a reason to check out Big Man Grimm. Never be the one who gets Big Man Grimm in the cop's crosshairs, trust me. He's avoided being pulled in for at least the twenty years I've known him. Plus, the big man will want to have a memorial service for his cousin."

Shel was biting her lower lip. "That makes sense. Have you?"

"Have I what?" Wolfe asked, confused.

"Avoided being pulled in by the police?"

"Not completely... I've had a few run-ins and been put in the back of a car once or twice, but I've never been held long enough to be booked and fingerprinted, except my sealed juvenile records, thanks to Big Man Grimm's connections. I'm a known associate though."

Wolfe pulled his own phone out and called Rich.

He didn't get an answer, and after half a minute, he hung up. *Fucker better be sleeping off the best sex ever.*

A sudden grim thought crossed Wolfe's mind. *I hope he didn't get killed in last night's fighting.*

Wolfe pushed it aside and dialed Harry, Big Man Grimm's personal guard, instead. Wolfe had business to take care of; he couldn't be worried about possible dead associates.

Harry answered, his own voice blurry. *This guy has almost an extra hour of sleep, maybe two, over me. He shouldn't be complaining.*

"Harry, it's Wolfe. I need you to get a couple of guys, a van, and a tarp. We're going to move a body."

"Uh... yeah, I'll get on it. Where are we moving it from and to?"

As he was talking, Wolfe's eye fell on something else. "From the Morning After Inn. I'll let you know about 'to' in a bit."

Wolfe hung up and kneeled down. One smear of blood went halfway under the nightstand. He reached down and grabbed the piece of furniture under its edge and lifted it.

On the floor, about dead center under where the nightstand had been, was a card. Wolfe stared at it. It had a bit of blood on the side, but it was the card itself that fascinated Wolfe the most.

An Escaped Damned.

Right, Heinrich's deck. Which they took... but somehow, they lost a card. Must have been knocked down here by the girl's flailing and missed by whoever grabbed the cards.

CHAPTER 11

LESSONS IN THE GRAVEYARD

"Great Game Rule #11: A "hand of cards" is three cards, unless increased through leveling."

"All right, girl, let's do this after all," Wolfe said, sitting down on the floor away from the blood and pulling out the ten cards from the deckbearer he had killed in the ambush with the Imp deck plus his own old cards. Then he added the ten from Frankie and the one he had picked off the floor. "We have to wait for Harry and his boys to get here."

He spread the twenty-one cards across the floor. The ones from the dead ambush guy were almost all imp related and in his current deck, but he hadn't seen Frankie's yet.

Shel sat down on the other side of the cards cross-legged, but her eyes went to the corpses not but six feet away. "Do we have to do this... here?"

Wolfe stopped arranging cards and glanced up. "It'll build character. Or at least a tolerance for bodies and the smell of death. Offer's still open if you want to just take the cash and get out. It's the smart move. As Confucius said, 'If you seek revenge, dig two graves.'"

Shel nervously chuckled. "Confucius didn't say that. It's a quote recorded in a book by some American guy that went to Japan and didn't attribute it to anyone. Whoever said it first is now lost to time."

He just stared at her, his eyes narrowed.

Shel's picks grew pink. "I did a report on Confucius."

"I'm sure it earned you a fancy gold star."

Shel folded her arms over her chest. "I think you're just mad I corrected you."

"Or maybe I just want to get this over with because we *are* in a room full of corpses." He lifted an eyebrow.

"R-Right."

Shel furrowed her brow and twisted a finger in her red hair, but didn't say anything else. Wolfe went back to arranging the cards with a huff. After they were arranged, he checked the cards he had on the ground while Shel watched.

Frankie's cards were nearly all useless to Wolfe, unless he wanted to add Corrupted power to his character sheet. Frankie had ten cards: His four Caustic Frog Demons, his mantle, the one-power Corrupted card that summoned a persistent brazier that reduced the power of all non-corrupted cards and deckbearers within a hundred feet, and two copies of a card that allowed a one-time acid attack that was about as strong as a pistol in terms of likely damage inflicted, but with far less range. Only thing that made that card useful, that Wolfe could see, was that the Caustic Frog Demons could heal from Corrupted damage.

But he had two cards that piqued Wolfe's interest. He stared at them for a moment.

Desperate Pact
Uncommon Tier-1 Corrupted Persistent(Aura)
2 Corrupted Power or 4 Health

Special: This card gives a +1 stat bonus to all Infernal, Undead, Elder, Corrupted, and Mortal that are on the Deckbearer's side.

"There are very few people that would willingly ally themselves with the dark without an incentive. And for good people, the thing that turns them to darkness is usually a truly desperate moment."

Wolfe put the remaining eight of Frankie's cards in his pocket—he could sell or trade them, and he was pretty sure the ten cards were worth just shy of a million dollars. Unfortunately, they weren't useful to him in the moment.

But he kept the two Desperate Pacts out, an idea toying at his mind. The awkward wording of the card's ability made him think of a possible build he might use.

Wolfe had twenty-one potentially useful cards, including the ones in his deck. Six Tormentor Imp and five Escaped Damned made up nearly half the useable cards. The Tiny Pitchfork was a persistent equipment card that made an imp stronger. He had two mantles—the Imp Master one that empowered imps and his own Soul Hunter which increased his stats and made him stronger against other Infernal cards. Then he had his persistent non-mantle cards: two Punish the Sinner cards and his two Return to the Pit cards.

Almost all Infernal. But his original deck had been Beast, and he still had those cards—one Loyal Guard Dogs and one Rescue Pup, as well as his companion card, Cereboo. Plus, his own perks made him stronger when he used Beast cards.

And in Shel's deck he had the strong, but dangerous to use, Fallen Angel card.

"Shel, how many of the Rookie EMT cards do you have in your deck?"

"Two," she replied, cocking her head at him.

Wolfe looked up. "I know I said we'd wait, but can I give you a useless card and take the Fallen Angel after all?"

Shel nodded, pulling her own deck. Wolfe ignored the notification of a deckbearer pulling their deck.

He gave her one of the Caustic Frog Demon cards, and Shel, breathing through her mouth and looking a bit green with the dead bodies and smell of blood, switched it into her deck—she touched the Fallen Angel card and then touched Frankie's old card. They switched places. Wolfe picked up the Fallen Angel card and added it and the two Desperate Pact cards to his deck of ten.

Wolfe glanced up to find Shel breathing through her mouth and staring at him. She watched him run his finger along each card as he read them. Her eyes had been flickering over the cards—reading them upside down, probably—but she had stopped.

Wolfe put aside his deck work for just a moment. He would make one of the card combinations he could just to show her how it worked.

"First thing we're going to talk about is combining cards, since I have enough here to demonstrate. You need three cards of the same tier to raise the card a single tier."

Wolfe took three Escaped Damned and put the three cards together, giving Shel enough time to see the three cards. She leaned over to take in the stats.

Escaped Damned
Common Infernal/Undead Creature Tier-1
1 Infernal Power
Health: 10
Attack: 0
Magical Attack: 3
Defense: 8
Magical Defense: 1

"A Soul that somehow escaped the Infernal realm and wants to remain free"

Wolfe took the three cards and *willed* them together. The three cards all glowed a fiery red and then merged. The card front burned away, leaving a new card behind: Escaped Damned, tier-two.

Escaped Damned
Common Infernal/Undead Creature Tier-2
1 Infernal Power
Health: 11
Attack: 0
Magical Attack: 4
Defense: 8
Magical Defense: 2

"A Soul that somehow escaped the Infernal realm and wants to remain free"

"That was... underwhelming," Shel said.

Wolfe laughed. "I suppose, but it's a permanent and unlimited method to make yourself stronger no matter your level. You never need more power to cast or more cards on field. Just get giant piles of other cards and combine."

Shel nodded. "I guess that makes sense... It works for anything?"

"If you get three of the same card at the same tier."

Shel scrunched her nose as she focused. "So it's a geometric progression? Three raised to the power of the tier you are raising the card to, minus one?"

Wolfe rolled his eyes. "You just need three cards of the same name and tier and you'll make a new one. Don't complicate it."

"Still... I can see how it would be hard. A tier-four card

would require twenty-seven tier-one cards. Imagine the crazy amount of zeros you would need on a tier-ten or something."

"Heh." Wolfe pulled his deck. While merging cards he had decided to make the huge change. Wolfe moved the Fallen Angel card, and the two Desperate Pact cards, into his deck. He switched out the Imp Mantle, and put back in his Soul Hunter Mantle.

Soul Hunter
Uncommon Tier-1 Persistent(Mantle)
1 Infernal Power
This card grants the Deckbearer 2 Attack, 2 Defense, and 2 Magical Defense. Additionally, the Deckbearer will do an additional 25% damage against Infernal cards, monsters, and Deckbearers

"Sometimes, the Infernal Realms want their own back. That's when they send a Soul Hunter to do their dirty work."

Wolfe smiled. His Fallen Angel was strong, and relatively cheap. Cereboo was strong and cost nothing. And with the Soul Hunter Mantle, Wolfe himself would be insanely dangerous. Best of all, without costing power, the two Desperate Pacts would make *any* of those options far more dangerous.

The real trick to his current deck, however, was an associated healer.

Wolfe added the tier-two Escaped Damned to his deck, and then added the Rescue Pup back in—it didn't synergize that well, but it was costless and did give some benefits to both Cereboo and himself, potentially.

He didn't have anything else that synergized that well yet. He was tempted to merge his Tormentor Imp cards, but he hesitated—he might need to use his imp deck again. He decided against merging them, put two of the Tormentor Imps in his deck, and threw the Loyal Guard Dog back in as well.

And I need to level. Wolfe glanced up at Shel. "Okay, since we're still waiting on Harry, let's talk leveling. I need to level up a lot, and you need to level a bit. So, pull your status sheet up and follow along."

Shel glanced at the bodies on the bed again but said nothing.

He pulled his status sheet up again himself, then quickly checked the values each stat could be increased by. Then he used the chart as a reference to talk to Shel.

Wolfe puffed on his cigarette, adding secondhand smoke to the miasma of terrible that floated through the air of the room. "Each time you level, you get a leveling pip. Each of the deckbearer stats can be increased for a pip, times how often you've increased it, including the one you're doing at the moment. What you had to start doesn't really matter."

Shel was nodding.

She probably understood, but Wolfe gave her an example anyway. "So, for my first level, I added a point of power—Infernal power. but it's not the total that's the stat for determining the cost to raise my power. It's how many times I've raised it. It cost me one point. I have four power now—one Fire, two Infernal, and one Beast. But I've raised my power one time only, so it only cost me one leveling pip to raise it, even though I had three already. Get it?"

Shel forced a smile.

"If someone who didn't have a perk granting an extra power had tried to raise to three power from their base two, it would have cost the same. One leveling pip. No matter which specific power type they raised."

Shel kept up the bobblehead nodding as he talked. Like she was automatically agreeable. He wondered why. "Now, when I go to five, if I get a second Beast instead of a third Infernal, or even if I bought my first point of Corrupted to use Frankie's cards, it'll take two leveling pips. Because even though it's my first Beast power raise, it's my second power raise ever."

"Got it," she said. "What are the values of each increase on the other stats?"

"For a leveling pip each, you can get the following: Each increase to your deck size is five. Each increase to cards in hand and cards in play is one per. Each increase to length of play is one minute. Each increase to power is one power of any type, whether you currently have it or not."

"And specialty card slots?" Shel asked. "How much do each of those cost?"

Wolfe quoted from his memory of what he had read on the internet. "It's different for each specialty card. For the most common three—buildings, minions, and enhancers—it's five, one, and one, respectively, modified by number purchased. Unlike power, this goes up per type, not for the whole category. So even if you had five specialty cards, if none were minions and you bought a minion card slot, it would still only cost one for your first."

"And Companion cards?"

"Five to add one, and then ten for the second, fifteen for the third, and so on. Having five amazing companion cards that cost no power on the field at all times would be insanely powerful, but you'll need fifty levels to pull it off. Well, actually, only thirty for you since your card combination would give you a bonus companion card slot. But fifty for most people."

Shel exhaled so hard she practically deflated, then nodded at Wolfe. But she didn't say anything.

When she breathed in again, deeply, she coughed and went a bit gray.

It is getting even grosser in here.

Even as Wolfe thought it, his phone rang—it was Harry.

Wolfe answered.

"We're here. Four guys and a tarp. Is it okay if we come up?"

"Yeah. Room D3. We'll be outside in the hall, right when you get off the elevators."

Wolfe stood up, walked over, and ground his cigarette out in the ashtray on the nightstand. He turned to hold his hand out to Shel but found her already standing.

He dropped his hand and motioned to the door. "Well, with fortuitous timing, Harry has arrived right at the end of our talk about the two ways to make yourself more powerful as a deckbearer. Although now I don't really have a chance to level—duty calls. Let's go see what we can work out with them though."

Shel nodded and followed Wolfe outside the room and back into the hall. She walked a bit from the door and breathed heavily.

Maybe asking her to stay in there was a dick move... but she does need to toughen up.

"So, tell me about your deck," Wolfe said.

Shel took another deep breath, then started in. "It's mostly Mortal cards, actually. I have the same perk you do—I got an extra power type as well. You have Infernal and Beast and Fire. I have Divine and Mortal and Light."

He nodded, feeling the sting of his gifted deck pretty much declaring him irredeemably bad. *At least I can get this precious little cinnamon roll out of the life, just as soon as she gets her revenge.*

"I have Sorenia, a separate card that empowers mortals while it's out called Guiding Light, the 'Fallen Angel,' two small direct damage Light cards, and five common Mortal creature cards—Pitiable Martyr, two Rookie EMT cards, and two Rookie Riot Police cards."

Wolfe wanted to take another cigarette out but held off, tapping his foot against the floor. He still felt wired and anxious. "What are your perks and flaws?"

Shel frowned at him but answered fairly quickly. "The extra

power is one, and my second is an increased-quality pull for one random card from any Divine or Mortal pack we win from monsters or a dungeon, or, for a mixed pack, a guarantee that at least one card will be from one of those types."

Wolfe almost face-palmed. Every Drop Night, the world also got inundated with new monsters and dungeons—it was a great source of new cards and experience both. Wolfe had literally thought about it last night, but he had been so tired he had forgotten this morning. He pulled his phone out, searching through it for the contact that owed him the most.

Shel was still talking. "My flaw is that I can't gain attack from mantles."

Victor Gaines. He owes me—big time. As soon as I have some actual free time, I need to try to get some levels and cards before this season's resources disappear. Half will disappear in the first month, and two-thirds of the remainder in the rest of the year.

Then Wolfe did a double take. "Wait, say that again."

"I can't gain attack from a mantle."

"Can you gain magic attack?" Wolfe asked.

Shel's eyes unfocused for a second, then she nodded.

"Okay... very few mantles add magic attack, and you can't really train yourself up for it, but that's not the worst thing you could have gotten. Still, it's a decently harsh flaw. You might need to really lean into a mantle that benefits your cards."

Shel pursed her lips but didn't say anything else.

Wolfe got back to what he had been doing, holding his phone up.

Shel watched him as he unlocked his phone, but before he could call, the elevator door opened and Harry stepped out with four other goons whom Wolfe only barely recognized—and Derek. Wolfe was glad he seemed not only *not dead*, but actively fine.

Wolfe hooked a thumb toward D3. "There're two bodies inside, boys. One is Heinrich, Big Man Grimm's cousin—"

Derek cussed, and Wolfe was reminded again that the new guy was extremely talented. He had instantly understood what that meant. An escalation.

"—and one is a working girl. I need you to wrap the girl in the sheet and drop her off in the dumpster behind the Venom Arena, and Heinrich's body has to go to Big Man Grimm's mansion—*not the club*. You knuckleheads got it?"

Everyone nodded. Wolfe noted with amusement that half of them were ogling Shel, despite her ridiculously unsexy outfit.

"Harry?" Wolfe asked, and the man faced him. "Repeat it back, please."

Harry, whose thick frame was mostly hidden by the wrinkled suit from yesterday he had put back on, obliged. "Put the dead girl in the sheet, take her to the dumpster behind the Venom Arena, and leave her. Take Heinrich to the boss at his house."

Wolfe nodded. "Good. Additionally, someone needs to get this mattress and the blankets out of here and clean the floor perfectly. You guys can handle that?"

"You've got it," Derek said.

"Thanks, Derek. You're one of the smart ones." Wolfe flipped his phone open. "In fact, you seem very competent, like you did last night. Also whole, which is a plus. But you know what doing good work means, right?"

"More work?" Derek guessed.

"Exactly. Give me your contact info before I blow this joint. I have business that needs attending to, but if I need someone, I might call you up."

Derek did so, and Wolfe walked into the elevator. Shel followed him in.

A moment later, he exited into the lobby. Melissa was still behind the counter. *I know she could hire someone to run this place for her. She had a party a year or two ago that I attended—*

she has a small McMansion. I wonder why she's practically always here.

Wolfe leaned onto the counter. "I should've asked earlier... but did you see anything?"

Melissa nodded. "Yeah. I saw a guy leaving right before I went to check on Heinrich—his time was up. He was an ugly guy, bald, wearing a wife beater. He had a devil tattoo on his neck and a snake on his shoulder. His license plate read 'MILF, C, K, R.'"

Classy. "Thanks, Melissa. I'll let Big Man Grimm know that you were a huge help."

Wolfe took a hundred out of his pocket and handed it over to her.

"Thanks for the tip, hun," Melissa said.

CHAPTER 12

PLANNING AN EYE FOR AN EYE

"**Great Game Rule #12**: Deckbearers use power to activate their cards. Once a card is brought forth, the power used to bring it forth remains used up as long as the card is in play. Once the card returns to the deck, the power is restored."

"**The Great Game, Rule #110**: Orphan subtype minion cards have been added to the game. Each will receive a bonus if they are kept alive as minion cards for a specified amount of time—they can transform into a more advanced minion, another card type, or give bonus cards—or any combination."

W   olfe pulled into traffic, his phone sitting in one of the cupholders. He ended up behind a FedEx truck that blocked most of his view of the road, which always made him a touch nervous.

"Why did you give her a hundred dollars?" Shel asked.

"Try to make nice with the little people when you can," Wolfe said. "It'll come back to help you some day."

"'Little people?'" Shel laughed. "You just told me she's crazy rich."

"Well, then consider it respect—I'd kinda been curt with her, so that was a way to make sure next time she has information she'll call me again."

"That makes sense."

They drove in silence for a bit before Shel asked another question. "When can we go after the people who killed Kevin?"

"Who the fuck is Kevin?" Wolfe asked, then he immediately knew who it had to have been. "Sorry. Your brother, right?"

"Yeah."

"Look, we got up a couple of hours ago after three hours' sleep. Let me touch base with Big Man Grimm—which needs to come first. Then I'll call my guy about card and leveling opportunities, which are gonna be gone very soon, as everyone is out looking for them, and then maybe we can take a nap. After that, if we don't have any other jobs, we'll put together a plan of attack to go after the Cobras and figure out which one killed your brother, and then kill that guy back. Sound like a plan?"

Shel bit her lip and nodded.

Good enough. Wolfe dialed Big Man Grimm.

His menacing voice came through the other side. "Wolfe?"

"Yeah."

"Talk to me, packmate."

"The Cobras got Heinrich and took most of his cards. It was obviously a fast job... The one card they missed had simply fallen under a nightstand. Not sure if they got lucky during last night's attacks, but I gotta admit—I'm getting suspicious. Especially with everything else that's been happening. First Johnny, then Heinrich. I'm your only senior guy left."

There was a pause on the other end. "Why do you have a young girl running around with you?"

Wolfe blinked, caught flatfooted. *Who would have told him?*

I mean, Harry, Derek, and the other two only saw her ten minutes ago... Maybe Melissa?

"What?" Wolfe asked, just a noise to buy time.

"Why do you have some girl with you while you work? Who is she?"

Shel stared at Wolfe. He would bet that she'd heard Big Man Grimm from where she was sitting.

"She's a deckbearer—Divine type—and she's out to get the Cobras. Since we've lost our new deckbearer, and the Cobras have *at least* five more, I thought it would help even the odds. She's working with me to take down the Cobra leadership."

"Have you considered she might be a mole? That maybe she's the reason the Cobras whacked Heinrich?" Big Man Grimm asked.

"No chance," Wolfe replied with confidence. "She was in a fight to the death with Frankie the Frog about the same time Heinrich was getting murdered—and had no way to know where your cousin was dipping his wick regardless."

There was a long pause on the end of the phone before the boss's heavy voice came through again. "She was in a fight to the death with Frankie? I assume she won?"

Wolfe smiled a shark's smile, even though Big Man Grimm couldn't see. "*I* won—she was nearly killed before I jumped in. But I've been training her. She'll be an asset."

"So Frankie is dead?" Big Man Grimm pressed.

"As a doornail."

"And the girl is for sure on our side?"

Wolfe hesitated for a second before answering. "I don't think she's on our side, per se, but her goals and ours align, and she owes me personally. She won't betray us. I'd stake a lot on it."

Shel was nodding rapidly as Wolfe talked.

"Hmm... very well. I trust you, Wolfe," Big Man Grimm muttered before switching subjects. "You know we have to retaliate for Heinrich, right? An eye for an eye."

"Yeah, I know how it works. I already killed Frankie."

"That was for Johnny. I want you to find, and kill, one of the Cobra lieutenants—one of their deckbearers," Big Man Grimm said. "Make sure you carve Heinrich's name in his chest when you're done. Also, kill whomever offed Heinrich regardless of whether they were a deckbearer or not."

Wolfe knew it was needed. "I'll do it."

Then he had a thought. "Speaking of deckbearers, I already killed a second one."

"What?" Big Man Grimm asked. "You killed another deckbearer? When? And how am I finding these things out so late? Why didn't you call me?"

"Sorry. It's been a crazy couple of hours." Wolfe paused. "I had Rich handle it—I'm surprised he didn't let you know. The guy I killed was a new deckbearer—I think he'd had his deck for less than an hour when he made the mistake of attacking me."

"Well... you already got two of their deckbearers. Kill another," Big Man Grimm said, then, after a second, "In fact, for now, it's open season on the Cobras. They've started this war— they attacked my best runner, my accountant and cousin, and now my best enforcer and friend. I know you'll make sure they pay for their hubris—I've seen you in action, after all."

Wolfe nodded before remembering he was on the phone. "I'll take care of it."

Shel smiled at him. That order coincided with her goal.

There was a long pause on the other end of the line, and after a moment, Wolfe asked, "Boss?"

Big Man Grimm spoke. "We have another serious problem. We're out of product, Wolfe. The legitimate profits of the Ekron Eternal, and some cash I have squirreled away, will keep us going for a bit. But our distributors, and our customers... they're going to go elsewhere."

"They're going to go to the Cobras," Wolfe said.

"Exactly," Big Man Grimm confirmed. "I don't know how

to fix this... except to try again and hope we can buy at full markup for a few weeks, distribute at a loss. But the screwup at the docks, however little it was your fault, has put us in a terrible position."

"I'll keep an eye out for a solution," Wolfe promised.

"Make sure you do," Big Man Grimm said. There was a brief pause. "But none of that is the actual reason I called you. I've been thinking this war was coming. I booked Miriam a plane ticket to Paris. A month-long trip through Europe. Can you escort her to the airport tonight?"

Miriam is always a handful, but I suspect I can manage for a couple hours. "What time's the plane leaving?"

"8:10 P.M."

"Yeah, I'll handle it—although I'll need to borrow your ride. My car was busted up pretty bad in the attacks last night."

"Done. Pick her up around 5:30 at the mansion. And Wolfe —thank you." Big Man Grimm hung up.

Wolfe thought about the conversation. *It's a really bad sign that we've fallen so far in the number-of-trustworthy-guys-left department that the boss is just counting on me to escort his daughter. It seems the Cobras somehow have a better set of men. Certainly, they have more deckbearers left, at least ones that can reasonably be expected to fight.*

Although Wolfe knew that if Big Man Grimm ever took the field directly, the Cobras were probably fucked. It had been a long time, but once, Big Man Grimm had been a killer as good as Wolfe. And his deck was *way* better. He had started with a god-gifted deck and he had been working on it for *forty years*, with a lot of killing and money to make levels and get really good cards both. But their side was down to Big Man Grimm himself, his three children, and Wolfe—and Miriam was exiting the field.

Plus, Big Man Grimm was near sixty—if he was needed, the family was probably already screwed.

After a moment, Shel asked, "So... what's the plan?"

"I'm going to put one more call in, to Victor—he owes me quite a lot and is a talented information broker. I'll see if he knows about who killed your brother or any odd happenings that might be Drop Night goodies running around. Unless he has immediately useful shit, next we'll go catch a nap."

Shel yawned with almost perfect timing and Wolfe chuckled before continuing. "After that, we take Miriam—Big Man Grimm's daughter—to the airport."

"To keep her safe? Isn't she a part of the gang?" Shel asked.

"Nah, Big Man Grimm kept her pretty sheltered, or tried to at least. He never keeps her around for the darkest parts of the business. There were rumors all around his lifestyle, of course. And while she's figured it all out by now, she doesn't seem interested—she's mostly into her goth life and school... and speaking of, she's studying the law. Pretty sure running a mob family precludes admission to the bar," Wolfe replied.

Wolfe turned onto Main, heading toward the part of town where he lived. *I've driven this street like five times in the last twelve hours.*

"Tonight, once we've handled Big Man Grimm's daughter, we'll take care of our own shit. Look for Cobra gang members. Find one and make him tell us where whomever killed your brother is. Along the way, try to get a few cards for our decks."

Shel gave a half smile. "That's a lot for one day."

"We'll be the most overachieving thugs the world has ever seen," Wolfe quipped, grabbing his phone.

"Should you be calling people while driving?"

"Girl, I've *killed* people while driving. I can handle a damned phone."

Wolfe expected her to make some snappy comeback or roll her eyes. But she just nodded.

Wolfe dialed Victor the fence—the guy who owed him.

Victor answered almost immediately. "Wolfe, my best of friends, what can I do you for?"

"Information, Victor. I want to know three things: First, if you know who killed a kid, some new gun carrier for the Cobras, name of Kevin Lyons."

"The second?" Victor asked.

"The name of a Cobra with a devil tattoo on his neck and a license plate that reads 'M I L F C K R.'"

Victor laughed. "What a douche. I don't know offhand, but I'll check on it. Anything else?"

"Anything really exciting that you've heard about Drop Night specials where I could get cards fast. Roaming monsters, dungeons, puzzles... whatever you've heard."

Victor sounded hesitant as he answered. "Well... I gave most of that information to Damian when he called a few hours ago."

Of course that card-hungry hobbit already called our contacts. Wolfe wished he'd called last night, although it was still only nine hours since the Drop.

Victor continued. "I did hold something really juicy back though..."

"What?"

Another pause. "Look, this one is pretty good, legit. Full dungeon, unusual appearance conditions, almost certainly not picked over yet. If I give it to you, we're square, okay?"

"Fine, if you also tell me about Kevin and M I L F C K R," Wolfe said. "You'll be in the clear for Janine."

"Not that I don't truly appreciate you saving my daughter, but I'll be glad when I don't owe you for that anymore—so this is a done deal. All right. You know the Noimoire City Pound on Industrial, near the airport?"

"Yeah. It's where I got my old dog, Pierce. Why?"

"Late last night, after the pound closed, while the moon was out, a dungeon entrance opened in the back near the kennels."

A moon-based dungeon in the pound? I'd bet anything it's a Beast dungeon, almost certainly werewolves. "How'd you find that out?"

"A janitor—sorry, *sanitation worker*—there sells me things sometimes. He sold me the information."

I've gotta get some more contacts myself. "And Kevin?"

"One second," Victor said. "Before we move on, some basics about the Drop you might not know yet. The set is called the 'Lonely and the Lost.' It has an entirely new type of card, called the companion."

"I know about companions," Wolfe said.

"In-ter-rest-ing," Victor drawled out. "Someone got a god-gifted deck, then? Only the god-gifted ones came with companions."

"Yeah, but what else? What does the lost refer to?" Wolfe asked.

"Well, lost refers to two new card subtypes—the minion subtype 'orphan' and the building subtype 'orphanage,'" Victor said, his voice going a lower as he talked. "But I don't think lonely only refers to the companion cards. A ton of cards are 'sets' now, and if you make them whole, they give crazy benefits. Any orphan, orphanage, companion, or set card will go for an insane amount of money right now."

Yeah, I was almost positive I wouldn't be able to buy my way through the quest my Infernal patron gave me. This confirms it.

"Orphans?" Shel mouthed at him, and Wolfe shrugged.

"I'll keep an eye out for those types of cards," Wolfe said. "Now, about who killed Kevin?"

Victor gave a long sigh over the phone. "I don't have a clue— I heard about it, but even the people in the Cobras that I talk to don't seem to know what happened. But I'll figure it out."

Shel, clearly able to hear still, grimaced at the news.

"That cover it?" Victor asked.

"Yeah."

"And we're square?"

Wolfe gritted his teeth. "We're square once you bring me

something of use on Kevin, Victor. You can charge me like everyone else now for everything else, but I still want that info."

"Understood. As thankful as I am that you saved my Janine, I'll be glad to be out from under your thumb on this."

"Sounds great." Wolfe hung up before Victor could get any other quips in and tossed his phone hard into the cupholder. He was home, and he turned his busted car into the driveway.

"What's wrong?" Shel asked.

Wolfe got out of the car and slammed the door, a tiny piece of glass shaking free from the window and landing on the cement with a plink. "No idea who killed your brother. I'm getting the sense this is going to turn into a whole *thing*. Also, the Cobras don't do stealth, subtlety, or subterfuge. Why is his death such a mystery?"

Shel's eyes widened. "How do we find out who killed him?"

Wolfe paused. "I'll think of something. But for now, I'm going to go sleep. You call Detective Amber, tell her what we talked about. Harry and the boys should've dropped the girl's body by now."

Shel nodded.

"Then make sure you get some sleep as well. We need to be up again in four hours or so. A lot of stuff needs doing."

Wolfe unlocked the door to his small house, turned right, and went down the hall to his room. He closed the door behind him and lay on his queen-sized bed, pulling the blanket over himself. He could still faintly smell his old dog, Pierce, and loneliness briefly struck him.

He rolled over, held his hand on his chest, and then pulled his cards forth.

A second later, Cereboo jumped onto his bed, licking his face from three angles. The giant, black boxer then circled on the bed before slumping down, his back facing Wolfe. Wolfe knew he would have to put Cereboo back in the deck when he got up, but he smiled to see the pup. His brief irritation melted away with his dog's presence.

Wolfe reached out and pet his new dog once, scratched the ear of the left head, and then settled into his bed, happier than he'd felt in a while.

He was asleep in less than a minute.

CHAPTER 13

WAGES OF SIN

"**Great Game Rule #13**: Deckbearers cannot overspend their power limit."

Shel let out a whistle as Wolfe pulled into the driveway of 111 Greenbow Way—the Grimm family mansion. Wolfe wasn't as exuberant. Despite four extra hours of sleep he was dragging a bit, more groggy than tired. But still tired.

A three-story mansion with over fifty rooms greeted them, done mostly in a sort of American suburbia look: white doors and a tiled, slanted roof with lots of arches. But the whole front had an awning over it—which ran around the side—with about twenty white Greek columns holding the awning up as the mansion's most distinguishing feature.

The driveway was blocked by a huge, wrought-iron gate with a tattooed guy in a cheap suit manning a booth. He recognized Wolfe on sight and the gate swung back to admit them. The rest of the driveway was quite long and bracketed by willow trees but eventually hit a huge, circular portion around a giant fountain in front of the mansion.

The mansion had three front entrances, each with its own

parking spaces and collection of marble columns. Wolfe didn't know where Miriam was at the moment, other than 'at the mansion,' and just settled for the left entrance, pulling into the parking stall. The main entrance was spectacular. But it was filled with Infernal imagery, and Wolfe doubted Shel would appreciate it.

He got out of his busted car and Shel trailed after him. Wolfe walked up to the front door, past immaculately maintained shrubs, and knocked on it hard.

It opened immediately, and Wolfe recognized the tall, wiry-thin guy with prematurely balding red hair who let them in—Bobby O'Hattery, one of Big Man Grimm's house guards.

Bobby held the door open as Wolfe entered. "Evening, Wolfe. Who's the new girl?"

"This is Shel," Wolfe said absently. "Where's Miriam at?"

"She's out back with some friends—finishing up a going-away party." Bobby hesitated for a moment, then sheepishly said, "All her friends are still here."

Wolfe pulled his phone out. 5:28 P.M. He was supposed to pick her up in two minutes, and she was still partying.

"All right, I'll check the veranda," Wolfe said. "Can you get Big Man Grimm's Hummer to the front, please?"

Bobby nodded and hurried out the front door.

Wolfe continued into the house, Shel still in tow like a baby duckling. He knew the way—he'd been here numerous times.

He went to the kitchen first on his way out back. As he walked into the giant kitchen, however, a tall woman stepped into his way—early fifties; long, black dress; black hair; and green eyes under furrowed brow. Guinevere, Miriam's mother.

"Wolfe! About time you showed up. You're here for my daughter?"

Wolfe restrained himself from rolling his eyes and instead nodded. "Of course, Mrs. Grimm."

Shel stepped forward and held her hand out. "I'm Shel Lyons, ma'am. Pleased to meet you."

Guinevere ignored her utterly, stepping closer to Wolfe. "You *need* to make sure Miriam makes it to the airport safely and promptly on time! I'll not have her exposed to the violence in this pestilential city."

That's exactly what Big Man Grimm asked me to do, ya Karen. "Of course, Mrs. Grimm."

Shel awkwardly let her hand fall.

Guinevere pointed her finger at Wolfe's, an inch from the end of his nose. "I mean it, Wolfe. If one hair on my daughter's head is harmed, I'll execute you myself."

Sure you will. Normally, you just threaten me with Big Man Grimm. You must be really worked up if you're pretending you'd come after me yourself.

He kept his opinions off his face though. "She'll be fine, Mrs. Grimm. I promise."

Guinevere removed her hand from Wolfe's mug and tapped one perfect, red nail against her lip for a second. "Since you *are* Thad's best thug, I need you to complete another job for me as well.

"Please, tell me."

Guinevere frowned at him. "Are you being sarcastic with me?"

Yes. "No."

She glared at him for a moment before continuing. "I need you to go handle a problem for one of my associates, a Ms. Greenwall."

Guinevere fished a small piece of paper from inside her dress —*where had she been keeping it?*—and handed it to him. It just had an address written on it.

"What problem?" Wolfe asked, putting the address in his pocket. He could vaguely remember Ms. Greenwall—she was a dentist that handled changing skeletons so that they matched certain dental records when the Grimms needed specific people to disappear.

"Rats," Guinevere replied.

"Rats?" Wolfe asked, startled out of any attempt at decorum. "I'm not a damn exterminator. What do you want me to do?"

Guinevere sneered at him. "We can't have anyone not in the family working on it. You'll understand when you get there. Now, be a good dog and take care of what I want."

She finally stepped out of his way. "My daughter is in the back. Make sure you keep her safe!"

Wolfe was seething inside, but he nodded again and slipped past her, Shel still following. They went to the near floor-to-ceiling glass windows and pulled the door open. He stepped out into the covered veranda.

It was a large space with multiple tables for entertaining, with a sloped roof leading from the middle of the second floor all the way down to the very edge of the pool—Big Man Grimm had used it multiple times for smaller formal parties when he wanted to appear the consummate businessman. Wolfe thought the super high, moderately slanted ceiling on the area looked silly, and they'd had a bat problem once.

But it was impressive, he supposed.

Wolfe could already see Miriam on the veranda, right at the edge closest to the pool. He was pleasantly surprised to see that the 'party' was just Big Man Grimm's daughter and three other girls having tea and cakes, and not some huge event.

He was less pleased to see what she was wearing, which still called a ton of attention to her—not something Wolfe really wanted. She wore a long black dress that was belted around her waist but otherwise hung loosely on her thin body. She also had on black net leggings and gloves, and had added a ton of mascara to her eyes. What appeared to be stylized manacles and a collar, with silvered chains connecting them, accessorized the whole insane outfit.

She went full goth. Never go full goth.

Her friends were dressed the same way for whatever reason. Wolfe had been pretty sure goth wasn't in, but he didn't know what the children were doing these days. Probably dumb shit. It had been dumb shit when he was that age.

Wolfe also noted the numerous wineglasses on the table. Compared to the usual standards of the Grimm family, underage drinking was practically behavior that would earn you a Divine card. But few things irritated Wolfe more than a drunk twenty-year-old girl.

They're obnoxious as fuck and you can't bang them when they're wasted, the only thing that normally makes girls that age bearable.

Although, maybe it's just the ones I know. Shel seems great.

Wolfe went outside and walked through the other tables and up to the one nearest the pool where the girls were, crossing his arms over his chest.

The four girls glanced up at him, and the blonde one turned to Miriam, her voice slurred. "Wow, he *is* good-looking. He works for your dad, right? He has to do anything you say?"

Miriam's eyes caught Wolfe's, but she simply stared into them, boldly, and licked her lips. "Yeah."

"Like... *anything*?" the blonde girl slurred further. "Cesear style? Make him fight people? Or sleep with someone?"

Wolfe frowned at Miriam and pinched the bridge of his nose, but didn't intervene.

Miriam smiled, still staring Wolfe dead in the eyes. "Yeah."

The blonde one kept going. "Could you make him sleep with another one of your guards? Yaoi is so hot."

Wolfe gritted his teeth but uncrossed his arms, leaning forward over the table. "That's enough of that crap. I'm here for Miriam. Go get your shit, girl."

Ignoring Wolfe, the black-haired girl pointed to Shel. "It looks like he already has a partner."

"Dressed like *that*?" the brunette asked, pointing at Shel's stained and slept-in clothing.

"Well, I think it's *his* shirt," the black-haired girl replied.

Shel nervously chuckled. "We're together. I mean, as, like partners. Deckbearer, uh, partners. Not anything else." She brought a hand to her face and half hid her growing redness. "Oh my goodness, Shel," she whispered to herself. "What's wrong with you? Just say no."

"So you *are* together?" one of the girls asked, clearly confused.

Wolfe growled, "We're whatever we want to be. *Stop asking damn questions.*"

The brunette snickered. "Such Daddy vibes. No wonder that girl is wearing his shirt."

Wolfe relaxed, but he didn't want to be part of this conversation any longer. "Miriam, go get your damned bags. I'll be in front of the house, entrance closest to the main driveway out. Don't make me wait."

"Bye!" the blonde girl called, drawing the vowel out a bit, probably a result of the alcohol.

Miriam got up from the table. "I'm going to go get my things. Meet me out front."

Wolfe frowned. *Is she repeating what I just said to look cool in front of her friends?* "Sounds great."

Wolfe turned and walked into the house again, thinking about all he needed to do. Shel followed him as he went.

What a colossal cockup—where are all the other competent fuckers? Is there really no one else that can handle any of this?

Wolfe was barely paying attention as he walked through the Grimm mansion, and as he did, he nearly crashed into Damian —the pudgy bastard yelled "Whoa!" and stumbled back into his older brother, Thaddeus Jr.

Damian straightened his suit and slicked his hair back with

his ring-encrusted hand, then fiddled with his fly cufflinks as he clearly took a moment to regain his composure.

"Hey," Thad said with an upward jut of his chin. Wolfe ignored him—the Big Man's oldest son was a near-irrelevancy.

Damian finished his little ritual and stared up at Wolfe. "I heard you were here, Wolfe. I need to talk to you. I have some things that need to be taken care of."

Does every single member of this family think they can order me around? Wolfe's hand involuntarily curled into a fist. "What do you want, Damian?"

CHAPTER 14

ROAD TO DAMNATION

"**The Great Game Rule #14**: Summoned creatures *must* attack opposing summoned creatures *first*, before they can target enemy deckbearers or mortals."

Damian's recessed eyes flickered to Wolfe's face, then down to his hands, then back. He held his fat hands up palm out, fingers spread. "No need to get upset, Wolfe. Sorry. Let me start again. I have some information on things that I think only you can handle, for the benefit of the family. I hope to convince you to handle them. But if you don't want to, that's fine."

The overdressed hobbit gave an ingratiating smile that didn't reach his eyes. "As Dad says, I'm not in charge, *yet*. I'm not presuming to order you around. I just know you're the family's best and most loyal enforcer."

Wolfe sighed and relaxed. *I should at least listen to him...* "Speak your piece."

Damian smiled more genuinely. "Thanks, Wolfe. However, would you mind if we spoke just a touch more privately?"

"Lead on."

Damian nodded and took them down the main hall, the one that connected the three main entrances. He went most of the way to the main entrance before stepping into Wolfe's favorite room—the library.

It was, quite literally, a library. Shelves lined the walls, filled with various tomes and folios. Although most of the books were fancy hardcovers or old editions, and everything was covered in dust—the family kept it to look fancy.

The real reason to come in here was the pool table in the middle, although there was also a rickety, borderline-antique metal stairway to the second floor. Wolfe remembered many a game with Big Man Grimm, Johnny, and some of the other enforcers, with fancy whisky in small glasses kept on the book shelves around them.

Wolfe grabbed the pool stick and the cue ball, and took a shot at it, knocking it around the table. Damian closed the door behind them.

"Wanna play a game?" Thad Jr. asked.

Wolfe rolled his eyes and set the pool cue down. "I've got a lot to do, sorry. What's going on, Damian?"

"The Jarvis Street Gang, which joined the Cobras a year or so back, still has a member that is loyal to me—at least loyal enough to give me information. He says that the product they're receiving have been in yellow packages marked with a fly symbol."

Wolfe grimaced. *The Grimm family uses those packages. It's Johnny's shipment.*

Shel walked over and backed up against the metal stair.

Damian nodded at Wolfe. "Exactly. If that was everything, I wouldn't come to you. But my contact *also* heard one of them say that they were out, and they needed to get more from News Street. I checked—News Street is short, and almost entirely empty. But there is a single warehouse next to an abandoned cannery there. Dan checked it out for me last night after everyone left. Javier was there, along with a couple of Cobra mooks. They were guarding a ton of our product."

Wolfe cussed. *Javier Garcia, Groom of the Dead. One of the five remaining Cobra lieutenants.*

Wolfe stared at Damian and leaned against the pool table. "The guy may dress like an insane Tim Burton met the Day of the Dead, but he's killed a lot of people, and has a powerful deck. Not to mention a powerful crew. I assume they're all over the warehouse?"

Damian nodded.

"Do I get a crew?" Wolfe asked.

Damian shrugged, looking down and fiddling with his cufflinks. "I assume so—ask Dad. Although make sure to take Piper. Piper's the most likely runner to move into Johnny's role now that Johnny is dead. In fact, I'd recommend taking people you know are loyal to the Grimm family. Older, trusted guys. Because I'm beginning to think we've been betrayed from the inside. Too many of the Cobras' hits have felt like they knew what they were doing."

Wolfe grimaced again and slapped at the cue ball, which spun around the table. *I've never really liked Damian, but maybe I'm letting my prejudices blind me. He's obviously smart as hell, and seems to have the family's best interests at heart...*

Wolfe glanced up to see Thad Jr. giving Wolfe a dog-like smile. *Probably assumes I'll just make everything better. He's probably right, but I wish these guys were a little better at handling shit. Or a lot better.*

He glanced back down at Damian. "Alright, I'll talk to your dad to get some guys, and we'll handle it. But I'll do it tomorrow —I assume the drugs aren't going anywhere?"

Damian frowned. "I don't think so, but why not tonight?"

"I have to take your sister to the airport, and then I have some personal business to take care of."

"What're you doing?" Damian asked, his eyes boring into Wolfe's.

"*Personal* business," Wolfe replied.

Damian frowned, but nodded. "I guess that's fair. Make sure you talk to Dad, take Piper and get some other loyal guys—we *need* to get the product back. We're in a bad state."

"I know. I'll handle it," Wolfe promised.

"I have something else to tell you, Wolfe. I got a card... it's part of a card set that claims that whomever has all the cards will gain additional, truly powerful Infernal cards. And it claimed that all of the cards are with deckbearers in the Noimoire crime groups."

Wolfe's blood chilled at the revelation, and his thoughts tumbled over one another. *Damian has one of the cards in the Cereboo set. He's one of the people I have to stop from assembling the cards. But he's the Big Man's son, and probable successor—and he's never done anything to me to deserve killing.*

Damian was still talking, but Wolfe had missed a bit. "—do find the cards when killing their deckbearers, I *need* you to give them to me."

Wolfe managed to choke out, "Yeah, of course."

Damian nodded. "Alright, well, thank you. I'm gonna go see my sister if she's leaving."

Wolfe's mind was turned from his previous thoughts. *He didn't know she was going? Weird.* "Sure, catch ya on the flip side."

Shel snorted. Damian's eyes fell on her, and lingered for a long time. Too long for Wolfe's taste.

"C'mon," Wolfe said, coming off the pool table and taking Shel's hand. He pulled her off the railing and then gently pushed her out of the room. "We need to get going."

Wolfe continued to guide Shel as they exited the mansion.

Once they were back outside, Bobby had pulled up Big Man Grimm's personal vehicle—a massive black Hummer that had been maintained long after the car style had gone out of production. Most of the inside was a custom job, and it had the same upgrades to windows and such that Wolfe's car had—or had had, since it had been shot and smashed to shit. But Big Man Grimm's car was probably the safest thing in Noimoire since the old military base had closed. You'd need a rocket launcher to take it out.

Wolfe walked up to the vehicle, Shel following. Bobby tossed Wolfe the keys, gave him an over-the-top salute, and headed back to the door he had been at. *Okay, at least someone is competent.*

Miriam wasn't there, and Wolfe just chilled for a moment, looking back at the house.

"You all right?" Shel asked.

Wolfe was honestly tempted to ask her to be quiet for a bit, but as he stared over the car at her kind, green eyes and soft, innocent face, he was reminded that everything about her was wholesome and good, in contrast to everything and everyone he normally dealt with. It made it clear why Raphael had chosen her to receive a Divine gifted deck.

She really is far too kind and caring to be a part of our life, a real cinnamon roll. I need to find her idiot brother's killer and get her out of here. It's the one real service I can do the world. Although if I'd been twenty years younger, I might have tried to run with her.

Wolfe exhaled through his nose. "I just learned a share a card set with my boss's son, Shel. Also, when I became a deckbearer, I heard a voice... it seemed to indicate I'm supposed to fight the other people that hold the set cards. That's what bothers me the most. But I'm also really busy. I have a ton of dangerous tasks—for you, for Big Man Grimm, his wife, his son... and one of my own making. But I don't want to burden you with it."

Shel smiled at Wolfe, her eyes sparkling. "I... I *want* to be burdened with your concerns. You're already doing so much for me. The least I can do is listen to your problems."

Wolfe pulled his cigarette pack out and lit one up. "I'm not really a feelings guy, Shel. Let's just do the job. Jobs. You know what I mean."

Shel nodded, hesitating, but then she met his eyes again. "You don't need to tell me about the voice or your thoughts on Damian... But can you at least tell me about the Cobras? The main ones, I mean. You seem to know a lot about them, and since we're going after them I'd like to know as well."

Wolfe took a long drag on his cigarette. *It's a fair request, and talking it through may help me as well.*

"Alright, so, if we're truly going all the way, there are five main guys we'll have to get rid of. In the process, I suspect we'll end up killing more people than I've killed in the twenty years ending on Drop Night."

Shel frowned and clutched a clump of her red hair to her chest, but nodded to Wolfe's words. "Who are the five?"

"You just heard about Javier Garcia. They call him the Groom of the Dead because he uses a bunch of Corpse Bride cards in a Psychic and Undead mixed deck. And he has other undead women—female vampires and the like—in his deck. He's like Frankie—an old gang banger that joined the Cobras as a founding member. Don't underestimate him, though. He has a lot of experience and some solid cards. Also, a lot of his gang stayed with him. A core group within the Cobras that are loyal to him."

Shel nodded.

"Then there are the three newer members."

"Newer?"

"I just mean that didn't join in the initial wave—they were recruited later, and aren't as loyal to Jason Klaus. The first two are the twins, Marko and Ramius. Both are pretty much pure enforcers for the Cobras that tend toward ultra violence. They have god-gifted decks from Aesthma, the Infernal of Wrath, and the chosen patron of the Cobras. They also have Beasts, and Death energy, in their decks. Close to my style, I guess."

"I doubt that," Shel said.

Wolfe ignored her as he continued. "They're both extremely talented fighters, probably a hair beneath my capabilities but with absolutely no hesitation or scruples—and they almost always travel together. If your brother's killer hadn't been subtle, I would have assumed one of these two assholes did it. But they never do *anything* subtle."

Wolfe paused, rubbing at his chest. "The last of the new members, and Klaus' right hand, is Nico. We don't even know his last name—he just goes by Nico. He's *evil*."

Wolfe paused again, meeting Shel's eyes. "I mean, we're all evil. Even me, obviously, since I got an Infernal Deck. But Nico—"

"I don't think you're evil," Shel interrupted, holding Wolfe's gaze.

Wolfe frowned and took another long drag on his cigarette. *Where the fuck is Miriam?*

He exhaled smoke. "Well, you're wrong—the Infernal thought I was a good bet. But thanks for the words."

Another drag, and Wolfe stared at the sky before continuing. "Well, whether I'm evil or not, I was trying to tell you that Nico takes it to a whole new and fucked-up level. I've heard stories of murder, rape, indiscriminate killings like drive-bys and terrorist bombings, torturing people. All of it. Just... all the evil. He makes his home in a magical building called the Mausoleum of Lost Souls—and in case you can't tell from that, he uses an Undead deck. Undead and Corruption both."

Shel shuddered.

Wolfe glanced down again. "Lastly, there is ol' Jason Klaus, the Big Snake himself."

Shel laughed. "His nickname is the Big Snake? They didn't think that sounded... um... sexual?"

Wolfe frowned again. "No, he doesn't have a nickname like that—I just called him that right now. Sorry."

Shel flushed. "Oh... um... it's a great name."

"Don't patronize me, girl," Wolfe growled out, then laughed.

Shel smiled back. "So, what's Jason's thing?"

"He was god-gifted with a deck from Aesthma twenty years ago, before the Cobras came about. He's been serving the Lord of Wrath ever since, growing his gang and territory by killing or chasing off all his enemies. He's got a deck that is probably valued in the tens of millions, he's very high level, and he has a lot of demon cards specific to the Lord of Wrath. *Very* deadly. He loves violence, in all its forms. Which is why he has the Venom Arena as his personal club, most likely."

Shel nodded. "You think you can take them out?"

Wolfe shrugged. "The first three, alone, with my skills and deck? Sure. Nico... maybe. Jason... I'd be worried, but I'd take the shot. But with all their mooks, their bases, all that crap? It's—"

"—gonna be a whole thing?" Shel finished, smiling at him.

Wolfe chuckled. "Yeah." Then he frowned. "I'll probably get killed." He held Shel's eyes. "Also, *you'll* probably get killed. Are you *sure* you don't wanna just take the money and go? I could send you to Paris with Miriam."

"Nah. I hate the goth look. Black isn't my color."

Wolfe stared for a moment, then laughed again.

Before he could continue what was becoming enjoyable repartee, Miriam came out. A guard was with her, carrying two suitcases, and Miriam had a...

"What's with the gods'-damned golf bag?" Wolfe asked.

"I play golf," Miriam said, tilting her head to the side, staring at him with her black-rimmed eyes. *Girl looks like a damned raccoon.*

Wolfe tossed his cigarette on the ground and stepped on it. "Of course you do. Well, get in the damned car. You have a plane to catch, and then I have a shit-ton of things I need to take care of for your family."

CHAPTER 15

DOMINION OVER THE BEASTS

"The Great Game Rule #15: Deckbearers require 100
experience points to gain a level."

Wolfe squinted in irritation at the setting sun—it
was a beautiful sunset, but it was still somehow
hitting him right in the face. Miriam sat in the
passenger seat and Shel in the back as they drove through
the city.

Miriam suddenly spoke without turning. "So how come
you're working with Wolfe, Shel? I mean, no offense, but you
appear utterly unsuited to the rigors of our world. Like, *really*
unsuited for it. *Naked* for it, even."

*'Our' world, you sheltered kitten? You put some balls on to go
with your mascara?* "Now that you're not making up stories
about holding my chain, you got all cocky again, Miriam?"

Miriam blushed slightly but still smiled at him. For some
insane reason, she had pulled a golf club out and was slowly
rubbing the part you hit the ball with.

Shel said, "I have a Divine and Mortal mixed deck. I'm a full blown deckbearer."

"Still doesn't mean you're ready for the streets," Miriam muttered.

"Well, Wolfe has also been training me. He taught me about the cards, and how to fight."

Miriam glanced over, her eyes narrowed. She seemed... irritated. But after a short moment, her calm demeanor returned. "Wolfe hasn't ever groomed me to be a fighter. I'm jealous."

"No one is grooming anything," Wolfe said through clenched teeth. "Shel needs to know how to fight."

"Why? She isn't your replacement, is she?" Miriam grazed her fingers over Wolfe's shoulder. "I'm fond of you. And you just got a deck. We don't need a replacement just yet."

"Um, I'm not a replacement," Shel awkwardly said. "I was trying to stop the Cobras from killing other people, like they did to my brother. I almost died. Wolfe saved me. Now we're working together to take out the remaining Cobras."

"Then why are you here while he's playing chauffeur for me?" Miriam asked.

Shel twirled her finger in her long hair. "I... guess it just sorta happened. And I can't go home, for, well, reasons."

"Reasons? Some fascinating drama?" Miriam shook her pale, slender arms and the silver manacles with chains on them she wore rattled.

"Just reasons. Nothing fascinating at all," Shel said, shaking her head. "In fact, my home life is grimy and mundane and dingy."

"Boo." Miriam settled back in her seat. "So you're just travelling with Wolfe because you've got nowhere else to be? That's a bit pathetic, wouldn't you say?"

"Watch your mouth," Wolfe growled.

He remembered the way Shel insisted on fighting, and how

she would do anything to make things right for her brother. Few people had that kind of determination.

"Oh, did I touch a nerve?" Miriam smiled. "Maybe you like her? Hm? Wolfe has a little kitten following him around."

He tightened his grip on the steering wheel. This was another one of Miriam's games. He was mad at himself for falling for it in the first place.

"Uh, well, we're going to a dungeon after we drop you off," Shel said. "So, I mean, I'm not totally pathetic. And I'm going to get stronger—with each level and card. This kitten will evolve into a wild jungle cat."

Miriam sat up like she had been shocked. "Wait, you guys are going to a dungeon? Really? I wanna go!"

Wolfe glared in the rearview mirror at Shel and mouthed "Why?"

Shel pulled her red hair in front of her face.

"I have to get you on a plane," Wolfe said.

"C'mon, its barely 5:40," Miriam said, pointing to the dashboard clock, her thin black sleeve hanging down. "I have a deck! I've never made so much as a single experience point, except for two victories in the arenas. I need new cards, and levels, and..."

"If you get so much as a scratch on you, your dad will hang me by my guts," Wolfe said.

Miriam smiled at him, leaning in a bit close, and licked her lips again. "Ah, big man like you can't take care of an itty-bitty girl like wittle ol' me?"

"Quit fucking around, Miriam. You're a gods' damned law student. The baby talk isn't gonna cut it."

Miriam leaned back, crossing her slender arms across her chest and hugging herself, her eyes staring at nothing. "Fine. The truth is, I don't want to feel weak anymore. I want to know if I can be powerful, and dangerous, and vicious for my *own* sake. So that no one and nothing will ever hurt me again."

"Who hurt you?" Wolfe asked, his own mind showing him the terrified brown eyes again.

Miriam didn't move, her eyes still staring at nothing. "Doesn't matter who it was. It could be anyone. Someday, it will be someone else, again and again, until I'm a killer myself."

I really hope this girl doesn't go supervillain. Wolfe exhaled noisily. "Fine. *Fine.* We'll do it your way. You can come with us."

Miriam rubbed her manacled hands across her legs, a look of maniacal glee returning to her face. "Thank you. I'll make it up to you somehow, I swear."

"Sure. Fortunately, the location is right near the airport, so we don't even have to switch directions."

A bit later, Wolfe pulled the car into the parking lot of the Noimoire Pound, which had two cars in it—and a few people clustered outside the pound entrance.

"Son of a an Infernal," Wolfe cussed with feeling.

"What?" Shel asked, sitting up at the sound of his vitriol.

"It's the Cobras—they somehow know about the dungeon I just gave up a major favor for!"

"How do you know?" Miriam asked, staring at the group.

Two of the thugs had pulled pistols out, but Wolfe was still quite distant—and in a borderline tank. He ignored them.

Instead, he pointed at the two fancy cars—each with a custom license plate. One read 'LeftOne,' and the other 'RigtOne.' "Those are the cars of the twins, Marko and Ramius. I recognize their idiot license plates. Which means that they somehow learned about a Beast dungeon—deep in their controlled portion of the city's territory, I might add—and decided to come augment their decks. Which means my trade to Victor was worthless."

"You think he sold it to them?" Shel asked.

Wolfe was briefly startled—the thought hadn't even crossed his mind. But he dismissed it. "No. I saved his daughter, and I'm almost positive he wouldn't betray me. This is just stupid bad luck, like most of my damn life."

"So, if we want the dungeon, there's gonna be a fight?" Shel asked as Wolfe idled the car.

"Yeah."

"What's your deck?" Shel asked Miriam as Wolfe circled the outer edge of the parking lot slowly.

She smiled and jangled the manacles on her wrist. "An Undead and Psychic mixed deck. It's vampire tribal specifically. Enslavement, power stealing, and creature stealing with some okay synergy. I've got a vampire mantle and a little extra trick up my skirt. I was hoping the Undead faction would see fit to give me a god-gifted deck, but I guess not. Gonna try hard for the next ten years to get on their good side."

Up her skirt?

"You've never killed anyone, have you?" Wolfe asked.

"Not yet," Miriam said, glee in her voice. She picked the club off the ground and held it up. "But I brought my trusty nine-iron."

Oh for fuck's sake. "Joy."

"Hit them with the car!" Miriam suddenly said, ghoulishly.

"What?" Wolfe asked.

"Let's do it!" Miriam said, leaning forward in the seat, her green eyes alight with ghoulish enthusiasm. "I wanna see someone die! These are the fuckers that killed Cousin Heinrich and have been fucking with us, right? Let's send them to the Gray Beyond!"

When did she start paying attention to the business? Wolfe thought. *Also, the Gray Beyond?*

Before he could analyze further though, Miriam continued. "We have to take them out. That way, whomever is left, we'll have the advantage! Three deckbearers against whomever isn't bumper jelly!"

She licked her lips again. "And I can collect my first soul."

Wolfe reached a decision. "Everyone duck, in case the glass doesn't hold!"

Wolfe hit the accelerator and the car rumbled forward, picking up speed rapidly.

"Oh fuck yeah," Miriam screamed.

But both Miriam and Shel ducked down, keeping their eyes barely above the dashboard level. Shel was braced, and Miriam staring avidly.

Two of the thugs pulled pistols as Wolfe drove at them, but both panicked and didn't fire—one ran to the side, and the other froze. Ramius got the door unlocked and ripped it open, and he, his brother Marko, and two thugs made it inside.

Wolfe barely noted when the Hummer hit the remaining thug, who disappeared under the car without fanfare—but he hit the metal door so hard it was ripped from its hinges and thrown inward into the pound, and the Hummer half-smashed through the building wall, lodging inside with the hood half in, and half out, of the pound.

Wolfe was thrown hard against his seatbelt but recovered quickly, dismissing the experience notification for Roadkill McThug. A quick glance showed him that both Miriam and Shel were fine, and his attention turned to the threats outside.

Wolfe hit the window down-switch and leaned out before it was even fully open, firing at the Cobra who had escaped vehicular manslaughter as he came off the ground.

Old-fashioned homicide-with-a-firearm put the second thug away, who slumped back with bullet holes in his chest.

Wolfe pushed the door open, got out, and leaned over the hood. He pulled his head back fast as Marko—or maybe Ramius, he couldn't exactly tell—fired at him.

He touched his chest, pulling forth his cards at the same

time *four* notifications of deckbearers pulling their decks flashed before his vision.

We've got a rather huge fight going here.

Constant howls, barks, and a single rapid-fire, high-pitched yapping from the back of the pound also greeted Wolfe as he checked his cards.

Wolfe had Cereboo, his Soul Hunter Mantle—finally—the Fallen Angel, and a Desperate Pact. *Shit. Everything good just popped in the first pull.*

"That you, Wolfe?" Ramius called from inside, his voice filled with rage. "I'm gonna fucking slit your throat, you piece of shit!"

"Yeah!" Marko called. "We're gonna fuck you up!"

"Wow, what wit," Wolfe cried back as bullets were slamming into the windshield of the Hummer. but Wolfe ignored them, touching his Mantle card instead.

Red energy ran around him, but this time, he barely changed. His skin gained a light dusting of red scales and two tiny horns poked from his head. That was it, visually. But Wolfe could feel power coursing through him.

And the Soul Hunter mantle, modified by Wolfe's perk, gave another thirty-seven and a half percent to his stats if he was fighting the Infernal—so nineteen without his Edge pistol and twenty-four with. Probably way more than anything the brothers had on the field at the moment.

Despite that, Wolfe didn't attack. Instead, he yelled out, "Shel, EMT next card!"

Sorenia appeared next to Wolfe, her lantern held high.

Miriam crawled out the side of the Hummer nearest Wolfe and crouched. She touched a gray-outlined card that floated in front of her and a thin, pale woman with a diaphanous black dress, red eyes, and extra-long canines appeared from a swirl of gray mist.

Wolfe glanced at it.

Sexy Spawn
Common Tier-1 Undead(Vampire) Creature
1 Undead Power
Health: 8
Attack: 4
Magical Attack: 0
Defense: 4
Magical Defense: 4

Special: Every point of damage dealt by the card restores a point of the card's health.
Special: +1 to every stat except Magical Attack for every Psychic persistent, including creatures, on the field.

"Newly embraced, this vampire was clearly chosen to join the night for their looks, not their fighting strength."

A huge, snarling Angry Hellhound leapt onto the short hood of the Hummer and then leapt at the unreasonably sexy vampire that Miriam had summoned. Wolfe raised his pistol and fired into the Hellhound's center of mass. Red swirled around the muzzle, and the Angry Hellhound's chest utterly exploded, blowing mangled chunks across the wall like Wolfe had hit it with a cannonball.

What the fuck was that?

The corpse dissolved into red light and flowed back into the pound.

There was a brief lull in combat, and Wolfe, his eyes wide, risked a glance at his combat notification. His natural eight attack had gained three from the mantle directly, thanks to the fifty percent his perk "In the thick of it" gave, raising him to an eleven—which in turn went to a fourteen when he used his pistol, and that raised to an eighteen thanks to his vicious killer perk. And *that* went to a twenty-four against other Infernals—

which the hellhound was—because Soul Hunter gave him further modifiers against his own kind.

The better of the two random rolls gave Wolfe a bonus six on his attack, raising him to a thirty—against the Hellhound's defense of seven. Thirty times thirty was nine hundred, divided by seven was *way* more than the Hellhound's measly twelve Health. Close to ten times as much, in fact.

Violent glee filled Wolfe. *Angel shit! I might just be able to handle them myself, since they rely on Infernal power!*

But he still didn't want to be an idiot. When the card timer was up, he hit the Desperate Pact card.

Wolfe grunted as pain ripped through him. Slight wounds opened across his body and his skin bruised all down one arm as the four-health cost came out. But Wolfe gained another point increase to his stats—modified by all his stacking perks to result in two more to everything. Additionally, all his Mortal and Undead allies—which was everything on his side except Sorenia at this point—gained an increase to every stat as well.

Then a woman with hair escaping from a hastily assembled bun wearing a blue jumpsuit and carrying a box with a white plus on it appeared. Wolfe felt health pour into him, and his bruising and most of his wounds disappeared.

As a two-deck synergy this is extremely effective—I can use cards that take health instead of power, and Shel heals me.

Wolfe glanced at his defense stat. It was a touch lower than his attack, but still fourteen. That meant an average thug with a gun would probably hit for three to four damage—which meant it would still only take about eight-to-ten sets of shots to finish him.

There were only four guys and their cards on the other side...

Wolfe threw Cereboo out. "Miriam, send your vampire across, and Shel, send Sorenia and the EMT, then summon to replace and send the next creatures."

A wall of bullets met the three creatures as they leapt onto the hood of the Hummer and slid down the front. Another Angry Hellhound leapt to intercept Sorenia—who took very little damage from it, swiping it aside with her arm and then hitting it with a beam of light.

Cereboo followed over the hood, leaping onto it and then bounding into the fray, all three heads howling in glee. Bullets that hit him did less, and he choked up the fight, giving Wolfe the opening he needed.

A kindred desire to hunt and take down the evil filled Wolfe, and he leapt across the hood and into the pound after the creatures that had paved the way.

He rolled across the hood and landed inside the pound in a crouch, then fired into one of the thugs shooting his team of cards. The man blew apart just in time for Wolfe to see a *third* Angry Hellhound join the fight, followed by seven small imps with tiny pitchforks—the card that appeared over the imp's head when Wolfe stared said they were collectively called Swarm of Imps.

He also saw the brothers, Marko and Ramius, cards floating in front of their chests and pistols out. Ramius also had claws, teeth, and an unfortunate amount of hair—a Beast mantle of some sort. But Marko—Marko had on an Infernal mantle that gave him scales, a tail, and a whip.

Behind them was a rectangular door made of moonlight that opened into a dark forest.

The vampire and Rookie EMT went down, but an emaciated male vampire followed over the hood—another Sexy Spawn, from the card popup—as well as a man in riot armor. Wolfe tried to keep card creatures between him and the human enemies, taking a moment to waste the second thug. *As long as we have at least one creature card on the field, the only danger to me is the Cobras themselves. I need to remove them first.*

The slightly stronger creatures of Marko and Ramius were

replaced at about the same rate Shel, Miriam, and Wolfe threw weaker creatures in, stalemating the fight with the cards.

Wolfe leaned out and fired at Marko, his Infernal power multiplied by fighting another Infernal. Marko shifted at the last second, and Wolfe shot clean through his adversary's upper arm, shattering the bone and leaving the arm hanging in tatters. Marko dived to the side, still alive thanks to his own mantle, and Wolfe stood to try and track him.

Ramius howled out "No!" and charged Wolfe, claws out. Wolfe shot at Marko again but missed as the Cobra lieutenant crawled through the moonlit door.

Ramius hit Wolfe, clawing across his chest and biting on his shoulder. They went down, hitting the ground hard, Ramius on top.

But he forgot to throw another creature out, and Marko was gone. Wolfe wedged an arm into Ramius' mouth, cussing as he did —it didn't hurt *as much* thanks to Wolfe's mantle, but it still hurt.

With his other arm, he carefully aimed and shot the remaining Angry Hellhound. The creature exploded from the power of Wolfe's magically enhanced bullet, much like the first.

Which left a wounded vampire, Sorenia, a guy in riot armor with a nightstick, and Cereboo all free to attack Ramius.

A light beam hit the Cobra lieutenant in the face, and he let go of Wolfe's arm. As he stood, a nightstick took him across the face, barely harming him but leveraging him in further off balance for Cereboo's attack, which ripped him off Wolfe in a fury of exchanged claws and bites.

The vampire kicking him in the side was rather superfluous.

Wolfe clambered to his feet. His side, shoulder, and arm leaked blood, but he ignored his pain in favor of his rage and shot Ramius in the face. Ramius's head nearly exploded, and Cereboo jumped aside with a loud bark. Two heads glared at Wolfe in obvious irritation while one scanned for danger.

"Sorry, but it ended the fight," Wolfe said, dismissing the experience and level notification and scooping up the cards that appeared.

A sudden feeling of health permeated Wolfe, and his new wounds partially closed.

He turned to see Shel climbing over the hood of the hummer, scrabbling up using the wheel. Standing on the hood was the Rookie EMT.

"I thought it only worked once?" Wolfe asked, poking his still tender but no longer bleeding shoulder.

"Once per card," Shel said, smiling at him as she dragged herself onto the hood and then over.

Miriam was staring at them from the other side.

"Don't climb over," Wolfe said. "Just pull the car back and face it the other way."

"Why?" Miriam asked. Her face was flushed.

First couple levels from combat, I'd guess. Or maybe she really does get off on death. Fuck if I know.

Wolfe pointed back at the moonlit gate. "We've probably got less than twenty minutes before the cops get here and this becomes a municipal dungeon. I want to get a run in as fast as possible, get a few packs to supplement what we just took from this jackass. I turned in a huge favor to get this dungeon, I want to get *something* from it even if it's far less than I'd hoped."

Miriam nodded and they all faced the gate.

"And maybe we'll run into Marko, as well," Miriam said, her eyes bright.

CHAPTER 16

THE DOG DUNGEON

"**The Great Game Rule #16**: Deckbearers gain experience by (1) killing mortals, (2) killing deckbearers, (3) defeating free-roaming or dungeon monsters, (4) winning arena duels, and (5) solving puzzle boxes."

A minute later, with the car no longer lodged in the entrance to the pound, the three of them faced the moonlit door.

"So you think this is a Beast dungeon?" Miriam asked, her golf club now in her hand.

"Yeah."

"What are its matchups?" Miriam continued, twirling her golf head and miming striking one of the dead thugs with it.

Shel frowned and shook her head at Miriam's macabre display.

As Wolfe looked at the most wholesome girl he had ever known, he was briefly distracted from Miriam's question. *I should have gotten Shel a gun and some training. That would make her a touch dangerous at least. Although I met her less than twenty hours ago—haven't had the fucking time, really.*

Miriam faced back to Wolfe. "The matchups?"

He whipped his phone out and quickly looked up the strengths and resistances of Beast-type creatures. He was almost positive that they would find a bunch of them in the dungeon.

Wolfe rattled off what came up on his phone. "Beast has a weakness to Corrupted, Undead, and Death. It resists nothing, and it is resisted by three types and an energy. Dragon, Mortal, and Nature resist it, as does Telekinetic."

"Well, looks like I'll be fine," Miriam said, laughing. "You guys might be fucked."

Wolfe pinched the bridge of his nose. "Not helping, Miriam."

Cereboo woofed at her as well, and Miriam looked at him.

After a moment, she started laughing. Wolfe's heart froze and sank into his stomach. "Uh..."

"By the gods, Wolfe, you have a card from the same set as my brother! That's too fucking delicious. You know if he finds out he's gonna kill you, right?"

Wolfe stared at her a moment. *Is she threatening me?*

"You can't tell him!" Shel said, stepping forward. Sorenia took a step forward as well.

Miriam held her hands up. "Whoa, whoa, don't get your panties in a twist. I'm not gonna turn your crush in. By the Divine, calm your tits."

Shel frowned and seemed to shrink in on herself a bit. "W-Well, okay. But if you did, I have his back." She hardened her voice for the last bit, like she was imitating a thug from a TV show.

Wolfe found it cute—if only because she said she had his back.

Miriam twirled her golf club around, stepping confidently back to them. "Like I said, I'm not planning to turn your boyfriend in."

Miriam gave Wolfe a half-smile that didn't reach her eyes.

"Damian's going to kill you, Wolfe. He takes what he wants, always, no matter what it costs someone else."

He's always seemed pretty reasonable to me—at least enough to not fuck himself over.

Wolfe frowned. "What do you want me to do about it, Miriam? Give up Cereboo?"

Cereboo woofed.

Miriam frowned, staring at nothing. "I want you to kill Damian."

"What the fuck?" Wolfe asked, his eyes widening.

"I hate Damian," Miriam muttered, giving her golf club a vicious swing at nothing.

"Why?" Shel asked, walking up to Miriam.

Miriam stepped away from her. "I'm not doing sob story time. I hate him and I hope you kill him. I'm certainly not going to rat you out, though. Your secret is utterly safe with me, I can promise you that much."

Wolfe accepted it—the alternative was pretty much 'murder Miriam,' which wasn't a real option for him. He hoped she was telling the truth about her intentions.

After a moment, Wolfe looked up. "All right, Shel, here's the deal. With Sorenia, your lantern angel companion out, you'll have amazing matchups against Beasts, as your Mortal cards will do twenty-five percent more damage and will also take half base damage from their natural resistance to Beast type. Your cards will be *way* stronger. Unfortunately, your mantle won't give you anything else personally, however. So try and stay out of the fight if you can."

Shel nodded. "Ever since our discussion about my fiasco with Frankie, I've been trying to do things that way regardless."

Actually, a Divine and Mortal deck would likely kick the shit out of my Infernal and Beast deck... Infernal wrecks Mortal, but Divine beats Infernal and Mortal beats Beast. Not like I plan to betray her or anything, but just something else to keep in the back of my mind.

"What about me?" Miriam asked.

"Well, Undead does fifty percent bonus damage to Beasts, so it's very likely you'll do amazingly as well. I don't know the details of your deck beyond that, however."

Miriam laughed, holding her nine-iron up. "I will claim their souls for the Gray Beyond!"

Wolfe eyed the horizon, where the moon was just coming up. "What's the Gray Beyond? You keep saying that."

"A lot of Undead deckbearers online are calling the Deadlands that, just like they've taken to calling themselves Necromancers. I thought it sounded cool."

Wolfe snorted. "On that amazing note, let's go. We've got, like, eighteen minutes max, I think. If we're focused, we can get to at least one sub-boss."

Wolfe started jogging inside, and the others followed.

As they approached the gate, a howl that was only half sound reverberated through their souls, pushing at Wolfe's will with a terrible fear.

Every dog in the pound went dead silent, even the one that had yapped since the first gunshot.

Miriam stumbled and Shel trembled, but Wolfe just pushed it aside. He'd been there and done that in a lot of life-and-death situations and knew how to act through fear.

"Still want to go in?" he asked them.

Both warily nodded, their expressions nervous.

Wolfe stepped into the gate.

With no sense of the passage of time or space, Wolfe found himself inside a forest. Ahead of him, he saw building tops through the forest canopy. Their lights cast a ruddy glow over the trees. A powerline on rickety poles ran from somewhere ahead of him toward the town, surprising Wolfe—the dungeons rarely acknowledged the advance of technology. From the same direction as the town, he heard screams.

Damn. I've read about dungeons, but this is something else entirely. Really different. The gods are powerful and strange as fuck both.

Wolfe glanced around. Behind him and to the side, Wolfe saw a huge moon, blood red. A glow came from the forest just 'below' the moon, from Wolfe's current position. An eldritch glow that spoke of magic. But more importantly, he saw blood smears on some leaves leading away from the town.

As Shel and Miriam materialized near him, Wolfe turned to face them. "Let's head to the town."

"Why?" Shel asked, staring back at the eldritch glow coming from behind them.

As Wolfe broke into a jog, he answered. "Nothing here is real, so this is just a choice over card types to get first. I can get Infernal cards from kicking Cobra ass, but you have no naturally available source of cards. So we should grab some Mortal cards by 'rescuing' whatever fake people are in the town," Wolfe said, holding air quotes up as he picked up speed. He strongly suspected there was no real reason to run in regards to saving people, but he wasn't a hundred percent sure. Perhaps the town had a timer before you lost amazing cards.

Wolfe continued to talk as they went. "Also, I saw what is almost certainly Marko's blood in the other direction. Despite what Miriam was saying, I'd rather not run into him as we fight whatever's in the dungeon—it could get very nasty."

"Ahhh," Miriam said, drawing the word out. "I wanted to finish him off."

Wolfe rolled his eyes. "We're about to lose all our mantles and cards, and he's probably crippled anyway—why are you so kill happy, girl?"

Shel scrunched her nose at Wolfe's comment.

Miriam shrugged as they ran. "I don't know... the Cobras

threaten me. I've been pushed around, abused, or ignored my whole life—I guess they represent a lot of that."

"I can understand that," Shel whispered, her words icy.

Half of Wolfe wanted to make some kind of *ah, poor princess* comment, but half of him was beginning to suspect both Shel and Miriam had suffered very real and significant abuse at some point. He settled on not saying anything as they approached the collection of buildings following the path and powerline.

They came around a bend into the outskirts of a tiny town. It had a gas station, a sheriff's office, a small post office, and a few homes. All were in nineteenth-century wooden style but with electricity added.

The sheriff's office was under attack by multiple werewolves, all howling and ripping at boarded-up windows and doors. Each werewolf was practically a carbon copy of the others. They were seven feet tall, bipedal humanoids with fur, wolf faces, and elongated jaws, as well as claws on their hands and feet.

The boards had been ripped from quite a few windows of the sheriff's office. But at the same time, a scream came from one of the houses along the street.

Sorenia lifted her lantern high.

Wolfe was torn. He wanted to keep Shel with him—but he also wanted to make sure that Miriam didn't get hurt. He *also*-also wanted all the cards they could get.

Shel had the highest net advantage against Beasts, so it was probably safest to send her off alone in this one situation. Probably. "Shel, go save whatever was in the house! Miriam, with me!"

Shel and Sorenia ran off toward the scream as Wolfe leveled his pistol at the mass of werewolves and pulled up his deck.

At that moment, his mantle fell from him. The red energy flowed back into his deck.

Fuck.

CHAPTER 17

SAVING THE MEEK

"The Great Game Rule #17: The equation for calculating experience is: divide the (level of the killed) by (the level of the killer) and then multiply by 100.

If experience if left over after being applied to bring the deckbearer's experience to 100 and making them level, remaining experience is multiplied by (old level)/(new level) before being applied to the next level, and this occurs ad infinitum at each new level"

Wolfe had a Rescue Pup, his Loyal Guard Dog, and a Tormentor Imp. He decided his initial hand skewed toward Beast cards more and brought forth the Rescue Pup card immediately, even though it made him cringe a bit—it was just a card, but it was clearly also a dog meant to die, which didn't sit well with Wolfe.

The creature that popped out appeared as a large, forty-pound dog that was emaciated beyond belief.

Poor puppy.

But between being a zero-drawdown card and its special

effect, the Rescue Pup was probably damn useful in a Beast deck, and Wolfe already had Cereboo out. He didn't want to risk any more injuries—or, Divine forbid, letting Miriam get injured.

Rescue Pup

Uncommon Tier-1 Beast(Canine) Creature
1 Beast Power [Available]
Health: 8
Attack: 3
Magical Attack: 0
Defense: 3
Magical Defense: 3

Special: Does not require upkeep—is a zero-cost monster.
Special: If slain, all Mortal and Beast cards in play gain +50% physical attack for the next 30 seconds.

"A sad puppy, but loyal now that it has found a new master who is kind and caring."

The emaciated dog appeared and began to bark. Then it charged the werewolves alongside Cereboo.

Wolfe really hoped the puppy would last until he could bring his Loyal Guard Dog out, but he was skeptical. It clearly had a lifespan that fruit flies looked at with pity.

Miriam touched her chest and brought out her cards. Three cards appeared—no fourth card for the companion. Two cards that glowed with an uncanny gray light, and one that glowed with a harsh purple light, appeared. Miriam touched a gray one and a thin, effeminate, and naked male vampire appeared next to Miriam.

"Really?" Wolfe asked. "Another Sexy Spawn?"

"I have female ones in the deck as well," Miriam said airily. "You've seen them. And it's part of a synergistic deck build."

Cereboo and the Rescue Pup hit the werewolves. Wolfe's companion was yapping joyfully as he leapt into the fray, like he usually did, and the ensuing chaos pulled Wolfe's attention from the vampire that was clearly the bottom in the relationship next to him.

"You get'im, Cereboo!" Miriam called excitedly.

Wolfe shook his head at her exuberance. *Cereboo always treats death and mayhem like a fun game. He can remember between deaths—but it doesn't seem to affect him. I wonder if it's because he's immortal, because he's a card, or because he's demonic.*

Some of the werewolves turned on Cereboo and the Rescue Pup, and one shot toward the undead nudist next to Miriam. The rest stayed clawing at the sheriff's office, but the rate at which boards were being ripped off went down, and the rate of return fire from the sheriff's office went up.

Cereboo damaged one werewolf and was raked by another, and the pup yipped, got a small bite in, and then died as a claw swipe from a separate werewolf eviscerated it.

Miriam swiped her cards and then touched one. True to her word, a second Sexy Spawn, this one a female vampire that looked like it was the personification of heroin chic, appeared.

Wolfe brought forth the Loyal Guard Dog, then shot another clawing at the sheriff's office down with multiple shots to its back. *Glad these don't have the 'silver and magic attacks only' special.*

Two more of the werewolves charged, one at Wolfe and one at Miriam. Wolfe thanked the gods for the 'fairness' mechanics they put into most dungeons. It seemed to have manifested in this case by not having the whole group charge, just the one per deckbearer.

But then the werewolves hit. Fortunately, they acted as summoned creature cards, attacking Wolfe's Dog companion and the new vampire instead of Wolfe and Miriam, respectively.

Unfortunately, both the lesser creatures went down like they couldn't wait to try on new coffins.

Miriam, however, wasn't above doing her own fighting. She gripped her nine-iron tight and swung for the fences. She slammed it into the knee of the first werewolf that had attacked her original Sexy Spawn card. The werewolf's leg buckled, and Miriam gave a happy laugh, then proceeded to try and club it to death, slamming it in the head over and over. She began to sing 'Poison,' the nineteen-eighties song, as she did.

I think she really is touched in her head.

Still, she has the right idea. Wolfe pulled his pistol up and shot the one near him in the chest three times. It managed to rip the heart out of the last Sexy Spawn before a fourth shot finished it off.

We need some tougher creature cards. Both of ours are going down like cheap whores... Or maybe this is just a stronger dungeon.

Only Cereboo was left of all their creatures, but of the werewolves that had detached to fight them only two were left— and one was being beaten to death by Miriam.

Wolfe fired into the chest of the other whole werewolf, but two more detached from the pack to come fight Wolfe and Miriam.

Gunfire was coming steadily from the sheriff's office now, as rifles were being poked through the slats from which werewolves had left. Cereboo finished his target off with the help of the dead doggo buff from the Rescue Pup before finally being torn apart by the werewolf himself.

Speaking of dropping too fast... could have used him for another minute or two.

Wolfe shifted his deck fast, cussing as no creatures came up. He got both the Desperate Pact cards, which he didn't want to use because Shel wasn't around to heal him. But he also got his Soul Hunter mantle.

The werewolf headed for him put on a sudden burst of

movement, racing through the tiny town square and launching himself for Wolfe claws first, fast as hell. Wolfe hit his mantle and lurched backward at the same time. He kicked out hard, hitting the werewolf in the stomach with his new boosted attack and punching it back—but it raked its claws down the shin of the leg he had kicked it with, and Wolfe grunted in agony.

Miriam took a break from aggravated assault and battery to bring forth a glowing purple rune, which hung in the air—the werewolves became a touch slower, and their eyes narrowed in pain.

The second werewolf was almost upon Miriam, and her eyes widened and she cowered back, nine-iron held in front of her. The one on the ground started to rise as well, crawling to its knees and hacking blood.

Cursing, Wolfe shifted from his own target and shot the one racing at Miriam in the head just as it reached her. It slewed sideways and hit the ground, dead.

But the one he had kicked back came in, slashing along his chest. His T-shirt shredded beneath the claws, as did Wolfe's skin. Wolfe howled as blood poured from three shallow but long gouges across his chest. He put his Edge into the chest of the werewolf and pulled the trigger, expecting the heavy recoil, but instead clicking on empty.

Fuck!

The werewolf raked Wolfe's arm. But Wolfe didn't retreat from his larger opponent, instead hooking his leg behind the werewolf and shoving as hard as he could. The werewolf went down. A quick glance over showed that Miriam was okay—with the one down, she had teed off on the other's head.

And unlike Wolfe, she had cards she could use—she touched one and a gray aura settled around her. Her eyes became red, her skin even paler, and she grew long teeth.

Wolfe stepped back, ejecting his clip but not yet reloading, trying to time it right. As the second werewolf leapt back to its feet, Wolfe leapt back from the claw *just* enough and then reversed his pistol, cussing as the barrel was hot enough to hurt even if not burn him, per se. He slammed the barrel in the werewolf's head, slewing it to the side, and then kicked it as hard as he could in the back of the knee. It dropped again for another half-second, then leapt back around, snarling—but Wolfe slapped a clip into his pistol and flipped his deck at the same time.

Wolfe shot the werewolf in the chest at point-blank range, pulling the trigger three times in quick succession. The bullets he fired had a slight red haze around them, similar to his mantle, and they blew through the werewolf's chest in a shower of gore.

A quick glance up showed him that two *more* werewolves were headed for them, although only one remained to attack the sheriff's office.

He glanced at his cards—Cereboo wasn't back yet, but he had his tier two Escaped Damned, his tier-one Escaped Damned, and the Fallen Angel. Not wanting to take any more damage in his chewed-up state, Wolfe tossed the Escaped Damned into the fight.

The Escaped Damned had barely materialized when another werewolf hit it—and if another one had reached Wolfe, that probably meant he had missed one headed for Miriam. Fearing the worst, Wolfe turned and glanced at his ward to find that she had been raked across the arm, probably before the Escaped Damned had appeared. But she had leapt onto the werewolf and wrapped her legs around its torso, sinking her teeth into its neck. Wolfe waited till the turning of the pair presented the creature's back, then shot that lycanthrope dead as well.

Miriam dropped off, her mouth dripping blood, her eyes wild with an excitement almost sexual. Still smiling wildly at Wolfe, she dragged her arm across her mouth and then picked up the nine-iron.

The people—so to speak—at the sheriff's office had killed

the remaining werewolves, all but the one that had just chewed on Wolfe's Escaped Damned.

Wolfe, suspicious that this wasn't really the end of the fight, summoned his weaker Escaped Damned even as Miriam touched a card and then screamed at the last werewolf. A beam of psychic energy flashed from her to the last werewolf, killing it —but not before the damn werewolf took Wolfe's Escaped Damned with it.

But Wolfe had been right—the obvious mook wave hadn't been the end of the fight. A larger werewolf, about ten feet tall, landed on the roof of the sheriff's office and *howled*, a sound that reverberated through Wolfe same as the howl from when the dungeon opened. Wolfe chuckled to himself darkly, pleased that he had predicted it and summoned another creature. The beast facing them had a pentagram carved into its chest that burned with fire, and after it howled, it stared with red eyes at Wolfe and Miriam.

Demonic Werewolf Alpha
Dungeon Monster Infernal/Beast[Canine, Lycanthrope]
Creature
Health: 60
Attack: 15
Magical Attack: 0
Defense: 15
Magical Defense: 7

Special: Will make an additional 8 strength attack against the deckbearer of any monster it slays.
Special: Will summon a hellhound as a free action at 50% and 25% Health

"A werewolf alpha that wasn't content to rule just its own pack, so it had to go and make a deal with the Infernal for even more power."

Wolfe was simultaneously impressed and not that worried—for himself. His Soul Hunter mantle gave him an additional twenty-five percent attack and defense since this thing was Infernal as well—thirty-seven percent once his special merit was taken into account. He had already experienced the power the mantle gave him against the Infernal—he would practically ignore the follow-up attack.

But it couldn't be allowed to hit Miriam. That would go extraordinarily poorly.

"Miriam, don't attack it with creatures!" Wolfe shouted, reloading and swiping his deck as the monster rushed him.

"Got it!" she yelled back. "I might still suck it dry, though!"

She's crazy, Wolfe thought as he emptied his clip at the monster. His shots were dead on, hitting it in the face. The Escaped Damned went down as the claws tore burning essence from it, and the werewolf leapt at Wolfe, slashing wildly. One claw caught Wolfe across his chest, a light slash that still drew blood. The notification popped up.

Deckbearer Ethan Wolfe engages in combat with Demonic Werewolf Alpha.

Ethan makes a ranged Physical Attack at 23 against Demonic Werewolf's Physical Defense of 15. Damage dealt is 35. (23 * (23/15)).

Demonic Werewolf Alpha makes a Physical Attack at 15 against the Escaped Damned's Physical Defense of 8. Damage dealt is 28. (15 * (15/8)). Escaped Damned is destroyed.

Demonic Werewolf Alpha makes a Physical Attack at 8 against Deckbearer Wolfe's Physical Defense of 16. Damage dealt is 4. (8 * (8/16)).

Deckbearer Wolfe has 10 of 30 Health remaining.

Wolfe cussed, not quite as free of danger as he had hoped. He swiped his cards, Cereboo finally returning, and pulled his pup—it got a bonus against the Infernal and would help a huge amount here.

But a pentagram also appeared on the ground and a huge, slavering hellhound crawled out of it and rushed Cereboo.

A flash of purple light came from Miriam, and blood ruptured from the huge lycanthrope's ear and nose.

Cereboo leapt onto the Demonic Werewolf Alpha and Wolfe unloaded his pistol at it again. His attack roll, even with his 'pick two and take the better' perk, was somehow worse and he didn't quite finish it off—but Cereboo, while having his back leg chewed on by the hellhound, still got three attacks at ten because of his anti-Infernal ability.

The demonic werewolf finished off Cereboo even as Cereboo chewed it to death.

Although it didn't get its follow-up attack once dead, Wolfe was pleased to see.

And the hellhound unsummoned.

Wolfe dismissed notifications that showed he had made another *four* levels—those had been some nasty monsters.

"My god that was fun!" Miriam exclaimed, running up and grabbing Wolfe by the shoulders. She tried to plant a kiss on him, but he swayed back.

"You just drank a werewolf's blood, Miriam. Maybe some other time."

Miriam gave another wild laugh, and her mantle dropped away from her, gray light swirling around and then sinking into her.

"Do you think the blood from cards stays in me once the mantle is gone?" Miriam asked, licking her lips as she glanced at him.

Wolfe raised an eyebrow but nodded toward the sheriff's

office, where the door was opening. Miriam turned with his nod to glance at the people leaving the building.

A sheriff who radiated an old-timey hick vibe walked out. He had a long piece of straw in his mouth and a silver star badge. He was followed by a lot of 'random hick citizen' types—and one angry-looking child of about twelve with a knife covered in blood.

"Thank ya fer savin' us." The sheriff held two packs of cards out. "We ain't got much in these here parts, but take this fer yer trouble."

Wolfe didn't even look, grabbing them all. "Thanks."

"Also, this boy here lost his parents. He's a right tough fighter, and I was hopin' you'd take him with you."

Wolfe stared at the kid for a second, and a card box appeared.

Vengeful Orphan
Rare, no-tier Mortal minion[orphan]
0 Power
Health: 8
Attack: N/A
Defense: 3
Magical Attack: N/A
Magical Defense: 3

Special: Will fetch normal objects and such with a decent degree of precision and help carry up to fifteen pounds.
Special: If kept 'alive' for five straight years, will turn into a legendary, Mortal, 3 power, tier-6, equivalent creature card. If ever 'killed,' the timer resets.

"This young boy tries to keep his chin up, even though he lost his parents to monsters. But in his heart, he yearns to seek vengeance."

Even as Wolfe stared at the kid, he dissolved, the particles rushing to Wolfe's hand and forming a card in it.

The sheriff kept talking, telling a story about a werewolf lair and a demon infecting them and the next step to saving the town, but Wolfe tuned him out.

Instead, he turned to Miriam. "Run out and get the car ready. Pull right to the door. If the police—or the Cobras—are here, just drive off and wait near the end of the road out of sight. Got it?"

"Yeah... what are you going to do?"

"Get Shel."

Miriam nodded, her face still flushed from the combat. She turned and started to run off, but even as she did, Shel showed up. She was carrying a card pack clutched in her left hand.

Before Wolfe could even ask, she said, "I rescued some people from a Werewolf Witch. It was a really easy fight, as it was considered Beast and Infernal, so every card I drew had advantages."

Wolfe nodded, thankful she was okay—Shel was really growing on him, and didn't deserve bad things happening to her. "Let's go."

The three of them turned and ran as fast as they could go back down the forest path. The moon was a touch higher, and Wolfe could still see the mystic glow deeper in the forest. But he wasn't staying around—the chances the police were coming was about the same as the sun rising tomorrow. He needed to get out of here before he was putting his reduced health pool up against a nine-millimeter.

He wondered where Marko was, and kept an eye out for an ambush. But nothing came.

He reached the point of entry—the moonlight portal—and stepped through. He appeared back in the pound to the same chorus of barks that he had left less than ten minutes ago, somehow. Shel and Miriam stumbled after him, and Wolfe rushed out to the hummer in the parking lot. He didn't see the police around, nor any more Cobras.

"About time we got a break," Wolfe murmured, and Miriam and Shel looked at him blankly for a moment, then both giggled.

Wolfe opened the driver's-side door, grabbing Miriam by the back of her black dress when she tried to climb in and pushing her, clanking with her silver chains, to the back left seat of the Hummer and taking the driver's seat for himself. They all got into the car, and Wolfe drove out onto Industrial, sped the two blocks to Main, and then calmly turned on it, heading for the airport.

Well, we got a few cards, and the Cobras are starting to hurt as bad as we are. That's something.

CHAPTER 18

LILITH FLEES THE GARDEN

"The Great Game Rule #18: All card specific rules supersede the general rules."

"You didn't do too badly for your first time," Wolfe said to Miriam as they all sat in the Hummer in the lamplit short-term parking at the Noimoire airport. "Maybe you have some acumen for the family business after all. I'm surprised. I hope I end up working for you and not your brother. If I have to choose between sexy death nut and obese hobbit card-obsessed nut, I choose the first nut."

"Ha ha," Miriam said. "It was your first time as well, at least for the dungeon."

Wolfe chuckled at her response. *I'm probably being a selfish prick, but if she takes over instead of Damian in a few years, I'll be in a far better position, I think.*

The airport was busy, the lights showing people scurrying to and fro. However, Wolfe was pretty sure that it wasn't so busy that Miriam would miss her flight if they took another thirty minutes to tend to her injuries and divvy up cards.

Wolfe sat in the back seat. Shel, up front, had turned around so that the three were all facing each other inside the car. Wolfe was examining Miriam's arm.

"Completely fine," he said. "Shel's EMT's fixed it right up."

Miriam smiled. "Good. I wouldn't have minded too much if I'd had a souvenir of the victory, but I do prefer being flawless and perfect."

Wolfe rolled his eyes.

"Still, I'm glad that I wasn't wounded mostly so that Mom and Dad wouldn't bitch when I got back."

Wolfe chuckled. He wouldn't have worried too much, but he didn't really want to be there when they theoretically learned Wolfe had let their precious daughter be hurt. Although given his lifestyle at the moment, it wasn't like he was terribly likely to still be around by the time Miriam got back.

Miriam was still talking. "Well, despite the pain of the wound, I'm glad we put down those doggos. For the longest time, I felt I was weak. I didn't think I could be strong. But I just stood in a fearsome fight, killed with my cards, my own hands, and even my teeth. I drank the blood of those that would harm me."

"Yeah, it's a liberating experience," Shel whispered, her gaze on the ground. She wasn't really speaking to anyone—just herself.

Wolfe knew how they both felt, although he had found his own strength years and years ago, with some follow-up help from her father.

Wolfe sat back and examined Wolfe, who was covered in blood still. "How are you holding up?"

Wolfe admitted to himself he was hurting. The long scrapes down his leg hurt like crazy, and would probably scar. They joined his partially healed shoulder, chest scrapes, and side to create a background of pain and ache to everything he was doing.

But he didn't have to admit that to anyone else. "I'm fine."

"So stoic." Miriam smiled at him and blatantly running her eyes up and down his body. "To answer the rest of your earlier question, I've got to be honest with you. I'm glad I know I can fight, but I'll have to think about what you said. Maybe I will try to take over. But I don't know if that's what I want, exactly. I mean, I'm already ahead in my law school work. I could live a good life as a lawyer as well."

"Stealing in the legal way," Wolfe quipped.

"Lawyers aren't really bad people." Shel glanced between them. "Are they?"

Wolfe huffed. "They're the worst. Trust me."

Miriam's grin turned mischievous. "Even if I quit being a lawyer, you might not *want* me to take over." She leaned in close to Wolfe and walked her fingers up his chest. "The way I feel right now, your job title might change from 'head enforcer' to 'boy toy.' I'd ride you hard enough to wake the dead. Watching you fight, having you save me... woof."

Wolfe tensed, his thoughts grinding to a halt. Miriam wasn't serious. She just wanted to fuck with him. With a sneer, he brushed her hand away, but his body remained tense, and his pulse high.

Shel cleared her throat and scooted further on the car seat so she was more present in the circle.

Miriam rolled her eyes at Wolfe—obviously irritated he never fell for her games—and then offered Shel a sweet smile. "Don't worry. You can join my harem, too."

Shel's face brightened redder than her hair. "Uh, thank you? I didn't know gangsters had harems... I guess it makes sense."

"Wow. She's so fresh." Miriam eyed Wolfe. "You better be nice to her. She pulled out her kitten claws to threaten me, and even protectively circled you. Girl has a little spunk that I like."

Shel half covered her face, clearly trying to hide her embarrassment. "I'd prefer if you didn't talk about me like I wasn't here."

"She does it to everyone," Wolfe grumbled. Then he glanced out the car window to stare at the airport.

Miriam reached down and touched the three packs and the card on the chair between them. Each had a different picture on the front, but all bore the words "Cycle of the Lost and the Lonely, Opening," on it.

Wolfe knew enough to know that cycles usually lasted multiple decades, with similarly themed cards. He wondered exactly what this cycle would bring.

Besides Orphans and Companion cards, of course.

Miriam coughed. "So, enough of me being weird. These are six-card packs, right? Eighteen new cards, each worth the yearly earnings of an average family, at least? Killing-someone-over-level money?"

"Yes," Wolfe said.

"What about Ramius' cards?" Miriam asked.

Wolfe shrugged. "Your dad said I could keep what I killed."

"And his deck was Beast and Infernal," Shel said, holding up a finger.

Miriam frowned. "Fine. Dad did say that. But how do you know about the deck, Cutey?"

Shel sighed. "Wolfe told me about the Cobra lieutenants. I've been trying to find out who killed my brother."

Miriam bit her lip for a moment, then reached down and touched the packs. "So just these three packs, then? A mixed, a Mortal, and a Beast?"

"Yes," Shel said. "Not the greatest packs ever, but still decent ones for Wolfe's deck."

"What about *your* deck?" Miriam asked.

Shel poked her fingers together. "Well, I mean, if I get cards, it's decent for my deck as well, since some will be Mortal type. But Wolfe is already doing so much for me."

Miriam rolled her eyes. "Such a goody two-shoes. Maybe you *can't* be in my harem."

Wolfe ignored the byplay and glanced at the packs again. They had two common packs—Mortal type and mixed. They also had a rare Beast pack.

And they had the Vengeful Orphan card. Minion cards were special card types that would create a summoned creature card that had a permanent effect and could never be attacked by other creature cards—and if killed by a person, they would reform the next day. But they still existed as cards inside a deck, making a deck 'weaker' since occasionally the pull would have the useless card in it.

The Vengeful Orphan card claimed it would exist for five years, and if not killed, would become a unique legendary Mortal three-power card at equivalent tier-six. In the meantime, it could carry out minor fetch commands.

"That could be ridiculously good for your deck down the road, Shel, if we make it that far," Wolfe said, touching the card. "But it would take a level pip just to open your first minion card slot."

Shel had a pensive look on her face as she stared at the card. "I actually made five levels fighting the werewolves... so I'm level ten now. But I don't know if I want to invest in a minion card. I could use more power, or perhaps I should open my next companion slot. I'm not sure."

"Your call," Wolfe replied.

They stared awkwardly at the packs for another moment.

Wolfe knew why. As Miriam had said, three card packs was an almost-unheard-of treasure for a normal person. The question of how to divide them would be interesting.

"So... how do packs work, exactly?" Miriam didn't appear as if she wanted to jump someone's bones anymore, and her wild flush had faded.

Shel pulled her phone up and searched while they waited. Less than thirty seconds later, she spoke. "It says that each pack has a distribution chance, based on the studies. A common pack has six common cards, each of which has a five percent chance to be an uncommon instead, and a one percent chance to be rare."

"Only a one percent chance to be rare? What bull," Miriam interjected.

Shel stuttered to a stop, but when no one else said anything, she continued. "A rare pack has three common cards with the same chance to upgrade, two uncommon with a twenty percent chance to downgrade to a common and a five percent chance to be a rare, and a rare card with a twenty percent chance to be an uncommon and a five percent chance to be a legendary."

"Five percent is *way* better," Miriam interjected.

"All rare or better cards have a half-percent chance to be unique, and all cards have a two percent chance to be 'special' card like a building or a minion, and a five percent chance to specifically be an enhancer card."

Shel put her phone back in her pocket. "And there is a twenty percent chance any card from a typed pack will be random instead of the pack's type."

"How are we doing this?" Miriam asked. "I mean, a weak tier, common card is usually fifty thousand dollars... a rare pack usually has a rare card, as well, which could, for the really good one, go for millions. Should we each take a pack?"

"I don't need a pack," Shel said. "You guys can have the cards."

"That's bullshit," Wolfe said, fishing in his pocket for a cigarette and pulling it out. "You earned a pack. I mean, you *literally* went off and earned one of the packs."

"Can you *not* create a haze of coughing and cancer in here?" Miriam lifted an eyebrow.

Wolfe sighed and pushed the cigarette back into the pack. *I'll be dropping her off in a few minutes. No need to piss her off first.*

"If we split the packs, Wolfe gets the rare one?" Miriam asked.

"I think he did the most work, judging by what you described, right?" Shel nodded. "You accomplished less?"

Miriam nodded, but then smiled at them and licked her lips. "I had more fun doing it though."

Shel giggled.

"Can I propose something different?" Wolfe asked.

Both the girls nodded.

"Let's open all three packs and look," he said. "And then we can decide what we want to take. One card at a time. But we'll have Shel open the two packs, the mixed and the Mortal one. She has a super-rare perk to upgrade one card anyway."

Miriam whistled, her weird fighting-and-killing-is-sexy vibe gone almost instantly. "That's an amazing perk, Shel. I think you could make money just pulling cards for people if you advertised that ability—I haven't heard of that."

"Th-Thanks."

Miriam continued. "I like the idea of Shel pulling... But you'll be going first?" Miriam glanced over at Wolfe.

"I really don't need any more cards," Shel offered. "I mean, you guys can just go. Wolfe's already doing so much for me."

"You sure you aren't sleeping with him?" Miriam asked.

Shel nervously chuckled. "I think I would know."

"You're such a virgin."

Shel immediately glanced away, but her ears were bright red, betraying her embarrassment.

Wolfe growled out, "Everyone *focus*. And Shel, stop being such a fucking martyr. You earned your share, like I *just fucking said*, and having a better deck can only help me and the Grimm family end the Cobras, anyway. If you really want to sacrifice for the good, how about you just pick third so that Miriam can be middle pick? That work for everyone?"

Shel nodded vigorously, but she didn't yet turn around.

Miriam thought about the offer, tapping one nail against her teeth, then nodded.

Shel reached out and took the common Mortal pack into her hand. It showed a man in riot gear on the front, his baton glinting with magic light. Wolfe was again surprised as the card packs, like the dungeons, rarely acknowledged technology.

She ripped the top open and took the cards out, a slight tan haze appearing extremely briefly before fading. She placed them down on the seat.

Four common and two uncommon. One was guaranteed to become uncommon from her power, but getting a second uncommon was decently unlikely. Not bad.

The four common cards were another Rookie Riot Police creature card; Rousing Speech, which buffed Mortal creature cards for a single round but only required available power, not drawdown; a third Rookie EMT card; and Urban Riot, a five-power persistent card that allowed all Mortal creature cards in play to deal their damage a second time, randomly assigned among enemy creatures, each combat round as an extra bonus damage that didn't invite counterattack. Useful, but the power cost to have it and enough creatures to make it worthwhile meant only very high-level deckbearers would likely ever use it.

The first uncommon was Barter the Soul, which would remove a Mortal creature from the caster but take control of one of a couple of different factions' creature cards, and the second was Main Street, a six-power persistent that would generate Mortal creatures every round—very useful in a lot of situations, but it took a lot to put on the field. It would only be really valuable in a very high-level deckbearer's deck.

"Nice," Miriam said, but she didn't sound that enthused.

They weren't really for her deck, Wolfe knew.

Shel reached to the next pack on the seat, the common mixed pack. She took it and tore the packaging—showing a small dragon hovering over a modern office building—and tore it open.

She placed the cards on the seat.

Six common.

The typing in the cards, though... It felt like it was tailormade for them. There was an angel card, Lantern Angel, which was basically a weak version of Shel's companion.

Then there was a Flameling, a weak Fire energy creature that strengthened from other Fire energy creatures.

Next was a Light energy equipment card, a Red Light Blade, able to be equipped by some creature cards.

A Putrefied Drake followed. It was a three-power Undead and Dragon mixed-type creature.

After that was the Imp Horde card, an Infernal, seven-power card that had huge attack and health and only took five max damage from non-AOE hits, but triple damage from any attack hitting more than one creature.

Last was another Rookie Riot Police card.

Miriam frowned as Wolfe picked the last pack up. From what Shel had described of her ability, they couldn't benefit from her opening a Beast-themed pack—only from Mortal, Divine, and to a lesser degree, mixed packs.

The front had a werewolf on top of a sheriff's office. Wolfe barked out a laugh. *Very on point.*

Wolfe tore the pack open and pulled the cards out.

He nearly gasped as two common, two uncommon, and *two* rare were revealed.

"Wow," Shel said as he spread the cards out. "There was only slightly less than one in six chance of an uncommon becoming rare. I mean, a legendary would have been better. But still... Wow."

Miriam also nodded.

Wolfe looked at the two rare cards first—he couldn't help it. One was a creature called a Fireborn Hellhound, and the other was a persistent called a No Kill Pound. Both were three power cards that could be used in his deck. One could dang near only be used in a deck very similar to his—and it was quite strong to boot.

Fireborn Hellhound
Rare Tier-1 Infernal[Canine] Creature
1 Beast, 1 Infernal, and 1 Fire power
Health: 23
Attack: 9
Magical Attack: 12
Defense: 9
Magical Defense: 12

Special: +100% magic Defense against Fire energy
Special: +1 Attack and magical Attack for every Escaped Damned card on the field within 100 feet, regardless of owner.

"An unusually tough and rare specimen of hellhound that makes its lair near Gehenna, the lake of fire. Only one large pack of these particular hellhounds is known to exist."

No Kill Pound
Rare Tier-1 Beast Persistent
1 Beast, 2 Any Power

Special: Any Beast with 'rescue' in its title has +50% Attack and Defense.
Special: Generates a Rescue Pup at no power cost every 30 seconds until Level/5 Rescue Pups are on the field, rounded up.
Special: If any opponent 'sacrifices' a creature card type Beast, that card joins you instead of being destroyed until the fight ends.
Special: You cannot sacrifice Beast cards.

"This card is a rare 'no-kill' pound that rescues dogs left by heartless masters who didn't appreciate their good boys."

Wolfe whistled.

Both of those would be quite fascinating in his deck, he felt. Although he was a touch low on power to be using them—either would drain more than half his power. He could increase his power since he had a lot of levels to make, however. Five power would make the cards useful in his deck useful—he imagined getting Cereboo, a Rescue Pup, and the No Kill Pound out.

The uncommon cards were also good—another Rescue Pup and a Squirrel! card. The Squirrel! card was a temporary card that would make all opposing Beast or Dragon creature cards lose their attack for thirty seconds and make them unable to defend their deckbearer for the same length of time.

Not that dissimilar to the Punish the Sinner card—although it was both more powerful and limited, since it only affected two enemy creature types.

The common cards weren't dog cards, which surprised Wolfe since the rest of the Beast pack had been pretty themed to its werewolf cover. The first was a Rapacious Raptor, a bird creature card that could attack a deckbearer directly but was quite weak for its two-power cost, and the second was a Giant Capybara, a two-power card with huge life and decent defense and almost no offense.

"Well, I'm feeling personally attacked by these cards," Miriam said sardonically. Then she turned to Wolfe. "What'll you be taking, Tall, Dark, and Grumpy?"

Wolfe frowned and then frowned even harder at the two rare cards.

He started to reach for the Fireborn Hellhound, but Shel gently took his hand. He glanced at her.

"You should take the No Kill Pound," she whispered.

"I'm running an Infernal deck—it's what the gods chose for me."

Shel shook her head. "You're running the deck of Cerberus, the being that keeps the demons in hell. I think there's a reason you got a deck that specializes in fighting the Infernal, even if the deck itself is Infernal. You can make it a true Infernal deck, or you can make it more of a puppy deck. Or try to hybridize it. That's on you. Don't forget your perk, though. You have an advantage with canine decks."

"'Puppy deck.'" Miriam snorted. "I'm dying. The wolf has a puppy deck."

Wolfe frowned at Shel again. "Beast decks aren't the strongest from type matchups, and my likely kills are going to be people with Infernal decks. If I focus on my own Infernal deck, that'll let me grow faster. And the Fireborn Hellhound has synergy with Escaped Damned."

Even as he said it, however, Wolfe remembered the voice. Shel might have a point.

Shel hung her head for a second but then looked up and met Wolfe's eyes. "I've been reading a lot on the internet about the card releases from this Drop Night and deck types and all of it. Beast decks have bad type matchups, it's true. But they have a huge number of dual card types and usually get a lot of cards out fast—something the No Kill Pound specializes in."

She spoke with a little more enthusiasm, like all this information had been fascinating. It seemed perhaps she had found something to be passionate about other than her brother's murderer.

"It grows more powerful as you do to boot," Shel said matter-of-factly. "Also, your only real Infernal synergy at the moment is in imps... why not go for the Rescue Pups?"

"You're killing me," Wolfe muttered. With a sigh, he picked up the No Kill Pound.

Miriam took the Fireborn Hellhound. "This'll make me less

money to trade for other cards since it's so specialized, but it'll still fetch a decent amount."

Shel took the Vengeful Orphan.

It went quickly after that, as nothing was so special as to warrant fighting over. Wolfe got the second Rescue Pup and another four cards. Shel took the two Rookie Riot Police cards and the EMT, as well as the Barter the Soul and Main Street. Miriam took mostly whatever seemed like it would sell the best at the moment.

Shel piped up. "Can we trade for the Fireborn Hellhound?"

"Hmm?" Miriam asked.

"Can we give you cards we need less to get the Fireborn Hellhound?"

Miriam thought, then pointed to Wolfe. "How about you give me all the cards except the No Kill Pound and the Rescue Pup you got, and I'll give you the Fireborn Hellhound?"

Wolfe barely needed to think about it. He handed the cards to Miriam.

She put them in her purse. "Well, I feel odd since I'm now transporting probably close to eight hundred thousand dollars in cards, but, given my family, at least it isn't cocaine, right? You two love-bunnies have fun."

Wolfe rolled his eyes at her smartass mouth but smiled. "Thanks, Miriam. Have a good flight."

She hesitated, then took a wrapper and a pen from her purse. She quickly scrawled something on the wrapper and handed it to Wolfe. "If you need me."

Before Wolfe could respond, she opened the door and stepped out into the airport, the moon looking down on her. She grabbed her bags, gave a half-salute, mouthed "I'll be back," and then turned and walked away.

CHAPTER 19

GOOD INTENTIONS

"**The Great Game Rule #19**: Every new deck shall contain a persistent mantle card."

olfe drove his car away from the airport, making sure to stick to the speed limit. His eyelids were heavy, and his thoughts drifted to his bed more than once.

Wolfe's phone buzzed in his pocket, and he almost threw the thing out the window. It was nearly nine p.m. on a day when he had gotten *maybe* six hours of sleep interrupted in the middle, and he was pretty sure between people and their cards he had killed close to fifty things and been killed in turn nearly twice, but for Shel's healing.

But he put aside his annoyance and glanced at the phone.

"Who is it?" Shel asked.

"Damian," Wolfe said. "No idea why the hobbit is calling me when I didn't even promise to take care of his shit until tomorrow."

"Are you going to answer?" Shel asked, her green eyes slightly wide.

"Ugh," Wolfe sighed. "Might as well. He'll just pout if I don't."

Shel laughed.

Wolfe slid the answer button and put the phone to his ear. "New phone, who dis?"

"What?" came Damian's confused voice from the other end.

Shel raised one eyebrow at Wolfe, her own green eyes quizzical.

Wolfe laughed. "Never mind, wrong generation. What can I do for you, Damian?"

"Ha ha," Damian said. "Right, well, I was originally calling for something else. But first off: I just heard that you were in a shootout with Marko and Ramius at the Noimoire pound. Why are you risking yourself on dumb stuff? I thought you were going to take care of the problem with the product and kill Javier Garcia. You shouldn't risk killing yourself over small stuff. It's imperative that we get the goods, and that Javier become one of his own dead. You're our only talented enforcer left."

Wolfe did his best to keep the nuclear sarcasm from his voice. "Well, your concern for my health is appreciated, but I was on my own time. I didn't expect Marko and his dead brother to be there, alright? Besides, why are you upset? I killed another Cobra lieutenant. Fuck, we've been dealing with these guys for nearly ten years, and I've taken out a third of their lieutenants in less than forty-eight hours. Doesn't that deserve an attaboy or something? Throw me a bone here."

Shel snickered at Wolfe's outburst.

Lights flashed over the car as Wolfe drove down a long road with dozens of street lamps. They were in darkness, then a flash of light. Darkness. Light. Over and over.

Damian gave a long sigh. "Alright, sorry, sorry. I'm just really excited for some stuff, but I need you for it to all work."

A sudden thought made Wolfe's blood go cold. "Wait, how do you know about my dust-up with the Cobras? That was barely three hours ago."

Damian chuckled. "Well, that brings me to the second thing —the real reason I called. While you were out playing shoot-im cowboy with Marko and poor Ramius, I was doing the work that'll put our family back on top for generations."

Damian paused dramatically.

"Well, don't break your arm jerking yourself off. Let me ooh and aah over it as well," Wolfe said, failing to keep the sarcasm from his voice this time. But he was gripping the wheel tight awaiting Damian's answer.

Damian chuckled again, like some bad B-movie villain. "Well, I've negotiated a deal with Nico that'll end the threat to us—and cripple the Cobras. That's how I heard about your shenanigans—Nico mentioned your rampage and said I had to call you off him as part of the deal."

Shel mouthed "Nico? The Cobra?" at Wolfe.

"You negotiated with... Nico?" Wolfe asked, briefly staring at the roof of the car as they drove. "Nico, the Cobras' head enforcer? Nico, the crazy guy that has murdered and raped a ton of people? Nico, the guy that gave me the scar across my chest?"

"I don't care about his personal foibles," Damian said, finally sounding irritated. "What I care about is that he will help you to murder the head Cobra, Jason Klaus himself. You already did Frankie and Ramius in... once you kill Javier and Jason, the Cobras will be nearly devoid of deckbearers, and we'll have Dad, Thad, me, and you, at the minimum. I've saved us."

Wolfe kept his eyes on the road, but relaxed—Damian having inside information made total sense under these circumstances.

Still, Wolfe couldn't help one sarcastic rejoinder. "So, no need for me then?"

"Don't be ridiculous. I'm the brains, you're the brawn,"

Damian said. "I need you to be the triggerman on Jason. We both know you're the guy that gets shit done. Why do you keep making me say it? I'm beginning to think what you really want is to have your ego stroked."

Wolfe was half irritated by the insinuation that he wasn't the brains. He had been the impetus behind quite a few of the family's plans, back in the day.

But the second half of him was amused by Damian's joke. That part won out, and Wolfe chuckled.

"You'll always have a place with the family, Wolfe," Damian said. "Don't worry."

"Sure, sounds good. What *is* my place in this scheme, though? You haven't explained it."

"Forty-eight hours from now, Jason Klaus will be hosting a mixed-martial arts event—but not at the Venom Arena, and this isn't some UFC event. This is going to be a bare-knuckle, no-rules-at-all, unsanctioned tournament. They're setting it up mostly to preview possible new Cobra thugs, to replace the ones they've lost. Lost mostly at your hand. You get an attaboy for that, for sure."

"Thanks."

"Anyway, Nico has a secret entrance that leads close to the underground fight ring—underground literally as well figuratively. You can get in through the sewers, plant a bomb, and blow the place to hell."

"Why me?" Wolfe asked. "Any jackass can do that. Hells, *Nico* can do that on his own."

"Two reasons. Less important is the fact that Nico will be publicly seen elsewhere, so none of the Cobras will hesitate to follow him after Jason is gone."

"Alright, that eliminates Nico, but it doesn't automatically nominate me."

Damian's voice lost its joviality and took on a slight note of pleading. "It *has* to be you, Wolfe. Jason has one of the cards that is a part of the set to make the Mythic Infernal card, like my own card. He told Nico about it. That's what Nico is giving me for his help. I need someone of your competence to make absolutely sure that I get that card, afterwards. Not some Cobra thug, not Nico. Not anyone but *me*, Wolfe."

Yeah, now why I'm needed makes sense.

Damian's voice returned to joviality. "Also, I don't want Nico or anyone else getting cold feet and not carrying it out. I know I can trust you—you've always had the family's best interests at heart."

Wolfe was beginning to regret his loyalty, if only because it was getting him multiple fourteen-plus-hour work days in a row. "Well, I'm almost home and it's been a hell of a day. I'm gonna hang up and go catch a few z's. I'll need to get my beauty sleep so I can be the best dog the family has ever had."

"Good," Damian said. "See that you are. I'm counting on you, Wolfe."

"Sure."

Wolfe hung his phone up as he pulled around the little building card type church that David Torres ran.

"Um, Wolfe, what do we do if Nico is the one that killed my brother?" Shel asked, tapping her steepled fingers together. "Are... Are you going to let him get away with what he's done?"

Wolfe didn't answer for a second, making the last turn and then pulling into his driveway.

He parked, but kept the engine on. He wanted the heat from the AC. The neighborhood was gloomy—barren and dark. Wolfe could barely make out all the details inside his car.

Wolfe leaned back, put his arm over his eyes, and finally answered Shel's dreaded question. "I don't know, Shel. Honestly, I hate Nico for a bunch of my own reasons, and I don't think the big man is going to let the Cobras survive at all, even in a reduced state. So I suspect we'll put Nico down, one way or another. But I'm honestly not sure."

"The whole reason I'm here is to avenge my brother. Can we at least question him before we turn him over?"

"I've made it past nearly every single deckbearer they have by the skin of my teeth, Shel. But if we can do it without endangering me—or you—I'll try to question one. Fair?"

Shel nodded. She perked up a bit and smiled a sly smile.

"What's that for?" he asked.

"Oh, you called me *Shel*. You usually call me *girl* or *that one* or *her* or something." She brightened a bit. "Does that mean you're coming to trust me? I'm a capable deckbearer now?"

"Don't get cocky," Wolfe said, though he couldn't help but smile.

"But... I am, right?"

"Well, the first time I met you, I had to carry your unconscious ass from the wreckage of the fight. Now, well, now you can help me in dungeons."

"And you think I'll be able to avenge Kevin, right? That this wasn't all for nothing?"

"Sure," he muttered.

Silence.

Shel rubbed her hands together, obviously wresting with words she couldn't articulate, but Wolfe was losing his grip on the waking world. If she wanted to say something, she'd have to do it fast. Sleep sounded so good.

"What is it?" he growled.

"Oh, uh, well..." Shel fumbled her words a bit before quickly saying, "I think you're very capable. And I really appreciate your, uh, strength. And being there for me."

"Okay. And?"

Wolfe sensed she wanted to say something else—he hated it when people beat around the bush for no damn reason.

"It's..." Shel turned away. "N-Nothing. Sorry. I forgot." She quickly leapt out of the car, practically fleeing.

Wolfe was too tired to interrupt any of that.

He exited the car, and Shel walked over to his side. She reached out, as though she were going to touch his arm—or maybe hold it—but at the last second, shoved her hands into her pockets. She kept her gaze down.

Wolfe unlocked the gate, passed through his old dog's space, and then entered the house. Blood dappled the floor behind him. His injured leg was still weeping crimson, it seemed. Wolfe ignored that as he stepped into the front room from the hall to give himself some space.

He pulled his deck and tossed a card out.

Cereboo woofed happily and put two paws, and three tongues, on Wolfe. He had to brace himself to stay upright, and pain flared from his injured leg all the way up to his spine.

Wolfe fended him off half-heartedly, and half-successfully, trying not to grimace. "Good to see you, too, boy. Thanks for handling all those werewolves for me. We got you a sibling out of it. Some rare breed of Hellhound."

Cereboo woofed excitedly, dropping to the carpet and zooming around the room in a tight circle.

Shel smiled. "I heard that if your dog has the zoomies, it means they trust you and feel comfortable around you."

Wolfe watched Cereboo make another circuit of the room. "I don't know if that applies to companion cards, but I hope it means Cereboo likes me. I do worry about the amount of times I've gotten him killed, which is twice in as many days. Really only a single day by hours."

"We already talked about this, but I still think he doesn't mind. I asked Sorenia about it. According to her, it doesn't affect our companions like it would us."

Wolfe raised an eyebrow. "They can remember getting torn to pieces by a werewolf but aren't traumatized by it?"

Shel nervously chuckled. "I, uh guess? That's a pretty good super power, actually. I'd love a *no trauma* perk."

"Yeah," Wolfe muttered. "I'm going to take a bath and try to clean up some of my own damage." He motioned to his blood-stained shirt and slashed leg. "There's a first-aid kit under the kitchen sink—"

"Why there?" Shel asked. "Do you have a lot of cooking accidents?"

"Cute. Just... hand it to me, will you?"

Shel lifted both eyebrows. "You can't bend over?"

"Just help me out, will you? I need to... soak."

"O-Okay."

Chapter 20

Chicken Soup for the Soul

"The Great Game, Rule #20: No Deckbearer may be equipped
with more than one mantle."

Wolfe left the front room, headed down the hall, and
entered his bedroom. He grabbed a pair of workout
shorts and a tank top from his closet, then hobbled
back into the hall. His leg hurt more and more, as though
his body's resistances to the agony were slowly fading.

And now that Shel wasn't looking, Wolfe didn't mind
leaning half his weight on the nearby wall to aid his walking.

Once he made it to the bathroom, he limped inside and shut
the door. He turned on the bath water until it was near-scolding,
the steam quickly filling the tiny space and making everything
warm. Wolfe stripped off his clothes, careful not to bother his
still-blooding leg.

Wolfe glanced at the mirror.

His image was a study in contrasts in many ways. Six-foot-
two, two hundred and thirty pounds of muscle, and he still had
abs. A body any man should have been proud of. His hair,

although balding enough to give him a widow's peak, was still dark brown.

But it was a body with damage. Maybe too much damage.

His hazel eyes were tired, and he had a flat stare. A huge scar ran from his navel to his neck, distended from his skin, the mark of the encounter with Nico that hadn't gone Wolfe's way.

That scar was bisected by three long, shallow slashes now. A few much smaller scars also crossed his body, each with a memory: A knife to the side, the burn mark on his thigh from a lab explosion and fire, another knife to the arm. A tin can lid he'd sliced his hand on. He smiled at the last one. Not his finest moment.

And now he had a claw slash to his leg.

Oh, and the acid burn on his arm.

Also, the puckered wound on his side that was the half-healed bullet he had taken in the bar fight against Frankie. It was a lot less of a normal gunshot wound, and more a puncture to the side, thanks to the healing from Shel, but it was still a puckered hole in his flesh.

It wasn't pretty.

Wolfe sighed at the crisscross of wounds across his body. *I'll just have to clean it off and see what Shel can do about it.* He grabbed his first aid kit and brought it to the edge of the tub.

Then Wolfe stepped into the bath, hissing as hot water washed over all his various wounds.

Crimson blood blossomed all around Wolfe as he slid deeper and deeper into the comforting arms of the tub. With a sigh, he leaned his head back and rested it on the tub edge. His heart beat hard enough for him to listen to it for a while as his body soaked.

He grabbed the first aid kit, but his grip was weak. The container, nothing more than a plastic briefcase of supplies, slipped from his fingers and crashed onto the bathroom floor. The contents spilled out across the tile.

Bandages. Painkillers. Antiseptics.

Wolfe groaned. He didn't have the strength to get up and deal with it. Fatigue ate at him. He just wanted the agony to go away—all of it. His physical agony, his mental agony.

I was strong when it mattered. I can afford to take a break now.

He closed his eyes, the anxiety of multiple life-or-death situations slowly draining from him.

The door creaked open.

"Wolfe?"

But he didn't have the willpower to respond. It could be a dream, it could be reality. Wolfe didn't want to think about it.

Someone stepped into the bathroom. Wolfe was vaguely aware they were cleaning up all the medical supplies. He refused to open his eyes. He didn't want to deal with it. He didn't need to be tough anymore—and he did need to heal. And rest. So much rest.

"Oh, no," he heard Shel whisper. It sounded close, but somehow far, like his consciousness was fleeing from the world as well.

A gentle yet strong hand touched his shoulder. Wolfe exhaled, still unwilling to deal with reality. More water entered the bath. Then something else. Soap? Ointment? Something. It soothed some of his aches.

Minutes passed in quiet contemplation. Wolfe breathed easy. He never really had... someone who had looked after him. Well, his dog had been there, but only as a dog could. The touch he felt on his leg, and on his shoulder, and down his side...

It was a gentle massaging, helping the injuries heal.

That was nice.

When Wolfe finally found the strength to open his eyes again, he found Shel sitting on the bathroom floor, leaning against the side of his bathtub. She had her phone up. She scrolled through pages and pages of cards, and occasionally stopped on *healing powers* to zoom in on the descriptions people had written up.

Occasionally, she dipped her fingers into the water, and when it was cold, she filled the tub up again.

Wolfe took a deep breath.

Shel glanced over, her brow furrowed. "Are you okay?" she whispered.

Wolfe didn't move from his spot in the tub. "I'm fine. Never been better."

He had expected a chuckle, but Shel obviously wasn't in the mood.

"I hope you don't mind I came in here. You were, uh, gone for so long. And I heard a crash." She pointed to the first aid kit. "I think you dropped this."

"Eh," Wolfe replied.

Shel brought her knees to her chest and smiled at him. "I was little worried about coming in here. I thought you might get excited and ravage me... Or something like that."

"Tsk. Right now, I don't think I could ravage a ham sandwich."

"Well, as you once told me, ham sandwiches have killed people." Shel chuckled at the joke. He liked her voice as it echoed around the small bathroom. It was as soothing as the water.

"I do think you should get out now," Shel said. "You're turning into a prune."

Wolfe grabbed the edge of the tub, but he didn't think he could lift his whole weight in one go. He struggled, and he hated himself for doing it in front of someone else. In his line of work, weakness just meant you were gonna die faster.

He clung to the fact he had been strong when it mattered.

But Shel didn't even make so much as a joke.

She took one of his arms and helped him to his feet. With all her strength, she supported half his weight and eased him out of the tub. Then she helped him to the towels. Wolfe grabbed one, and although he hadn't asked, Shel left his side to retrieve his clothing.

Once dry, Shel carefully wrapped his injuries in bandages. First his leg, then his side, and lastly, his arm. Wolfe kept his eyes closed through most of it, trying to rest, even while standing.

"You have a lot of... interesting marks," Shel whispered. "You must have a lot of good stories. Or maybe scary stories, depending."

"Eh."

Once she was done, she tapped his shoulder. That was when Wolfe fumbled with his clothing. He was... numb. Whatever had been in the water had dulled a lot of the agony—and he was grateful for that.

He got dressed in the sloppiest manner possible, though. Wolfe leaned against the wall, slowly got his pants on, and then lazily slid on the tank top. Shel walked over for the last part of it, and smoothed his clothing over his body, mindful of the bandages.

"There," she said in an upbeat tone. "You're as good as new."

"Woo," he sarcastically groaned in response.

"Let's get you to bed."

Shel helped Wolfe out of the bathroom and down the hall. They entered his room together, though Wolfe hated every second he needed to lean on her. He just wanted this day to be over. He wanted to sleep.

His room was nothing fancy, but at least he had a large bed.

Shel helped him onto the mattress. Then her gaze traveled over to the wall just above the headboard, where Wolfe's Grim Reaper band poster hung.

"I like this," Shel stated.

"The painting of one of the strongest cards of a dark god?" Wolfe quipped.

"W-Well. I don't like the subject matter. But... I think it says something about you. The fact you had a favorite band and even got this signed by them once. It says, *I have a sensitive side too— it's just buried beneath layers of 'no witnesses.'*"

Wolfe snorted back a laugh as he rolled onto his non-injured side. "Look, before I slip away into slumberland, why don't we talk about your levels?"

"Why?" Shel asked.

"Just so... we can be productive." Wolfe didn't want to talk about anything in his room. "What level are you?"

"I'm level eleven. I made level five from Frankie—thank you again—and then made level nine against Ramius and his cards, and the Werewolf Witch pushed me the rest of the way to my current lofty heights."

Wolfe fluffed his pillow, fighting sleep. "Is that sarcasm?"

She paused in her ministrations. "Not really. The best way I can say it is, I never thought I would be level anything, and level eleven is a lot. I would have had to beat multiple deckbearers quite a few levels above me in the arena to achieve that if we were making levels even slightly legally, so this is a double surprise—surprise that I'm a deckbearer, and surprise that I'm level eleven. At the same time, I mean, we've heard of the champions. Those people are mostly over level one-hundred."

"Deckbearers usually hit somewhere around level twenty, average, over their life," Wolfe said. "So already being level eleven is pretty fucking impressive."

"That statistic includes deckbearers that died in their first fight outside the arena, or that got their deck when they were eighty and just sat on it for five years. Things like that," Shel said. "But still... you're right. Making ten levels in two days is insanely good. Thank you for giving me that."

Wolfe nodded, smiling. He liked to hear compliments from Shel, he admitted in the privacy of his own mind. "Well, even if I did most of the heavy lifting, you didn't do nothing, that's for sure. Kept me alive, at least. And the last two you earned on your own."

Shel took a seat on the edge of the bed and smiled.

"How come your brother meant so much to you?"

Shel tapped her fingers on her knees. "We had a hard life. Dad was physically abusive. Our oldest brother was the same. My mom left the family and took my younger sister with her. Everyone except Kevin either beat me... or left me."

A single tear slid down her cheek.

Fucking Divine, I don't know how to handle weeping women. "I'm sorry," Wolfe whispered. He painfully forced himself into a sitting position.

Awkwardly, he reached for her, like he would comfort her, but he wasn't entirely sure what to do.

So he stopped.

"Anyway," Shel said, wiping her face dry, "at some level, I know Kevin was awful. He screwed up all the time, stealing, doing drugs, things like that. He failed out of high school. He was self-destructive even before he got killed, like the rest of the family had convinced him he really was just a piece of shit. But he was the one family member who was maybe redeemable, who also needed me. And now that opportunity is gone forever. I'll never make things right for him, you know?"

"I do," Wolfe said.

He thought he had covered his emotions better, but Shel must've heard something in his voice because she met his eyes. "Something happen with your family?"

Wolfe didn't answer immediately, his mind seeing the terrified hazel eyes, hearing high-pitched and feminine screaming, and deep-voiced male shouting. Cereboo must have sensed something, all the way from the living room, because the three-headed pooch bounded down the hall and into his bedroom.

Cereboo walked over, all three heads up and alert.

Wolfe petted his companion, then looked over at Shel. "I... I don't want to talk about that right now."

Shel raised her eyebrow.

Wolfe changed the subject. "You going to bring your companion out?"

Shel frowned slightly. "I don't want to bring Sorenia out right now—she'll just lecture me. Or you. Probably both of us."

Wolfe snorted laughter.

"Why do you work for Big Man Grimm?" she asked as she scooted closer to him on the bed.

"I owe him everything," Wolfe said simply. It was the truth, and he owned it.

"Did he save your life or something?" Shel asked. "Like in a big gunfight? That's how gangsters accrue life debts, right?"

Wolfe laughed but then grimaced as his wounds twinged. "He did save my life, but there was no gunfight. Not even a little bit. We've had quite a few adventures together since where he shot various idiots, but that was in the early days. He hasn't fired a gun in anger in fifteen years."

"Then... why?" Shel asked, putting her hand on his shoulder and not moving away from him.

Wolfe exhaled.

It was an unpleasant memory.

"I ended up with a murder rap as a teenager. They were going to try me as an adult, and Big Man Grimm... Well, he had a personal connection to the case. When he heard about it, he leaned on some people and threw some simoleons around toon town, and the lawyers and jury suddenly found my self-defense case compelling, got it dropped to an insufficient self-defense manslaughter rap, and I did less than a year at juvie."

"*Was* it self-defense?" Shel asked.

"No."

Shel stared at him for a long moment. "Why did you kill... whomever you killed?"

"He truly had it coming," Wolfe said darkly. "I've never regretted the death of any man less than him... even if I've regretted the fallout."

"Why?" Shel asked again, staring at him with wide eyes.

Wolfe huffed again. "Look—I don't like talking about this. In a couple days, once we get justice for your brother, you're on a plane to wherever the fuck. So it doesn't matter, okay?"

Shel said nothing.

The conversation died, and with it went Wolfe's last tatters of the will to stay awake. He leaned back down on the pillow and relaxed. He didn't want to be conscious anymore.

For a long while, Shel didn't move.

Ceraboo walked in a circle three times before lying down on the floor. He had curled himself into a loaf as best he could for a doggo his size.

Then Shel stood, walked over to the light switch, and turned it off. Once the room was dark, and cold, she returned to the side of the bed. Wolfe didn't have the energy to get up, or discuss much else.

Thankfully, Shel didn't say anything to him.

She just... lied on the bed. At first, she was a few inches from his side, but then she scooted closer, until her body was pressed against his side. She grazed her fingers over his arm.

It was nice to have her company.

Wolfe sighed and fell asleep to the soft rhythm of her breathing.

CHAPTER 21

CALM BEFORE THE STORM

"The Great Game, Rule #21: There are 12 faction types: Beast, Divine, Dragon, Elder, Elemental, Golem, Infernal, Mortal, Nature, Plant, Shadow, and Undead. Each is weak to or resists one or more types."

Wolfe woke up, warm and comfortable. He blinked back his grogginess and found Shel sleeping next to him, her head tucked against his chest. She had a scent of honey about her that reminded Wolfe of soothing tea. Memories of quiet breakfasts at home played at the edge of his mind, no doubt fueled by his fatigue.

A quick glance at his phone showed it was 8 a.m.

He was still exhausted, even though he had been asleep for most of ten hours—he was pretty sure it was lag from all the fighting, being wounded, and stress of the previous day. He was half tempted to sleep longer, feeling he had earned it, but his bladder insisted he visit the toilet, so Wolfe gave up on that thought.

Without disturbing Shel too much, Wolfe carefully slid off his bed.

Clad only in his work-out shorts, he crept toward the door. His everything hurt, but he pushed that aside.

A low-volume woof from the foot of his bed reminded him that Cereboo was still here.

"Shh!" Wolfe resummoned the pup into his deck.

Then he grabbed his T-shirt and tiptoed from the room, feeling absurd as he did so. He couldn't remember the last time he had tiptoed. He wasn't sure he ever had.

But it must have worked, because Shel didn't so much as shift in her sleep as he left. He quietly closed the door behind him.

Once outside in the hall, Wolfe pulled Cereboo again.

The dog woofed at him indignantly.

Wolfe rolled his eyes at his companion. "There was no way we were both getting out of there without waking Shel—suck it up. At least when you go back in the deck, you heal. I'm going to have to deal with all my wounds for days or weeks."

Cereboo woofed again, but started panting happily from all three heads. Wolfe rubbed the center head and scratched behind the ear. "Good boy! Besides, I'll make it up to you."

Wolfe went into the kitchen, and pulled twelve eggs and some cheese from the fridge. Then he opened a drawer, pulled out a spare pack of cigarettes and his ashtray, and lit one up.

Cereboo sneezed.

"Hey, I don't need my dog judging me, buddy. If you don't like it, wait in the other room."

Cereboo gave a three-headed, atonal warble but sat on the ground, occasionally rubbing one of his noses with a paw.

Wolfe set to cooking, breaking all twelve eggs into a bowl and throwing away the shells in the garbage beside the sink. Wolfe was by no means a good cook, but years as a bachelor—and a very financially poor one for his earliest years alone—had taught him a few basics. He got a pan, started scrambled eggs on the stove, but added a bit of milk, salt, butter, and some cheese to make a fattier but tastier version.

As he finished, he stubbed out his cigarette, then divided the eggs: a third for him, two thirds for Cereboo, both served on one of his cheap ceramic plates.

"Do you even eat, boy?" Wolfe asked, wondering. *I mean, he's a magic card, not a biological animal.*

Cereboo woofed again, and the left head grabbed half the eggs from the plate. The two others got in a fight with themselves, and lefty gobbled the second half as well a moment later.

Wolfe laughed so hard to see his dog fight himself and then steal from himself that tears rolled down his face. He had needed it. "I guess you *do* eat."

Feeling refreshed, Wolfe decided he was okay enough to do the rest of his usual morning routine. He went into the front room and belted out a light set of push-ups and sit-ups, then decided to just make it a chest and arm day, doing low-weight curls, shoulder shrugs, and various weighted arm thrusts. It hurt, thanks to his wounds. But not too badly.

Afterwards, a quick shower and shave, and Wolfe was starting to feel the tension of the last couple days leave him.

It was nearly 9 a.m., and Shel still wasn't awake. Wolfe was deciding between waking her so they could start the day and trying to handle a few things before she woke when his phone rang, making the decision for him.

Victor. Maybe he has info on her brother's killer.

Wolfe swiped, put the phone to his ear, and said, "Talk to me."

Victor laughed. "Straight to business, huh? Well, good news. I found out about the guy you asked for—Milf Fucker. He's an enforcer for the Cobras. Real bad dude. Rap sheet is crazy long —attempted murder, rape, assault with G.B.I, even a fucking child molestation charge. I was gonna charge you through the nose for the info, since the Cobras might take exception, but I'll give it to you for a cool five K, given who this guy is... and one other piece of information."

Big Man Grimm is good for it.

"Yeah, you'll get your money."

Shel, once again dressed in jeans and Wolfe's T-shirt, chose that moment to walk into the room, rubbing the sleep from her eyes. She stared at him questioningly.

Wolfe mouthed, "I'll tell you in a minute," at her.

Victor was still talking. "So, the guy's real name is Billy Jenson. He doesn't have a place. He's been staying in different motels and shit. He's not keeping a low profile or anything, but just given how mobile he's been, it's hard to track him down."

Wolfe frowned at his phone. "That's not much."

"I know, but it should get you started—and I do have one more odd piece of information... and the real reason I can sell the info cheap. Apparently, Jason Klaus, head of the Cobras—whom Billy supposedly works for—has put out the word that he'll give an uncommon card or fifty thousand cash to anyone who brings him Billy, dead or alive. Apparently, Billy was acting without orders from the top."

Wolfe thought about it. *That... makes almost no sense. The Cobras have wiped out half our leadership team—if it isn't on the orders of their head, then who? Wouldn't some fucker trying to overstep the Cobras' head honcho just try to help him kick the bucket rather than trying to help him win his street war without orders?*

Wolfe shook his head. *I just need to kill the fucker who murdered Heinrich and the poor girl, not worry about all this crazy shit.* "Well, I appreciate it, Victor. Also, I'll still pay if you get some really good tips on anything else to help me get better cards."

"Will do," Victor said.

"Good," Wolfe said, then hung up.

"That was Victor?" Shel asked. "Did he find out about Kevin?"

Wolfe shook his head. "He only had some information about Heinrich's killer."

Shel blinked. "Wow, I'd honestly forgotten about that, even though it was only twenty-four hours ago. I can't believe things have been so crazy I managed to forget about learning to level next to two corpses. Is your life always crazy like this?"

Wolfe laughed. "Not so much, no. Crazier than most peoples, I suspect, but way less than this most of the time."

"So, what are the plans for today then?"

"How about, first you heal me with those EMTs of yours?"

Shel hung her head. "It hasn't been twenty-four hours since I last used them on you. But even more importantly, they won't heal *injury* debuffs, just damage to health. So, once they're available, I can heal damage—but not the underlying issues. I need stronger cards for that."

Wolfe grimaced. *Joy.*

Then he glanced over at Shel, who was now petting Cereboo. *She* was beautiful, but her outfit was gross—Shel had been wearing it for a very stressful thirty-six hours straight.

"Then I guess, first, we go and get you some clothes. You look like a refugee from the hobo nation. Then we'll see. Everyone and their sister have errands for me: you want me to find your brother's killer, Big Man Grimm wants to find this Billy Jenson guy—that's the one who killed Heinrich and the working girl—and deep six him, Ms. Grimm wants me to help with the dentist lady, and Damian wants me to go kill Javier and steal back the drugs they stole from us."

"But first, clothes?" Shel asked.

Then her stomach rumbled, and she blushed.

"First, I'll make you some cheesy scrambled eggs, a specialty of mine."

Cereboo whined.

Wolfe rolled his eyes. "Alright, you and my new dog's two idiot heads some."

Cereboo woofed happily.

Wolfe traveled down Main Street again. He was starting to develop an utterly irrational dislike for the stupid road, since he had been down it so many times recently to do things he didn't want to. But he just kept driving it, multiple times a day.

"So, as we were talking about yesterday, I'm sitting on ten leveling pips," Shel said. "How do you think I should spend them?"

"How a deckbearer levels is a very personal decision, Shel. You ought to give it some deep thought before you decide on the path to take."

"Aren't we going to go kill Javier tonight? I think I ought to make the levels, and consider how to upgrade my deck. Aside from putting the Caustic Frog Demon in, I haven't made any changes at all."

"Sensible suggestions like that were certainly why you were a valedictorian. Yeah, I ought to make my levels as well, and look at my own deck. How about, we make the levels here, since we can just see our charts at will, and we work on decks when we stop for lunch later today?"

"Alright, tell me about the leveling again."

Wolfe pulled up his chart and stared at it, trying to remember all the stuff he had looked up that long thirty-six hours ago.

"Alright, so, quick recap. The things you can increase are as follows: You can increase your power by one, either current types or new types. You can increase your cards in deck by five. You can increase your cards each draw by one. You can increase the time a card spends in play by a minute. You can add a minion card or enhancer slot for one as well. For five, you can add a building or companion card slot. Each of those numbers is multiplied by the number of times you've made the buy, including the one you're making at the moment."

Shel nodded. "What if I added two Mortal power for three of my leveling pips, a minion card slot for one, cards drawn into hand by one, and then added a companion slot?"

"Do you have a new companion card?"

Shel shook her head, her red hair swishing back and forth now that it was in its new ponytail.

"Then just up your power and card draw, get your minion card slot, and then save the other five. If you get to the point you have a second companion, just spend your points then."

Shel nodded thoughtfully. "That sounds better."

"Why two Mortal power? Why not a Mortal and a Divine?"

"Well, if I do get some of Sorenia's, um, sisters I guess, then my best cards will be Mortal ones... and since companions don't cost power, I don't need Divine power even if I get all four of them."

Wolfe mulled that over. "You're bright as well as decent-looking. Did you make a deal with a demon in your previous life?"

Shel rolled her eyes. "So droll."

Wolfe moved on. "Do you think you'll ever actually get any more of the Sorenia-style angel cards?" Wolfe grimaced. "I mean, I might get more of the Infernal set cards because, at the end of the day, we're bad people that are killing each other. But why would Divine deckbearers fight each other?"

Shel twisted her finger in her hair. "I thought about that, but, well... we've been getting *a lot* of cards. If I manage to get some more, maybe I can just trade whole stacks of them for cash and *buy* the companions. Or get other Divine companions and trade them? You pull off amazing shit practically every day, Wolfe. You think I could do that much, right?"

Wolfe laughed. "Your opinion of me is in the dictionary under 'overrating,' but I like it. I don't think I pull very much amazing shit off, and certainly not every day."

"But do you think my plan is okay?"

Wolfe started to say something sarcastic, but stopped himself. "It'll be a very hard road, but you're young and bright as hell. If you really want it, and really work at it, I think you can probably pull it off."

Shel smiled. "Thanks, Wolfe. What are you going to pick for your levels? What level are you?"

"Fourteen. I think I'm going to up power again, twice. One Infernal and one Beast power, so that I have six total power— three Infernal, two Beast, and one Fire. That'll use five more pips, so six total of my thirteen, leaving seven. I think I'll also spend one to up cards in draw—I want to get the cards I need in the moment more often, especially my damn mantle, which I feel has it out for me personally."

Shel laughed at his musings.

"Hey, it hasn't come to me in way too many fights. For me, the mantle is my *most* important card, even more so than for most deckbearers."

"The big bad wolf needs to be even bigger and badder?" Shel smiled at him. "You know, I've seen everything. You don't need to compensate so hard."

"You're a laugh a minute," Wolfe drawled.

Shel offered a playful smirk. "I'm just sayin'."

Wolfe chuckled. "Anyway, after that, I'll probably save my six remaining points, in case I get a companion, building, enhancer, or minion myself. Until I get some of those, I don't think increasing my deck size will help me, and most of my fights don't last more than five minutes, so I don't want to spend the points there."

Shel nodded. "That makes sense."
Wolfe made the changes and stared at his status sheet.

Ethan Madison Wolfe Status:
Level 8 Mortal (6 Levels pending)

Deckbearer Perks:
Deckbearer Perk 1: In the Thick of it: +50% to all numerical benefits gained from mantles
Deckbearer Perk 2: Man's Best Friend's Best Friend: Gain 1 Beast Power. May have one extra card in play so long as it's a Beast(Canine or Hybrid Canine).
Deckbearer Flaw: Fallen: May not gain Divine Power, nor use Divine cards unless they are also Infernal or Corrupted.

Deckbearer Stats:
Cards in Deck: 10
Cards in Hand: 4 (1 pip)
Cards in Play: 2
Length of Play: 5 minutes
Specialty Cards: Companion: 1
Type 1 and Power: 3 Infernal (3 pips)
Type 2 and Power: 2 Beast (3 pips)
Energy 1 and Power: 1 Fire

Personal Perks:
Inborn Perk 1: Vicious Killer: +25% to all Attack and Defense, check twice for attack modifier and take the best
Inborn Perk 2: Tough as Nails: +10 Health
Acquired Perk 1: Crafty Street Fighter: +3 Attack and Defense

Personal Stats:
Health: 20/30(25) (moderately injured debuff applied—maximum Health -5 till healed)

Attack: 10
Magical Attack [None]: 0
Defense: 10
Magical Defense [None]: 5

Wolfe grimaced. *I have an injured debuff. Joy.*

But he had reached his destination. He turned off Main into the collection of stores that he had chosen to shop at for Shel.

Deal with the injuries later—not much you can do anyways.

I just hope it doesn't affect me too much in the fights going forward, since I still have quite a few, most likely.

Chapter 22

Victuals

"**The Great Game, Rule #22**: There are 12 energy types: Corrupt, Death, Fire, Ice, Life, Light, Lightning, Meta, Psychic, and Telekinetic. Most are weak or resist one or more types."

Wolfe whistled—*heh*—as Shel came out of the changing room door.

She smiled and twirled.

Shel wore a new pair of slightly baggy cargo denim jeans and a white, button-up crop top with long sleeves and lace around the edges that showed her belly off. It wasn't the most practical combat outfit Wolfe had ever seen, but it wasn't bad, per se, and he had to admit it was pleasantly eye-catching.

"You like it?" Shel smiled at him wide enough to show her pearly whites and fiddling with her long red ponytail.

"Quite a bit."

Wolfe stood from the bench near the changing room in the Nordstrom they were in. He enjoyed giving things to Shel—things he was pretty sure she hadn't really had before. *But...*

Wolfe sighed. "That makes five outfits—more than enough

for us to handle everything, I'd warrant. Let's pay for these so we can go take care of business."

"Warrant?" she asked. "Pretty decent language for a high school dropout. At least when used that way."

"What are you, some amateur Sherlock Holmes?" Wolfe bit down his irritation and sighed. "I already told you, my dad was an attorney, an extremely successful mob lawyer. I've got a lot of his language in my vocabulary, stuff I learned when I was at home, before... everything."

Shel started to open her mouth, but Wolfe held his hand up. "Uh-uh. No more tricking me into talking about this. Let's go pay."

They followed the aisles back to an escalator and took it down, a lot of the people staring at Wolfe, whose exposed and scarred arms and muscles made him not quite fit the local scene. He sneered back at a few as they descended. *Stuck-up pricks. They're likely to call the police on me for being surly.*

Wolfe's eyes widened. *The police!*

"Hey, Shel?" Wolfe asked.

"Yeah?"

They reached the bottom and Wolfe stepped off, almost plowing over a well-dressed, heavy-set woman in a suit who dodged to the side as Wolfe continued excitedly. "How did your conversation with Detective Young go? I know it's not likely at all, but any chance you think she'd do a license check for you?"

"A license check?" Shel asked, her brow furrowed, obviously confused.

Wolfe walked up to the counter and tossed the clothes Shel had picked on it. "These, plus the set she's wearing," he told the beanpole-thin old lady at the front.

He turned to respond to Shel. "Like at a motel. I mean, M.I.L.F.C.K.R. has to be a noticeable license plate. Maybe caught on camera or something?"

"M.I.L.F.C.K.R.?" Shel asked, her brow furrowing further.

"Sorry, the license plate on the guy that killed Heinrich—Victor told me his name is Billy Jenson."

"I don't think police can get that information easily, and I'm almost positive they won't give it out..." Shel trailed off. "Wait, don't you have people?"

Wolfe watched the lady scanning clothes, who came around the counter, frowning, to scan Shel's worn items. "What? I don't have 'people,'" he said, holding up air quotes.

"But... you could get some people to look around, at the motels in the parts of town the families are in, see what they can find, right?"

Wolfe grimaced at the price, nearly five hundred, that came up on the counter but forked the cash over, thinking about what she'd said.

Then he got his phone out and started slowly adding people to a huge group text—all the enforcers he knew in the family, both senior and a few others. Then he typed out a simple message:

Keep an I out 4 car w/ M.I.L.F.C.K.R. license, at motels, tell me ASAP if U C it.

Shel giggled again. "Do people still text like that?"

Wolfe glared at her. "Obviously. Now zip it."

The lady bagged everything and gave Wolfe his change, and Wolfe started to walk out of the store. Almost immediately, his phone buzzed. He pulled it out, and Shel stared over his arm at it.

He had a message from Derek, the new guy who had fought with him in the dock ambush and impressed him back at the Morning After Inn. *"We saw the car outside the Lucky Fifty-Two last night. I remember joking about it. Might still be there. Also, do people really still type like that?"*

Shel giggled again. Wolfe gave her the eye. She only giggled harder.

Wolfe glanced at his watch. Between getting ready, getting

food, and getting clothing, they had killed over three hours since they'd gotten up, and it was nearing eleven in the morning. The gambling den didn't open until six p.m. Wolfe had time, most likely, before he needed to head over.

Time enough to take care of Mrs. Grimm's stupid errand, he hoped. Then, in the evening, he could handle Billy. Lastly, at night, he could handle Javier.

That would only leave blowing the head of the Cobras up and this chapter of Wolfe's life would be done.

But first, an early lunch and working on his deck. He still hadn't even looked at what cards he had gotten from Ramius.

"Let's get lunch," Wolfe said to Shel.

"We ate like three hours ago. I'm not really hungry yet," Shel said.

Wolfe frowned. "Well, given how I suspect today might go, this could well be our only remaining meal. We need the fuel."

"Well, when you sell it like that..."

Wolfe spread the new cards out on the plastic table inside the Deckburger. The inside of the fast-food chain was both garish and zany—a terrible combination. The booths were bright yellow, and the walls were an electric blue, everything so bright it practically hurt to gaze upon it all.

The Deckburger mascot, a three-eyed burger holding a milkshake and a hand of three cards, was slapped across everything—the windows, the garbage cans, and even the cash registers. Her name was "Patty the Deckbearer," which was the most creatively bankrupt name anyone could think up, in Wolfe's humble opinion.

He glanced up at Shel, who sat across from him. "Don't ever tell me I don't take you to all the nicest places."

Shel gave a perfunctory chuckle, took a bite of her burger. After she took a bite, she jokingly said, "Thank you for the c-c-combo."

"*Don't*," he growled. "If I have to hear that one more time, I'll put my own gun to my head."

Shel chuckled as she turned her attention to his cards.

There were ten, and they were considerably more interesting than Wolfe had suspected they would be.

Four Angry Hellhounds stared at him as some of the least interesting cards in the deck. They had been ubiquitous last season. So ubiquitous that even Wolfe knew about them. They were a two-power common card that could be used by both Infernal and Beast decks separately. Despite their common quality, they kind of worked for Wolfe and his deck, and he was giving honest thought to using them.

Angry Hellhound

Common Tier-One Beast/Infernal(Canine) Creature
Two Beast or Infernal Power
Health: 12
Attack: 6
Defense: 5
Magical Attack: 3 (bonus)
Magical Defense: 5

Special: When this creature makes a physical attack, it also makes a magical attack of either Fire or Infernal typing on the same target.
Special: +1 to all attacks for every other canine on the field.
Special: Must attack every thirty seconds or it returns to the deck.

"It could be argued that most things in the Infernal realms are angry, but these hellhounds take it to an entirely new level."

Shel read along with him. "That seems *very* weak for a two-power creature."

Wolfe nodded. "Yeah, but it essentially makes two weak attacks with every normal attack. So power-ups have double the effect—and it gets its own canine powerup. Imagine if I had a couple bonuses to both attacks and a Rescue Pup died on the field."

"Still..." Shel said, obviously unconvinced.

Wolfe didn't blame her—but he could also merge the cards. He took three of the four and pushed them together. They fused and another card appeared.

Angry Hellhound

Common Tier-Two Beast/Infernal(Canine) Creature
Two Beast or Infernal Power
Health: 12
Attack: 7
Defense: 5
Magical Attack: 7 (bonus)
Magical Defense: 5

Special: When this creature makes a physical attack, it also makes a Magical Attack of either Fire or Infernal typing on the same target.
Special: Immune to all mind-affecting debuffs.
Special: +1 to all attacks for every other canine on the field.
Special: Gains +1 Attack for every Escaped Damned on the field.

"It could be argued that most things in the Infernal realms are angry, but these hellhounds take it to an entirely new level."

"See, he's a better doggo already," Wolfe said. "An extra point of attack in each category, given it's a multiplying thing—"

"Geometric progression, or just the square," Shel said.

"Enough of your sass," Wolfe said with a chuckle. "The point is, it increases the damage a lot—about a third, I think. Especially if I'm throwing Escaped Damned out as well. Nearly everything in my deck makes the card stronger."

Wolfe decided, given his new power, to substitute a Tier-One and a Tier-Two Angry Hellhound into his deck and removing the two Tier-One Tormentor Imps. He still had what was essentially an entire imp deck in his pocket—but it wasn't what his deck was focused on at the moment.

A voice came from beside Wolfe, who nearly grabbed his pistol.

"Hey, um, can I watch? I've never seen a real deck before."

Wolfe turned to see a boy, about seven or eight, standing next to him with a smear of ketchup on his face.

A slightly pudgy woman in her late twenties or early thirties rushed up. "I'm so sorry!" she said, grabbing the boy.

Wolfe remembered being young. "It's okay, he can stay if he wants."

The mother stared at Wolfe, obviously distrusting, but her eyes fell on Shel, who was smiling up at her. "Well, um, I suppose it's fine."

"Alright, let's look at the other six cards," Wolfe said.

The next two were both enhancer cards, "Deal with the Devil," that gave a month of life for every Infernal card in the deck. *In a large deck, that could add up to a lot of extra time,* Wolfe thought, vaguely impressed.

"You should take those two—you said you were worried about getting old, and each could add another half year or so."

"At the cost of three leveling pips," Wolfe said. "Remember, each enhancer is still a specialty card. And in my deck of ten, that means that I get maybe another year of life for three levels—assuming I'm not killed in a shoot-out or drive-by, which is way more likely at this point."

The boy gasped, and the mother frowned, at Wolfe's words.

Shel twisted her finger in her red hair and shrugged, looking away. Wolfe wasn't sure why she was reacting so much to a tiny rejection of a small idea.

He stared down at the cards again. Wolfe wondered if Ramius had gotten the cards recently, since he hadn't increased his deck size at all, which would have really made them special.

The next card convinced him of the truth of his 'got them recently' theory. It was a card called Possessed Orphan. As the name suggested, it was a minion subtype orphan card—unique to the drop that had just happened.

"Wow, that card is scary," the boy next to Wolfe said.

Wolfe stared at the card. The image was of a girl, dressed in dirty and ragged clothes, staring at her hands from which eldritch black smoke was rising. Her face looked horrified.

"It kinda is," Shel replied.

Wolfe's eyes tracked down to the stats.

Possessed Orphan
Rare, no-tier Mortal minion[orphan]

0 Power

Health: 6

Attack: N/A

Defense: 2

Magical Attack: N/A

Magical Defense: 4

Special: Will fetch normal objects and such with a decent degree of precision and help carry up to ten pounds.

Special: If kept 'alive' for five straight years, will turn into a legendary, 2 power, tier-6, equivalent creature card. It will have typing the same as the most common of the Infernal, Undead, Elder, or Mortal cards in its deckbearer's deck, and differing powers based on its type. If ever 'killed,' the timer resets.

"This young girl has been possessed by the other, and has no memory of who she is, where her parents are—or what happened to them."

"Wow, that's sad," the boy said. "She doesn't know who she is or where her parents are?"

"Uh..." Shel said, then looked up at the mother.

"Okay, I don't think this is the deck you should be looking at," the woman said, then glanced at Shel. "Thanks for letting him look, but I think I'll take George home now."

"Ah, Mom..." the boy whined as he was dragged away.

"Have fun!" Shel called after him.

Wolfe shrugged. "I coulda told her that no one should leave their rugrats around me. My life is rated M for mature."

"I can't decide if that was funny or cringe."

"I repeat—enough of your sass," Wolfe said with a roll of his eyes. *They can't all be winners.*

Wolfe glanced down at the next three cards. There was an Infernal Werewolf mantle that gave a lot of attack and a low amount of defense. It was a touch stronger than the Soul Hunter Mantle, but cost more and didn't give the bonus against other Infernal cards. Wolfe decided to keep his existing mantle.

Then there were two Pack Howl cards. Each required an existing Beast power but didn't have any drawdown—and each gave all canine cards plus two to all stats for a single round.

Wolfe was legitimately tempted to add the Howls and the orphan card. Although he had just subbed out the Tormentor Imps, and his deck was now a bit tight.

He decided to spend two more of his leveling pips—one on a minion card slot and one to go to fifteen cards. He winced as he did. Larger decks were good for many things, but rarely direct combat. Still, he had raised his cards in hand to four per draw, and he had Cereboo, so he could cycle his whole deck in three rounds, or near enough.

233

He did a quick restructuring, moving some cards in and others out, focusing on his canine cards now. He ended with a deck that had the following: Cereboo, two Rescue Pups, the Loyal Guard Dog, the Fireborn Hellhound, a tier-one and a tier-two Angry Hellhound, two Pack Howls, his Soul Hunter Mantle, his No Kill Pound, the Possessed Orphan, a Return to the Pit, an Escaped Damned, and a Tier-Two Escaped Damned.

"You've got a real 'hounds of hell' deck going," Shel said, holding her fingers up in air quotes.

Wolfe nodded, decently satisfied with the deck. "Yeah. It doesn't have as many crazy tricks as some of the previous builds I've run through, but it seems pretty solid, and it still has relatively high utility against Infernal decks as well. Between the moderately strong tribal elements and said anti-Infernal elements, I think it'll do."

He passed the Fallen Angel back to Shel.

"Thanks, although I don't think I'm going to use it at the moment."

Wolfe shrugged. "Hold it in case you need it."

"You know that was payment to you, right?" Shel asked. "You can sell it or something."

"Just use it for now, okay?"

Shel nodded.

"What're you doing with your deck, then? Since you aren't using the Fallen Angel."

"I subbed out the basic direct-damage Light cards to add in an extra Rookie Riot Police and Rookie EMT each, and then I got rid of that Caustic Frog to put in the Barter the Soul card," Shel said.

Wolfe raised an eyebrow. "The Barter the Soul?"

Shel nodded. "Yeah, it's fairly situational, but it could be insanely clutch in the right moment. Even if someone had a ten-power creature on the field, if it was the right type, I could take control of it by sacrificing my one-power Mortal creature. And I have six Mortal creatures—they're more than half my deck."

Wolfe huffed.

Then he glanced up. Shel had only taken three bites from her burger, and eaten a couple fries. "You done with your burger?"

She offered him half a smile. "Yeah. I wasn't that hungry, sorry."

"That's fine. Let's go see about an old lady."

Shel raised a surprised eyebrow at him. "What?"

CHAPTER 23

PLAGUE OF RATS

"The Great Game, Rule #23: Beast is weak to the Undead Faction and the Corrupt and Death energies. It is resisted by Dragon, Mortal, Nature, and Telekinetic."

"Where're we going?" Shel asked as they got into Wolfe's car.

Wolfe handed Shel a piece of paper. "This is the address. I want to get Guinevere off my back, so we're gonna go handle her associate's rat problem. Put that address into your phone and get me directions—I know about where we're headed, but not exactly."

Shel pulled her phone out, entering the destination.

The residential neighborhoods in Noimoire were really hit and miss, some filled with huge, ornate houses with giant gardens, and some filled with hovels or giant subsidized apartment complexes for the poor. But the neighborhood Shel's phone took them to was a rare case—something in between. It was an older neighborhood of large brick and wood houses that was slowly losing to entropy.

As they drove, Shel pointed to a pile of garbage on the side of the road with a man sleeping on it and laughed. "Heh, check that out."

Wolfe grunted out a single laugh.

"Ever just drive around looking at how disgusting Noimoire is?" Shel asked.

"Not really—I'm usually driving somewhere and have a goal. Can't just look around."

"You should. In its own weird and gross way, it's kinda pretty. Like that," Shel said, pointing at an entire squad of pigeons fighting over a discarded pizza box with the uneaten crusts spilling out.

Wolfe drove by slowly, enjoying the idiot pigeons.

As he drove, Shel continued to point things out to him. There wasn't much that was exciting, but a woman dressed in actual curtains, a man with a funny sign asking for cash, and even half a couch—just a couch torn in half—thrown to the side of the road all made for inane talk.

Wolfe found himself admiring the view. Despite his rapport with Big Man Grimm and a few benders and other types of 'nights out with the boys,' he had spent most of the last twenty years lonely. He found himself enjoying having an impromptu partner far more than he'd thought he would.

By the time Wolfe had pulled into the driveway at their destination, next to a beat-up old Volkswagen that would have been out of style in the '80s, he was feeling decent about life.

Ms. Greenwall's house was on par with the houses around it, but larger. It had a brick lower half of the first story, and then a dark wooden second half of the first story and entire second story. The front was 'plants gone wild,' rose bushes and hedges raging out of control. But for the most part, the house had a relatively opulent look to it, worn down by time.

Wolfe knocked on the big, dark wooden door with a metal knocker hanging from it.

The door opened and an old lady, probably nearly seventy and using a cane, stared up at him from a diminutive five-foot height. "Who're you hooligans?"

Guinevere and her fucking assignments. I swear she finds all the least likeable asshats in the entire city.

The woman's white hair was so frizzy, it looked like she had tried for an afro, but it was thinning notably. Her brown eyes were intelligent, however, and flicked easily across Wolfe and Shel, taking them in. Her mouth was set in a permanent sneer that proclaimed her contempt to the world.

"Sorry to bother you, Ms. Greenwall. We're here about the rats," Shel offered before Wolfe could speak. "Guinevere said we were to help you, so..."

"Call me 'Juliet.' Never liked my damn last name. Should've gotten married just to change the stupid thing. Well, it's about time someone got here. Follow me. The problem is this way."

She turned and limped into the house with all the speed of a maimed turtle but still called out, "Hurry up! No lollygagging!"

Wolfe, torn between amusement at the caustic old biddy and his remaining irritation over the menial task, entered the house. As soon as he did, he encountered the smell of death. Wolfe glanced over at Juliet. *She isn't so old she should smell like this or leave a smell like it around. Also, the place looks clean and well-kept.*

Juliet slowly led them out of the front room, a geriatric hellscape of floral print and Ansel Adams—even hard candy in a bowl. Then through a hall with pictures of numerous award ceremonies but no family members, and into a large kitchen. "This way! This way!"

The smell kept getting worse as they went.

She walked over to a door in the back of the kitchen and rapped on it with her cane. "Problem is through here. Handle it better than the last people Guinevere sent. They were all idiots."

"Of course, ma'am," Shel said.

"*Juliet*!" The old biddy whacked Shel on her calf.

Shel gave a startled yelp and reached down to rub her leg.

Wolfe was torn between irritation and laughing at the situation. *Lady is crazier than a soup sandwich.*

"I'll look the situation over and see what I can do, but I'm not promising anything," Wolfe said.

The lady thwapped Wolfe in his ankle. "You have to handle it!"

"Son of an Infernal!" *Don't kill the old lady. Don't kill the old lady,* Wolfe repeated to himself as a mantra.

She went to thwap him again and Wolfe caught the cane. He looked her dead in the eye and spat out, "Stop."

Shel stepped in and gently took the cane from Wolfe's hands. "Of course, Juliet. Guinevere wouldn't have asked us if she didn't think we can handle it. We *will* handle it."

Juliet frowned. "Hmph. I guess I have no choice but to trust you. The last people she sent only made things worse. You guys had better handle it though, or Guinevere will hear my opinion in no uncertain terms! I'll be in the living room." She walked away, her cane giving off an odd, punctuating thump each time.

Wolfe opened the door and then pulled back, almost gagging. Shel did gag, and turned to the side, her face green. Then she reached over and flipped the switch by the door. Light flooded the entire basement as multiple floodlights turned on. The basement was huge, some old bomb-shelter. But that just made the horror of the situation worse.

Rats covered the floor. The entire floor, squirming and wriggling over each other. Wolfe could immediately see why. There were two bodies chained to chairs, now half eaten, their remaining rotten flesh liquified by decay, rat saliva, and the insufficiently cooled basement. At least the mystery of the death smell was solved.

Tada! It was actual dead people. For my next trick I'll shoot someone.

"They made me hold two Cobra thugs in the basement!" Juliet yelled from the other room. "And then they forgot about them! And then the rats got in! It's not my fault—I was barely a part of this!"

Wolfe wondered which brainless shit nugget enforcer had originally been in charge of this clusterfuck. He owed that guy a beating.

His eyes were drawn to small rat traps and empty poison boxes around the floor. *Or which idiot enforcers just let it get worse.* There were hundreds and hundreds of rats, and such small-scale solutions had likely only killed off the most idiotic of the rats. Wolfe resolved to find out who had screwed the pooch on fixing this situation and throw them a beating as well.

Later though. I have too much shit to do.

Wolfe pulled out his deck and then brought Cereboo out. The puppy woofed and jumped on him but then wrinkled all three noses. The left head sneezed hard, blowing snot onto Wolfe, which fortunately dissipated.

"Hey, boy! Glad to see you too. Sorry to pull you into this. Don't let any rats past this door."

With that, Wolfe walked down the stairs, taking in the rest of the basement as he did. He saw an entire lab down here— skeletons, gurneys, a medical table, bone saws, a computer... a bunch of stuff.

Shel followed him down, her hand covering her mouth and still half-gagging.

"So, what do we do?" she asked.

Wolfe hefted his STI Edge, ejecting the magazine and glancing at the limited bullets he had left. Then he thought about his deck. *Could I just summon a creature and tell it to go to town on rodent ass? Would it even succeed? How the fuck long would it take?*

Wolfe glanced up and met Shel's gaze. "I have no fucking idea what to do."

Shel's eyes widened. "Really? You don't have a plan? You always have a plan."

"Woman, I'm standing in a basement full of corpses and rats. Clearly, I don't have all the answers in life."

Shel laughed once and smiled at him.

Wolfe contemplated calling an exterminator, but the dead bodies would get the cops called so fast, he might as well tap his heels and wish to be sent straight to jail. He couldn't help but figure that Guinevere had given him the assignment because she hated him. Why, he didn't know, but she'd always seemed to have it out for him.

Juliet stuck her head back around the basement door, over Cereboo. "Have you started yet?!"

Wolfe bet himself that it was just a matter of time until he snapped and killed her.

Shel must have sensed his deep irritation because she turned up to her and forced a smile despite being green around the gills. "We're going over our options."

Wolfe glared up at the old lady. "We'll tell *you* when we're done. Keep to yourself until then."

"I've worked for the Grimm family for thirty years," she said, poking her cane at Wolfe over Cereboo's shoulder as if *Crochety Old Lady* were her legal first, middle, and last name. "If I wanted, I could call in favors and have you two dealt with!"

Cereboo barked and Juliet shrieked and actually whacked the companion card with her cane. Cereboo woofed again from three heads, and Juliet backed up, shrieking curses. It was Wolfe's turn to laugh, and he called up, "Good boy!"

After Wolfe stopped chortling, Shel turned to him. "What if we just pour a ton of bleach and ammonia down here?"

"I'm not physically cleaning this place, no matter what the old woman is threatening. She's full of crap, anyway—in the twenty years I've worked for the Grimm family, I've heard her mentioned maybe ten times. But even if she weren't, I'd let them put a bullet in the back of my head before I pick up a damn scrub brush and try to fix this mess."

"So dramatic," Shel said with a roll of her eyes and a smile. "But I wasn't talking about cleaning the place."

"Then why?" Wolfe asked.

"When you mix ammonia and bleach, you make chlorine gas. It's deadly—burns your lungs and stuff. If we poured it all over the floor, I'm sure it'd kill the rats... but then we'd have hundreds of rat corpses here."

"Where'd you learn that?" Wolfe asked, vaguely impressed.

"Chemistry class *and* history class. The ones I took getting a high school diploma that *everyone* can get and isn't that impressive."

Wolfe scoffed at her. "You're becoming a regular smartass."

"I learned from the best."

Wolfe laughed. She had a point. "How dangerous is this gas?"

Shel pushed her tongue against the inside of her cheek for half a second, then said, "Fairly dangerous. People die from it from time to time when cleaning their houses. I think Juliet would need to live elsewhere for a week or so, and then the basement would need to be *very* thoroughly cleaned, but the pests will be dead."

"Fine. I'll get the chemicals. You deal with the old lady."

"I can do that," Shel said, smiling a brilliant smile at Wolfe again. "Despite the whole cane thing, and general attitude, I think she just wants company."

Shel walked back up the stairs quickly. Cereboo woofed quietly and licked her repetitively as she passed. Juliet was just behind Wolfe's companion again.

"We have a plan," Shel said, her voice filled with cheer. "We'll be taking you to a hotel for a week. We'll make sure it's an excellent one, so you can think of it as taking a vacation. When you get back, everything will be fixed."

"No one better steal my stuff," Juliet said. "I was an orthodontic surgeon! I'm friends with the Grimm family. Did dentist work and rearranged corpses for them. They owe me a ton of favors for making it look like specific men turned up dead. Seriously, you better not steal my stuff!"

Shel took her elbow and led her back into the main portion of the large house. "No need to worry. Guinevere made it *very* clear that you were a dear friend."

"She did?"

"Oh, yes. We know what'll happen to us if we take your stuff, no need to worry. We just want to make sure your basement is clear."

"Good... good. That's what I want to hear."

Shel led her to the kitchen, and Wolfe followed. When she arrived, she guided Juliet to a chair and then asked, "Would you like some coffee?"

"Yes, please. Hmm. I was skeptical at first, but it seems Guinevere picked well this time. You should have been the first ones she sent."

Wolfe caught Shel's eye and motioned her over with a tilt of his head. She jumped to his side without hesitation.

"What're you doing?" he hissed. "Leave crotchety-klaus alone—she doesn't need to like us for this to work."

"Didn't you tell me just a day ago how we should make sure we make nice with people so they'll think of us and have our backs?"

Wolfe chuckled to hear his lessons taken seriously—and shoved back in his face. "I guess I did. Point made. Never mind me, you keep doing what you're doing."

CHAPTER 24

SMITING THE WICKED

"The Great Game, Rule #24: Divine is weak to Corrupt and resists Infernal."

It took most of the morning and afternoon, until around 5 P.M., for Wolfe and Shel to get everything set up for Juliet's house.

By the time Shel and Wolfe had dropped her off, Juliet sang Shel's praises and was not actively upset with Wolfe. She even said she hoped they would be a part of the family for long time to come.

The old lady was now resting at a resort hotel on Big Man Grimm's dime, praising both of them to the stars. She had even texted Guinevere about what a good job they had done, which Wolfe somehow doubted would help him much in the long run. Although he doubted it would hurt, either. The chemicals had all been placed in the house as well—also at the expense of the Grimm family.

There were going to be a large number of unhappy rats quite soon.

But now... Wolfe snorted to himself as he stared out the

passenger-side window of his car, past Shel. The Lucky Fifty-Two was the least well-disguised illegal gambling den he could have ever imagined. Even the name was insanely obvious.

The roulette table easily visible through the giant front window was just the icing on the 'no one gives a fuck about the law' cake.

Wolfe fingered the collection of handcuffs he'd bought as he wondered how much the bribes were to keep the police away—he had never needed to find out. What he didn't need to wonder about was who was paying the bribes. Illegal gambling in Noimoire was run by the Renfeldt family, who were beloved of the Infernal Lord of Greed, Mammon. That illegal gambling *included* this little place.

Wolfe wasn't sure why the Renfeldt family was letting Billy Jenson hide here after murdering a member of the Grimm family. The two families got along, and the Renfeldts sold drugs at some of their gambling dens, drugs they got from the Grimm family. Why were they willing to risk trouble?

But none of that shit really mattered right now. What mattered was that Wolfe had orders from Big Man Grimm to take care of Billy, orders he intended, and was happy, to carry out. The license plate MILFCKR stared at him from just inside the trash-filled, chain-link-surrounded parking lot of the not-so-subtle illegal gambling den, mixed in with a few other cars. Its sheer brazenness spurred Wolfe to want to take care of business. The little murderer obviously thought he couldn't be touched.

The gambling den hadn't formally opened yet, but people had entered, and Wolfe saw a guy smoking around the back, near a rear door that was propped open, inside the parking lot. That was his target.

Wolfe turned to his partner-in-crime. "Shel, stay here. Be prepared to drive off fast if I come running. I'm going to go handle business."

She nodded as Wolfe left the car and headed around the side.

He watched to make sure she was complying with the orders. She moved to the driver's seat and he assumed this was the best he would get from her without hanging around and watching.

Wolfe knew that he needed to get the jump on his target, and just walking up as himself was sure to spook the guy. So he waited till the guy's head faced the other direction, then ran behind a car in the parking lot. Praying to whichever gods would listen that no one would call him out for his suspicious behavior, Wolfe quickly moved from behind one old clunker to the next. When he was a mere fifteen feet from the door, he peeked around the side of the last car.

Luck, or the gods' favor, had his target facing away from him. Wolfe exploded into a run, his knees twinging but obeying as he launched himself forward. The guy must have heard the slap of Wolfe's shoes on the asphalt because he started to turn.

Wolfe hit him with an elbow in his temple and slammed him against the wall. The guy stiffened and fell like a damn fainting goat, but unlike those misbegotten failures, the thug stayed unconscious.

Can't kill what are probably Renfeldt's stooges. Leave him.

Still, he was sure that 'leave him' could quickly become a mistake.

To mitigate that chance, Wolfe searched the guy and took his pistol, then rolled him onto his stomach and handcuffed his hands behind his back. He wasn't worried about the thug escaping—but Wolfe was a tad nervous about his victim coming out of his beating-induced nap and trying to exact vengeance by surprise. With his hands cuffed, he could run but couldn't enact vengeance, most likely.

Wolfe opened the door and went in the back. He found himself in a small hall with a bathroom and a kitchen and some random building supplies—pipes and such.

From the bathroom, someone called out, "Julio? Everything okay?"

Grabbing one of the pipes, Wolfe rushed to the side of the bathroom door. A moment later, the door opened and Wolfe smashed the person coming out with a powerful swing of his improvised weapon. The man had just enough time for his eyes to widen before Wolfe slammed him so hard, blood hit the doorframe he had been exiting.

"That one is out of the ballpark," Wolfe quipped with black humor as he repeated his de-gun process and then handcuffed the guy around the toilet.

Two down—how many motherfuckers are in this place?

Wolfe snuck back down the hallway, exiting into the kitchen. A tall, older, umber-skinned man in a dirty chef's apron was busy unpacking frozen food and happened to stare right at Wolfe as he came around the corner.

Wolfe stood and drew his pistol, pointing it at the man. "Freeze! And keep quiet!"

The man froze in place, staring at Wolfe with hard, slightly narrowed eyes that flickered around—looking for a way out, an ally, or a weapon. Wolfe recognized the look—the look of a warrior that wasn't defeated.

Wolfe's instincts were almost always on point—this guy wasn't a chump like most of the thugs Wolfe dealt with, he could feel it in his bones.

Fuck, fuck, fuck! Those guards were pussies, but this cook is an ex-military guy or something—thank the Divine he looks sixty. I need a moment.

"What's your name?" Wolfe asked, touching his own chest and feeling the hunger and fire of his deck as he did.

"James," the man said curtly.

Feeling as if the situation was already halfway escaping him and hoping that there weren't any deckbearers around, Wolfe brought forth his deck and summoned Cereboo.

His dog licked him with three tongues and then did a full circle, its tail wagging wildly. Not the impressive mastiff-ofdoom that Wolfe was hoping for, but it was still a three-headed demon dog. Well, puppy. Wolfe hoped it would be good enough.

He kept his pistol trained on James as he petted his dog with one hand. "Cereboo, make sure this nice military man doesn't leave or call for help. If he does either of those things, kill him. If he doesn't, leave him alone."

Wolfe winced as Cereboo gave a bark.

"How do you know I served in the military?" James asked.

Wolfe was already moving. "The way you carry yourself and how your eyes move. Now shut up. I don't have time for fucking twenty questions."

"Why are you here?" James asked.

"Gotta grab someone. Not one of your people—not the Renfeldt people or the people working at the business, either."

"Billy?" James asked.

Wolfe, interest piqued, turned and faced the cook. "Yeah, how'd you know?"

"The way you carry yourself and how your eyes move," James quipped.

Wolfe snorted back a laugh. "Ha, ha. This is serious, old man."

"I knew you were looking for him because who wouldn't be?" James tilted his head. "Main room is empty. Take the hall leading back from the front door—first one on the left as you exit from the kitchen—and follow it back. He's in the second door on the right. Shouldn't be a problem."

Wolfe turned and faced the man, dropping his pistol to his side. "Why are you helping me?"

James grimaced. "Certain people shouldn't be allowed to roam free."

Wolfe thought back to the working girl who had been traumatized before being murdered, and what he surmised of this guy's background. He was almost positive he could trust him. Almost. "I appreciate it. Gonna leave Cereboo on you—I'll be back soon."

The man gave another single tilt of his head, this time to Wolfe.

Wolfe cautiously walked into the main room. No one was there, just as promised. A few rows of tables, a giant roulette wheel, and a ton of slot machines graced the room—but no people.

Wolfe shook his head. *Fucking slot machines, openly, in a city that banned gambling. I'm surprised every Infernal and Corrupted gifted deck didn't get sent here.*

There was a larger hall heading to the back, and Wolfe followed it. As he got close, he immediately understood why James had been willing to help him—the sound of flesh striking flesh and whimpering was coming from the second door on the right.

Wolfe took his pistol out and pushed the door open. He stepped into a fancy bedroom—Wolfe wondered what architectural insanity had led to that being placed here—with a nice queen bed, plush carpet, and a huge plasma TV on the wall.

He found two people fucking—huge guy on top with a devil on his neck and snake on his shoulder, slapping the tiny woman beneath him with one hand and holding her wrists pinned with his other. The woman yelled even louder as Wolfe busted in, but the man didn't immediately notice the intruder to his private space.

"Get off!" Wolfe shouted, pointing his gun at them, then he almost choked with the black humor of his comment.

The man rolled from the woman, his pock-marked, pig-eyed face glaring at Wolfe from beneath thick, black hair. Wolfe walked close, but not within easy lunging distance, pistol pointed at the man's rather unimpressive dick. The woman let out a second scream and grabbed covers, pulling them over herself. Wolfe sighed.

"Who're you?" the man asked belligerently, but he didn't move except to shake slightly.

"I'm Wolfe," Wolfe replied, pleased to see that the man's eyes went wide with fear. "Now, stay there for one moment."

Wolfe walked sideways until he was near the man's pants, then rummaged through his pockets one-handed. He found a huge wad of cash, thick, over ten thousand if the inner bills were of the same denomination as the outer hundred-dollar bill.

He put the cash on the ground, keeping his Edge trained on Billy the whole time. Then he tossed Billy his pants.

"Put those on. We're going for a ride," Wolfe said.

"I'm not going anywhere," Billy replied.

Wolfe sighed and extended his pistol a few inches toward Billy's now utterly tiny dick. Billy flinched. "Wait!"

"I've got orders to kill you if you don't cooperate," Wolfe said, just making shit up to get Billy to do what he wanted. "So get the pants on and then handcuff your hands behind your back."

"You're just going to kill me later," Billy said, not moving.

Wolfe, still talking out his ass, said, "I might. On the other hand, I might not. Depends on what the boss says."

For some reason, that seemed to make Billy relax, and he smiled a smug smile at Wolfe, showing off a mouth of incredibly gross teeth that ten of ten dentists recommended suicide for. "Got it. You'll get no trouble from me."

Billy pulled his pants up and Wolfe threw him handcuffs, which the murderer willingly put on. Billy stared at Wolfe with that same yellow-toothed, gag-inducing, smug smile the whole time. Like he had some advantage Wolfe didn't know about.

Wolfe resisted the urge to punch the woman-abusing bastard in his gross mouth—he would get his.

Once Billy was done half-dressing himself, Wolfe motioned to the door. "March. We're going out through the exit behind the kitchens. Start shit and you'll die in a pool of your own blood and shit."

Billy managed to glare without losing his smug smile, the first mildly impressive accomplishment that Wolfe had seen from him.

Wolfe turned to the occupant of the bed. "You, lady. Money is yours—I recommend you take it and get out of here, and don't say anything for a few hours if you know what's good for you."

Billy walked out past the girl, who didn't move from behind the blankets, leering at her. "I'll be back for you, cunt."

"Shut up and walk faster!" Wolfe ground out. He smacked Billy in the back of the head now that he was handcuffed and it wasn't as dangerous to be close to him.

Billy didn't say anything else, just walking out.

They walked past the front room and to the kitchen, where Wolfe found Cereboo, James... and Shel.

"What're you doing here?" Wolfe demanded.

"I got the notification you had pulled your deck. I thought you might be in trouble and came to... um... came to..." Shel trailed off, touching the ends of her fingers together and staring up at Wolfe through her long eyelashes.

Wolfe snorted. "You came to rescue me. I don't need rescuing, Shel."

Shel whispered, "I have a Divine deck... but Mr. Washington explained the situation."

"Mr. Washington?"

James raised his hand, his other now scratching Cereboo's left head, which was panting heavily, the dog's tail wagging.

"Well, I'm fine," Wolfe said, simultaneously irritated, insulted, and touched by Shel's concern. "What I need is a getaway driver. Let's go."

Wolfe was tempted to say something like, "Thanks," to James, but it would probably be better if his help was never acknowledged, so he just gave him a very slight tilt of the head and pushed Billy out the back. He held his pistol close. "Get in the back of the car and make it look casual."

Billy complied, and Wolfe got in the driver's seat, holding his gun on Billy the whole time. "Shel, drive us back to the warehouse, please."

Shel's face might have been carved from stone—sad stone, but still stone—as she got in the driver's seat.

CHAPTER 25

BEELZEBUB, LORD OF LIES

"The Great Game, Rule #29: Infernal is weak to Divine and resists Mortal. It is resisted by Divine."

The warehouse was an actual warehouse—but it never housed goods.

It was a location on the docks that the Grimm family kept for the purpose of interrogating people and making bodies disappear. It was pretty far from anything else, and right out the back was a deep, fast-moving part of the river. A part where, if you dropped bodies with bricks attached to them, the freshwater crabs tended to get to them long before the police did.

The interior of the warehouse was just one chair, a table with cheap torture instruments, a bag of netting and bricks, and a single lightbulb hanging from a central pole.

"Sit," Wolfe commanded.

Billy sat in the chair, still smiling smugly.

"Cuff him to the chair," Wolfe said.

Shel took some handcuffs from him and cuffed Billy's legs, then released his hands and re-cuffed them to the chair's arms.

Billy kept the same expression the whole time. *Boy is acting like he just won the lottery, and not like he's just been captured by his enemies.*

"So, talk to me." Wolfe knelt in front of Billy. "Why kill Heinrich?"

Billy laughed, still strangely at ease. "Good one."

What?

Wolfe pulled his pistol out and smashed the butt down on Billy's hand. He felt parts within the Cobra's fingers crunch, even through his Edge.

Billy screamed. After a moment, he calmed, but tears were running down his eyes. "What the fuck, man? What're you doing? Why'd you hurt me?"

"Answer the question if you don't want to get hurt further."

"What? I followed orders! I was doing what I was told!" Billy now struggled against his bonds.

Shel gave a slight sob and fled from the warehouse, out the front door. *Shit. I'll deal with her in a bit.*

"Told by whom?" Wolfe asked his victim.

"By Nico! Nico told me to do it."

Why is the head enforcer of the Cobras ordering hits on us? Is Nico trying to kill everyone, take over everything himself? He just asked us to help him kill his boss!

"Not Jason Klaus?" Wolfe asked.

Billy chuckled. "No, of course not."

What?

"Of course not?" Wolfe asked. "Why of course not?"

Before Billy could answer, Wolfe's phone rang. He was tempted to ignore it, but he reached down and checked.

Damian Grimm. What the fuck does he want now?

Wolfe stared at the phone for a moment but finally stepped a bit away from Billy in the darkened warehouse and then hit 'accept.' He placed the phone to his ear.

"Wolfe here."

"Wolfe," Damian said, "I heard you captured one of the Cobras."

"Yeah, Billy Jenson. The jackass who murdered your Uncle Heinrich. I got him."

There was a brief pause on the other side in which the receiver was obviously covered, then Damian said, "I need you to let him go."

"What?" Wolfe said, stunned. *Let him go?*

"Yeah. I heard you snatched him from the Lucky Fifty-Two, beat up some of the Reinfeldt family guys. I'm seriously impressed with you as always, but the Renfeldt family—they're pissed, threatening a street war. If we let him go now, it'll be no harm, no foul, and I can smooth everything over."

"None of their people got hurt," Wolfe said through clenched teeth.

There was another pause of silence, then Damian said, "Well, two of their guys got beat up badly, and one has a fractured skull. Besides, you have more important matters to deal with than some low-ranking thug."

'Low-ranking thug'? Wolfe thought, reflecting that he felt behind the curve on everything that was happening. *How is the guy who murdered Heinrich a low-ranking thug?*

"I don't know if I can do that, Damian. I mean, he killed Heinrich."

"Wolfe, c'mon. Punishing a street thug isn't worth getting into a war with one of the other families. Please, be smart about this. Your loyalty to the family has always been extremely high, and you've taken care of us. Don't throw that away now because you're mad about one street thug."

Wolfe frowned. He was loyal to Big Man Grimm because of what Big Man Grimm had done for him, not to the family, per se. And Big Man Grimm had called for the guy's death.

But Damian was right, they couldn't afford a second street war...

Wolfe didn't want to cause problems until he could speak to Big Man Grimm himself, get renewed marching orders. So he just threw Damian a platitude. "I'm always loyal to the Grimm family."

"Good. That's what I want to hear from my best hunting dog. I'm legit sorry you need to release this one back into the wild."

Wolfe rolled his eyes. *Way to really milk the wolf metaphor every single time we talk.*

"What's the other thing you needed to talk to me about?" Wolfe asked.

"Did you drop my sister off at the airport? She never made it to her scheduled pick-up in Europe. I'm worried about her."

"What?" Wolfe asked, his blood running cold.

"Where is she?"

Wolfe blinked. Why would Damian think Wolfe knew where she was? "I have no fucking clue. I dropped her off at the airport, exactly like I said I would. I have no idea why she didn't get on the plane, either."

"I want to know she's safe, Wolfe."

"If I find her, I'll be sure to give her your number," Wolfe quipped. "But I still have no fucking clue where she is—I'll look for her once everything else is done though."

There was a long silence on the other end, but Damian finally managed a, "Fine."

Wolfe waited, but when nothing else came, he asked, "Anything else?"

"Just the two biggest ones—take out Javier tonight, and Jason tomorrow night."

"I'll get it done," Wolfe said. "They're good plans."

"Thank you, Wolfe. Please see that you do," Damian said. "I don't want to nag, but this is the most important thing we're doing. Get that card for me."

Wolfe frowned at his phone. *Getting the product and getting rid of the Cobras leader is more important than the cards.*

"Heard," was all Wolfe responded.

"One more thing," Damian said. "You don't have one of the special cards yourself, right? That's what you told me?"

Wolfe nearly cussed, but managed to get out a semi-casual, "Nope, I don't have one."

"You know the set cards can be on special types, like minions or companions, right?"

Does he know? How could he? "Nope, nothing like that."

There was another long pause.

Finally, Damian spoke again. "Fine. Here's the plan. Let Billy go so I can smooth things over with the Renfeldt family, let me know when you find my sister, go get the product back for us, and start prepping to explode the underground fight ring. Got it?"

"Yeah, I got it, Damian. You don't need to repeat things—I'm not Harry."

"Thank you. Good hunting," Damian said, then hung up.

Wolfe stared at Billy, tapping his foot. Then he pulled his second-to-last cigarette out and lit it up, taking a drag on it, thinking about everything he'd heard. It felt as if Damian was taking over more and more of the business, and for whatever reason, Big Man Grimm seemed distracted and out of the loop both—maybe he was just getting old.

Theoretically, Wolfe should have been happy, but in his heart, it felt off to him.

Damian was quite smart, and seemed to be well connected, but Big Man Grimm believed you had to earn power, and he had a certain amount of honor and restraint to him, even if he also had an Infernal deck. Wolfe didn't feel that from Damian.

Can his cunning and smarts make up for it? Wolfe didn't know.

Still, Big Man Grimm was in charge for the moment, and that was what mattered.

Wolfe dialed his phone.

"Wolfe?" The Big Man's heavy voice came over the phone.

"Yeah, I need some clarification. Clarification on a lot of things, actually."

"What do you need, Wolfe? Did you get the man that killed Heinrich?"

"Actually, yes. That's the first thing I'm calling about. I've got him at the warehouse. I captured him from the Lucky Fifty-Two—you know, the illegal gambling parlor that the Renfeldt run? The one that would barely be more obvious if they put up a neon sign declaring its purpose?"

Big Man Grimm didn't laugh. "Go on."

Everyone's a critic. "Right. Anyway, I busted a couple of their guys up fairly badly, but they were all alive. When I got here, Damian called, said the Renfeldt family is pissed about it as a violation of their territory, and want us to let him go as some sort of apology. My orders were from you, but if this is a serious thing..."

Wolfe trailed off, and Big Man Grimm didn't talk for a bit.

"No. I appreciate that Damian is looking out for us, but we're on our back heel here. We can't afford to show any weakness. You put the guy in the river, I'll take the heat for the call—and I'll talk to Damian, he shouldn't be making these decisions, or talking to the heads of the other families."

Wolfe really appreciated how decisive Big Man Grimm was. "And the Renfeldts?"

"I'll call Ben myself, smooth this over. I don't think he'll be *that* upset by the loss of some two-bit Cobra gangbanger, even if it was in his territory. What else do you need?"

"Some guys for tonight," Wolfe responded.

"What's tonight?" Big Man Grimm asked, surprised.

"The product recovery? Killing Javier the Corpse Bride?"

"I have no idea what you're talking about," Big Man Grimm said. "Explain."

Wolfe gave him a really quick rundown of Damian's plan.

Afterwards, Big Man Grimm was quiet for a while before finally speaking. "My fucking kid. So brilliant—but so disrespectful. I had no idea this was happening. Damian is my probable successor, and I want to give him the chance to spread his wings... but he doesn't run things yet, you understand what I'm saying?"

"I do," Wolfe said. "So... am I attacking the Cobras, then?"

"Of course," Big Man Grimm snarled. "Of course. We're out of product, Wolfe. We can get by on the money for a while, but every two-bit street gang will turn to someone else—most likely the Cobras themselves—unless we remedy that. You go handle this, right now. My son's plan is a good one."

Wolfe glanced back at Billy, who was *still* smiling at him. "Can I get some guys? I mean, it's a guarded facility—I really don't want to attack it alone. Hell, if nothing else, I'll probably need help loading the product."

"Yeah, of course. Sorry, I know you just said that—I'm still a bit shocked that I'm learning about everything now. Take Pete and the Frederick brothers."

"Can I take Derek as well? New guy Derek?"

"Yeah, as long as you trust him. I don't want anyone on this that isn't a hundred percent."

Wolfe thought about all the situations they had been in where Derek could have betrayed them easily. "I trust him."

"Then, like I said, take him. Anything else?"

"Did Miriam ever talk to you?"

"No... why?" Big Man Grimm asked.

"She didn't get on the plane, apparently."

"Son of an Infernal!" Big Man Grimm snarled. "Go, Wolfe. Fuck the river—just put a bullet in the head of Heinrich's killer as fast as you can, then get the product, right fucking now. The second you're done, come meet me at the club. We have a lot to discuss—about my daughter and her whereabouts, my son and his future, and everything else. In the meantime, I'll see what I can find out where she went."

"Yeah, I'll handle it all."

Wolfe hung up and walked back to Billy, looking at him contemplatively. Despite what the Big Man had ordered, Wolfe didn't really want to put a bullet in his head and then clean up the mess. It left a lot more evidence than dropping him into the drink.

Although, between the shootout at Frankie's club, which almost certainly left evidence despite me burning it, and the fight at the pound, I've probably put a ton of ballistics into the world that can connect my pistol to the about twenty murders. Hell, even the impact on the door probably left evidence that would lead back to Big Man Grimm.

I doubt this is really that much worse.

Something had been nagging at Wolfe. "What did you do with Heinrich's cards, after you killed him?"

"What?" Billy asked. "I gave them to Nico, just like he said to do. He was really butt-hurt that I only had nine, wanted to know what the last card was really bad. Took half the bonus back just for missing that one card. Why?"

Something about that didn't sit right with Wolfe, but his instincts were telling him that Billy wasn't lying.

"So, you gonna scare me and pretend to send me to sleep with the fishes now? Or just let me go?" Billy asked.

Wolfe made his decision. "Neither."

Wolfe's pistol rose, and Billy's eyes widened in genuine surprise, as if the situation being real, and him being in actual danger, had never crossed his mind for some reason.

The sound of Wolfe blowing the murdering rapist's brains out echoed through the empty warehouse.

Chapter 26

Sins of the Father

"**The Great Game, Rule #30**: Mortal is weak to Corrupt and Infernal, and Resists Beast. It is resisted by Infernal."

Wolfe pulled on the door handle of his car, and finding it locked, reached in through the busted window and unlocked it. He paused, took a cigarette from his pocket, lit it up, and took a draft.

Then he got into the car.

"You okay?" Shel asked.

Wolfe took another long drag of his cigarette before responding. "Better than Billy."

Shel's eyes widened at Wolfe's black humor, but after a moment, she nodded, her face somber.

Wolfe took out his phone and dialed his favorite clean-up guy.

"Wolfe?" the voice answered.

"Yeah, it's me. Get a cleaning crew out to the warehouse.

Clean up for blood and a body, and make sure you get any bullet casings—things like that. You got it, Rich?"

Rich's voice came through the phone, clearly irritated. "Yeah, I've got it."

"Good," Wolfe said and hung up.

"You killed Billy?" Shel asked.

"You're bright, Shel. What do you think?"

Shel leaned back in the chair. Wolfe picked the phone up and called Peter "Piper"—one of the two guys that had taken over moving the product after Johnny had been killed.

"Wolfe, my good boi, what can I do you for?" came Peter's boyish tone over the phone after a single ring.

"None of your supposed charm right now, Piper—we've got a job to do. A serious job. I need you to get ahold of the new guy, Derek, and the Frederick brothers. Once you've gotten ahold of them, have one of them get the big truck, then have everyone meet me at the Q.T. Mart on 4th and Industrial, got it?"

"Of course, Wolfe. Is that the one near your place?"

Wolfe frowned. He didn't hide where he lived, per se, but he didn't advertise it either. He hadn't had a lot of parties for his fellow enforcers and their little thuglets at his place, so not that many people knew where he lived. It weirded him out a bit that Piper did. "Yeah, it's about two minutes from me. Why?"

"Just making sure I've got the right one. What're we meeting for?"

Wolfe looked over at Shel, whose eyes glistened with unshed tears for some reason. "I'll tell you once we're there. But come strapped."

Wolfe hung up before Piper could respond. He would do what was needed. Piper was also a good boy.

Wolfe turned the car on and pulled out, heading for Main for the quick jump to the meeting spot. Then he half-turned to Shel, keeping his eyes on the road. "What's wrong?"

She exhaled. "I'm sorry, Wolfe, I guess it just caught up with me. Killing Billy... Look, I know he was evil. Really evil. I saw firsthand the wages of his sin, and Mr. Washington told me he was up abusing a girl when you captured him. He deserved to die. But it just takes a toll, you know? I mean, you just murdered someone I cuffed to a chair. Killed them in cold blood."

Wolfe understood—he had only killed a very few people that weren't actively trying to end his life, and each one felt like it took something from him as well.

But Billy... Wolfe shook his head.

Billy had deserved it more than anyone.

"I get it, Shel. But I don't regret Billy. If he had just murdered Heinrich, I guess I would have felt something when I killed him, even if it was necessary. But when he murdered the other girl, when I found him abusing a crying woman... He wasn't human to me anymore. He was just an Escaped Damned with a meat shell. I don't regret his death one bit. I don't even regret how it went down."

"You said that you didn't regret the death of the man you got a murder rap for... the one that Big Man Grimm helped you not go to jail for."

"Yeah. What's your point?"

"Can I ask what happened that got you in trouble, when you were a kid?" Shel asked, tapping her fingers together in a steepled pattern again.

Wolfe briefly lost control of his own mind, involuntarily seeing a flash of brown hair and terrified eyes again.

Wolfe gripped the wheel tight. "We're driving like a bat out of hell to go kill more people—why do you need to know? What does it matter?"

"You've... been a hero to me."

Wolfe was caught so off guard he snorted. "Are you fuckin' with me, Shel? A hero?"

Shel put her hand on his shoulder. "No, truly. You saved my life, not knowing who I was, at risk to yourself from what you said, when we first met. Since then, you've helped me with my goals, gotten me cards, helped me make levels, taken care of me in all ways. Even bought me clothes, and you never take anything in return when I offer. Not even... me. You're the first person who ever did things like that for me. I just wanna know about your origin story. Where you came from, why you are as you are. How you ended up here when you're obviously amazing."

Wolfe shook his head. *Idiot nonsense. I'm hardly amazing, except at fucking a dude up.* Wolfe smiled a shark's smile. *I'm damn good at that though.*

"'Origin story'? Like a freaking hero in a comic book?"

Shel shrugged and took her hand back. "Please."

Wolfe sighed. She *was* gonna be gone soon, hopefully. He was likely to kill the rest of the Cobra leadership in the next thirty-six hours, give or take. So what harm did telling her do? "I killed my father."

Shel gasped. "Why?"

"You said your father was physically abusive, right?" Wolfe asked.

Shel nodded. "Sometimes, yeah. He's not... the worst, I guess. But he beat us a lot for very little, and he's a drunk who wastes most of his money on booze. Was your dad like that?"

Wolfe was gripping the wheel and accelerating even harder. "Worse. He... He started to rape my sister when we were young. I found out later. The fucker had always beaten my mother, constantly, for the slightest thing. 'To keep her in her place' was his usual reason. He had a lot of really fucked-up notions about being a man. But he would fly off the handle for anything— because Mom had backtalked, for a bad dinner, you name it. But the fucker had never hit us."

"Never?" Shel asked.

"Well, not till later. When I confronted him and tried to stop him from raping Mel, I learned his forbearance hadn't been out of love or anything. The bastard beat me to within an inch of my life."

"I'm so sorry," Shel said, her eyes watering. "Didn't anyone do anything?"

Wolfe winced, remembering the week spent in the hospital afterward. "At first, he was taken to jail—for one night. After that, the investigation went away. All the cops were apparently on the take. They said I was a liar. Various judges made rulings that kept everything out of court. Records were even falsified."

"That must have been hard," Shel said softly.

Wolfe's grip on the steering wheel was white-knuckled. "Yeah, him being who he was, and me having done the supposed right thing, then having the whole world think I was a liar... it was hard. But the bastard was friends with everyone, including people in our current business. *Lots* of people in our business— he was a lawyer making over a million a year working for the three big crime families. More importantly, he knew about *all* the skeletons in three families' closets. I learned that that kind of pull can make problems go away—and I learned that *I* was a problem. Saving two kids wasn't worth upsetting my dad."

Shel was just watching Wolfe as he drove and talked, saying nothing else. Wolfe wished he had left Cereboo out, but he didn't want his companion card being seen by any deckbearers.

He kept talking as he drove through town, heading into worse and worse areas. "So, afterward, I spent a lot of time working out and in fighting gyms. I learned my lesson the hard way: People don't give a shit when you're powerless. So I did my best to get power."

"By being good at violence?" Shel asked.

"All power comes down to violence, if you dig far enough," Wolfe said. "If you don't think so, try not paying your taxes someday, then try resisting being sent to jail for not paying said taxes. Even the Grimm family pays their damned taxes."

"Hmm..."

Wolfe continued. "Dad, evil fucker that he was, stopped... hiding things from me after that. Tried to *teach* me, about how to be a man, his kind of man. To take what I wanted. He beat Mom and Mel in front of me and wasn't... shy... about his abuse of either of them. He reveled in the fact we all witnessed it, knew it, and were helpless before him."

In his mind's eye Wolfe again saw his sister, brown hair, hazel eyes, cowering in terror from their father. The failure that haunted him. He knew it was the reason he never, ever felt sympathy for killing scum like Billy. They deserved to be sent to the Infernal realms.

Silent tears, of sympathy Wolfe supposed, started running down Shel's face.

"But Dad was wrong about one thing—*I wasn't helpless*," Wolfe said, a savage satisfaction in his words. "One day, a year later, after all the working out and training, I felt ready. When he pushed Mel down, I grabbed him. We ended up in a fight, but this time, I won. But I won... too much. I killed him when I kicked him in the head after I had knocked the asshole to the ground. I'll never forget it, the rapist fucker down, on his hands and knees, staring at me with hatred and still struggling to get to his feet. I wanted him to stay down, and he did."

"I'm so, so sorry," Shel said, reaching out and putting her hand on his shoulder again. "That must have been so hard."

"Whatever," Wolfe said, suddenly tired of the conversation. "It was twenty years ago. I've moved on—and speaking of, we're nearly there, and have real shit to deal with."

CHAPTER 27

SIX DARK DISCIPLES

"The Great Game, Rule #34: Undead is weak to Life and immune to Death."

Wolfe pulled into the Q.T. Mart. There were two cars in the parking lot, but he didn't recognize either one. He suspected no one else had shown up yet.

He parked and got out of his car, pulling a cigarette out and lighting it up, taking a deep drag on it, his hand shaking slightly with rage.

Shel got out behind him. Before she could ask anything else, however, a scion—a box car—with a stylized picture of the pied piper pulled into the parking lot.

Wolfe snorted with laughter, his mood almost instantly better as he saw the ridiculous vehicle.

As the boyishly good-looking man driving got out of the car, Wolfe waved. "Hey, Piper, good to see you. The others coming?"

The man walked over, grinning. Piper always seemed happy,

and it was infectious. Wolfe didn't know why the loon had joined their life, or the Grimm family specifically, but he had. A lot of the time Wolfe found his happy-go-lucky attitude—and his ridiculous blonde ponytail—irritating. Wolfe figured Piper's lax attitude and distinct appearance would get him caught by the police or DEA someday. At the moment, however, he was glad for the lift to his spirits.

"Yeah, they'll be here in two shakes of a tail," Piper said. "So, what's this crazy project you've got us on?"

"We're going to be doing your job, Piper—getting product."

Piper raised an eyebrow. "From where?"

"From the Cobras, actually. Damian managed to locate the place they took all the stuff they stole from us when they killed Johnny."

"Clever girl," Piper said, drawing it out a touch.

He's not even old enough to have seen that in theatres, how does he know the reference? Wolfe wondered. "Yeah, Damian's a bright kid. He has a couple plots going that'll put us ahead of the Cobras. But he *is* a fat hobbit, so he needs us orcs to do the grunt work."

Piper laughed. "And I bet he wants all the cards we get."

"Just the important ones," Wolfe responded.

Piper nodded. "That's in character."

"Also, don't repeat any of that," Wolfe said. "It's beginning to look pretty heavily like Damian's going to be the boss in a decade or so... and he's a bit prickly."

"You won't be the same if you start keeping your opinions to yourself," Piper said. "I'll miss the old Wolfe." He wiped a fake tear from his eye.

Shel giggled at his display, her own melancholy dissolving in the face of Piper's antics.

"Ass."

Before the bantering could continue, another car—a large Ford F-150 truck—pulled into the parking lot.

The Frederick brothers got out, and the older one, cradling a shotgun against his broad chest, called out, "Hey, Wolfe."

Wolfe nodded respectfully at them. "Liam, Larry, good to see you."

The Frederick brothers nodded in unison. Each was about two inches shy of six feet, and nearly as wide. But it wasn't fat that gave them width, like it would be with most Americans. They were almost solid muscle, with squat legs and biceps almost as large as their thighs. Each had been a mechanic when they were younger, before the recession had driven them into the family—and they had built and rebuilt cars with old-fashioned machinery, relying on their raw strength for much of the work.

They were basically built like tall dwarves, and Wolfe wouldn't have wanted to try hand-to-hand combat with either. Even if he won, they certainly wouldn't go down easy.

Both also managed to be bald with magnificent beards they had put large rings in, as if they had consciously decided to play up their dwarven image.

The contrast between them and the tall, blonde-ponytailed, thin pretty-boy Piper could not have been more pronounced.

And Piper couldn't resist pointing it out. "We look like a discount Lord of the Rings fellowship."

"So, who we killin'?" Liam asked, utterly ignoring Piper.

Wolfe quietly chuckled. Straight to the point as always, the Frederick brothers never had patience for anyone's antics. "Javier Garcia."

Larry whistled, and Liam asked, "The ol' Groom of the Dead himself, huh? 'Bout time we did some damage to the Cobras. They need to learn respect for the family."

A massive truck, a sixteen-wheeler, pulled into the parking lot. From the window, Derek waved to the group, his smile almost pure white in his umber face.

Wolfe's brief good humor faded, even though he was happy to see Derek. The guy had demonstrated very high levels of competence, and Wolfe wasn't surprised he was the one Piper had sent to get the truck.

But it was time.

"So this is the place, huh?" Piper asked as the six of them stared across the street at a huge warehouse from the side of the truck they had parked.

Wolfe was nervous—News Street was entirely empty of buildings except for a large, abandoned cannery to the side of the warehouse. Four cars and a large gray van were in the parking lot of the warehouse.

What it told Wolfe was that there were between five and ten guys inside the warehouse that they would need to deal with... and that those guys would likely know they were coming if they had even semi-competent people on the inside, since no one would ever park here for any reason not related to the warehouse and its illicit purpose. He could see a thin strip of windows around the top of the warehouse, about twenty feet from the ground—and bet someone was watching them in turn from those very windows.

"We're not going to get surprise on anyone this time," Wolfe said. "Shel, pull your deck and get Sorenia out. Javier has to know we're coming, we might as well get the advantage of having our companions."

"I wondered why you brought the random hot chick," Piper said as Shel touched her heart and then pulled her cards out. "But, since you're the Wolfe, I assumed you knew what you were doing."

Wolfe pulled his own deck, ignoring both Piper and the notification about a deckbearer pulling a deck. He got four cards in his 'main draw' this time thanks to his recent spend of leveling pips, but ignored them to pull Cereboo.

His companion appeared with a series of happy woofs. Wolfe winced at the noise despite his firm belief that they had already been spotted.

Sorenia appeared next to them as well, her light killing any remaining pretense at stealth.

"A vision of heaven," Piper said, miming taking an arrow to the heart.

"Knock it off, ya goof, that's an angel!" Liam said.

Wolfe forestalled any further issues. "You guys ready?"

Derek held up a set of heavy-duty bolt cutters. "Ready." Everyone else nodded.

"Alright," Wolfe said. "Shel, do you have your mantle?"

She nodded and touched a card. The golden light flowed over her and she sprouted her third eye.

Wolfe glanced at his deck, noting that even though he had drawn a third of his deck he still didn't have his mantle. *Of course.*

He turned to his team. "Run fast, move to the sides, and try not to let yourself be a target. I seriously doubt they'll start firing on us before we get to the warehouse itself from those thin windows, but it's not worth risking dying on that bet."

The six of them ran across the street, jinking at random moments with spastic movement. They ran over the tiny strip of grass by the street, through the parking lot, and hit the warehouse walls at the edge of the huge loading door, which was locked with a large padlock.

Derek hefted the bolt cutters and raised an eyebrow.

Wolfe stared at the loading door. Every instinct in his body screamed that they would hit a wall of bullets fired from prepared positions as soon as they opened that door.

He swiped his cards, pushing four of his remaining ten into

view, and smiled to see his mantle. He touched it and the red energy flowed across him, increasing his stats—and making him 'Infernal,' which lowered the damage from bullets.

But his eyes wandered down to the slight claws the new form had given him, then up to the thin windows in the top of the warehouse wall, fifteen feet above him.

I wonder...

Wolfe jumped up and hooked his claws into the warehouse wall, gripping as hard as he could, and pulled himself up, blessing all his mornings spent working out at home. He reached the top and rapidly poked his head up.

The inside of the warehouse was dimly lit by overhead lights, and to Wolfe's dark-adjusted eyes, it was plenty to see that there were multiple pallets and forklifts arranged to give ten guys cover, all of whom were facing the door, guns held at their sides, or in one case, pointed directly at the door.

But worst of all, Javier already had his deck out—and a mantle on. He appeared to be a 'Day of the Dead' skeleton, with fancy designs across his body. He stood on a pile of pallets like he had no concern in the world. Four corpses, all zombie women in white dresses, were near him.

Yeah, if we go through there in a normal manner, we're fucked. Probably fucked regardless.

Also, how come I didn't get a notification of his deck being pulled?

Wolfe dropped to the floor. "They're burrowed in there like this was the zombie apocalypse, ironically. Javier already has his deck out. If we go through that door, we're all as good as dead. We'll be running into a defensive position while outnumbered."

"So... come back a different day?" Piper asked, a quavering smile on his face.

Wolfe shook his head. "If they know we're here, they know we know—they'll move the stuff. It has to be now, and it has to be fast—they've most likely summoned backup."

Wolfe's eyes roamed around the parking lot, then fell to his own bulging wallet, barely visible in his pocket.

"Alright, I have a plan, and it's gonna make one of you fuckers very rich…"

CHAPTER 28

THE DEAD RISE

"The Great Game, Rule #37: Fire is weak to Ice. It is resisted by Golem."

W olfe waited at the front cargo-loading door, occasionally kicking at the sheet metal and rattling it, hoping that the people inside would stay focused on him and his team. With him waited Larry with the shotgun, Piper with the bolt cutters, and Shel, her golden cards floating in front of her.

Wolfe kept his eyes to the windows, so that if someone came to see what they were doing he could discourage peeking out. He let out a black chuckle. *This would be insanely boring if it wasn't liable to result in dead people at any second.*

He heard muttered talking from inside, and quietly backed away from his original spot. He flipped his cards and put his mantle back on for the second time, and Shel did the same.

Finally, the sound he had been waiting almost ten minutes for came. In the parking lot, an engine roared to life. Wolfe stepped back away from the wall, keeping his eyes on the window above.

Sure enough, a head poked up into the window above them.

"Son of an Infernal!" Wolfe snarled as his shot missed, blowing the glass out of the window but killing nothing. The head ducked back down, however, so Wolfe supposed he had accomplished the main purpose of his attack.

The screeching of tires on pavement filled the night, and Wolfe turned. The van was flying across the parking lot, accelerating as it came toward the left side of the warehouse.

Wolfe didn't have a good eye for estimating speed, but he would have bet it was over sixty miles an hour when it passed the angle he could see it at.

"Now!" Wolfe said to Piper.

A fraction of a second later, a resounding crash came from the side of the warehouse. A fraction of a second after that, Piper cut the padlock.

Gunfire sounded, and Wolfe took the opportunity to push the loading door open slightly.

He stuck his head in. All of the Cobra thugs he had seen from the window were now facing the van—which had crashed through the wall. They were firing their guns over and over at it.

Wolfe took a breath, stepped into the warehouse, and shot the guy closest to him. The red-haze-covered bullet exploded through the man, and Wolfe noted that basic humans no longer gave him any experience.

Before anyone could react, Wolfe ran as fast as he could toward the nearest cover: a pallet that was about forty-feet from the door. Bullets snapped around him for the last few feet and he leapt, crashing to the ground and rolling to his feet behind the cover. Wolfe pointed carefully through the pallet and fired a single bullet at one of the remaining Cobra thugs.

It pinged off the pallet *that* guy was hiding behind, and Wolfe dropped as more bullets headed his way, just in case they got a lucky shot that passed unimpeded between the boards of Wolfe's pallet. One or two of the bullets blew through the wood, and Wolfe hissed as one hit, stinging and leaving a welt. But between the wood, Wolfe's mantle, and his new Infernal resistance to Mortal sources of damage, the bullet had lost most of its stopping power.

But it reminded him he wasn't exactly safe behind his impromptu barricade.

Cereboo woofed excitedly and charged in roughly thirty seconds after Wolfe had, as planned—and then Sorenia joined the fight, firing off a beam of light that blasted the edge of a pallet about as effectively as a gun would have.

We're gonna do it! Wolfe exulted as Larry leaned around the corner and fired his gun, and Cereboo took a couple hits from bullets before leaping over a forklift and rushing past to drive a Corpse Bride to the ground.

Then the remaining three corpse brides opened their mouths, and each sang a crooning melody of loss.

Wolfe's head felt as if it was going to explode, and blood leaked from his nose.

All four of the Corpse Brides did damage—each as a mere three-point magical attack. But Wolfe's magic defense, unlike his physical defense, was barely enhanced—it was an eight. The Corpse Brides did nine damage. That meant that most 'attacks' each did a point of damage to Wolfe net. Also to his team, since he could see Larry wincing, blood running from his ear.

Ice flowed through Wolfe's veins. "Fuck me, they'll kill me in less than three minutes if I just sit here!"

Wolfe leapt up, running forward. He lost six health as he ran into a storm of lead, but his ridiculous physical defense kept him going. He leapt the barricade himself while flipping his deck, shot one of Javier's men who blew apart, and threw down the Fireborn Hellhound all in less than ten seconds.

"Everyone, go now!" Wolfe screamed. He hadn't expected

the magical AOE, and his plan was in shambles—but a full-out assault, now that he and his two doggos were in the very center of their enemies, might salvage it.

Javier looked down at Wolfe, and the old man steepled his fingers and stared at Wolfe with faux sad eyes. "You don't have the numbers, friend. If you surrender now—"

A notification popped into Wolfe's sight. *A deckbearer has pulled their deck near you.*

"Don't I?" Wolfe quipped, turning and firing at another thug, blowing him near in half with his mantle-enhanced bullets.

Don't zombies take bonus damage from fire?

"Use your magical attacks, doggos!" Wolfe screamed, then grimaced because he doubted they needed yelling to follow his orders—he was just letting the enemies know what he planned.

Shel ran into the room, her eyes wide. She tossed a Rookie EMT down, and Wolfe's health ticked up, his head clearing and the pain fading a bit.

Cereboo pulled back and breathed fire on his zombie chew toy, which was finished by the attack. The Fireborn Hellhound let loose an impressive gout of flame that nearly disintegrated his target.

At the same time, a tiny Tormentor Imp flew over and poked Javier.

"What the fuck!" Javier yelled, his faux calm gone in an instant. "What did you do?"

Wolfe stumbled and fell as two bullets hit him in the leg, feeling more like getting kicked really hard than shot, and returned fire, putting another Cobra permanently out of commission. From the floor, however, he couldn't resist a bit of sarcasm. "We just shut you down for a full minute, asshole. How about *you* surrender now?"

Liam and Derek—who had three red cards floating in front of his chest—charged into the warehouse through the hole the van had made. The second change to the direction the attacks were coming managed to throw the Cobras for a loop, and another one was killed. Three ran toward the back of the warehouse.

Javier snarled and touched another card. A flash of purple came from him and Wolfe saw stars. He found himself on the ground retching, blood pouring from his nose, ears, and eyes.

Eight health of thirty remaining, Wolfe saw on the notification. The Imp had shut down Javier's Undead cards, but not his use of Psychic ones. Wolfe prayed to whatever being gave a fuck about him that Javier didn't have a similar second card.

Wolfe held his pistol out, jumped to his feet, and rushed the Cobra lieutenant, pulling the trigger repetitively until he clicked on empty. Javier jerked with each shot, blood spewing from his wounds, and collapsed back off the pile of pallets he had been grand-standing from.

Three more health poured into Wolfe from a second Rookie EMT, and he thanked whatever gods were listening for the small favors. Cereboo and the Fireborn Hellhound finished off the last two Corpse Brides with fire.

Wolfe rushed around the pallet to find Javier with blood pouring from him, swiping his cards while he was on hands and knees.

A soccer kick to the head knocked Javier out of consciousness, as well as a few of his teeth out of his head.

Wolfe glanced around. The last two Cobra thugs that hadn't run had their hands up.

"Now what?" Wolfe wondered. Somehow, he hadn't ended up with normal prisoners before in this street war, and he wasn't actually sure what to do with them.

Shel walked over, touching him gently. "By the Divine, Wolfe. For someone that wins every fight they get in, you sure get hurt *a lot*."

Derek laughed, and Wolfe turned, surprised, to see him

coming around the corner. Derek's face was flushed—impressive on a guy with his skin color—in his excitement.

Wolfe smiled. "Good to be a deckbearer, huh?"

"Shit yeah, man. I can't believe you were sitting on a spare deck—a fully themed one, even. And I can't believe you just gave it to me. Damn. It's been pretty fucking rough, being in the Grimm family these last couple weeks. But this makes everything worthwhile and then some."

There was a pause in which Wolfe couldn't help but smile at Derek's enthusiasm, even if Wolfe had given away what was probably a cool half million dollars' worth of cards. *I'll just claim Javier's cards as my 'share' of the booty to make up for it. I don't think anyone will argue the point.*

"I'm a deckbearer," Derek whispered again, smiling.

"Well, keep it in your pants," Wolfe quipped. "Point one, we've got work to do. A lot of work, and quickly. Point two, it's an imp deck."

Shel put her hand on Derek's shoulder. "Congratulations."

Derek turned to face Wolfe and held his hand out. "I owe you, man. Whatever you might need, I owe you."

Wolfe turned away and growled. "In your pants, I said. C'mon, let's go get the brothers and Piper—we've got work to do."

Wolfe reached down, grabbed the unconscious Javier, and dragged him back around the pile of pallets. He felt briefly guilty, as Javier looked less like an undead god and more like the fifty-year-old man he was now that his mantle was gone. On the other hand, he had certainly been willing to kill Wolfe, Shel, and the others.

Wolfe found Liam standing guard over the Cobra thugs, tears streaming down his face.

A sinking feeling filled Wolfe's stomach. "Larry?"

Liam shook his head, and a sob tore awkwardly from his body, like he had never made the sound before.

Wolfe shook his head. *Fuck. Fuck fuck fuck.*

"I'm sorry, man," Wolfe said awkwardly.

"Should never have gotten into the business," Liam said. "Larry said it was a bad idea, no matter how bad our shop was underwater. I told him it'd be okay. We've been doing this for years—I thought he was wrong. Now..."

Liam gave another wracking sob. "Sorry, Wolfe. I've got this. I can handle business."

Wolfe brusquely nodded. It wasn't like they hadn't lost people before, but somehow, he had never been around anyone that lost a sibling before this very moment.

Shel ran up and threw her arms around Liam, who stood, shocked, for a moment before he gathered her into his bulk, nearly causing her to disappear, and burst into sobs.

Wolfe pulled his pistol and faced it vaguely in the direction of the Cobra thugs. *Someone has to keep their eye on the ball.* "Nobody get any stupid ideas during this touching personal moment."

The thugs, who hadn't been moving much, stilled completely.

"Where's Piper?" Derek asked.

Wolfe glanced around. "Piper!"

No one answered. Wolfe couldn't even remember him joining the fight, after he had cut the bolts from the door.

"Derek, keep an eye on things here."

Wolfe walked outside and glanced around. No Piper. Everything else was as they'd left it. *What the fuck?*

CHAPTER 29

ASK THE WIND

"The Great Game, Rule #40: Light resists Shadow."

Wolfe walked back inside again and pointed his pistol at the five Cobra thugs that had surrendered sooner or later. "Alright, get off the floor. Since my team is dead, missing, or suffering through a personal crisis, you guys are loaders. Derek, search them, take all their guns and phones, then go get the truck and back it up to the loading door. Odds are they called backup and we have very limited time."

"It's already been over ten minutes, do you think we're gonna get ambushed?" Derek asked.

"Don't know, but we've got little choice—we need to get the product to Big Man Grimm. That isn't an optional assignment."

"What're we doing about Piper?" Liam asked, sniffling.

Wolfe turned to see that he had let go of Shel and stopped weeping—mostly. "No idea. Keep a gun on these jackasses. I need to talk to Javier."

Wolfe walked over to Javier and gently slapped him. Shel

raised an eyebrow at him, but Wolfe wasn't sure what she was trying to communicate.

After a moment, Javier groaned and rolled over. Wolfe put a pistol in his face. "If you pull your deck, I'm gonna re*dec*orate in brain."

Shel groaned.

Javier coughed, and Wolfe saw his mouth bulge around his missing teeth, almost certainly from him running his tongue over the holes.

"Wha... what happened?" he asked.

Wolfe had a vague sense of déjà vu to his meeting with Shel two days okay. "What do you remember last?"

"I was waiting for you to bust into the—"

"Right, so blah blah, long story, I did and we kicked your ass —and I specifically kicked you in your face, hard. Which is why you're missing teeth and memories. Now I'm the one asking questions."

Javier grimaced and looked up at Wolfe. "Everyone always said you were a hit at all the parties. I can see why—your rapier wit."

Wolfe could appreciate the guy joking in the face of disaster, and his respect for him went up. But Wolfe had business to take care of.

"Kid joined the Cobras a few months back, name of Kevin..." Wolfe snapped his fingers. "Kevin Lyons. He turned up dead a week ago. I need to know who killed him and why."

"That's your question?" Javier asked, his eyes wide. "Not how we... I mean... something else?"

"You're just the worst at being interrogated, aren't you?" Wolfe asked with a laugh, his opinion of Javier plummeting back into the pit again. "Whichever god picked you to be a deckbearer was asleep at the cosmic wheel."

Javier glared at him.

Wolfe rolled his eyes. "Just answer my question, numb nuts."

"That's a new one," Shel muttered, and Wolfe gave her a quick glare. She looked away and twisted her finger in her hair.

"I know the kid—and I have no idea who killed him, or how. Best guess is overdose, but it was... weird. No visible marks, nothing we could see... but no one reported him overdosing, no one remembers even being with him when he took drugs in the last couple days. Last time anyone saw him, he was with Nico—"

"He was with Nico?" Shel butted in.

Javier glanced at her. "Who's the chick?"

Wolfe grimaced. "If you can't get the instruction to 'just answer questions' down, I'm gonna start hitting you."

Javier transferred his glare back to Wolfe but started talking again. "Yeah, he was the last person who was seen with Kevin. But that was *days* before the kid disappeared, and Nico said he left the same day. Besides, Nico was the one who hired the kid."

Wolfe changed tactics. "Alright, so tell me how you guys knew about the drugs now."

Javier scowled, and a bit of blood dribbled from the side of his mouth. He wiped it away with his hand, slowly. "Nico has an inside source—someone that knew about the drug movements. I don't know who it is, but he knew about this shipment, and he knew about the last one."

Wolfe turned and stared at the door.

"Piper?" Shel asked.

Wolfe scowled. Piper was missing, now, and he had been one of the guys working directly under Johnny—one of the few people that knew when and where the drugs were coming in.

"Why would he betray us, though?" Wolfe asked, honestly confused. Piper never had beef with anyone that Wolfe knew about.

"Money?" Shel asked. "A sick family member?"

"Maybe..."

"We're almost loaded!" Derek called.

And I'm almost surprised the Cobras haven't shown up yet.

287

I've got to wrap this up. "Alright, Javier, you've got to drop your deck and give up being a deckbearer. And be *really* careful with anything you say even remotely close to 'over my dead body.'"

Javier scowled at him but didn't move.

Wolfe raised his pistol and put it to Javier's temple. "You know who Billy Jenson is, Javier?"

Javier nodded.

Wolfe tried to make himself sound as bored as possible. "It was about four hours ago that I ended his life, seconds after we were in this exact position, my Edge, here, held to his head and him not believing me. Which is weird, given my reputation. Why *wouldn't* someone believe I'd kill a person? Big Man Grimm always says that past patterns predict future results. Anyway, enough of my random musings. Last chance."

Javier's teeth clenched so hard Wolfe was honestly surprised he didn't lose another one, and the Cobra lieutenant bit out, "I hope you burn in Gehenna!"

But his deck appeared—fifteen cards, all with gray or purple energy surrounding them.

"Good choice," Wolfe said, picking the cards up.

He turned to Liam and Derek. "Get all their phones, then let's go."

"You already had me do that," Derek said, holding up five phones.

"Good on past me," Wolfe quipped, not remembering giving that order.

"You're not going to kill the Cobras?" Liam asked. "One of them might have killed Larry!"

Wolfe sighed. He understood, he truly did. But if they killed every punk that dropped his gun, no one would drop their guns when fighting them ever again. But this wasn't the moment to be explaining that. "Look, it's needful. Plus, half their friends are dead and they lost a deckbearer. It has to be enough."

For a wonder, Liam didn't fly off the handle. A moment

later, he nodded. "Yeah, they lost far more than us. It sucks, but I guess it's not fair to just kill the rest of them."

He hesitated, then said, "Sucks though." A few more tears fell down his face.

"That it does," Wolfe said.

"So, where are we heading to?" Liam asked, wiping at his face and getting snot in his thick arm hair.

"I'll tell you once we're outside," Wolfe said with a nod to Javier.

Liam nodded again. "Right, of course. Sorry, I'm not at my best."

The four remaining members of the Grimm crime family—Wolfe, Shel, Derek, and Liam—met outside, and the second they were there, Wolfe pointed to Derek. "I need you to drive us back to the Q.T. Mart and then take the drugs to one of the hidden locations."

"Which one?" Derek asked. "I don't know most of them."

Wolfe started to answer, then stopped. "I... don't know," he said, slowly. "If Piper really has betrayed us, he knows all the locations... and if he hasn't, but got nabbed, somehow, during the fight, they might get the information from him anyway." *Although when would someone have had the chance to—and not shoot us from behind?*

"What about the warehouse?" Shel asked, suddenly.

"He knows about the warehouse," Wolfe said.

Shel leaned forward, her green eyes intense. "But does he know you would put the drugs there? Wouldn't it be one of the last places he searched?"

Wolfe scratched at his chest, at the intersection of the old scar Nico had given him and the new one he had gotten from the werewolf. "That... isn't the worst idea. And we only need to store it for a day or so before we can move it again. I just need to talk to Big Man Grimm tonight, and he can figure it out as soon as he wants."

Wolfe nodded to Shel and snapped his fingers. "We'll do it. Thanks. Derek, Liam, get the truck and take it to the warehouse. *The* warehouse, know what I mean."

"I know what you're talking about, Wolfe," Liam replied. "We can handle it. Can I ask a favor, though?"

Wolfe nodded.

"Can you help me put my brother in the truck, so I can take his body home?"

This is up there with cleaning out rats in the list of 'activities I did today to remind me I'm really living the high life.'

But Wolfe couldn't say that to someone who had made the ultimate sacrifice for the family—he deserved better. For that matter, so did Larry himself. "Of course, Liam. It would be my honor."

CHAPTER 30

DARK DISCUSSION

"The Great Game, Rule #43: Psychic has no effect on Elemental and Golem."

"Where are we going?" Shel asked, shivering as the night air blew through Wolfe's car thanks to the two missing windows. Her sexy blouse might be cute, but it wasn't doing much to keep the cold from her now that day had turned to night.

Wolfe flipped the heater on. "To see Big Man Grimm at the Ekron Eternal. He called me while I was in the warehouse with Billy, after you left, and asked me to come talk to him."

Shel nodded slowly. "We... didn't learn much about who killed Kevin, did we?"

"Do you think Javier did it?" Wolfe asked, fishing in his pocket for a cigarette.

"Those will kill you, you know," Shel said.

"Not likely," Wolfe replied, pulling the cigarette out and fumbling to light it while he drove. It wasn't normally a problem, but he was pretty damn beat up, and his body wasn't quite responding perfectly. He pulled up his status chart, briefly, and saw that he had penalties to his attack and defense from his wounds now.

He hurt as well.

"Well, statistically, smoking—" Shel began.

"I know the risks of smoking, Shel. But it mostly kills you late in life and makes the later parts miserable. I'm not likely to live that long. And nicotine calms me, stops me from being too twitchy."

Shel's eyebrows knitted as she gazed into his eyes.

"Don't feel sorry for me, woman. I'm a big boy and made my choices. Worry about yourself."

"I want to worry about you," Shel said, echoing her statements from the day prior.

Wolfe snorted irritably and rubbed his own arms where the wind was blowing across him. *It is getting cold out.*

"I don't think Javier did it," Shel said, returning to the earlier point.

"Well, there you are."

Shel appeared nervous, twisting her finger in her hair and biting her lip. But she didn't say anything else.

The silence was awkward, and Wolfe reached over and turned the radio on as well.

An announcer was talking. "—died in the new dungeon that appeared in the mall food court today. He took with him all twenty cards that had been in his family for four generations. This left the sprawling and mostly destitute Vanderbilt family, once famous, with no deckbearers among Cornelius Vanderbilt's over three hundred great-grandchildren."

"That's sad, that they lost their family's cards along with... whomever that was," Shel volunteered. To fill the silence, Wolfe bet.

But he snorted. "Even with most of the families passing down decks to their kids, sooner or later, if you're stupid enough, it'll catch up with you. I mean, it's hard to lose cards. The Great Game Rule #5: Cards will vanish from the world ONLY if the deckbearer is killed by a free-roaming monster, a dungeon, or their own hand. Any other way and they all drop, ready for someone else to pick up."

"Deckbearers commit suicide?" Shel asked.

"Yeah." Wolfe didn't say anything else, just leaning back in his chair, his mind drifting into more general thoughts about the situation and his life as he near autonomously drove the familiar route to the Ekron Eternal.

Once upon a time, I thought about it. A lot, as a teenager. When my father was abusing us and when I was in juvie... but the answer is to get strong and try to make the world the way you want it to be, not leave it.

Wolfe was vaguely aware of Shel staring at him with pity-filled eyes again, but he stayed with his own thoughts.

How much have I really made my world what I want, though? I'm a deckbearer, I've got like a million dollars in spare cards now —probably closer to millions with Javier's cards. I've dealt the Cobras some really bad blows, and I'm going to be cutting their head off. Soon, I'll finish my good deed, and then I can focus on working on my deck and minor shit for the Grimm family, live the easy life.

But do I want that? Especially since I'll have to give Damian Cereboo for that to happen?

He sighed. *I wish Miriam was more willing to take over, or that Big Man Grimm were a lot younger.*

But even then, Wolfe couldn't deny a certain restlessness. A discontentment with his situation... he had only felt truly alive lately when he was hunting the Cobras and taking care of Shel, and the thought of returning to his old life rankled.

"Are you okay?" Shel asked, cutting into Wolfe's thoughts.

They were almost there, and Wolfe sighed. "Doesn't matter if I am or I ain't, we've got shit to do."

"O-Okay," Shel said.

After a few seconds, Wolfe pulled up to the front of Big Man Grimm's club. They exited the car at the same time. He had been there countless times, once or twice a week for nearly twenty years. He still glanced at the front. It was lit up like a neon Christmas tree, and a giant sign in garish, crimson neon on the front read, "Ekron Eternal."

Wolfe had heard—from about seventy people who thought they were smart and didn't realize they were just regurgitating the fundamental lore for the Grimm family—that Ekron was the philistine city first associated with the cards Beelzebub dropped.

He was honestly surprised some religious fanatic hadn't taken the club out yet. Few things advertised their Infernal association quite so openly as Big Man Grimm's club. And Wolfe couldn't even claim he wouldn't have a lot of sympathy for the hypothetical religious dudes' position.

The two girls dancing in their underwear in cages as Wolfe entered probably didn't help the general vibe, either.

Wolfe nodded to the guard at the front—Josh Devonshire, another enforcer—and passed him two hundred cash as he passed the door. Then he handed his keys over. "Have someone take my car to the garage, please."

Josh's eyes widened at the state of Wolfe's clothes—which had enough blood on them to feed a vampire family for a month. But he wisely kept his mouth shut, nodded, and touched a mic on his shirt, speaking into it quietly.

Wolfe knew that the real reason the club existed was to launder money. Most of the cash that the Grimm family made was passed to its associates, who went and bought ridiculously overpriced drinks and various other things from the club. And that didn't even count the hundred-dollar cover charge to get in for men and not-hot-enough women. Ekron Eternal was the funnel through which the millions of dollars a year made it into the Grimm's pockets safely every year—for almost twenty-five years now. The huge lines and massive earnings also made the club itself appear popular, and Wolfe wouldn't be surprised if he learned that a lot of money was made legally as well.

Hell, the Grimm family even paid their fucking taxes religiously. They weren't going out like that one Prohibition-era gangster had.

Wolfe entered the dance floor—the same one that he had been at for the Drop Night party. Now, as then, it was filled with statues of demons and flies, as well as fog and half-naked dancers. Wolfe wove his way through the club to the table at the back, Shel following him half a step behind.

Harry and Dan were both here, in new suits that were matching navy blue for some reason, but otherwise, they appeared as they always did. They nodded to Wolfe as he moved past them and slipped into Big Man Grimm's personal booth. But when Shel tried to follow, Harry held his hand in front of her and shook his head *no*.

Wolfe glanced at her, then nodded slightly. She obviously interpreted his gesture as one to accept the denial and took a step back. But she stood watching him as he turned back to the table.

The Big Man himself was the only person in the booth, except for the same tiny, East Asian girl Wolfe had seen here on Drop Night. Big Man Grimm was drinking from a glass that smoked, and he had dilated pupils. Every time the glass dipped low, the girl refilled it.

Joy. He's been using the product.

It was extremely rare for Big Man Grimm to use their product, but occasionally, he partook. Normally, he only did so under controlled conditions. Not when leadership was needed, like now.

"Honey, I need to talk to Wolfe," Big Man Grimm said. "Give us a moment, please."

The girl smiled and left the booth, putting some wiggle into her rear as she did. Big Man Grimm watched her walk away. "You're late."

"Sorry, I got held up a bit," Wolfe replied easily. One of the things he really appreciated about Big Man Grimm was that he never put much stock in pretenses. As long as Wolfe got the job done, Wolfe could say damn near whatever he wanted.

Big Man Grimm turned back to Wolfe. He took in the condition of his best enforcer, including the blood-soaked shirt he was wearing. "What the fuck happened to you?"

Wolfe placed the fifteen new cards face-up on the table. "You should see the other guy."

Big Man Grimm gave a dark chuckle. "I always liked your sense of humor. Dark. It fits us."

"Thanks," Wolfe said, re-pocketing the cards.

Thaddeus Senior's smile dropped from his face and he leaned toward Wolfe. "Javier is dead, then?"

Wolfe shook his head. "Javier lost his deck, and the Cobras lost another five mooks as well. But I didn't kill him—he answered questions from me. Which was important—it'll make sense in a moment. Because this wasn't without cost. I'm nearly dead, Larry *is* dead, Liam's a mental wreck... and Piper's disappeared."

"Piper has... disappeared?" Big Man Grimm asked.

Wolfe nodded. "Like a fart in the wind."

The Big Man frowned. "Okay, I take it back. None of your humor for a moment, Wolfe. Just explain."

"He was in on the fight, and during the fight—which couldn't have lasted more than three minutes—he disappeared. All the cars were there, and I didn't see any sign of struggle, or blood, or a corpse, or anything. We figure he ran—but out of fear or because he's betraying us, I have no idea. Javier did say they had been getting inside information on us from someone that knew all the drug movements... so he might be our guy. But I just don't know."

"Son of an Infernal," Big Man Grimm said. "We've got ourselves a mole. It might be Piper, but if so, he knows damn near everything. But it also might be someone else—running in the middle of the fight doesn't make a lot of sense, unless he thought Javier would live and finger him. But that seems unlikely."

Wolfe nodded. It lined up with his thoughts as well.

"And the product?" Big Man Grimm asked.

"Well, in good news, we're once again the ones committing multiple felonies."

Big Man Grimm's brow furrowed, but then he rolled his eyes. "So, they're in our possession, then?"

"Yup. It went to the warehouse—*the* warehouse, not *a* warehouse. If Piper really was a traitor, those other locations are about as secure as a whore's... well, you know. But since most people wouldn't search the warehouse first, you'll probably have a time before they try and take it back to move it to someplace totally new."

The Big Man slowly nodded. "Good thinking, Wolfe. You are, as always, my best and most loyal packmate."

Wolfe smiled, thinking about the subtle difference in the way Big Man Grimm joked about his name and the way Damian used it. One with respect, and one with condescension.

Big Man Grimm's face broke into an actual smile, an expression not dissimilar from what an antelope saw on the face of the lion that ate it. "Excellent indeed. You really *are* the best. No one else can seem to accomplish a gods' damned thing around here, and you've managed to waste four of their deckbearers, and who knows how many of their thugs. Not to mention kill the guy that got Heinrich."

"What happened with that, by the way? Please tell me we aren't in a fight with the Renfeldts. I already hurt, just, *everywhere.*"

Big Man Grimm glanced at Wolfe, again taking in his blood-stained and bruised state. "I can see that. As to whether we are in another war, I don't think so."

Wolfe raised an eyebrow and mimicked his boss's voice. "'You don't think so?'"

"I called, but Ben Renfeldt wasn't in. His son, Mort, told me he didn't know about his father being upset, but said our understanding and deals would hold. So I think we're okay."

Benjamin Renfeldt, *head of the* Renfeldt *family, called Damian but didn't talk to the family head when he called? The creepy little meatball really does have some crazy skills at wheeling and dealing.*

"Well, I guess that's good." Wolfe nodded and sniffed the drink in front of him. He wasn't sure what was in it, but it smelled off to him, and he put it back down. Then he glanced over at Harry. "Get me a drink, Harry. Whisky please. Ask the bartender—Clive, not Matt—for my usual."

Harry nodded and ambled off, content as a cow chewing its cud, and with an expression nearly as blank.

Big Man Grimm reached out and grabbed Wolfe's shoulder. "Wolfe... do you know what happened to my daughter?"

Wolfe winced slightly. Big Man Grimm was still ridiculously strong, especially for a sixty-year-old. Wolfe wasn't sure if his deck gave him a slightly expanded life or if he was just that much of a workout-aholic, but even his grip was still powerful.

"I'm sorry, Thad," Wolfe said. "Truly. But I have no idea. I dropped her off at the airport and she was fine. Better than fine. After that, like I said, I simply have no idea."

Big Man Grimm let go and leaned back in the booth, putting his huge hands over his face, then running them back through his salt-and-pepper, mostly salt, hair. "Damn. I should have known she'd do something stupid."

He slammed his fist on the table again, knocking most of the remaining bottles and glasses over. "Damn!"

"Sorry," Wolfe said again. It was a sufficiently awkward

conversation and moment that Wolfe stared out into the club, watching all the hot, half-dressed young people dancing together amid the demon statues and fake fog.

Big Man Grimm sighed and gathered himself. "We should find her, first priority. The Cobras have been going after everyone."

Wolfe nodded and offered what solace he could to his mentor. "Well, it shouldn't be a problem much longer, right?"

"What?" Big Man Grimm asked, staring at Wolfe.

"Damian's plan, our own inside guy..." Wolfe trailed off at the obvious confusion on Big Man Grimm's face.

"What plan?" Big Man Grimm asked. "What plan has my son concocted?"

"Nico is turning on his boss, Jason Klaus. They're letting me in to assassinate him tomorrow, at some underground fight ring. You knew, right?"

Big Man Grimm leaned forward, his hands and teeth clenched. He stared into Wolfe's eyes and spoke in a menacing whisper. "I've never heard of this. Tell me everything."

Wolfe did. Partway through, Harry brought him his drink, and he sipped at the whisky, which went down smooth as always, warming him and taking the edge off. As he spoke, Big Man Grimm got angrier and angrier.

Finally, Wolfe finished. Big Man Grimm drummed his fingers on the rich darkwood table before speaking. "Do you think this plan is legit?"

"Yeah... I mean, I'm not sure I trust Nico frankly. But Damian really stepped up on this last one. It was his plan to take out Javier, and get the drugs back. I assume he knows what he's doing here. And Damian clearly got a lot of inside information from Nico, so at some level Nico is betraying his boss for sure."

Big Man Grimm sat for a moment, fuming. "Fine... Carry my damn son's plan out—it has merit."

"Yeah," Wolfe said.

Big Man Grimm gave a huge sigh, his anger leaving him, and leaned back against the booth's leather backing.

They both sat, quietly, for a moment.

Then Big Man Grimm spoke again. "I'm tired, Wolfe. Old in my bones. When I was young... remember *Vito's Toy*?"

Wolfe smiled. "Of course I remember *Vito's Toy*. Our finest moment together."

Big Man Grimm was staring at nothing. "I was determined, back then. I wanted the entirety of the Noimoire drug trade, and when he took that shipment..."

"We tracked it to his ship, and you, me, Johnny, and a couple other boys took it back and killed Vito. Even though it turned out to be an ambush. You've run the scene ever since, basically." Wolfe sipped his whisky. "Man, we must've been outnumbered four-to-one for most of that situation—and we only lost Anderson, Heinrich's brother."

Big Man Grimm sighed again. "Everyone that went with us on that ship is dead now, Wolfe, except me and you. And half the guys working for us back then as well—although I'll admit, booze, drugs, and age got more of them than bullets."

Wolfe blinked, thinking about it. Big Man Grimm was right —not one of the people that had been with them at the *Vito's Toy* were still alive.

"Exactly," Big Man Grimm said, staring at Wolfe's face. "Exactly. I think... I think I want out, Wolfe. I really didn't want Damian to take over yet. He's my son and I love him, but he's done some things... things I've never told you about. Things that make me worry about giving him the reins of the family."

Wolfe blinked again, wondering if Big Man Grimm was referring to the hints Miriam had dropped.

"He's smart though. Very smart. And weirdly effective at getting people to do what he wants. But mostly... mostly I'm done, Wolfe."

Wolfe nodded and took another sip.

"I've treated you right, right, Wolfe?" Big Man Grimm asked.

"Always," Wolfe said and meant it.

"I own an island, you know. Super small, just a few acres. Off the coast of Thailand. It's beautiful there—warm water, sun, beaches. If I retired, and gave you half the island and a house, would you go with me? Think of helping me in my retirement as your next job. I'd pay, of course. And I think getting the rest of the family away from Damian would be best."

Wolfe was floored. Big Man Grimm had always taken care of him, and Wolfe had enough money to *buy* a medium-sized house outright. But not an island.

"I... don't speak Thai," Wolfe said.

Big Man Grimm sighed. "Well, give it some thought. I want to be done with all this."

"So... you really are going to hand it all over to Damian? The family?"

Big Man Grimm nodded. "Yeah. I want to finish this all up, make sure the family is intact and whole and stable. We have to end the Cobras."

Wolfe nodded.

"But afterwards, I think I'll sit down with my boy and pass the reins on, give him most of the accounts, and I'll blow out of here with a couple million, spend my last couple decades relaxing on a beach and reading. Besides, it'll be a better life for Thad and Miriam, I'm sure. Neither one seems cut out for this life."

Miriam might be more suited for it than you suspect, Wolfe couldn't help but think to himself.

Big Man Grimm took a large gulp of his own drink. "Like I said, I'll incentivize you to join me. But we've got to finish this first."

That pretty much means I'll retire when the big man does, Wolfe thought, with a surprising amount of happiness at the thought. He didn't want to work for Damian... and he really didn't want this life anymore, Wolfe realized with a shock. He loved hunting the Cobras, at least the evil ones. But the rest of it... not so much.

You couldn't normally retire from being a mafia enforcer, but Big Man Grimm was offering him a path out.

Although Wolfe had absolutely no skills, so he would need to save up an incredible amount of money or live a very low-key lifestyle if he was making it another forty years. Even the cool million or so he had in cards was only twenty-five thousand a year over forty years... Maybe that went way further in Thailand. Wolfe would have to look it up.

Big Man Grimm interrupted his thoughts, seemingly unaware of Wolfe's musings. "Also, we're not letting Nico take over the Cobras—that just extends the problem we're trying to solve. I'll be in contact, but we're putting a plan together to sweep his people—buy out the low-level drug pushers as their new source, kill anyone we think will be a serious problem. A lot of that is going to fall on you."

Okay, so, retire if I make it that far, Wolfe thought.

Big Man Grimm smiled, a terrible thing of cruelty. "In fact... Once you've taken care of Jason, I want you to capture Nico and bring him back to me as well. I need to demonstrate our power. One last grand demonstration of the dangers of opposing us before we turn everything over to Damian."

Wolfe sighed. *At least watching Nico fall will be nice. If anyone deserves to go to the Infernal, it's him. Plus, it'll help me level and get some more cards to sell. So that's a bonus as well.*

Big Man Grimm settled back in the booth again.

Even as Wolfe was thinking, screams came from the dance floor. Wolfe glanced over and saw two men with honest-to-god *Tommy guns*, like old-time gangsters, pushing toward the front of the club. Gunshots and screams rang out throughout the rest of the club as the Tommy guns came up.

CHAPTER 31

FALL OF EKRON

"**The Great Game, Rule #65**: Enhancer cards shall cost 1 leveling pip to add one slot to the deck for the current and each previous pick. These cards provide permanent, magical benefits to the Deckbearer or the other cards in the deck."

"Under the table!" Wolfe screamed as he grabbed the edges of the darkwood table.

Shel dove under the table, joined by Big Man Grimm. Harry and Pete were slower. Wolfe threw the table over behind Shel and dropped as the two Tommy guns erupted. Wood splintered and the table shook, but Wolfe was already moving. He had one hand on his chest while he pulled the pistol with the other.

A deckbearer has pulled their deck near you.

Damn.

When the initial spray stopped, Wolfe leaned around the side of the table.

Dan was down, multiple gunshots to the chest, in a spreading pool of his own blood. But Harry appeared somehow completely untouched, one of those freak luck things, and he shot one of the assailants in the chest while Wolfe shot the other. To his disgust, he hit the thigh instead of the torso of his target, but it was ultimately irrelevant as his target went down while trying to reload, and Harry and Wolfe each put a few more bullets into the guy.

Wolfe glanced around, taking stock. Enforcers at various points around the club were dead or missing. *We've been betrayed—someone let them in.*

It isn't Piper. Wolfe had a terrible thought. *Or not just Piper.*

Wolfe also noted that quite a few party-goers were also down, many screaming as they bled, and a few unmoving. *This is going to fuck Big Man Grimm's operations for months, if not years.*

He turned back around to find that Big Man Grimm had three fiery red cards in front of him. Even as he watched, a card disappeared and a red aura settled over Big Man Grimm, giving him horns, bat wings, a tail, and cloven feet as an aura around him. His eyes glowed red.

Wolfe took in the mantle.

Infernal Baron
Legendary Tier-1 Infernal Persistent (Mantle)
5 Infernal Power
Gain 15 Magic Attack and an additional 7 to each Defense. Gain 30 Health. Gain a fly movement capability. All Infernal creature cards gain 25% to their stats.

"The hierarchy of the various hells has accepted you, and you receive a portion of their power, making you an almost unstoppable killing force."

Well, fuck, I guess our enemies missed their chance, and holy crap, if I had that card with my perk... were the only two thoughts in Wolfe's head as he stared at his boss. He hadn't known that Big Man Grimm had upgraded his mantle since the last time Wolfe had seen it.

"It's time to reap," Big Man Grimm said, his already menacing voice seeming to reverberate from the very pit.

A person with a handgun typically rated about an eight to ten attack, so...

A massive gout of flame hit the thug that came through the crowd and left a chunk of charred meat that the coroners would have a hell of a time identifying—the thug didn't even scream.

But the flame washed around, the air superheating to the point that people around the target screamed and yelled, and many staggered away cradling burns. As Wolfe glanced around, he saw a couple of people with camera phones filming. *Damn! He's gonna get himself arrested for accidentally killing the clubgoers!*

"Be more careful!" Wolfe yelled. "Don't hurt your clientele!"

Big Man Grimm glanced around. "Got it."

Another thug came running up and Big Man Grimm touched one of his cards. An extremely sexy succubus sprung into existence, and the man stopped moving, just staring at her.

"We should go!" Wolfe shouted. "We're not doing any good sitting here and fighting! We need to be where we can tell friend from foe!"

Big Man Grimm nodded. "Fine. We'll take the evacuation plan and head for the garage. Call Rich—he's on garage duty—and make sure that everything is fine. For now, let's get to the elevators on the assumption it is."

The four of them—Shel, Wolfe, Big Man Grimm, and Harry—all rushed toward the back wall of the club, where the elevators were, dodging or pushing through the screaming party-goers as they did. At the same time, Wolfe dialed Rich.

"Wolfe?" came Rich's voice. "What's going on?"

A gunshot went off amid the general cacophony around them.

"Was that a gunshot?" Rich asked.

Wolfe nodded. "Yes. Is the garage clear of Cobras?"

"Yeah."

"We'll be there shortly," Wolfe said and then ended the call.

A few more gunshots went off, but the attack seemed disorganized, and nothing else came at them before the elevators arrived. The four of them jumped in, and Wolfe hit the *down* button.

"When this is all done," Big Man Grimm growled out, his voice heavy, "I want you to make absolutely sure you kill every Cobra lieutenant."

"I figured," Wolfe responded.

"We need to hire new people—people we can trust."

Wolfe nodded, but he knew that part of the conversation wasn't really for him. The elevator reached the garage level and everyone exited. It was like entering a new world—no screams, no gunshots, everything was clear, like what was happening above was a distant nightmare. They headed for the Hummer that Big Man Grimm kept in the garage for just this emergency.

Wolfe was uneasy, but it took him a moment to figure out why. He held his hand up. "Wait."

Everyone, even Big Man Grimm, stopped.

"What's going on?" Wolfe's boss asked. As he did, the mantle faded from him and rushed back into the deck. He pulled more cards and began to cycle through them, most likely looking for his mantle again.

Wolfe was looking around, his own gun half-raised. He also touched his chest, bringing his cards out and looking for his own mantle. "It's too quiet here. They had guys all over the club, for fuck's sake! Practically coming out of the damn woodwork. Now it's just peaceful and safe here? I don't buy it."

Shel's eyes darted between Big Man Grimm and Wolfe, and she brought her own deck forth.

"What's happening?" Harry asked.

"Maybe just walk up to the street and call an Uber?" Wolfe asked.

"If there's someone out there, we'll definitely be dead if we do that," Big Man Grimm said, his tone still matching his last name.

As they were speaking, Rich walked over to them, his brow furrowed over brown eyes. "What's going on?"

"The club is under attack," Wolfe replied. Then an idea struck him. "Did you bring your car, Rich?"

Rich nodded, his eyes quizzical.

"And you, Harry?" Wolfe asked.

"No."

Wolfe took his keys out and held them out to Harry. "Take my car."

"What?" Harry asked.

Wolfe rolled his eyes. "Look, let's have Rich here take the Hummer, we'll take Rich's car at the back of the pack, and Harry can lead us out. If nothing happens, we can switch cars a couple of blocks down."

"What do you think will happen?" Rich asked nervously.

Wolfe shrugged. "I don't know, but they knew enough to get past the guards here... so they might know which car is the boss's."

"Well, fuck that!"

"If things go really bad, the family'll take care of Tiffany," Wolfe said sweetly.

"Look, Wolfe—" Rich began.

Big Man Grimm leaned in. "I'll pay you ten thousand extra to do this one thing—something you should already be handling. I didn't pay you to spend most of your life dancing in my club and fucking teeny-boppers."

Teeny-boppers?

Rich's eyes filled with greed and he nodded, then fished his keys from his pocket and handed them to Wolfe with a frown.

Wolfe flipped his cards and his mantle showed. He grabbed it and the familiar red aura settled around him, forming tiny horns on his head, small claws on his hands, and turning his skin red and scaled.

Shel also found her aura, and a golden radiance rushed into her and then emanated from her body.

Rich pointed to a boring sedan-style car in blue. "That's mine there."

Big Man Grimm handed Rich his own keys, and everyone scattered. Big Man Grimm, Shel, and Wolfe all got into the blue sedan. The floor was filled with wrappers and empty plastic drink bottles, both front and back, and Big Man Grimm frowned at the mess as he got in the front. Shel went to the back.

Harry drove out in Wolfe's car. He drove to the exit, paused, and then turned onto the street, heading left.

It was late enough—or early enough, depending on your perspective—that the street was empty outside, well-lit by the two fancy clubs on either side. The one across the street was a lot tamer than the Ekron Eternal, with a floral theme, including a row of bushes around the outside. Rich went next, driving the same black Hummer Wolfe had taken the boss's daughter, Miriam, to the airport—among other places—in.

He stopped at the exit, paused, and then drove out onto the road as Wolfe inched the blue sedan toward the exit behind the Hummer.

A brief flash came from behind the bushes across the street, and the Hummer blew apart in a fiery explosion. A piece of metal flew through the front window of Wolfe's temporary car, blowing the entire front windshield apart and lashing glass across Wolfe's eyes in a flash of agony despite his red aura adding protection. He heard Big Man Grimm cussing, Shel's scream, and gunfire as he opened the door and tried to roll to safety while blind.

CHAPTER 32

WAR OF THE DAMNED

"**The Great Game, Rule #68**: Arena's shall appear with each Drop Night. At any arena, a deckbearer may fight another deckbearer for experience up to three times without either needing to die. All wounds sustained shall be merely illusory."

W olfe rolled to the concrete and kept rolling until he hit the wall.

He couldn't see, a condition that tightened his gut with fear even more than the whole 'rocket launcher' thing, and he didn't know if that condition was permanent. Thankfully, he could remember that the inside wall was out of sight of his assailants. Wolfe stood and touched his deck again. There wasn't time to worry about anything else in the moment. He sensed his cards despite his blindness and he pulled Cereboo. He instinctually knew where his card was, as well as the other cards he could pull.

A notification popped into his mind's eye. *Deckbearer Rachel Lyons has summoned her creature card Rookie EMT and used its special ability on you. You gain 3 health.*

The agony left Wolfe's eyes and he wiped blood from them, managing to stare out again. Despite the situation, relief filled him. *Thank the gods Shel wasn't killed. Also, that she got that third Rookie EMT card from the werewolf dungeon. Never been so glad I stopped to take care of some shit for myself in my entire damned life.*

"Go fuck those guys up," Wolfe whispered to Cereboo, who was barking angrily in the direction of the assailants.

The dog ran out, stumbling as gunfire hit him, but guns were still far less effective against Cereboo. As had been the case many times before, his Infernal type resisting Mortal damage was a massive advantage.

Wolfe briefly glanced at his cards—No Kill Pound, Loyal Guard Dog, an Angry Hellhound, and his Rescue Pup. He decided to bet on the Rescue Pup since he only got one pull before his cards switched—it was the zero-power cost option and he was hoping to get the Fireborn Hellhound next round.

He touched the card and chestnut-colored energy left it and poured downward, coalescing on the ground into a thirty- or forty-pound dog, slightly emaciated despite its large size. It followed Cereboo out to the street, rushing the bushes across the street where the gunfire—and the rocket attack—had come from.

Wolfe checked that Shel and Big Man Grimm were okay— and both appeared to be—before rushing out from behind the wall. A bullet flew by his ear, causing his testicles to draw up as he ran. He made it behind the burning Hummer without being shot, bringing him closer to his enemies. A combat log popped up, but only the last part interested him.

...Rescue Pup slain. Cereboo gains +50% attack for the next thirty seconds.

As the snarls and screams from the bushes intensified, Wolfe swiped his deck. He got his Fireborn Hellhound, as well as his second Rescue Pup.

Should have brought out the No Kill Pound, Wolfe thought to himself as screams, barking, snarls, and the *ping* of gunshots on metal filled the burning-car-warmed air around him. He tossed the second Rescue Pup down. If it could last a single round, the boost it would provide by dying would be huge, hopefully helping Cereboo and the Fireborn Hellhound both.

The second emaciated dog ran into the bushes as well.

Big Man Grimm came flying over the car—literally flying. Red bat wings propelled his huge form across the entire street. Gunfire slammed into Wolfe's boss, doing almost nothing as he descended. He landed, and the screams intensified. A few people came running out of the bushes, two being chased by Cereboo and the Rescue Pup and one running off on his own down the glittering main street with the club complexes on either side.

The charred corpse of a fourth man blew out of the bushes and hit the street at the same time the bushes themselves lit on fire.

Well, I guess the Big Man can handle this himself.

Wolfe glanced at the lone guy running away. *Fuck that guy.*

Wolfe ran after the lone Cobra. He threw his Fireborn Hellhound down, using up all but two of his remaining power, and flipped his cards away, bringing up four new options.

The guy saw Wolfe and his new doggo coming and tried to curve down an alley—a loading area behind two of the clubs. But while Wolfe was a bit older, he was in great shape, cut and lean. The man he was chasing could give any hobo on the street a run for his money in the 'strung-out tweaker' look as he tried to escape through the puddles in the alley, turning back to stare at Wolfe as he did, his eyes wide and fearful in the dim light provided by the bulbs at the top of the loading gates.

The Fireborn Hellhound splashed through the last puddle between them, letting off a tiny bit of steam. It grabbed the thug by his left leg, chomped down... and then shook. The guy screamed, long and hoarse, and fell to the ground, trying to turn over and shooting the mutt repetitively. Before the hellhound could finish the thug off, Wolfe mentally ordered him to let go. The hellhound did, and Wolfe ran up and kicked the pistol from the screaming thug's hand.

Wolfe grabbed the guy by his shirt and lifted him off the ground, slamming him into the railing on the outer edge of a loading dock.

"No, no, no!" the thug cried out, putting his hands up as if to push Wolfe away while tears ran down his face.

Wolfe slapped him, hard, and the guy stopped his wailing. Wolfe immediately heard faint sirens, which he guessed meant he had about thirty seconds to ask questions.

"Who gave the order to attack us?" Wolfe shouted as he shook the man.

"Not you. The target wasn't you!" the thug cried out. "Just Big Man Grimm. You weren't supposed to be there! We had reports you were at the drug storage site!"

It was Nico, Wolfe guessed with near certainty. *That's why no one showed up to help defend Javier—they were all here, and they didn't have spare guys. Why would Nico do that? We were going to help him!*

Wolfe paused. *And then betray him, per Big Man Grimm's orders. I guess he just tried to get the drop on the Big Man first...*

Wolfe released the thug, who landed on his two legs, screamed, and collapsed to the ground clutching the ravaged left leg.

A notification popped up, telling Wolfe that his Rescue Pup had died, and that Cereboo had killed two more thugs. Wolfe mentally called Cereboo back as he stared at the wailing embarrassment to all manhood huddled at his feet.

He felt... tired, despite the adrenaline still running through his veins. Tired physically from multiple life-and-death fights over the last two days, and tired from the sheer and utter pointlessness of it all. *This life is shit. We can't even betray each other without betraying each other.*

But as Wolfe thought about it, he clung to one fact. *I can trust Big Man Grimm. He saved my life, and he's always treated me right. He didn't betray me, or even Nico, technically. As long the Big Man lives, there is honor among thieves. If I can win this street war, we can both leave this life. Just hang in a bit longer, Wolfe.*

Wolfe's mantle faded out, having presumably hit the end of the time a card could remain out. *That was only five minutes?*

As he was thinking, he heard Shel calling, "Wolfe! Wolfe, where are you?"

Wolfe turned. Shel was running down the street, Sorenia beside her. She was clearly looking down alleys, but Wolfe figured the glittering lights of the clubs on the main street blinded her to him in the dim alley.

"I'm here!" Wolfe raised his hand.

Shel turned and ran down the alley, quite lithe and quick for the intellectual thing she was, her red hair appearing almost crimson in the lights of the alley, as if she too were stained by blood. She was backlit by Sorenia, who held her lantern high as she ran down the alley after her deckbearer.

"Wolfe!" Shel cried, throwing her arms around him. "You're okay!"

Wolfe disentangled himself, holding the girl back at arm's length. "I'm fine, Shel. Look to yourself and don't worry about me. I'm harder to kill than a damn cockroach."

"And almost as unlikeable," Sorenia said, but she was smiling.

Wolfe hadn't known angels were allowed senses of humor, and certainly she had never displayed one before. He gave her the thumbs up.

Shel nodded, a grin practically splitting her face in what

Wolfe thought was relief. Before they could continue the conversation, however, flashing lights flew past the alley.

"Run!" Wolfe said, turning and rushing down the alley.

"But we have committed no injustice," Sorenia protested indignantly. "The fiends attacked us!"

Shel followed Wolfe's advice and started running as well. Sighing, Sorenia started to follow before Shel called, "Into the deck, Sorenia. I can't have your lantern giving us away."

Sorenia turned into a diffuse, golden glow—ironically decreasing the total light—and sped back into Shel.

Just as she did, a police car turned down the alley, its lights flashing. A megaphone blared out, "Stop! You're being detained!"

Wolfe didn't stop—if anything, the call spurred him to greater action and he flew down the alley. The police car maneuvered around the thug on the ground, giving Wolfe and Shel a chance to make some distance, but then it sped down the alley after them, closing the distance rapidly.

Wolfe reached a chain-link fence and leapt onto it just before the police caught up. He kicked once and reached the top almost instantly. He turned back to see Shel, who called out, "Help!" and ran at him, throwing herself partway up the fence. Wolfe caught her hand and yanked her onto the fence.

The police car slowed with a screech of brakes but hit a puddle and slid into the fence, hurling them off on the other side. Wolfe grabbed Shel and made sure he hit the ground first, yelling as the impact bruised him further and reopened old wounds.

Wolfe was down to a mere five health, and he climbed to his feet, half-limping as his whole back hurt. Shel started to run even as the police officer threw his door open and jumped out. "Stop! I'm commanding you!"

Wolfe didn't stop, awkwardly speed-hobbling down the alleyway as he tried to get the pain from his back.

A notification popped up: *Unknown Deckbearer Officer has pulled a deck.*

Are you fucking shitting me? Wolfe thought, completely exasperated. *We're the ones who got one of the elite Card Police? Not the people on the street with the burning vehicle?*

He swiped his cards again as the officer threw a Fiery Angel card into play. A man with fiery wings and a sword of pure flame appeared. Wolfe glanced back at it, noting its four power and commensurate stats, and grimaced.

Fiery Angel

Uncommon Tier-2 Divine Creature
2 Divine, 2 Any Power
Health: 35
Attack: 12
Magical Attack: 16
Defense: 14
Magical Defense: 14

Special: Immune to Fire Energy
Special: Double all bonuses, including type bonuses, against Infernal

"A lieutenant in the armies of the divine, this angel is powerful and dedicated to the elimination of all evil—and some of the merely not good."

Ah, fuck, Wolfe thought, tempted to surrender.

At the same time, a Rookie EMT card appeared next to Shel but was unable to heal any targets, since all three in her deck had already healed Wolfe in the last twenty-four hours and Shel remained unwounded.

"Stop! Last warning!" the officer screamed. He pointed his pistol down the alley. It was a Glock 17, a very standard police gun, slightly weaker than Wolfe's own Edge but more than enough to put Wolfe away in his current state. The Fiery Angel likewise leveled its sword.

Wolfe raised his hands, hating himself, and slowed to a walk. He saw no alternative.

"*Put the cards away and let your decks down,*" the officer screamed.

Before Wolfe could take any action, Shel slapped one of her cards. Wolfe briefly saw Barter the Soul flash, and the Rookie EMT suddenly faced up, a silhouette of blue leaving her and flying skyward. At the same time, the Fiery Angel suddenly turned and slammed its sword down on the shocked officer's Glock, which discharged into the ground.

"Run!" Shel yelled, grabbing Wolfe's arm and yanking. He winced but followed her, hobble-running down the alley and into the next street over.

Before they had even fully stopped running, Wolfe's phone rang. Out of instinct, he grabbed it. It was Big Man Grimm.

"Boss?" Wolfe asked as they jogged into another alley and headed for the third street over.

"I'm about to be arrested, Wolfe. *Finish the Cobras.* That's your highest priority. If I don't get out in time, end Klaus and take the Cobras' leadership out. Those are your orders. Don't let anyone else stop you, don't let anyone else countermand those orders. Don't accept any other jobs. You know what's at stake."

Wolfe heard yells to get down and drop the phone in the background through the receiver.

"Handle it," Big Man Grimm said, and the phone went dead.

Handle it, Wolfe thought, glancing at himself. Ragged clothing, blood everywhere, and he could barely maintain his jog.

Sure.

"What now?" Shel asked as they slowed to a stop on the third major street over.

"Call an Uber," Wolfe said, handing her his phone as he stared around the street at the less glitzy, and mostly closed for the night, buildings around them. A single gas station appeared to be open. "I'll wash up, then we need to get out of here. We still have work to do."

"Hell of a job you have," Shel said soberly.

Wolfe chuckled sardonically. "Yeah. Hell of a job."

CHAPTER 33

MEANDERING THOUGHTS OF REDEMPTION ON THE SIDE OF THE ROAD

"**The Great Game, Rule #70**: Minion cards shall cost 1 leveling pip to add one slot to the deck for the current and each previous pick. They must be in a deck to take effect, and each shall be a null card for the active portion of the Great Game. They will create a magical construct in the world with a permanent presence and a permanent effect."

Wolfe crossed the street and entered the gas station mart through a sliding glass door where only one half opened. A huge woman, close to six feet tall and probably nearly three hundred pounds, was working the front counter. She gave him the eye as he entered, but he ignored her and headed to the back, pushing into the bathroom.

The inside was trashed, and the mirror shattered, but the faucet poured cold water. Wolfe ran it over his face and hands, mostly trying to clear the smear of blood across his face. His results were somewhat mixed, and his shirt was a total loss, but he could pass for 'not a chainsaw murderer,' he was fairly sure. For a moment or two, at least.

He walked back out of the bathroom and grabbed a six-pack of Yuengling Lager and took it up to the lady running the place. The clock above her head declared it was nearly two in the morning, and Wolfe grimaced.

He put the beer on the counter. "Give me a pack of Marlboro Reds. too. And a lighter, please."

The lady complied, and Wolfe fished the mangled bills from his pants to pay before heading outside.

Shel was waiting on the sidewalk when he came out.

Wolfe stared at her for a moment. "I think you should get out of here, for your own safety. Now, I mean. I'll let you know what happens with Nico and Jason, but I'm supposed to be putting an end to both of them tomorrow evening. I think it's getting—no, it *has gotten*—far too dangerous for you. We should get you out of town tonight."

Shel's happiness collapsed, and she raised a hand, nervously fiddling with her ponytail. "Do I... have to?"

Wolfe took another drag of his cigarette as he contemplated this development. "What?"

"Do I have to go? What if I wanted to stay and help you?" Shel's green eyes bored into his.

"Shel..." Wolfe hesitated before continuing, gathering his thoughts. "This life isn't for you. I'll avenge your brother, but even that... it isn't *you*. If Sorenia were out of the deck right now, she'd be encouraging you to get out of here. You've got an angel deck, you're smart, and you're pretty. But you're also *soft*. This life is the kind of thing a good man would protect you from, not involve you in."

"Because I'm a woman?" Shel asked.

Wolfe frowned at her. "No, because you're *you*. I don't try to save the drugged-out whores, or the girls obviously looking for a walk on the wild side, or the people like good ol' Julia—"

"Juliet," Shel interjected.

"—the crazy orthodontic surgeon lady with the rats, who

322

got involved to make some extra money. I believe in Big Man Grimm's rule, deeply. The ones who got involved for selfish reasons, or because they're too stupid to stay away, well... they were all adults and they can save themselves."

Shel listened, rapt, as he talked.

"But you... well, you got involved to make sure that whomever hurt your brother can't do it again. But I've run through most of the Cobra street gang, and I'm gonna kill everyone else that matters tomorrow, most likely. 'Cept maybe Marko. No idea where that jackass ended up."

Wolfe paused. "He's probably trying to hunt me down. I'd bet money on it. Damn."

"One more thing?" Shel asked with a smile.

"You're speaking my language. But that's not the point. The point is, you've got no reason to stay. So get the fuck out while you can."

Shel was silent a bit longer.

"Will you come with me?" she asked.

Wolfe was so surprised, he half-sucked his cigarette in and then choked and spit it out onto the concrete parking lot they were standing in. After a few moments of hacking, he stared at her from watery eyes like she'd grown another head. "What? Go with you *where*?"

"Away from here." Shel waved her arms around the nighttime city street like that explained a damn thing.

"You don't *have* anywhere," Wolfe said. "That's why I was giving you the extra cash the first time we met. You're trying to pay me in monopoly money."

"I just meant... out of this life."

Shel walked a step closer and threw her arms around Wolfe, her head pressed up against him, her red-hair-ponytail pressed up under his chin.

"Whatever happened when you were a kid, you've paid enough, Wolfe. You don't belong here. You can leave now."

Wolfe sighed and stroked her hair. He was tempted, he truly was. But he had just had almost this same talk with Big Man Grimm, and he couldn't leave yet.

He tried to explain everything. "Look, Shel... I *haven't* been feeling this damn life lately. I can remember when I did feel it. I was younger once, fresh from my sentence in juvie, and I was keen to fight the street wars."

"Why?" Shel asked.

"Because I was clearly tainted, but I was also bringing down other people who were evil. I thought that in a weird way, I was still doing good, kinda. But the whole time I was also working for Big Man Grimm, a man I deeply respect."

Shel's voice was muffled against his chest, but Wolfe could still understand her as he stared over her head at the nighttime streets around them. "Because he helped you?"

"Partially. But that's not all. Big Man Grimm is evil, I know that—I'm not a fool. He's a genteel and honorable evil, one that keeps the evil confined to the shadows and to people who have decided to play in our world." Wolfe laughed. "He is a devil who only comes when summoned. Sure, if you call him, you're liable to get burnt. But I honestly believe, even now, that he made the streets less dangerous than they would have been if he hadn't been there."

"By selling drugs?" Shel pulled back a little and stared up at Wolfe with narrowed eyes.

"By selling them with, until recently, almost no violence. Someone is gonna do it. He does it... less horribly," Wolfe finished.

"Even if that's true, why can't you leave? I mean, most of that speech makes it sound like you want to go now, anyway."

Wolfe gave a tired chuckle. "Yeah, I guess I wasn't selling 'staying.' But the point is, I'm still tainted, Shel. I've killed a dozen guys in the last couple of days. Dozens, plural. I know you laughed at me the first time I said it, but I'm heading toward cancer levels here. Like they're just mooks in a B action movie and I've got a minigun."

"They were bad people," Shel said.

Wolfe sighed. "The gods themselves let me know, Shel. The Infernal chose me to receive a deck. Everything I touch turns to crap or dies—I belong in this world. Whether I want to or not, I serve the Infernal. I tried to fight for justice, to defend the weak and helpless. It all turned to crap. Only thing good I do is keep other bad people in line."

Shel touched the side of Wolfe's stubble-roughened cheek with one delicate hand. "Wolfe... you're not evil. You're just surrounded by it. Soaking in it."

Wolfe laughed again so abruptly, he was glad he hadn't relit a cigarette—a cigarette going down his windpipe would probably remove the last tiny shreds of his health. "What?"

"*The Infernal* didn't pick you, *Cerberus* did," Shel said. "I've seen pretty much your entire deck at this point, right?"

Wolfe nodded.

Shel spoke with intensity. "Well, Cerberus keeps people out of hell... *but he also keeps the demons in*. Your companion, your mantle... they're all made to fight *other Infernals*. I looked up the Infernal lords, Wolfe. Beelzebub gives decks to corrupters, those who use the desires of others against them. Aeshma gives decks to the violent. Asmodeus to rapists and those who use women's sexuality for their own gain. Every infernal lord, nearly, gives decks to evil people. But whom does Cerberus give decks to?"

Wolfe didn't know, but he could guess. "Bad people who hunt down worse people?"

Shel shrugged while still touching the side of Wolfe's face. He took her hand and pressed it down slowly, not to reject her but because he felt that her holding her hand up to his face was starting to look awkward to any passersby.

"I don't know, actually," Shel said. "There are almost no Cerberus cards out there. But it stands to reason. Also, each of the crime organizations got one of the cards, Wolfe. But so did you—the wildcard, so to speak. Each of five Infernal lords chose their champion, and Cerberus chose you—and only one can complete the set. You once joked that the gods are sadistic, and make it so deckbearers fight each other. Well, you've been pitted against the other Infernal, to bring them down."

Wolfe thought about it for a moment, but ultimately, there was still one core truth about him that stood in the way. "I won't kill Big Man Grimm's son, so killing all the other set deckbearers is moot anyway."

"Doesn't mean you aren't still on the side of good, even if not the angels."

Wolfe reached out and ruffled her hair. "Shel, once all of this war is done, I'm actually probably going to retire. Big Man Grimm wants out—and he wants me to follow him. His retirement sounds a little boring to me, but I think I'll leave the Grimm family. But *only* when the war is done. I owe Big Man Grimm that much, and he's counting on me."

Shel smiled wide. "You're going to leave the family? Really? Why didn't you start with that?"

Wolfe laughed. "Sorry, I'm tired and beat to shit. However, I talked about all that stuff to explain why I started and stayed in this life. I can go now... but not till we win this fight, so the Big Man can pass his business on to his son without shit hanging over it."

"That's wonderful!" Shel said. "Truly."

"Okay, but until then, I need to know you're okay. I need this one thing to go right."

"Why is me leaving such a big deal?" Shel asked. "I've been helpful, kinda, in some of your fights. I mean... you'd probably be blind now without me. I'm a deckbearer. Why are you pushing me away so hard?"

Wolfe hesitated. "Look... I told you about my mother and sister, right? What happened with my dad?"

Shel nodded. "Yeah. This evening, I think. Or maybe this morning. It's all a big blur at this point, a blur of odd schedules and terror."

Wolfe laughed. "It has been pretty fucking wretched, hasn't it?"

Shel nodded, smiling. "It's had its moments though."

Wolfe sobered again. "Look... the story with Dad ended terribly across the board. After I killed that abusive molester, well... Mom and Mel hated me for it."

"What?" Shel asked, her eyes widening. "Why?"

"They were so programmed, or used to it, that they didn't even see the horror. That's the best I can guess, anyway, but I never found out for sure. Them hating me was the one outcome I never expected. The first night I was in juvie, they came and told me that I'd ruined their lives and killed the one man who'd taken care of them." Wolfe's face twisted. "That I'd killed the one man who'd *loved* them. He had programmed them so well that they didn't even want to be rescued..."

"They never forgave you? Or tried to reconcile?" Shel asked.

Wolfe exhaled through his nose. "Maybe they would have, I don't know. But they died in a car accident less than two months later, before I was released. That conversation, in juvie, was the last I ever heard of them. But my mom had hated me so much, she'd even changed the will, so I got nothing... so I think they still hated me when they died, at least."

"I'm so, so sorry," Shel said quietly.

An old, red Volkswagen pulled up to the curb and honked.

"Our Uber?" Wolfe asked.

Shel nodded.

"Well, there you go," Wolfe said, staring at the car but not moving. "The last tiny bit of Wolfe's story. No more secrets, no more crazy events in my life. You know it all, Shel. Something only Big Man Grimm has ever heard before in its entirety. But that's why I need you to go once you can. I *must* save someone and have it go right for real. Just once. Please."

Shel's brow was narrowed, and her nose scrunched. It took a moment, but she sighed and her face relaxed. "Wolfe... If you tell me that this is the most important thing to you, I'll leave. But I'm asking you not to send me."

Wolfe opened his mouth, but Shel held her hand up.

"Not only for your sake, but for mine, too," she said. "I also need to see something go right, to save someone. My brother died—I tried to keep him around, but I failed. He left and died. Now you're about to leave, or make me leave. I'm not as strong as you, Wolfe, or as good at killing. But I can heal, and Sorenia can fight. You might need us."

"I'm just going to assassinate the head of the Cobras... I don't think I'll even be in a fight."

"Then there's no risk to me." Shel gave him a playful wink.

Wolfe hesitated, torn. "Alright. You're mental, wanting to stay and help me, like committed-to-an-asylum level mental, but sure. We'll finish this together."

Shel smiled. "Thank you."

The red Volkswagen honked, and Wolfe turned to it with narrowed eyes. It was that kind of day.

"Play nice," Shel said.

"I'm already regretting not asking you to fly out," Wolfe said with a half-laugh.

CHAPTER 34

THE PRODIGAL CHILDREN

"**The Great Game Rule #74**: Cards may have an (available) power cost—these take no power, and will have a single action effect."

Wolfe reached over the seat and passed the Uber driver forty bucks. "Keep the change."

"Thanks," the man muttered, already poking at his phone set-up. To get his next fare, Wolfe assumed.

Wolfe stepped from the car, and Shel followed on the other side, then came around to him. "Aren't you going to call Harry to get your car back?"

"Fuck, I'm tired," Wolfe muttered, pulling his phone out. "I should have done that forty bucks ago."

He glanced over at Shel as the phone rang. "In my defense, I've been hit with everything from a rocket blast wave to a police car since I gave him the keys. Well, a fence via police car, but still."

"Thanks for, um, saving me even though you were already super wounded."

"Yeah, sure." Wolfe opened the latch to the low chain-link gate and entered his yard. He reached the door and paused. "Shit."

"What?" Shel asked, nervously glancing around.

"I forgot—I gave the keys to Harry, remember? The same keys that are on a ring with my house keys."

Shel smiled with relief. "Oh, I thought it was a real problem."

Wolfe stared for a moment, then started laughing so hard it hurt. Shel furrowed her brow in concern as Wolfe doubled over, wheezing.

After a moment, he straightened. "A real problem? Oh, Shel, this is the closest I've felt to you. Being locked out of your house in the early morning hours while it's cold outside and your partner is bleeding is, in fact, not a real problem by our sad current standards."

Shel giggled. "Yeah."

The door handle jiggled, and Wolfe tensed again, reaching for his pistol. The door pulled open, and Miriam, still in yesterday's—had it only been a day?—black dress, but with her face scrubbed clean of makeup, stared out at them, a golf club in her left hand.

"Wolfe, is that you I hear cackling like a hyena? Good. I was worried that one of your many enemies had come to your house." Miriam rested the golf club on her shoulder and smiled.

Wolfe stared, as surprised by this turn of events as he had been by anything that had happened over the last couple days, besides getting a deck in the first place. "Miriam... what in the Infernal? Why didn't you get on the plane, and what are you doing here?"

She rolled her eyes and huffed. "Well, I decided that all the interesting things would be happening here. Maybe I didn't get a god-gifted deck, but with your help, I made a few levels, and gained a ton of cards to trade or sell. If I want more strength, in the form of levels and cards, I think this is the place to be."

Her smile widened even further. "And I think around you is the place to do it."

Wolfe jutted his chin at the golf club. "What's that for?"

She held it up, and Wolfe could see it still had faint red smears of blood on it. Her eyes widened to the point that her vibe went straight to psycho. "My nine-iron? It turns out that you can make all the way to level ten by killing mortals. Did you know that, Wolfe?"

He nodded. "Yeah."

She placed the golf club back on her shoulder. "If someone came through one of your windows unannounced, and without permission, I was gonna send them straight to whichever set of gods would take them. Perfectly justified homicide."

Wolfe shook his head. "It's, um, good to see you, Miriam. Please don't sneak into my house again."

"Oh, Wolfy... we both know I won't promise that."

Shel giggled.

Miriam was... impossible, at some level. Wolfe pointed at her. "Never use that nickname again."

Miriam laughed richly, smiling at him with friendly cruelty. "Oh, Wolfy... we both know I won't promise that, either."

Shel's giggle was heading for full laughter, but she sounded nervous.

"Just be glad you're too old to spank," Wolfe said, gently pushing past Miriam with ease. She started to open her mouth, but Wolfe held his hand up. "Nope. I realized, about two seconds too late, that I just walked into some weird sexual joke you're about to make, but no. Too tired, and far too beat up. Sleeping now. We'll talk in the morning, when I can deal with you."

"Ah, but Wolfy, I want you to tell me everything that's been happening."

"Tell Shel."

"Wolfe?" Damian asked on the other end of the line, sounding surprised. "You never call."

Shel sat up in the pile of blankets of Wolfe's floor, staring at him as he talked.

Wolfe stared at the poorly curtained window as he sat on his bed, Cereboo next to him. His whole body was tired and sore. "It's your big day coming up—you're turning eighteen. I need to know where we're having the fireworks display, and how I'm getting them."

There was a brief pause, and Shel raised an eyebrow.

"What?" Damian asked, clearly baffled.

"You want a pony or a donkey for everyone to play with? Ponies are more traditional, but I think a donkey would be more appropriate."

"Are you being funny or trying to use code?" Damian asked in clipped tones.

Wolfe groaned. "Neither, I'm trying, so hard, to find the humor in my life. It's like my quest at this point. But never mind. Where can I meet you to get directions and supplies is all I'm asking."

"Ah. Right... Meet me at the mansion. Also, have you seen my sister? No one has been able to find her."

Wolfe knew that Miriam didn't like her brother, and the hints he had gotten from her indicated she had good reason. His discussion with Big Man Grimm had given him a few more hints that all was not well between the siblings. Whimsically, he said, "I'll let you know when I've got eyeballs on her."

"You're being really odd this morning," Damian said. "Did something happen?"

"I'm a bit punch drunk."

Shel giggled.

"What?" Damian asked after a moment.

"Have you not heard about last night?" Wolfe asked with surprise. "I mean, your dad was arrested, the club got shot up—I was intimately involved in all that. Hell, I assume whatever sources you had told you, but I also thought the news might just be covering it. You get the news still, right?"

"Of course I still get the news," Damian said, sounding vexed. "I heard about that, for the Divine's sake. Everyone heard about that. That's not what I'm talking about. Did something else happen to you? You sound off, Wolfe. Almost as whimsical as Piper. I need to know that you're at your best before you do this. I won't lose that card."

Wolfe pulled himself together.

His status chart said his injured penalty had increased. Wolfe was now at a ten health, two attack, and two defense penalty. But he was back to twenty health of his thirty—his current maximum with the injury penalty. He should be able to get his shit together.

Never mind Damian—the Big Man himself was counting on Wolfe to get this right. He needed to quit fucking around.

Wolfe put as much sincerity into his voice as he could manage. "Sorry, Damian, I'll pull myself together. I'm ready for tonight. I got in a lot of fights and took a lot of damage yesterday—but I also completed everything the family asked of me except this—and I'm the only one that did damn near anything except you. I can handle it."

"I'm glad to hear it. I can't have the family's best dog losing himself."

Wolfe couldn't bring himself to respond with more than a "right" to that insulting statement. He was pretty sure the hobbit was trying to be friendly and make jokes with Wolfe's name, like his dad did, but his efforts always felt stilted and a touch insulting.

Damian continued. "Alright, so, meet me at the mansion. I'll have the directions and the tools that you need both."

"I'll be there," Wolfe said, then ended the call. He turned to Shel. "He may be the big up-and-comer, but on the one to ten creepy scale, that guy hits eleven faster than most pedophiles. Am I right, or am I super right?"

Shel giggled, but Cereboo just growled.

"I think you're funny," Shel said.

"I should've been a comedian," Wolfe quipped. Then he stood, trying to work some of the pain out.

The fire alarm went off, and Wolfe grabbed his pistol from the computer table and hit the ground, cussing, in just his boxers.

"What in the fresh Infernal is this nonsense?" Wolfe called over the alarm, walking out of his room, his weapon in his hand.

He was met by a miasma of bacon-flavored smoke. He coughed and pushed into the other room, no longer too worried, although he kept his trusty Edge out just in case.

"Sorry, Wolfe," Miriam yelled, now dressed in black jeans and a white lace top, her silver-chain cuffs and manacles replaced with bone bracelets. Her black mascara was on again, however.

"By all that is Divine, Miriam, what are you doing?"

"Bacon and eggs?" she said loudly, her voice rising up at the end like it was a question.

"How are you fucking up bacon and eggs?" Wolfe asked exasperatedly, taking the pan, which was pouring black smoke, by its handle.

"Well, technically, it was just bacon—I never got to the eggs," Miriam replied. "But to answer your question, we have servants for this stuff."

Wolfe opened a window and threw the whole pan onto the

cement walkway in his backyard. "Then *why*, by all the gods of the Great Game, are you trying to cook?"

"It looked easy."

Wolfe pinched the bridge of his nose. "It's too early for you."

"Sorry."

Wolfe sighed, reached up, unscrewed the alarm, then took the battery out. The screech-and-beep ground to a halt.

He reached under his sink and pulled another pan out. "I'll make the eggs."

Shel came walking out. "He makes good eggs."

Miriam arched her eyebrow at Shel. "I take it you didn't choose to have your eggs unfertilized."

Wolfe pinched the bridge of his nose again. "Miriam…"

Shel smiled. "We're not sleeping together, promise. I've kinda tried twice. He keeps saying no."

Miriam ran her eyes up and down Shel. "No accounting for some men's taste. I'd do you."

Shel flushed which caused Miriam to laugh.

Wolfe rolled his eyes at Miriam's shenanigans. "Look, your family is freaking out, Miriam. Not that I haven't loved having you over, but you should probably go see them. Your dad was worried sick."

"He's in jail at the moment, so that's hardly a practical solution."

Wolfe shrugged. "Damian keeps calling as well."

All of Miriam's manic energy seemed to leave her, and she slumped slightly. In a far more monotonous voice, she muttered, "I *really* don't want to see him."

"What happened between you two?"

Miriam frowned. "You wanna talk about what Dad did for you that made you so loyal? I asked him why a guy like you worked for him, and he said it was a terrible secret—he didn't say it like that, but that's what he meant—and that it was personal. I've been curious ever since."

Wolfe sprinkled some cheese over the eggs. "Not really."

Miriam crossed her arms over her chest. "Neither do I. I'm sure you can guess the outlines, and beyond that, no one needs to know."

"Fair. I'm gonna be doing some extremely dangerous stuff for the family. You can either go home, or you can stay here—but either way, I've got to go as soon as the food is done."

Miriam hugged herself, her demeanor still not restored. Shel walked up to her and put her arms around her from behind, gently hugging her.

"It's okay," she said. "Or it will be."

Miriam smirked, her demeanor coming back. She hooked a thumb backwards at Shel. "No wonder she got an angel deck, right?"

"Yeah, she's pretty good."

Wolfe turned, put the eggs on three plates, and held them out to the other two. "Breakfast is served. Eat fast. I'm gonna go see your brother about killing a man."

Miriam chuckled, took the plate, and then shoved some eggs in her mouth, chewing and making an appreciative noise.

After a moment she glanced up. "I'll go see about getting Dad out of jail pending his arraignment. Kinda wish I was gonna go with you to kill people, so I can make some levels, but I *really* don't want to see my brothers. So I'll just handle Dad's court stuff."

"Sure."

CHAPTER 35

INSTRUMENT OF THE DEVIL

"The Great Game Rule #77: Perks have been added to the game. Every person that becomes a deckbearer shall have one magical perk. Every person that becomes a deckbearer chosen by a named faction member shall have two magical perks."

"I'm surprised she decided to stay at your place," Shel said, her teeth chattering a bit despite the heater being on full blast. It was a sunny morning, but the air was still cool with the memory of night, and the grass had frosted dew on it.

"Hmm."

Wolfe turned his dented and shot-up car into 111 Greenbow Way, the Grimm family mansion. It was weird to be coming here without intending to meet Big Man Grimm—Wolfe couldn't honestly remember doing that before. But the big man was still in jail—Miriam had texted, saying she had gone to the courts and found out Thaddeus Sr. was being taken to a bail hearing in the morning—which in a court would apparently usually mean anything from eight-thirty a.m. to noon, and sometimes even later.

"It's still crazy beautiful, isn't it?" Shel asked, gazing at the twenty columns in the front of the mansion that supported the wrap-around overhang. Then she grinned at him. "I guess crime does pay."

"So clever, woman," Wolfe replied with a laugh.

It was a very large mansion—close to fifty rooms, with three main entrances and a circular driveway with fountains in the center fronting it.

He pulled into a parking space in front of the mansion, and a man that Wolfe didn't recognize came out.

"Name?" the man asked.

"I'm Wolfe, but the question is, who the fuck are you?" Wolfe had his hand on his pistol.

The man—although Wolfe doubted he was more than a year or two into his twenties—looked up, his face a morass of small craters left over from terrible acne. "I'm Aaron. I work for the Grimm family."

"How come I've never heard of you?"

"I was hired yesterday to be a guard at the house. Damian hired me—he said you guys have a manpower shortage."

Wolfe relaxed. "I suppose we do."

"So you're Wolfe, huh? People say you're some kind of badass. Been killing the Cobras."

"Something like that."

The man nodded. "Well, pleased to meet you. Hopefully everything settles down again soon. I've got a daughter—be a shame if I wasn't around to support her."

Wolfe frowned. "Sure, whatever. Just take me to Damian."

The man nodded and walked Wolfe to the same door that he had been to last time. He held it open, and Wolfe walked into the house. He walked the same path back toward the main kitchen, where he found Damian, Thaddeus Jr., and six guys with guns he didn't recognize.

Damian wore another suit, although at least this one was

black instead of burgundy. He had saved the burgundy for his tie.

Although he still had the idiotic fly cufflinks.

Thaddeus Junior wore a gi, complete with the uwagi jacket and thick belt. He smiled wide at Wolfe.

"What's with *Karate Kid* here?" Wolfe asked.

One of the guards snickered.

Thaddeus walked up and held his hand out. "I know you're the big man on the street, but I've been training. I'm hoping to be as tough and respected as you some day."

"I'm glad you know what you wanna be when you grow up," Wolfe quipped.

He quickly shook Thad's hand—*idiot thing to do when we've known each other for twenty years*—then deliberately turned away from him. The Big Man's oldest son and his half worshipful, half idiotic conversation was making Wolfe uncomfortable.

He addressed Damian. "Speaking of questionable decisions, what's with all the new guys?"

"Good to see you too, Wolfe," Damian said with a snort. "So, we'll skip the pleasantries and just get right to you acting the tough guy?"

Wolfe chuckled. *At least the sleazy bastard has a sense of wit. Unlike himbo, there.* "Sorry. But seriously, who are the new guys?"

"Well, we *are* in a street war, and we've lost at least twenty guys in the last couple weeks," Damian said. "Felt like I ought to replace some people."

"Touching."

"Speaking of other new faces, who's the girl?" Damian blatantly ran his lust-filled eyes up and down Shel. "We weren't properly introduced last time, but I would never forget a body like that."

Shel wore jeans that looked sprayed on and a pink top that

exposed her midriff, and Wolfe had to admit, he couldn't fault Damian's taste.

He still didn't like the man looking at Shel, though.

Shel didn't either, apparently. She folded her arms across her chest and turned away from Damian a bit.

"She's with me," Wolfe said, his voice on edge.

It took Damian a moment, but he ripped his eyes from Shel, met Wolfe's, and nodded.

Wolfe was surprised—he didn't think the bastard would recognize when his authority had limits. But Damian was proving to be far smarter than Wolfe had once thought, and he proved it again here.

Damian coughed. "Sorry, I have a weakness for gorgeous women. In my defense, it's shared by many men. However, talking about my foibles isn't the reason you're here."

"True. I need to know how I'm supposed to sneak into the underground fighting ring, and I need to know how I'm supposed to kill Jason. You said Nico had a plan for all that."

Damian smiled. "Nico knew some things, but I'm the one that had the plan."

"I'm sorry, I forgot my gold stickers today."

Shel snorted, and Damian's eyes narrowed. "Wolfe, we both know you'll be a good dog when I'm in charge, so how about not insulting me now?"

"Yeah, sure. Sorry. Tell me what I need to know to get you your card."

Damian frowned. "Well, here's my plan—there is an entrance to an old sewer system near the Venom Arena, and it connects to the underground fight ring the Cobras are using for their recruiting event."

"So... I need to sneak into the fight via the sewers?" Wolfe asked. "That sounds like the plot to a bad Saturday morning cartoon."

"You don't need to sneak into the event—you just need to

get close. One of the tunnels gets right to where the event is being held. Once close, well..."

Damian paused dramatically. "Charles, go get the special."

These guys sound like thirteen-year-olds that made a plan.

One of the guards walked out of the room, and a moment later, came back struggling under the weight of a large, obvious explosive—a detonator with a clock attached to a huge mess of plastique.

The guy dropped it to the ground, and Thad Jr. jumped. "Fucking Infernal, Charles! Don't do that, you'll kill us all!"

Damian rolled his eyes. "It's C4—only an electrical charge can set it off. No amount of jostling will do it. The timer is the only way to make the fireworks happen."

Wolfe knew very little about explosives, but the bomb was larger than many of the explosives he had seen in the movies. "How big is this explosion?"

Damian waddled up and put one pudgy, ring-encrusted hand on the device. "This is twenty-five kilograms, or about fifty-five pounds. It would blow this mansion down, most likely. If you set it, I would get hundreds of feet away at a minimum, or perhaps thousands would be better."

"Wouldn't that kill a lot of people?" Shel asked. "Innocent people?"

Damian nodded. "It would, if you set it off above ground. But from where you'll be setting it off, underground, I'd just be out of the actual arena and the building above it. That's probably everything that will be destroyed."

Wolfe raised an eyebrow. *Probably?*

Damian bent down and flipped a toggle on the device. "All you need to do is set the timer, here, like this. I had it made so that it can't be turned off if someone finds it—so make damn sure that you want to set it off before you turn it on."

One of the guards giggled at Damian's inadvertent wordplay.

Wolfe watched as Damian fiddled with the dials and then pointed to the switch to turn it on. Once he had demonstrated, he turned the timer off.

"The device won't accidentally set if the timer isn't on?" Wolfe asked.

"No, it's a double failsafe. The timer has to be set to something and clicked on, and only then can you arm the bomb truly, with the other switch."

Damian snapped his fingers, and one of the new guys brought a huge rucksack and stuffed the bomb into it. The thug carried the backpack over to Wolfe, who shrugged it on.

"Weight okay?" Damian asked.

"It's damn uncomfortable with all the damage I've taken over the last couple days, but it's doable," Wolfe responded.

Damian nodded, then walked up to Wolfe. He put his hand on Wolfe's arm. "Wolfe—I need that card. Each part of the set is powerful by itself, and all six would make any deck extraordinarily powerful. I will have all six. But even just the card that Jason has will make me far stronger. *Far* stronger."

"Alright, keep it in your pants. I'll get it for you."

Wolfe thought about Cereboo. His pup was quite an impressive card. Just Cereboo's ability to let Wolfe use two forms of power interchangeably was huge—a lot of cards that were all one type of power were stronger than less-picky but otherwise equivalent cards.

Wolfe wasn't exactly sure, but he'd bet a rare, all-specific-power card would be about as powerful as a common generic card two full total power above it, give or take.

Wolfe frowned, disappointed that he was going to have to give Jason's card to Damian. *Although, in the long run, it's a bit moot. I'll never kill Big Man Grimm's kid, so I'll never complete the set anyway—unless the Cobras kill Damian first or something. Then I'll get his card. But unless that happens, I might as well just give the card to Pudgy McPlan over there.*

Damian adjusted his cufflink and smiled at Wolfe. "Thank you. I really appreciate your loyalty and your competence. I'll be sure to reward you as well as my father did once he is gone and I'm in charge."

Then he reached into his suit coat and took a large piece of paper into his hand and held it out to Wolfe. "This is the exact locations of the entrance to the sewers, with written directions on how to navigate them."

Wolfe took the paper, glanced at it—it was a Google Maps printout with a circle on a street beside the Venom Arena and written notes at the bottom—and then handed it to Shel.

"Can I get a flashlight as well? A strong one?"

Damian snapped his fingers and one man hurried off. "It'll be here soon."

Damian paused before leaning in and speaking more intensely. "Wolfe... I need that card. And the family needs Jason to be dead. Please don't fail us. Not to sound corny, but you're our only hope at this point."

"Well, I can promise I don't want to fail. Anyway, as soon as the flashlight is here, I'm off—it's going to be a busy day."

CHAPTER 36

THE LIGHT IN THE DARKNESS

"**The Great Game, Rule #80**: Creature cards may now have an (available) power cost. These have zero drawdown once on the field."

Wolfe pulled his car into the parking lot of George's Bistro across the street from the Venom Arena. He parked it so that two cars would shield the view of his vehicle from across the street—he doubted many people recognized it on sight, but he wasn't risking exposure over something dumb. He was already conspicuous enough because of his giant backpack.

"You still want to come?" Wolfe asked Shel, knowing the likely answer, but feeling compelled to give her the chance to exit the situation.

She took a deep breath. "Yes."

"Alright, let's do this. Remember, don't pull cards unless you absolutely have to. It will instantly give us away, or at least make Jason pull his. If he has a mantle on, a strong enough one, the blast probably won't kill him."

"I know."

Wolfe stepped from his car, avoiding dinging the red Nissan next to him with his door, and then shrugged the backpack on. It was almost four in the evening, and the very first fights would start in about an hour—which meant that was the latest that Jason Klaus would be in place.

Wolfe walked out of the parking lot and waited street side as a few cars passed.

"What're you doing?" Shel asked. "The light is down there!"

Wolfe laughed. "Seriously? After everything we've done, you're worried about jay walking? You're accessory to at least a couple murders."

Shel flushed and looked down. "I'm liable for at least five first-degree murders under the felony murder rule, according to Miriam, since I was part of the felony break-in when we hit Javier. If we're ever caught, I'll spend the rest of my life in prison."

Wolfe stepped out into the street as a break in traffic presented itself, and Shel followed, nervously glancing around.

They reached the other side, and Wolfe continued the conversation. "I'm skeptical they'd send a young, innocent-looking girl like you to prison for life, but I get what you're saying. So why worry about jay walking?"

"You're carrying an illegal *bomb* in your backpack!" Shel whispered furiously. "What if a cop had happened to drive by right then, and stopped you and conducted a pat-down search? We'd both go to jail!"

Wolfe scratched his head, feeling like an idiot. "Yeah, that makes sense. Sorry, I'll think about it a bit more going forward."

Shel nodded.

The two of them walked around the back of the Venom Arena and across that parking lot, next to a rundown building of indeterminate use with patchy weeds around the base and across the dirt around it. Wolfe saw the open entrance, presumably to the sewers, next to the building.

He took a deep breath, hoping it wouldn't be too bad. "Shall we?"

Shel nodded and Wolfe walked over and bent down, putting one foot on the top rung.

His phone buzzed in his pocket, giving him a slight start. He stepped back up and pulled it out. *Miriam.*

She had sent a text message.

Wolfe grimaced at the comment. *I'm not even going to get a break after Jason. Still, it's needful.*

"Who is it?" Shel asked. "It's beginning to worry me whenever you make that expression. It always turns into a 'whole thing' to quote you."

"Yeah, it's gonna be a whole thing indeed. Miriam said that she got the Big Man out on bail, and they're headed to the mansion."

"That doesn't sound—"

Wolfe sighed loudly enough to cut her off. "And the Big Man said to capture Nico and bring him to the mansion after we kill Jason."

"Wow, they aren't giving you a break at all."

Wolfe gave her a sardonic grin. "I was literally just thinking the same thing."

Shel smiled at him, but it was forced—her eyes were flicking from side to side, and she was tapping her fingers together.

Wolfe put his foot on the rung again, half expecting something else, but when nothing happened, he descended into the darkness, being extremely careful due to the extra weight on his shoulders.

To his surprise, there was barely any odor at all down in the sewers. He could smell some earth, with an undertone of decay and old dust, but that was it. The sewer was a huge metal pipe, corroded in places and obviously stained in others—but it had a mesh-metal walkway along the sides. Wolfe wondered why the city had abandoned it.

He was in the middle of a large tunnel. It was faced toward the Venom Arena ahead of him, and away from it behind him.

Wolfe turned his flashlight on and pulled his piece of paper out. He began walking along the tunnel toward the Venom Arena, prepared to take the turns described on the paper.

After twenty minutes of walking, occasionally seeing rats and bug nests, but little else, Shel asked, "Shouldn't we have found it already? I mean, it wouldn't have taken close to this long to just walk to the underground portion of the Venom Arena."

Wolfe had already come to that conclusion and was irritated —his backpack was *heavy*. He thrust the paper at her and growled out, "Well, *you* tell me what I did wrong then."

Shel took the map and looked at the directions for a moment. "Well, on the third step, we didn't take a left, we took a right."

"There *was* no left! I assumed he just wrote the wrong direction down."

Shel didn't respond, just looking at the map for a bit. After a moment, she glanced up at him. "I found the problem."

"Do tell," Wolfe said, sarcastically.

"When we went down the hatch in the first place, I'm pretty sure you were supposed to start walking away from the Venom Arena. The next two turns, before the third step left, were both rights, followed by a long tunnel."

"So?" Wolfe asked.

Shel half smiled at him in the glow cast by the flashlight. "*So*, two lefts faces us backwards—we needed to get to some other pipe headed that way."

"Fucking joy."

Shel looked back down at the paper. "I think if we head down the connecting pipe in the other direction at step four we'll get back on track and cut about ten minutes off the total return trip."

"Alright, *you* lead us," Wolfe replied, adjusting the weight of the backpack on his shoulders.

Shel took the flashlight and headed back, carefully following the path back for about ten minutes. At the rough halfway mark, she cut a different direction than Wolfe had come from down an even larger pipe.

As they walked along the path, however, Wolfe noticed a slight green glow coming from the ground ahead of them.

"Stop!"

Shel stopped. Wolfe stepped up and took the flashlight from her, then shrugged off the backpack and pulled his Edge out.

"What is it?" Shel asked, briefly glancing at Wolfe's pistol and then staring forward.

"I'm... not sure," Wolfe replied. "But I'm not taking chances."

Wolfe stalked forward. The metal tunnel was perfectly cut on one side by a stacked-rock entrance way, with a shimmer of toxic green across the entrance, and an old stone hallway covered in vines visible past it.

Wolfe stared at the entrance as Shel walked up behind him.

"Is... is that a dungeon entrance?" she asked, awed.

"I think it is," Wolfe replied. "I can't believe we just stumbled upon it, now of all times."

"Yeah," Shel said.

Wolfe continued. "I wonder if it's from this season or if it's an undiscovered one from an earlier season."

"It could have gone undiscovered for a decade or two," Shel said. "Or even longer. Some of these tunnels were built when Noimoire was first being built, and never put into use. There are a lot of abandoned M line tunnels as well, although I think homeless people started using those ones almost immediately."

"Huh."

The two stared at the entrance for a bit longer.

"Are we going to... go in?" Shel asked. "Get more cards?"

Wolfe shook his head. "No. Just remember how we got here, and write it down once we're out. We'll come back in a few days or weeks, after this is all over, to get cards and make levels. This is a huge find—and makes up for the one I lost to the city because of the Cobras. But we have more important things to do."

Shel nodded, and the two turned from the dungeon entrance. Wolfe grabbed his backpack, grunting as he put it on, and then they headed the rest of the way down Shel's shortcut. It cut back out into another abandoned sewer tunnel, not very different than the rest, that Shel claimed would take them to their destination.

When the next three directions were all able to be followed correctly, Wolfe was also convinced she had found the path, and a few minutes after that, they started to hear cheering, clapping, and the sound of an announcer calling out the play-by-play on a fight.

It was less than sixty seconds after that when Wolfe and Shel arrived at their destination—a grate in the side of the sewer wall, blocked up with thin, rusted iron bars.

Wolfe looked out on the underground fight ring. Two guys, both beefy white dudes dressed in nothing but workout shorts, were whaling on each other in the center of a ring, with an announcer at the side calling it out. "Looks like Raffio is getting hit in the head way too often! He's gonna go down soon, I think, and if he doesn't, I'm sure this isn't doing his last few brain cells any good!"

Wolfe snorted. "Everyone thinks they're a joker."

Shel raised an eyebrow at him.

"Hey, *I'm* good at it," Wolfe said.

He turned back. The space was obviously a converted underground gym, with a couple workout mats and smaller rings surrounding a larger one. High school gym stands had been set up around the place, and about a hundred people were there, mostly sitting in the stands—Cobra thugs as well as a bunch of guys in obvious fighting clothes. But there were a few others, as well—older people that didn't appear at all to be part of the gang.

Who are they? Why are they here?

Wolfe put it from his mind, and took the pack of his back with a sigh of relief. He slowly and quietly unzipped it and took the C4 bomb out, placing it up against the vent. He knelt down and prepared to set the timer, giving him ample ability to get out.

"Wolfe, please... wait," Shel said, putting her hand on his as he started to set it up.

Wolfe looked up into her green eyes. "What?"

"You can't. You can't do this, I mean. It'll kill everyone. All those people. You have to find another way."

Are you fucking kidding me? Now this?

CHAPTER 37

FALL OF THE FIRST CHAMPION

"**The Great Game, Rule #93**: Building cards cost 5 leveling pips for the current and each previous picked. Building cards occupy a slot and have no cost. They create a physical, magical structure that can bring magic into the world, either directly or by altering deckbearers and their cards."

"Are you serious, Shel? You don't want me to kill Jason? *Everyone* will be after me if we don't!"

"Not that, Wolfe. I... I just don't want you to bomb everyone. For your soul."

Wolfe snorted loudly, then glanced around. In a quieter voice, but one as sarcastic as he could make it, he addressed Shel. "My *soul*? Are you kidding me? I've killed upwards of forty people, Shel. My soul is stained beyond black."

Shel shook her head. "No. Everyone you killed was part of the Cobras, right?"

Wolfe nodded. "That or some earlier gang that tried to kill or steal from us."

"So, they had already openly declared war on you. *All* the

Cobras knew about it, and most participated in the attacks on Drop Night, right?"

Wolfe nodded a second time. "Yeah, so?"

"Everyone we attacked was engaged in Cobra business—guarding drugs they took, attacking you and your friends, or with known, ultra-violent lieutenants, things like that. So they were enemies, Wolfe. Legitimate targets. When a man kills another on the battlefield, does his soul belong to the Infernal?"

"No."

"Exactly. So you're not gone, not yet. But this is evil, Wolfe. It's indiscriminate, and some of those people will never be Cobras. I think some are just family members here to support a guy in his fighting career. If we bomb them... we're lost. I mean, would even Cereboo want this?"

Wolfe sighed. He thought about it for a moment, but his gut was telling him she was right—and his mind saw Cereboo's disapproving expression. And the lost one on Shel's face. She would feel forever tainted by his actions if he went forward. He would ruin her life more thoroughly than anyone if he killed all these people.

Wolfe took the bomb and placed it back in his large rucksack and stood. "Alright, well, let's go find Nico. I mean, I *really* don't want to tell Big Man Grimm I failed without having something to show for it if at all possible."

Shel was staring at the grate now. "What... what if there was another way to kill Jason?"

"You want to kill him?" Wolfe asked.

Shel nodded. "I've seen the darkness the Cobras spread. Even if Jason wasn't the one that killed my brother himself, his gang obviously doesn't care at all. And *they're* the real reason that all this death is happening. We should stop him."

"And you have a plan?"

"I... it's not a great plan, but..." she trailed off.

"Spit it out," Wolfe said.

"Well... these bars are really rusted. What if, during some cheering or something, you busted them open and we went in? No one will really check us if we're already inside."

"A lot of them know my face, Shel. You weren't there, but in the ambush that led me to learning about Frankie, one of the Cobras flat out knew me on sight, even in the rain and darkness."

Shel blushed and twirled her finger in her long red hair. "So, you go to one of the side rooms, a storage space or something. I'll go... um... flirt with Jason. He can't be interested in every fight—I'll proposition him and take him to you. Then you can jump him before he can get his deck out."

"You think he'll just follow you back?" Wolfe asked. "Just like that?"

Shel nodded. "Yeah. Most of the thugs we've met, whether Cobra or Grimm, have given me the eye. A lot of eye in some cases. You said this Jason guy is super violent, right? Well, it frequently tracks with male sexual desire—he'll probably follow me back. And when he does—Pow."

"Pow, huh?" Wolfe asked.

Shel nodded.

The idea of Shel allowing the Cobra leader to paw all over her really angered Wolfe—it felt wrong to use her that way, to allow that to happen to her.

On the other hand... Wolfe had done the vast, vast majority of the work in "bringing her brother's killers to justice." Maybe mattering in the outcome, and sacrificing a little bit, in the process was important to Shel.

And, Wolfe had to admit to himself, it was better than bombing everyone or going back to the Grimm family with Jason *unkilled* because Wolfe had a crisis of conscience.

He still hated it, though. On a lot of levels.

"You know there's a decent chance this half-assed plan falls through, right? That I get caught, that he doesn't follow you, something. That ends *really* badly. Are you sure you want to do this? Really sure?"

Shel met his eyes with her deep green ones, and conviction shown. "I do, Wolfe. I want to bring my brother's killers to justice. I want to help you complete your mission. And I don't want us to be evil. I'm sorry I didn't say things earlier, when we could have a better plan, but I think this one has at least a better than fifty-fifty chance of success."

Five fifty-fifty plans in a row and you're dead like ninety-five percent of the time, Wolfe thought, but he supposed this was important enough to take the chance. "All right. Let's do it."

Twenty-five minutes later, Wolfe was in a large supply room, with wrestling mats, weight-lifting gear, cleaning supplies, and other various sundries. Wolfe himself was hidden deep behind a whole stack of mats near the door, on the side away from them.

He was being as still as possible, controlling his breathing, so he would make no noise. He was ducked low behind the mat so no one would find him without making two turns. Wolfe had even spilled a bit of cleaner to try and make sure his smell was covered up. He didn't want to give away his position as he crouched, a wrench he had found clenched in his right hand.

Wolfe was beyond antsy, though. Perhaps, he admitted to himself, even scared. It had been nerve-wracking, trying to break through the rusted bars "quietly," during moments the crowd was cheering. It had been nerve-wracking walking back here. And waiting for nearly twenty minutes so far, occasionally hearing the muted cheers of the crowd through the walls and footsteps outside, was nerve-wracking.

His nerves were well past wracked and into completely shot at this point.

C'mon, pull yourself together! You've been in plenty of tough spots.

Wolfe quietly rubbed his left hand on his pants, trying to lose the sweat. He knew why he was so out-of-sorts. In most cases when he was in a "tough situation," he could simply work his way out with violence. But in this case, if he was caught, he was well and truly fucked. There was no "fight your way free" option. He had to rely on stealth, and he hated it.

He *also* had to rely on Shel. To get manhandled or ogled enough to get here without getting caught or otherwise hurt. And Wolfe could do almost nothing about it. When they had made the plan, Wolfe had forgotten that he had let five people go that knew what Shel looked like. He was sweating bullets now, worried sick.

But it had been only twenty minutes, and he had to give her time.

A few minutes later, when Wolfe was at about the point of a futile charge to save Shel, the door popped open, and the muted sounds of the crowd, none too excited at the moment, seeped in. Along with a couple footsteps—one heavy, one light.

"C'mon, girlie, we're here now."

"Just let me shut the door," Shel said.

"I've got it," the other voice said and the door slammed.

From his angle, Wolfe watched. After a moment, Shel was pushed past the point where he could see her around the mats. She was facing Wolfe, walking backward as a huge bear of a man with graying hair, around Wolfe's age, pushed her up against a shelf filled with tools. The man was dressed in a cheap suit, and he shrugged out of the coat as he nuzzled at Shel's neck. As Wolfe slowly stood, the man started to push Shel's pink crop top up, exposing the underside of a white satin bra despite Shel pushing downward on the man's hands.

Wolfe rushed the last few steps, and Jason—Wolfe hoped—started to rise. But Wolfe brought the wrench down as hard as he could on the base of Jason's head. The resounding crack was loud, and the spray of blood got Wolfe across his arm and black shirt.

Jason dropped bonelessly to the ground.

Shel pushed her shirt down and shuddered, then looked at the man at their feet.

Wolfe pushed his combat log away—it only told him what he could have guessed, that Jason was seriously hurt and knocked out, but not dead.

"Is... is that it?" Shel asked. "We won? Just like that?"

Wolfe was breathing hard, more from the adrenaline dump and his nerves than the tiny bit of exhaustion. He was in full fight mode, and things did appear to be over.

He was both profoundly relieved and a tiny bit disappointed. Every other Cobra guy of any significance that Wolfe had finished off had been a huge battle, with some crazy deck fights. Wolfe figured he was owed an easy one, but didn't trust that the easy one was the Cobra's leader.

Jason had gone down to a slightly fancy mugging. It seemed surreal.

Although it wasn't quite done. Wolfe reared back and kicked Jason in the back of the neck as hard as he could with his heel. Shel gasped and turned away, and Wolfe dismissed the notification telling him that he had made another level.

A pile of cards appeared on Jason's back.

"Did... did you have to?" Shel asked, then, before Wolfe could answer, "Wait, nevermind. Of course you did. We can't lug him out of here for the police. Sorry. It was just... so sudden. And brutal. I'm not used to this yet."

Wolfe nodded, pleased she hadn't gone retarded on him. "He was a very bad man. Like my boss, with a pile of violence and rage issues added on, and no sense of self-restraint. We were better off without him."

Shel nodded, shuddering. "Yeah, I know. I know."

Wolfe reached down and took the pile of cards. There were twenty, and he quickly flipped through them. A bunch of named Aesthma, Infernal lord of wrath cards were present in the deck. And almost all were either rare, or higher than tier-1. It was an extremely expensive deck. But Wolfe was looking for one card in particular, and after a second, he found it.

Shel glanced over as Wolfe examined the card.

Infernal Rift
Unique tier-8 equivalent Enhancer/Persistent card
1 Infernal Power (permanent)

Special: When this card is played, any one deckbearer that has no creature cards on the field is banished to a faux Infernal realm for 90 seconds

Special: When this card is added to your deck, one persistent card may be permanently made into an Infernal card, gaining benefits and a second typing. This card will reflect the named Infernal most represented in the deck if any is. Any modified sub-cards are affected as well.

Special: When this card is added to your deck, one minion card may be made into an Infernal card, becoming a 2-power equivalent companion with a free card slot and gaining benefits and a second typing. This card will reflect the named Infernal most represented in the deck if any is. Any modified sub-cards are affected as well.

Special: When this card is added to your deck, one building card may be made into and Infernal building with a free card slot and gaining a second typing. This card will reflect the named Infernal most represented in the deck if any is. Any modified sub-cards are affected as well.

Special: Any benefit may take place after the fact if it has not taken effect, but afterward it may never happen a second time.

Special: If the card leaves the deck, all benefits are lost, and all cards revert.

"A permanent rift to the realm of an Infernal Lord, this hole between dimensions influences everything around it, tainting it all with demonic influence."

Shel whistled, her green eyes wide as she took it in.

Wolfe knew he was bug-eyed as well. "That is a *very* powerful card, Damian wasn't kidding. I can see why he wants it."

Shel nodded. "Even though it weakens you by a power, a free companion slot is insanely good. And making other cards in your deck stronger is nice as well."

"What do you think 'modified sub-cards' are?" Wolfe asked.

"No idea," Shel replied. "It seems like the weakest part of the power."

Wolfe held the card up. "As soon as we're back in the tunnels, I'm going to sub this in. We still have to go get Nico. I'll look at the rest of the cards later, but this is far too good to pass up heading into that fight."

Wolfe sighed. "Assuming we can get out of here without getting ourselves caught."

CHAPTER 38

AND THEN THERE WAS ONE

"**The Great Game, Rule #101**: Persistent(Equipment) cards may be found. Each adds to either the deckbearers stats or the stats of a card, and must be attached to one or the other. No card may have more than one equipment on it at a time."

"Do you think we're far enough away from the place to use this yet," Wolfe asked, holding the Infernal Rift card up.

"Give it a bit more distance, maybe?" Shel asked.

Wolfe sighed.

"Wonder what happened to Marko?" Shel asked, probably to distract him.

"Not really," Wolfe replied, looking distractedly at the Infernal Rift card in his hand. "He's probably sworn vengeance on me and my little pooch too, and is hunting me at the moment. I'll probably need to shoot him or move soon. Why?"

"I don't know... it's just him and Nico left, right?"

Wolfe nodded. "Yup. If they both go down, the Cobras will absolutely fall apart. Although if Nico goes down, I'm pretty sure the Cobras will fall apart regardless. Marko has less organizational skills than a rabid meerkat. They kept him around for the ultra-violence."

"So, if we take Nico out of the picture..."

"You've gotten vengeance for your brother and made the world safer as well," Wolfe said. "The whole gang will fall, partially as a result of attacking your brother. I think there are one or two points that I would have died without your healing and support—or at least would have backed off, like in the pound."

Shel smiled. "I... I like to think that I mattered."

"Well... pretty sure I'd have bombed this whole facility if you hadn't been here, so you likely mattered a lot from that standpoint, even if nothing else you did tipped the situation."

Wolfe held the card up again. "Think that we're far enough away from the place to use this?"

"Are we there yet?" Shel asked in a whiny, child-like voice.

Wolfe laughed. "Fair, ya ingrate. But are we?"

Shel chuckled as well. "Yeah, probably."

Wolfe smiled and touched his chest, pulling his deck out. He doubted strongly anyone got a *deckbearer has pulled a deck* type notification, and doubted they would have a minute ago. Still, he was a tiny bit nervous.

But not enough to stop him from trading out the Tier-one Escaped Damned for the Infernal Rift.

Immediately, his mind was flooded with options—options that were then picked for him. Wolfe had no building cards, but he had a ton of other cards. He could only add the Infernal to one persistent card that wasn't Infernal—which made the only choice in his current deck the No Kill Pound. Then it looked for a non-Infernal minion card, and found his only qualifying card —the Possessed Orphan.

Wolfe stared at the two new cards.

Cerberus's Home For Wayward Hellhounds

Unique Tier-1 equivalent Persistent
1 Infernal, 1 Beast, and 1 Any power

Special: Any Beast with 'Puppy' or 'Rescue' in its title has +50%
Attack and Defense.
Special: Generates a Lost Hellhound Puppy at no power cost
every 30 seconds until Level/5 Lost Hellhound Puppies are on
the field, rounded up.
Special: If any opponent 'sacrifices' a creature card type Beast,
that card joins you instead of being destroyed until the fight
ends.
Special: You cannot sacrifice Beast cards.

"This card is the only pound in existence that tries to find homes
for the few Bad Doggos in the universe. Perhaps with proper
attention, they too can be Good Boys."

Wolfe could feel something else in his deck change, and
flipped until he found his Rescue Pup cards. They had changed
to match his new demonic pound.

Lost Hellhound Puppy
Rare Tier-1 Beast/Infernal(Canine) Creature
1 Beast or Infernal Power [Available]
Health: 8
Attack: 4
Magical Attack: 3
Defense: 4
Magical Defense: 4

Special: Does not require upkeep—is a zero-cost monster.
Special: If slain, all Mortal and Beast cards in play gain +50%
Physical Attack for the next 30 seconds.

Special: May be merged with Rescue Pup cards, but advances as
if Rare in quality.

"A poor lost Hellhound, outside its normal realm."

Excited, Wolfe flipped to his new minion card.

Malviere, Conduit of Cerberus
Unqiue, no-tier Mortal/Infernal companion[Orphan, Canine]
0 Power
Health: 13
Attack: N/A
Defense: 3
Magical Attack: N/A
Magical Defense: 5

Special: Will fetch normal objects and such with a decent degree
of precision and help carry up to ten pounds.
Special: If kept 'alive' for five straight years, will turn into a tier-6
equivalent companion card, gaining notable power. If ever
'killed,' the timer resets.
Special: So long as she is on the field, all [Canine] creature cards
gain +1 to all stats.
Special: Once every 30 seconds, the most powerful Beast card on
the field will make a second attack or magical attack, whichever
is its highest score.
Special: Is liked by all canines, and can command them to do her
bidding—including the [Canine] creature cards of other
deckbearers, which, if summoned, will switch sides without
returning their power.

"Malviere cannot remember any life except that of acting as a
conduit for the great guardian of the gates of the Infernal,
Cerberus. She aids his chosen hunters on the Mortal plane, to

bring back those that Hell has lost. And she gets to play with *all* the doggos. Good, and bad."

Wolfe whistled at his new card, but didn't summon it. He stared at the picture, with its brown hair and hazel eyes. It reminded him far too much of his sister, although the resemblance wasn't strong.

"Bring her out!" Shel said, excitedly.

Wolfe shook his head. "I don't want to get attached. A little girl, with brown hair and an actual personality? I *really* don't want to do that. I have to give this card back to Damian, remember?"

Shel sighed. "Yeah... that makes sense."

Then she glanced up at him again. "You're always asking me if I'm sure I don't want to just leave... Are you sure you don't just want to kill Nico and then we can leave together? I mean, you'll have saved the Grimm family, and you'll have a ton of fancy new cards you can sell."

Wolfe almost tripped as he thought about it. He was so very tempted.

He shook his head. "No. Damian would still come after me, and the Big Man wouldn't trust me. I need to do this right, Shel. It'll be worth it in the long run."

She nodded. "Well, it'll get you out of the gang, get us safe, and then... we'll see. That's all I really want, now, besides finishing the Cobras off."

Wolfe heaved a sigh. "Man, not that Damian hasn't had some great ideas—including the one that got us this card—but it rankles, to have him getting what was the reward for my risk."

She nodded sympathetically.

Wolfe exhaled nosily a second time. "I will *really* miss this card. Let's go find Nico and get this over with."

The two of them followed the path the rest of the way back until they found the metal ladder that led to the surface. Wolfe reached up to grab a rung and start climbing. As he did, he caught a whiff of his own armpit and grimaced—he was rank from all the stress-sweat.

Then he chuckled. *For a trip through the sewers in which I killed someone, I smell like a fucking flower garden.*

Wolfe climbed out of the hole and took a deep breath. The sewers might not have been smelly per se, but they had still been stuffy—and making it back to the surface felt like freedom.

Wolfe held his hand down and grasped Shel's wrist, and gave a heave, bringing her the rest of the way out and moving her over solid ground before dropping her again.

Wolfe glanced around. It was late in the evening, and the sun was down, but the last dregs of red streaks still lit the sky. The lights of the Venom Arena lit the large parking lot he was in and the numerous cars now occupying it. As Wolfe took in his surroundings, his eyes fell on a man standing at a car in the back of the Venom parking lot, watching the front of the arena and smoking. He was about five-foot-ten, with a black ponytail over thinning, salt-and-pepper hair, dressed in a leather jacket with the arms torn off. On one arm was the symbol Wolfe most hated now—the flared snake of the Cobra gang. On the back of the jacket was a skull with five cards spread below it.

Wolfe reached out and put his hand over Shel's mouth, even though she hadn't said a thing. "That's Nico! I swear to all the gods, that's Nico right there!"

She stared, then looked up at him and raised an eyebrow.

Wolfe took his hand away from her mouth. "Seriously? Nico just happens to be here?"

Wolfe frowned. "Or maybe it isn't happenstance. Maybe he's here, waiting for the Venom Arena to blow up so he can ambush and kill me on the way out. He took the opportunity to hit the Ekron Eternal when he was formally allied with us."

"Why doesn't he have his people with him?" Shel asked.

"His people? You mean, the Cobras whose leader he would

be acting like he knew was assassinated as he just waited around? That's the only part I'm sure of in all this—he doesn't want to be seen being dirty."

Shel nodded. "So... what do we do?"

Wolfe smiled and pulled his pistol, reversing it and grabbing the handle. "I can't believe how easy this shit is, but I'm not going to spurn a gifted card."

Shel nodded. Wolfe shrugged out of the backpack with the bomb, then put his hand beside him, keeping his Edge down and hopefully out of view, since he was now back in the open. He was glad it was evening and at least a bit dark, but he didn't want to take chances.

"Watch the backpack," Wolfe said to Shel, who nodded.

Wolfe walked quickly but carefully, heading for the person that was closest to a nemesis he had in the world.

CHAPTER 39

CHASING THE END

"**The Great Game, Rule #108**: Companion cards have been added to the game. Each requires a slot purchased at a cost of 5 leveling pips plus 5 per previous pick. Each card may be present in the world at all times and is costless and unique."

Wolfe tried to remain quiet until he closed with Nico. At the last moment, he accelerated his run and raised his pistol, swinging the butt down toward the Cobra lieutenant's head.

Nico must have heard something, because he started to turn. Wolfe clocked him in the back of the head with the butt of his Edge, knocking the Cobra lieutenant down to the ground, but Nico immediately rolled, his eyes scanning as he awkwardly scrabbled at his gun and touching his chest, pushing five cards out of his chest that mixed a fiery red, bone white, and black, somehow, glow, depending on the card. He reached for one with a shaking hand, obviously stunned from the blow.

But Wolfe didn't give the half-conscious man a chance to

recover. His shoe met Nico's jaw, and the man's arms dropped limply to the ground, his legs spasming once then stilling as well.

The cards hovering in front of Nico's chest faded, and Wolfe couldn't help but not be surprised that someone with Nico's history had Infernal, Undead, and Death as his power types.

"Shel! Give me a hand!" Wolfe called, and Shel hurried over.

"Is...is that it, then?" Shel asked, staring down at Nico. "After all this, you've won—the last two Cobra bosses went down without a fight?"

Wolfe shrugged, feeling elated at his victory. "Seems like it, but how about we focus on what's in front of us? We still have things we need to take care of."

I've taken five of the Cobra leaders down in three days. I may only have one real skill, but gods' damned am I good at it.

Shel was watching him, her eyes knowing. "Feeling your oats, huh?"

"Something like that," Wolfe said.

Shel kept smiling as she stared at him. "Well, don't forget the lesson here—being a good person kept you alive."

"What are you talking about?" Wolfe asked, quirking his eyes at her.

"Well, obviously he was waiting for the Venom Arena to blow up. It was his information that gave us the path to plant the bomb, so he knew about the sewer entrance. If the Arena had exploded, I'm sure he would have been waiting to fill you with holes once you exited the tunnel."

Wolfe's blood went cold. *She's almost certainly right. Fuck. I need to be more careful. And crap do we all betray each other. I think I'll miss the lifestyle to some degree, and certainly the thrill of victory, when I leave. But I won't miss this shit at all.*

He shook off the moment. "Well, I keep some rope in my trunk—grab that for me and let's get him trussed up like a Thanksgiving turkey. I want to get him to Big Man Grimm as soon as possible, and I don't want him waking up able to pull cards along the way."

Wolfe pulled his keys from his pocket and tossed them to Shel, who fumbled and dropped them, flushed, then picked them up and headed off to the car.

Wolfe glanced down at Nico, keeping his pistol vaguely pointed at the Cobra lieutenant. He was half-tempted to pull the trigger and explain his way out of the situation with Big Man Grimm and Damian—after all, this was the man that had given Wolfe his chest scar, and Wolfe knew of the sheer horror Nico had perpetuated on others as well—including innocent others.

He was even the main culprit for the death of Shel's brother.

On the other hand, Wolfe was in the open, and someone would likely hear a gunshot.

Wolfe sighed. "I might as well take you back to the Grimm family. You were disappointing in the end, Nico. I didn't need my deck for you after all."

Shel came running back with the rope. Wolfe took it from her and they trussed Nico utterly, tying feet, hands, knees, and elbows together, and then linking all of those in a single hog-tie. Shel went and got the car, and once there, the two of them loaded Nico into the back.

Wolfe took the driver's seat and they headed out of the parking lot, pulling carefully into traffic, heading toward Main.

"Do you think your boss is going to kill Nico?" Shel asked from the passenger seat, tapping her fingers together.

"Yeah," Wolfe said. "He's gonna make a statement out of it. Johnny, Heinrich, the Ekron Eternal—Nico's done an absolute *ton* of damage. He won't be allowed to get away with it."

"Uh," came a voice from the back, and some shuffling. Wolfe glanced into his rearview mirror. Nico was squirming like crazy, somehow managing to get into a half-sitting position despite being tied like crazy.

He looked like some insane rope-bondage fetishist in his

later years. Given his size and age, Wolfe was surprised he was flexible enough to pull it off. Wolfe took him in again—two inches under six feet with salt-and-pepper hair that led to a more purely black ponytail. He was almost emaciated thin, but he was wiry—the arms exposed by his sleeveless jacket were muscled.

"I thought I might have kicked you so hard you woke up in 6g," Wolfe quipped. "Glad to see you'll be awake for your execution."

Nico smiled at Wolfe with a superior smile. "My execution. Sure."

Then he grimaced and worked his jaw for a moment. "You caught me good though, I can't deny, Wolfe," Nico said.

Then he spit blood onto Wolfe's seat.

Wolfe gripped the wheel tighter. His car was pretty much beyond saving at this point—smashed, shot up, windows blown out, and the back seat had blood from Shel and now Nico in it. Half of Wolfe was tempted to pull over and throw Nico a beating, but he knew that's what the Cobra wanted—a chance to escape, or yell for help, or something.

"Spit on the seat all you want," Wolfe said. "Car's a loss anyway. It was a price I happily paid to put an end to your sad gang."

Nico worked his mouth again and spit forward. Wolfe half-dodged, and the mixed globule of spit and blood landed on his shoulder.

Nico giggled insanely.

Wolfe tapped the brake hard and Nico flew forward, his face smashing into the seat. Inventive cursing followed, and Wolfe laughed.

"I like this new game," he mused. "Let's keep playing it."

"I'm going to enjoy watching you die," Nico ground out.

"Did you kill my brother?" Shel blurted. "Kevin Lyons?"

Nico squirmed back into his semi-sitting position and faced

her, his eyes considering, as if he were seeing her for the first time.

"Did you!" Shel half screamed. "I have to know!"

Nico was silent for a moment longer, but then he smiled. "I'm tempted not to answer, just to hurt you—but there'll be time for that later. I did kill him. Like breaking a chicken's neck —there was almost no fuss."

Wolfe stared back at Nico. "Billy was confident too, right before I redecorated in brain. You Cobras—what few of you are left now, I mean, you're kind of an endangered species—need to stop using your own product. Cuts into the margins."

Before Nico could respond, Shel cut in again, her voice raw, on the verge of sobbing. "Why kill him?"

Nico shrugged. "It wasn't personal, truly. I just needed a life —well, I needed someone to die—for one of my cards. Perhaps you'll get to see him one last time soon."

Tears began leaking down Shel's face, and her voice was choked. "You're a monster. He was my brother. The only one that was even halfway nice to me."

Nico smiled beatifically, as if utterly untouched by her comments, or her pain. "I *am* a monster—and I'm going to be the most powerful monster that ever lived. But *everyone* is someone's brother, or daughter, or father, or whatever."

"Christ, you have more unjustified confidence than a French general," Wolfe said.

Nico shrugged again, still smiling. It was starting to get on Wolfe's nerves.

"How about we play the quiet game until we reach the Grimm family, huh?"

"It's your dollar," Nico said, grinning up at the ceiling from his awkward sitting position.

Wolfe pulled his phone out and dialed Thad Sr.

"Wolfe? Is everything okay? Are you okay?" came the Big Man's voice.

"I'm fine. Jason is dead. I'm bringing Nico in."

Fifteen minutes later, Wolfe pulled into 111 Greenbow Way, the Grimm family mansion. It was well lit, but some of the lights were red, giving it a demonic feel. Wolfe had to admit that it worked—the place had an entirely different vibe at night, all alone by itself in the darkness and lit up with blood red light.

"Wow, there are a *lot* of other cars here," Shel said.

Wolfe gritted his teeth. "The Big Man said he wanted a spectacle. Given everything Nico has done, I can't say I blame him."

"Ah, I'm touched you noticed," Nico muttered from the back.

Wolfe parked the car in front of the main entrance and got out, followed by Shel, who stood looking up at the mansion.

"They really do lean into their image, don't they?" Shel asked.

Wolfe went to the trunk of the car and opened it up, taking the backpack with the bomb from it and shrugging it on, grimacing as the old wounds in his side twinged.

In just a few minutes, I won't need to lug this blasted thing around anymore.

He stepped back around the car to the rear passenger side as Shel waited. He pulled open the door, and then dragged Nico out. The Cobra promptly fell on his face and cussed.

Wolfe sighed. *No chance this fucker gets away now.* He bent down and undid the foot ropes—but not the knee ones. Nico could stand and barely shuffle forward. Wolfe grabbed the ropes around his back and pushed him onward while simultaneously holding him from falling.

Nico shuffled forward like a penguin on crack, taking a ton

of rapid, tiny steps as they approached the door. Bobby stood waiting there, and he gave a salute—unironically, Wolfe thought —and opened the door, permitting Wolfe and Shel to enter, still pushing Nico in front of them.

Inside the mansion was the same blood-red lighting. Wolfe knew the Big Man was going for theatricality, but it was simultaneously garish and nerve-wracking.

Shel gave one quiet, "Whoa!" to the décor of the front foyer —giant oil paintings and statues of the Infernal. *Right, she only ever went into the left side entrance with me. Shel hasn't seen all the amazing art Big Man Grimm likes to collect.*

While Shel was distracted, Wolfe shrugged the bomb off and left it, inside its backpack, in the front foyer. He stretched his back out.

"That the thing you were supposed to set off?" Nico asked.

"It doesn't matter to you anymore," Wolfe said. "Keep moving."

Wolfe pushed Nico forward into the main hall. It was even more garish than the front room, with tons of statues, rich red carpets, and two giant, wide stairs with huge bannisters that led up to the second story.

All around the room were numerous members of the Grimm mob family, most of them wearing suits. Wolfe barely knew one in five, and frowned at all the holes in their ranks. Who were these new *nameless thugs*? Wolfe didn't like being surrounded by new blood.

His eyes automatically searched for his boss, and Wolfe saw him at the top of the stairs flanked by his two sons, huge curtains behind them on the balcony with demons displayed. Damian was back in his burgundy suit, and Thad Jr. had finally managed to put on a suit with a normal tie.

I wonder where Miriam is? Did she get sent away? Big Man Grimm doesn't normally like her around this part of the family business.

Wolfe's boss stared down on them, a tight smile on his face.

"Wolfe, my best and most loyal packmate! You've brought our enemies low, I see—cast them down into *our* pit, to burn in *our* fires. The fate that will be shared by all who would contest the family favored of Beelzebub."

Wolfe wanted to make a crack, but here in the red light, surrounded by statues of demons, he just nodded to Big Man Grimm's over-the-top declaration.

Big Man Grimm walked along the balcony, his hand on the railing, and stepped onto the first step of stairs down. All eyes were on him.

"Nico, I will have your life for your crimes against the family, as I will have the life of *everyone* that moves against us." Big Man Grimm theatrically took another step.

"You ordered the hit on Johnny, and pulled the trigger yourself." Another step.

"You ordered the hit on Heinrich, my cousin." Another step.

"You ordered the attack on all our men on Drop Night." Another step.

Big Man Grimm stopped. "What do you have to say for yourself, if anything?"

Nico smiled. "Just two things. One, I didn't order *anything*. And two, well..." He glanced up to the balcony. "Anytime now."

"Clean house," Damian said, his voice dark and grim and sounding entirely too much like his father.

Damian pulled a massive Desert Eagle 50 caliber pistol from beneath his suit coat, a heavier gun than even Wolfe's Edge. Damian touched his own chest.

Deckbearer Damian Grimm has pulled his deck near you.

Wolfe felt trapped in a surreal nightmare, or perhaps the Infernal realm the Grimm were trying to emulate. He desperately yanked his own pistol from his pants.

All around them, the *nameless thugs* drew their own handguns and faced them at the Grimm men nearest them.

Damian leveled his massive pistol at the back of his father's head and pulled the trigger, almost falling over with the recoil. But Big Man Grimm's face exploded outward in a shower of blood, bone, and gore.

The once-leader of the Grimm family tumbled down the stairs as his cards flew out all around him.

CHAPTER 40

FALL FROM GRACE

"**The Great Game, Rule #109**: Deckbearers chosen by a named faction member on Drop Night shall henceforth have one additional companion card slot and faction associated companion."

A ll around Wolfe, guns erupted. Almost a fifth of the people in the room—many older family members that had been around for years if not decades—were killed instantly, but there were enough loyalists left that a fire fight started.

Thad Jr. touched his chest as well, bringing his deck out.

Then Damian touched his mantle card. A glowing red aura sprang around him before settling back, giving the tubby little traitor black scales, horns, and wings—and a glowing crown of fire.

Duke of the Legion
Unique Tier-5 equivalent Infernal Persistent(Mantle)
2 Infernal Power

Special: the wearer gains +7 Defense
Special: Wearer gains +15 Health
Special: All Infernal Cards cost 1 less power
Special: All Infernal Cards gain +25% to all stats
Special: One of the 'Gate to the Underworld' cards. If all 6 are
possessed in the same deck, the bearer will gain 7 Legendary
Infernal or Beast card pulls. Additionally, the deckbearer may
either gain the Mythic 'Gate to the Underworld' Building Card
or evolve Cereboo. One card is held by each of the crime families
of Noimoire, and the sixth is held within the city by another.

"This person has been chosen to lead the demons of the
Infernal, and they have been given the power to do so. Demons
come extremely cheaply and are far more powerful."

Damian's eyes were wide as he stared at Wolfe, however, and
he held his hands up and yelled down to Wolfe amid the red
light, gunfire, and screams. "No need for that, Wolfe. You're a
loyal dog, and you've told me multiple times that you're loyal to
the Grimm family. *I'm* the Grimm family now, and you'll have
your rightful place by my side, not the side of my soft father. But
you have to give me your card, Cereboo—I *will* complete that
set, Wolfe."

Wolfe knew that Javier must have told Nico, who told
Damian, about Cereboo. But it didn't matter one damn bit.
Wolfe was gonna kill the patricidal dwarf no matter what, and
cards had nothing to do with it.

"How could you, Damian?" Wolfe roared. "*How could you
kill your own father? He* was my friend! We were thinking of
leaving the business and turning it over to you!"

"Not fast enough," Damian said with a sneer.

Wolfe touched his own chest and fired rapidly at Damian,
who yelled in fear as one bullet took him in the chest—although
it did little. He dropped behind the balcony, and screamed out,

"You would spurn me, Wolfe! You want the cards for yourself, don't you? Fine. We'll do it your way!"

Wolfe glanced at his cards. *No mantle.* He grabbed his Fireborn Hellhound and tossed it into the fray.

A flash of golden light told him that Shel had pulled her deck as well.

Damian wasn't done yelling, and his voice rose even louder. "A hundred thousand to anyone that brings me Wolfe's corpse!"

Multiple people trained their guns on Wolfe.

Wolfe sprinted to the side as bullets shot around him, miraculously only taking a single glancing hit to his thigh as he did. He leapt the last bit, sliding on the cool marble floor into the side hall.

As he slid, he turned onto his side and fired back, just over his own legs, at the people chasing him. One went down almost comically, his top half slewing backwards as he ran after Wolfe, and the other couple dived to the side.

Shel ran into the room as well, Sorenia beside her.

Wolfe leapt to his feet. "Put your mantle on!"

"It's not in the draw," she screamed back, still running.

Wolfe threw a Lost Hellhound Puppy out. His notifications informed him that the Fireborn Hellhound had heavily damaged a thug but was eating bullets rapidly.

Wolfe saw Nico hobbling away and shot at him, but Nico managed to dive into the very front hall.

Thad Jr. ran down the stairs and pointed his pistol, a Glock 17 police issue, at Wolfe. Wolfe pulled his trigger first, and the Big Man's eldest son lost his own head in a shower of gore, dying as easily and pointlessly as he had lived, not even high enough level to give Wolfe experience.

But behind him stood Damian, whose tiny, rotund frame had been hidden by his much larger brother. He pointed his huge pistol down the hall—not at Wolfe, but at Shel.

"Checkmate, Wolfe. Brains beats brawn." Damian's finger tightened on the trigger.

"No!" Wolfe screamed, leaping in the way. The first shot passed through his chest, and he gasped in agony and then choked, coughed, and sprayed blood. The second bullet hit him high in the shoulder.

The sound of the bullets striking his flesh was almost lost in the screaming of Shel. "No, Raphael, *please*! Anyone but *him*!"

Nice to know she cares, Wolfe thought sardonically as he fell to his knees, bleeding. His notifications showed him that he had massive attack and defense penalties, and was down to three health.

And he had a bleeding debuff that would kill him in a few minutes.

A beam of light from Sorenia hit Damian. The cowardly dwarf cussed and threw himself to the side. "Someone finish them for fuck's sake! What am I paying you all for?"

A brief sense of wellness permeated Wolfe, and his health ticked to seven. He struggled to his feet, to see a blubbering Shel, her beautiful face marred by tears and a line of snot. Beside her was the nervous-looking Rookie EMT card.

"Get it together and get your mantle!" Wolfe hissed, swiping his own cards at the same time. "I can't have you dying."

Wolfe pointed his pistol and shot the first person that came into view—more to scare people and buy them a few seconds than kill people per se. There were too many, and Wolfe was too wounded. They had to escape.

His mantle came up in the second pull—*thank all the gods*—and Wolfe slapped it on. He got a notification of both his summoned monsters dying.

"Go around and cut them off!" Damian screamed. "And someone capture my sister before she escapes! She'll die or serve me like everyone in this traitorous family!"

Based on what Miriam told me, that ends extremely poorly

for her. Wolfe pointed to a door in the hall—the one that led to the library. "Through there and up the stairs!" he whispered to Shel, coughing again. *Her healing wasn't enough to fully fix my lung.* "They won't expect us to go up!"

They ran into the other room. As they went, Damian was screaming behind him. "I'm going to kill you, Wolfe! I'm going to kill you, take your cards, and everything you love!"

"That guy needs professional help," Wolfe muttered as he ran past the pool table and up the nearly antique stairs, stumbling into the metal railing and hissing once. He was almost immediately winded, his normal lung capacity—*heh*—shot.

As he as climbing, another *deckbearer has pulled their deck* notification came.

Miriam or Nico? Neither means good things.

They reached the second story. "To Miriam's bedroom," Wolfe said, pointing. The sound of gunfire was slowly petering off, but it wasn't ending yet. A fight for control of the Grimm family still raged. *Maybe I can help Miriam take over?*

"H-How do you know where Miriam's bedroom is?" Shel asked, her face still a complete mess.

Wolfe paused to catch his breath, wheezing in agony. "I've known the Grimms since the Big Man's daughter was still in diapers. Now isn't the time for jealousy!"

"I wasn't jealous!" Shel hissed back, bringing forth a second Rookie EMT. Wolfe took a deep breath, relieved beyond words, as the healing washed through him. *Ten health of my thirty max.*

Wolfe, for his action, threw Cereboo down.

Wolfe cautiously but quickly stalked forward in a crouch, pistol out. They were about to exit onto the balcony above the first room, and it was quite probable there were some men down below—he didn't want them to notice him.

A deckbearer has pulled a deck. Wolfe grimaced. *That's both of them. Miriam is under attack and Nico has his deck out. Joy.*

He looked out onto the balcony and didn't see anyone—he

could still hear the gunfire throughout the house, and calls to locate himself, but the balcony was empty—a few statues and the hanging banners were accented by some blood spatters and a few bodies, but Wolfe didn't see anyone standing.

He sprinted as fast as he could, Shel following. About halfway across, one of the banners swung back and Nico stepped out, whole body covered in a bone exoskeleton, his pistol pointed at Wolfe.

"Goodbye, hero," Nico said, an insane smile on his face behind his bone mask.

Wolfe grabbed Shel and flung them both behind a statue as bullets whizzed by—one catching him in the leg, feeling more like a hefty kick than being shot now that Wolfe's mantle was on.

It still put his health back to eight.

Wolfe didn't stop rolling—he dropped Shel behind the statue and kept going, firing repetitively as he did. Nico took the hits and used the opportunity to shoot Wolfe again, dropping him back to six health as Wolfe made it behind another statue.

"Missed me, fuckface!" Nico screamed.

At the same time Cereboo slammed into Nico, dragging the deckbearer to the ground and biting at him. Sorenia yelled, "Die, foul villain!" and hit the Cobra with a light beam.

Neither seemed to hurt him a whole lot, the bites and beam merely bruising and lightly burning him.

"Want to see something fun?" Nico screamed as Wolfe came to a knee and tried to get a bead on the Cobra enforcer while he fought with Cereboo. "You're going to love this, Ms. Lyons! I'm gonna let you see your brother again!"

Nico touched a card, and a massive skeleton, about twenty feet tall, appeared in the center of the room. Its chest was more of a cage than a normal set of ribs, and inside... a soul was there, a lean, blueish outline of an eighteen-year-old with thin wrists gripping the ribs from the inside. The hair was a mess, and the features were fine... in fact, it looked like—

"Kevin," Shel whispered, her voice broken.

Wolfe winced, knowing how bad this had to be for Shel. But he was taking in the stats on the monster. It had over fifteen in almost every stat, and seventy-two health.

No way I can fight that! No way we can fight it at all, even together!

Cereboo and Sorenia turned their attention to the giant skeleton—a Soul Cage Knight, it was called—and attacked it, rushing away from Nico.

Who was briefly left without cover.

The deckbearer is the actual target, and Shel and I are safe until our companions die. Wolfe squeezed off three rounds from his kneeling position. The first took Nico in the face, cracking the bone exoskeleton over his face and slamming into his eye. Nico screamed, grabbing at his face, as the next two caught the edges of the skull mask he wore, whipping him around.

The Cobra enforcer hit the ground but crawled behind a statue. "Not good enough, Wolfe! You're pathetic! You're not the monster I am!"

Not dead yet, then. "We need to go!" Wolfe screamed, pulling Shel standing and then pushing her in front of him, rushing forward.

"I'll kill you, Wolfe! You're my prey!" Nico fired with one hand over half his face.

Most of the bullets went wide, but one caught Wolfe dead in the back—the same lung he had been hit in before. The bullet slammed him forward, but didn't rip through him thanks to his mantle. Wolfe was still pitched to the ground, yelling as the force of the blow tore his back and reopened the wound. He scrabbled, desperately and in agony, into the hall on the far side, behind the edge of the door, and fired back around the corner a couple of times.

Damian's yelling floated up from the first floor. "He's

upstairs, you fools! Get up there and kill him! Bring me his cards!"

A quick glance at his notification told Wolfe he had three health and was bleeding—he had perhaps five minutes to live. He doubted Nico was a whole lot better after the bullets to the face, but that was cold comfort.

The loss of the closest thing to a decent father figure washed through Wolfe again. *I can't die till I murder Damian.*

Coughing again, Wolfe lurched to his feet and stumbled down the hall. He threw an Angry Hellhound down to give him some cover if the Soul Cage came after him.

Shel helped him along. "Wolfe, he has Kevin's soul. His *soul*!"

Wolfe coughed. "I know. He'll get his. I'm going to personally murder Nico and Damian both. But we need to *live* first."

"Why aren't we escaping then?"

The Angry Hellhound growled and raced backward, and Wolfe saw that a thug had entered the hall. He dropped to the ground to avoid the gunfire and pulled Shel after him, grunting as she jostled him.

The thug screamed and ran. The Angry Hellhound ran past him, headed for the Soul Cage.

Wolfe lurched to his feet. "We need to save Miriam. Last thing I can do for Big Man Grimm. I owe him that much for failing him."

"You didn't—"

Wolfe half-slashed his hand through the air, cutting her off. "I did! But don't talk about it now. We have to live!"

He went down the hall, half-carried by Shel, to a door with a couple corpses outside it—and bullet holes in it. A notification popped up that he had lost another health. As if to counterpoint his notification, Wolfe coughed blood onto the floor.

Cereboo died.

"Miriam, it's me, Wolfe! Don't shoot! I'm at my limit of bullets-to-the-face for the day!"

The door opened, and Miriam stood in a long-sleeve black dress, her eyes red and fangs coming from her mouth. Her eyes weren't just red—they were wild. Her arm leaked blood from a graze, an almost perfect match to the werewolf claw on the other side she had received two days ago.

But she still managed to smile at him. "Sardonic to the last, huh?"

Even as she said it, Wolfe heard crashing and turned. The Soul Cage was pushing into the hall, too big for it but smashing its way through regardless.

"What is that?" Miriam asked, staring wide-eyed.

Wolfe pushed forward into the room. "Too much to handle."

There were a couple Sexy Spawn inside the room, and Wolfe threw out Malviere, his newest companion.

"You called, hunter?" she asked, her words incongruous on her eight-year-old frame. Then her eyes widened. "Where are my doggos?"

The Angry Hellhound picked that moment to die. Malviere flinched.

"Gone," Wolfe managed.

Healing passed through him, and he returned to five health.

"Last one," Shel whispered.

Wolfe nodded. He couldn't receive any more healing from Shel today.

He glanced around. The whole bedroom was goth. Black curtains, opened to look down over the veranda roof to the pool, with a handprint 'dragging' down the massive bay window like someone had tried to escape. The blankets on Miriam's bed were black, and her walls were covered in posters, many of undead creatures, many of women in states of... sexy faux distress, Wolfe supposed.

Shel pulled her mantle, and a soft golden glow surrounded her.

"Open up, Wolfe!" a voice cried from outside, one Wolfe didn't recognize.

"Don't warn him you're coming, fool, get the door open!" Damian yelled.

Wolfe ignored them both, his mind on the problem of victory —or as close as he could get. The crashing was still coming from the hall, but it was joined by kicks to the outside of the door.

"Shel, Miriam, I need you to go out the window and run down and jump in the pool, then run out into the backyard as fast as you can!"

Both of them stepped toward the window, glancing out. The door cracked at the bottom.

Shel glanced nervously at the door then turned back to Wolfe. "What are you going to do?"

"End Damian, no matter the cost," Wolfe shouted. "None of us will be safe until he is dead—or no longer has a reason to come after you."

"Then I'm coming with you," Shel whispered.

"And I'm not running from Damian, ever again," Miriam added, turning to face Wolfe as well.

Wolfe didn't have time for their noble shit. He glanced at them. Both had their mantles on...

Wolfe turned, fired into the door. "I'm killing the first motherfucker that comes through!"

The he turned, took a step toward the girls, placing his hand high on each of their chests, and whispered, "If I don't make it, live to avenge me. If I do live, you'll find me where Heinrich died, sometime tomorrow."

Then Wolfe *pushed*, his power augmented by his own mantle. Both girls screamed as they exploded through the window, went sailing a few feet, and then crashed onto the veranda ceiling, rolling comically until they fell off the roof and landed in the pool.

But Wolfe hadn't waited. Hoping the sound of Shel and Miriam's 'escape' was covered by the crashing of the Soul Cage outside, he ran onto the veranda and went around the side of the house, easily making the transition to the overhand in the front that the columns all supported. He quickly sent a mental order to Malviere to attack the Soul Cage—she was a liability for his new plan as anything but a distraction that died.

Wolfe ran along the side, noting the couple thugs wandering the front. Calmly wandering. There were no more gunshots. *My side lost. Me and the girls are all that's left.*

Wolfe ran around the house, across the overhang roof—still half-hobbling—until he was right in front of the main entrance, looking down on the parking lot. Then he lay flat and checked under the front. He only saw two guys.

Wolfe took a deep breath, and squeezed out two sets of two shots, killing both. Then, grimacing, he dropped down, landing hard. *Another health lost.* But Wolfe didn't have time to be careful.

He pulled the door to the front open a crack and glanced inside. Wolfe only saw one person. He opened the door, firing as he entered. He took another bullet in a glancing hit, but his mantle protected him.

The thug, in turn, dropped, his leg twitching. Wolfe pointed his pistol and shot again, but clicked on empty.

Still, between the first shot, and the firing out front, everyone should have been summoned at this point.

Wolfe dropped to his knees next to the backpack he had left, cycling his cards.

The one he wanted appeared. At the same time, he got a notification that Malviere had died.

He ripped the bomb out of the backpack and put it on the

ground, going through the motions furiously. He set it for five seconds.

Just as he finished, Damian and Nico came running into the hall, surrounded by what appeared to be almost half the thugs that had fought them. Damian, aside from a rumpled and slightly blood-spattered suit, appeared fine... and still covered in his powerful mantle. But Nico had no mantle, and was covered in small wounds and a massive gaping one where his eye had been.

Damian's deep-set eyes widened as he stared at Wolfe. "Wolfe... what are you doing?"

"Making sure none of you live to see the light of day," Wolfe muttered, grabbing the bomb with both hands and flipping it around so they could all see the five-second timer.

A couple of the thugs began running.

"You'll die, Wolfe!" Damian screamed, shaking.

"I know," Wolfe replied, taking the final arming switch in his fingers.

"You can't. Your cards will die with you! I won't be able to complete the set."

"The Great Game Rule Number Five," Wolfe said, and gently flicked the switch.

The countdown began.

"Damn you!" Damian screamed, turning and waddling as fast as he could away from the bomb. "Why would you do this to me? What did I ever do to you?"

Wolfe glanced up, making sure everyone was running, and no one was looking back.

He touched a card.

CHAPTER 41

THE END OF THE BEGINNING

"**The Great Game Rule #111**: Set cards have been added to the game. If all cards of a specific set are in one deck, that deckbearer shall receive a powerful enumerated bonus. Set cards may be of any type."

Infernal Rift activated, with Wolfe targeting himself, now that all his creatures had been defeated. The card sent *any* deckbearer, not just an enemy one, to a faux infernal realm for ninety seconds, so long as they had no creature card out.

Wolfe fell into nothingness. There was a brief sense of movement, and a lake of fire appeared before him.

Then something *shifted*, and Wolfe found himself standing in a cave. He was staring up at a wall—a furry wall. His eyes tracked up, and up more, almost a hundred feet until the huge body branched out into three massive heads.

It was a three-headed dog, but one larger than the greatest sauropod that had ever lived.

Cerberus, Wolfe knew without thought. *He must have changed something—this doesn't feel like a 'faux' Infernal Realm.*

Each of Cerberus' heads chewed... something. Or multiple

somethings. Wolfe focused. Demons and souls both occupied the great mutt's mouths, and all three heads stared down at Wolfe as they masticated the damned.

Wolfe tried to speak, but no words would form. Somehow, he knew it was forbidden.

But he felt a kindred spirit, a desire to hunt—to find those that would escape the fate of their evil. Wolfe wanted to hunt them as well... to hunt and end them.

Cerberus was sitting now, but only because a worthy escapee had not presented itself.

Wolfe tried to tell the giant dog that he would hunt Damian to the ends of the earth for what he had done, but even the failed attempt rang hollow. Vengeance wasn't what Wolfe wanted.

Purpose was. The purpose that he had chosen twenty years ago—to remove those that were evil from the world, and send them onward.

Cerberus nodded one giant head, his red eyes boring into Wolfe as if he knew what Wolfe was thinking.

Wolfe was back in the mansion—or the fragments of it. He briefly reeled from a combination of the sudden switch of scenery and his wounds. The front of the house was *gone*, with only the back wall still standing, a pile of upper floors collapsed in front of it. Dust swirled about him, and occasional flaming particulate matter floated down around him. He heard a few screams—but nothing feminine, which was all he cared about at the moment.

He saw a red glow from a couple parts of the shattered mansion, and assumed something flammable had caught.

Wolfe had a notification informing him of a ton of dead

people—and another level gained from killing Nico. But not a notification for Shel or Miriam.

Thank the gods.

Damian also wasn't a killed notification. It seemed like he was the only person, beside a few remaining low-ranking thugs, that Wolfe hadn't gotten with his bomb—at least of those whose crimes included what had happened to Big Man Grimm.

Wolfe was briefly tempted to try and hunt Damian. But he was out of bullets, out of health, and stood almost no chance. Shel's and Miriam's fates were unknown, beyond the fact that they were alive. They might need him as well.

And he had no idea where Damian was.

A fire peeked out above one pile of house wreckage, rapidly spreading. Wolfe stood and started to walk away, through the shattered parking lot and the exploded cars, most tossed a few feet and lying on their sides.

Big Man Grimm's grave would be a pyre, and it would be fed by the corpses of almost everyone that had betrayed him. Wolfe was still filled with a deep sadness, but at some level, he had at least taken vengeance. And the remaining people that had harmed him would not escape Wolfe's justice either.

Wolfe passed his own car, which was finally dead—every window was smashed, and its engine block was half out of the car. One entire side was both pancaked and peppered with holes. It was unsalvageable.

Wolfe turned and limped from the house, heading toward Greenbow Way across the lawn at an oblique angle. He still had things to do, and didn't want to meet Damian or his stooges in his current condition.

Not yet, at least. But I'll come back for the evil little dwarf. He won't get away. I promise it.

He reached for his phone, to call an Uber, but winced as his hand hit the spot where it *had* been. Instead of his pocket, he met a bullet graze across his thigh.

He had no phone, and the last cards he had gotten, from Jason, were missing.

Wolfe looked up at the sky. "Really? Even now?"

Wolfe smiled at the door to D3, tired beyond belief and half asleep. He'd been up for almost twenty-four hours, and they had been crazy hours indeed.

He had his duffel bag with him—the one he usually kept his weights in. But at the moment, he had two changes of clothes, roughly $350,000 in cash, and the cards he had managed to keep. As well as an old bone that his first dog, Pierce, hadn't finished before he died.

The rest didn't matter.

He knocked on the door.

The door cracked open a few moments later, and a pair of red-rimmed green eyes stared at him. The door was flung open, and Shel, her eyes so sunken-in that she looked like a raccoon mid-boss. Behind her, Miriam was pointing a pistol out the door.

"Wolfe!" Shel managed before she flung herself onto him, wrapping her legs around him and hugging him tight, her head pressed against his shoulder. "By the Divine, you lived! You came back! I thought I had lost you, like everyone else!"

Wolfe shook his head, which, at the current angle, was more like running his chin through Shel's red hair. "Nah, harder to kill than a cockroach, like I said."

Shel gave a near-hysterical laugh, then sobbed. "By the gods, you're back. You're back."

Wolfe nodded.

Shel let go and dropped to the floor, but she took his hand, holding it. She stared deep into his eyes. "What now?"

"It's good to see you," Miriam said from behind Shel, her voice sardonic, and maybe a touch jealous.

Wolfe gave an upward jut of his chin to Miriam.

"Well, what *is* your plan now, as our cute friend asked?" Miriam asked.

Wolfe stepped into the room and shut the door. It was the same room as before, but the bed had been completely changed out, and the floor cleaned. Wolfe could still see a spot tinted red, however.

He pulled his deck and brought Cereboo forth. His first companion in everything that had happened deserved to be here. Then he tossed his new magical pooch the old bone.

"Well, first, I need to find a place to live," Wolfe said. "I think I need to get out of town for a bit—it won't take long for Damian to figure out my corpse isn't there. He'll go to the trouble of doing the dental records."

Shel and Miriam both nodded.

"Once out of town, I need to take some time to heal. Real time—a couple months, at least. I have bullet holes through me, and the EMT cards don't heal the injury penalties I've noticed."

"Yeah, I need stronger cards for that I think," Shel said.

"Right, well, like I said, I need to heal. We should go run the dungeon we found in the sewers once I'm partway healed."

Miriam clapped her hands. "Can I come?"

"Sure."

"Good," Miriam said. "Dad's fortune is heavily reduced, and I'll contest Damian in court for it. But at the same time, I want to make sure that if I need to fight him for control of the crime family, I can. Cards I can use or sell will go a long way to helping me accomplish that."

"And after we run the dungeon?" Shel asked Wolfe, twisting her red hair around her finger.

"Damian," Wolfe said, all mirth gone from his voice. "I have enough money and cards to support myself while I go after him."

"Wolfe... He has my dad's cards, as well as whatever special ones he got himself," Miriam said. "He's going to be *dangerous*."

Wolfe sighed. It was worse than that. Damian had his own cards, Big Man Grimm's cards, and Jason's cards all.

"I'll be stronger as well," Wolfe said. "I have two of the set cards, and we have a dungeon to run."

"I'll make sure I get stronger as well," Shel said, squeezing Wolfe's hand.

Thad's daughter came up and took the free hand of each. "We all will."

Miriam's pocket rang, and she stepped back, taking the phone out. "Hello?"

Shel took Wolfe's other hand in hers. "You're going to seek vengeance?"

Wolfe sighed. "Not just vengeance, Shel. You really might want to leave. I'm going to start with Damian. But that will only be the beginning. I'm going to end them all." He stared at Shel. "I know what you said... but I understand if you want out. It almost certainly won't end well for me."

Shel gave him another smile and leaned up, kissed him on the cheek, then whispered in his ear. "I knew you would say that. But what if you did it the right way for once?"

She leaned back down, and Wolfe stared at her quizzically. "What?"

"You went off half-cocked on your father. Then you killed thugs for other thugs. Now you're talking about some kind of anti-hero rampage. What if you just... did it the right way, instead? So you could be happy as well."

"Like become a cop?" Wolfe snorted. "Be serious, Shel. They're not gonna hire me. And here in Noimoire, at least, they're pretty corrupt."

"What about becoming a private investigator? Stay inside

the law, at least most of the time... but use your knowledge to take out the worst of the worst. In jail for life... or, if you must, six feet under."

Wolfe thought about it. It sounded preposterous—and limiting. But at the same time, Shel was right... he'd done the right things the wrong way every time. And it had cost him.

"Maybe. I'll think about it."

"Guys?" Miriam called, holding up the phone.

They both looked over. "So, Ms. Greenwall is on the phone... Damian is asking her to identify whether a body is Wolfe's. She wants to know if it is Wolfe's body."

Wolfe looked at Shel, and they both laughed.

"Be nice to the little guy, huh?" Shel asked.

Wolfe glanced at Miriam. "Hell yeah, make me dead. I don't want the bastard to see me coming." His eyes hardened. "Because I *am* coming. For him and everyone in Noimoire like him."

End Book 1

THANK YOU SO MUCH FOR READING!

If you're interested in more work from me, please check out my author page for other series, or sign up for the newsletter! I have a lot of other books, all LitRPG but with a great deal of variance therein.

If you'd like to contact me directly, the easiest way is my Discord. You can also find me on Facebook (be prepared for questionable photography skills), or can email me at John.W.Stovall@gmail.com. You can also support me and read advance chapters on my Patreon.

The story continues with the sequel...

Please consider leaving a review—any and all feedback is much appreciated!

Also, check out these super helpful Facebook groups!

https://www.facebook.com/groups/LitRPG.books
https://www.facebook.com/groups/Dungeonstories
https://www.facebook.com/groups/LitRPGsociety
https://www.facebook.com/groups/litrpgforum
https://www.facebook.com/groups/LitRPGReleases

ABOUT THE AUTHOR

John Stovall loves Shami, gaming, reading, math, his friends, his family, and his dog, and probably a whole lot of other things he can't think of right now. He obtained his BA in political science, and then later his JD from Humphrey's School of Law, but his real passion lies in writing. When he isn't thinking up number systems for his own homebrew Dungeons & Dragons game, he's thinking up cool plot lines for his books.

www.ingramcontent.com/pod-product-compliance
Lightning Source LLC
Chambersburg PA
CBHW021426240626
47153CB00001B/37